What the Heart Wants

T0352225

What the Heart Wants

JEANELL BOLTON

FOREVER
YOURS

New York   Boston

Forever Yours
Hachette Book Group
237 Park Avenue
New York, NY 10017
hachettebookgroup.com
twitter.com/foreverromance

First published as an ebook and as a print on demand: September 2014

Forever Yours is an imprint of Grand Central Publishing.
The Forever Yours name and logo are trademarks of Hachette Book Group, Inc.

The publisher is not responsible for websites (or their content) that are not owned by the publisher.

The Hachette Speakers Bureau provides a wide range of authors for speaking events. To find out more, go to www.hachettespeakersbureau.com or call (866) 376-6591.

ISBN: 978-1-4555-5729-5 (ebook edition)
ISBN: 978-1-4555-5726-4 (print on demand edition)

*In memory of my mother, Eileen Button
Buida, who encouraged me to read anything
I could get my hands on.*

Acknowledgments

It takes a village to write a book.

A big thank you to the Austin, Texas, chapter of Romance Writers of America, especially Janece Hudson, Jane Myers Perrine, April Kihlstrom, Louisa Edwards, and Jessica Scott. And a special shout-out to my RWA guardian angels, Liana Lefey and Colleen Thompson.

I also appreciate the encouragement of beta readers Joan Barton, Tina Bolick, Sharon Kite, Suzy Millar Miller, Ashley Vining, and Linda Wiles, as well as the enthusiasm of literary friends Paula Mitchell Marks, Carol Fox, and Suzy Gregory. Musical friends Mary Bedrich and Marion Mayfield were my expert sources on child prodigies.

Thank you also to my fabulous literary agent, Liza Dawson, who believed in me, and my ever-patient editor, Michele Bidelspach, who made my dream come true.

And, as always, thank you to my long-suffering husband, because he has been unfailingly supportive of my writing career, and my three wonderful children, because they have allowed me to write under my own name.

What the Heart Wants

Chapter One

Laurel held the long rope of pearls up to the brilliant mid-summer sunset shining in her bedroom window.

Here she was, sitting at her dressing table and wondering if pawning Gramma's necklace would provide enough money to pay the bills for the next couple of months. Her finances would straighten themselves out once she sold the house, but she'd had it on the market for almost seven weeks now, and not one soul had expressed interest in her six-thousand-square-foot white elephant.

She should have tried to sell it last fall, but managing her mother's funeral was all she could accomplish back then. Besides, she'd had another year to go on her teaching contract, and her work had become her life after Dave left her and Daddy died.

The past three years had been mind-numbing, one blow after another. Not that she really missed Dave. She'd married him because it was time for Bosque Bend's favorite daughter to march down the aisle, and he'd seemed like the logical choice. Too bad he'd ditched her when being married to Laurel Harlow became a liability rather than an asset.

The last blow came seven weeks ago, when her principal told her she wouldn't get another contract. She should have seen it coming, but she'd thought she was safe in the elementary school across the river, in Lynnwood, the new subdivision populated by new people who didn't know the protocols of old Bosque Bend, and who seemed to care more about her effectiveness as a teacher than her family history.

She'd driven home in a trance from the meeting with her principal, and as soon as she entered the safety of the house and locked the door, she'd whirled into a spate of activity to counteract the numbness that fogged her brain and made her feel like she was dragging around a fifty-pound weight. First she called the Realtor father of one of her students and put the house she'd lived in for most of her life on the market. Next she started contacting school districts in the Rio Grande Valley for jobs. Her days of servitude to Kinkaid House and her family legacy were over.

She rolled the pearls between her fingers. Living alone was the pits. Mrs. Bridges, across the street, employed a live-in maid, had a daughter who visited regularly, and was followed by a big, happy-looking dog everywhere she went. Laurel was her own maid, had no friends anymore, and Kinkaid House hadn't housed a dog since Mama's older sister died of rabies seventy-five years ago.

The doorbell chimed from downstairs. She sighed and nestled the rope of glowing beads back in its padded box. Who was it? Prince Charming magically appearing to rescue her from Bosque Bend?

She stood up and squared her shoulders. She didn't need Prince Charming. She'd make her own happy ending.

The bell rang again as she headed down the hall toward

the stairs. Probably the ill-mannered paperboy come collecting, though it didn't seem time for him yet. He always peered behind her down the hall as she handed him the money, then ran as if all the demons in hell were chasing him.

Her overactive conscience, part and parcel of being a preacher's daughter, charged into action. Of course the paperboy was afraid. Who could blame him? This house was notorious. Everyone in town knew what had happened here.

She started down the wide stairway.

If she could just mail in her payment, like when she used to take the *Dallas Morning News*, but Art Sawyer, who put out the town's biweekly newspaper, had never met an innovation he didn't dislike. Thus the *Bosque Bend Retriever* was printed on the same press he'd been using for the last forty years and was still hand-delivered by an army of schoolboys on bikes.

The doorbell pealed a third time. She gritted her teeth.

Sorry, whoever you are. I'm not about to break into a gallop. I might not have anything else left, but I can still muster a shred of dignity.

Three generations of family portraits on the staircase wall watched in approval as she regally descended the steps. As a child, she'd sped past them as fast as she could go to avoid their see-all stares, but now she drew strength from them. She might have to sell the house out from under their gilded frames, but she'd do it with her head held high.

And she'd burn the house down to the ground before she'd let it go for taxes.

Think positively, Laurel Elizabeth. Maybe your caller is a prospective buyer that the Realtor has sent over to look at the house.

She opened the heavy oak door a few cautious inches. Just

last week someone had lobbed a string of firecrackers at her when she was out in the yard, searching for her newspaper. Of course, it was right before the Fourth, but she doubted that those firecrackers were a patriotic salute.

Dear God in heaven, who was this on her doorstep?

Her caller was a giant, a big man darkly silhouetted against the red blaze of the high-summer Texas sunset. She couldn't make out his face because of the glare behind him, but he was built like a tank and stood maybe six four, six five. Definitely not Prince Charming. More like the Incredible Hulk. She glanced down to make sure the screen door was still locked.

"Laurel? Laurel Harlow?"

The voice seemed familiar. She couldn't quite place it, but her visitor sounded more surprised than dangerous. She pushed the door open wider, and the man's face came into focus as he moved forward to examine her through the wire mesh.

She stepped back a pace. He responded by taking off his dark glasses and smiling, a slight baring of his teeth.

"It's Jase Redlander, from old Bosque Bend High."

Her heart did a quick rabbit hop. Jase Redlander, of course. His voice was deeper now, his shoulders broader, and he'd grown a good three inches in height, but it was definitely Jase.

Jase, whom she'd loved to distraction. Jase whom she thought she'd never see again. Jase, who sixteen years ago had been run out of town for having sex with his English teacher.

He folded his sunglasses and put them in his pocket. "Sorry to bother you, but I just drove in from Dallas and I've got sort of a... well, a family emergency that might end up in your lap." He grimaced and glanced behind himself at the evening traffic moving along Austin Avenue. "Can we talk inside?"

The noise got bad this time of day, with everyone driving home from work and out to play. Back in the 1880s, when Great-Grampa Erasmus built Kinkaid House on a narrow dirt road that headed toward the state capital, he never could have imagined that it would one day be widened to four lanes, with a central turn lane being proposed for next year.

Laurel tried to keep her hand from shaking as she unlocked the screen.

"Of course. Come in." Her voice got stuck somewhere in the back of her throat. "How nice to see you," she managed to murmur.

But, standing aside as he entered, she saw that this was a different Jase Redlander than the teenager she'd fallen in love with sixteen years ago. The cut of his coal-black hair, the upscale Levi's and European-style polo shirt, the set of his shoulders—everything about him signaled money and power and confidence. Obviously he'd wrestled with life and won. She, on the other hand, had lost big-time. Could he tell?

Not if she could help it.

She relocked both outside doors, led him down the wide central hall, and unfolded the doors into the drawing room.

Three generations of her mother's people, Kinkaid women with money to burn, had managed to make the overlarge room, originally a double parlor, into a popular gathering place for Bosque Bend's moneyed elite in times past. Victorian sofas, heavy chairs, and grotesquely carved little tables, all flanked by potted greenery, formed intimate conversation groups, while fragile undercurtains, confections of snowy lace, filtered the harsh Texas sun coming in the front windows into fantastic arabesques on the oriental carpet.

Jase had always loved this room. Years ago, he'd told her

that if he ever died and sneaked into heaven, God's front room would look like this.

She hoped he wouldn't notice that heaven was somewhat the worse for wear. The upholstery was threadbare, the drapes faded, and the windows dingy. She glanced uneasily at the dark rectangles on the far wall, where the more saleable paintings had hung, then at the entrance to Daddy's study, which looked positively naked since she'd sold the fig-leafed marble youths who'd guarded the doorway for as long as she could remember.

The antiquities man from Austin had almost salivated as he loaded them into his van, and the money had, fittingly, paid off the last of Daddy's obligations.

Claiming a spindly ribbon-back chair for herself, Laurel gestured Jase toward the same velvet-upholstered sofa on which the two of them would sit and talk while Jase was waiting for Daddy to emerge from his study and summon him for his weekly counseling session. At first they had discussed school events in stilted little conversations, but after a while, when he started coming half an hour early, they'd relaxed with each other and began talking about what was going on in their lives. Jase had shared her joy when she made straight As and was elected sophomore representative to student council, and he'd consoled her when Mama and Daddy said she couldn't have unchaperoned dates until her next birthday.

In turn, she tried not to look shocked as she learned about the way he lived. Everyone in Baptist-dry Bosque Bend knew that Jase's father was a bad-tempered bully who kept a rowdy tavern just over the county line, but Laurel had been horrified to learn that Growler Redlander was such a poor excuse for a parent that his son had been working odd jobs since he was nine to support himself.

Jase had shrugged off her concern. "Laurel, I was five six when I was in the fourth grade. By the time I hit middle school, I was five ten and could pass for an eighteen-year-old any day of the week. The car wash is easy, and it's only one night a week. The only problem with the yard work is hiding the mower from my father so he can't toss it in the river like he does everything else."

Laurel's fifteen-year-old heart had opened to him. He was so brave, so valiant—and so handsome, just like the heroes on the covers of the romances she borrowed from Mrs. Bridges's extensive collection of paperbacks.

But that was sixteen years ago. What had brought Jase back to Bosque Bend? What sort of "family emergency" could possibly involve her?

She watched him deposit himself carefully on the delicately carved sofa, as if afraid it would break under his weight. He focused his gaze on her, and she took a quick breath. She'd forgotten how dark his eyes were—so black that iris and pupil seemed to blend into one. But why was he staring at her like that? Was something wrong? She glanced down at her silky white blouse. None of the buttons had come undone, and the zipper of her gray slacks was still closed tight.

He blinked, waved his hand in apology, and shifted his gaze. "I'm sorry. It's just that you seem so much the same. Somehow I expected you to look, well, *older.*"

Suddenly nervous, she pushed a heavy sheaf of dark hair back behind her ear and gave a little laugh, flattered but disbelieving. She was thirty-one years old, had been through hell, and didn't doubt that every bit of it showed on her face.

Nothing to do but seize the conversational bull by the horns. "You said you have an emergency?"

He exhaled deeply and rubbed his fingers along the nap of the sofa. "It's my daughter. She ran away from home this morning and left a note saying she was going to Bosque Bend to find her roots. I think she might try to contact you."

His daughter? Jase had a *child*?

Through the years, Laurel's mind had frozen him at age sixteen, standing alone against the world, her tragic lost love. The idea that he would marry one day and have a family had never even entered her head. Jase Redlander hadn't seemed to be the type to settle down. Instead, she'd pictured him as an unshaven roughneck putting out oil fires—or maybe a steeljawed hero fighting off a Mexican drug cartel. Year by year, he'd become a fantasy figure to her—a heroic dark knight. Certainly not a father.

He pulled a photo from his wallet. "Here's a picture of Lolly from last year. She looks a lot older than she is, but don't be fooled—she's only fifteen."

Using a thick-barreled pen, he scrawled something on the back of the picture before offering it to her. Laurel reached for it. Their fingers touched and a sizzle of awareness shot through her. The picture fell to the carpet.

Jase bent down to retrieve the photo and placed it on the rococo table beside her, his eyes catching hers for one long moment. "I'm at the old house," he said, his voice a bit deeper. "It's between renters right now." His gaze moved to her mouth, and his pitch dropped even lower. "You remember it. You were there... once."

Laurel picked the photograph up from the table, willing her hand not to tremble, and forced herself to study it. Jase was right. His daughter did look older than she had any right to, but that was how fifteen-year-old girls always looked, even when she herself was in high school. Probably back to caveman times. Lolly was lovely, just as pretty as Jase was handsome. Butter-yellow hair swooped down across her forehead, almost covering her right eye, while her pouting lips and lazy-lidded eyes were studiously sexy. Her eyebrows were long, like her father's—Hollywood eyebrows.

But did she have her father's smile? Jase didn't smile often in the old days, but when he did, it was like the sun coming out—a wide, brilliant, heartbreaking grin, perhaps more effective because it was so rare.

Well, from the looks of him, he had a lot more to smile about these days.

Laurel raised her eyes from the photo and held it out to him, this time careful to avoid all contact of the flesh. *He's married. Off limits.*

"If she does show up, I'll be sure to let you know."

Jase put up a refusing hand. "No, keep it. I wrote my number on the back. Show it to your parents too, in case she comes by when you're not here."

Laurel froze.

"Mama and Daddy are dead." She kept her voice steady as she placed the photo on the little table again. "I'm living here alone now, and I'm between jobs, so I spend most of my time at the house."

Jase's mouth opened and closed. She'd caught him by surprise. Apparently he hadn't kept up with the goings-on in his old home town. Who could blame him? He'd been all but ridden out on a rail.

"I'm sorry about that. I'd meant to come back here sometime to visit with your dad. Reverend Ed's support meant a lot to me. He's the only one who believed in me through that whole mess, you know. I guess I thought he was eternal."

Laurel shrugged. "Nothing lasts forever." And Daddy, her wonderful Daddy, had died in spirit long before his body finally gave out. She studied the philodendron in the wicker stand beside her guest. How long had it been since she'd watered the local vegetation? And why on earth had she focused on the stupid plant? Because she didn't want to think about Daddy.

Jase exhaled softly. "I thought maybe you were here visiting your parents, but you and Dave are living in this house now? Aunt Maxie said you two—"

"Dave Carson and I were divorced three years ago," she interrupted. "And we didn't have any children. I've been teaching music for the past six years at Lynnwood Elementary, a new school over on the east side of the river, but my contract wasn't renewed. I'm trying to sell the house so I can get a fresh start somewhere else."

He leaned forward to lay his big hand gently on hers. His voice was soft and comforting.

"I'm sorry for that too. It's hard to start over in a new place."

Her eyelids quivered. What was this man doing to her? She refused to let herself dissolve into tears just because Jase Redlander had gotten her libido going, then offered her sympathy when no one else had.

Withdrawing her hand, she directed the subject back to Jase's truant daughter. "What makes you think Lolly will come here?"

"Her history class did a unit on personal roots last semester, and she's been after me ever since, wanting to know about my family." He paused as if trying to decide what to say. "And her mother's."

His eyes avoided her questioning glance and wandered around the room.

Laurel held her breath. Had he noticed the Greek statues were gone? Daddy would have called it false pride, but she didn't want anyone to realize she was pawning jewelry and selling off family heirlooms to buy her bread and butter. Having the FOR SALE sign in front of the house was different—the more people who knew she was planning to leave Bosque Bend, the better. Maybe then they'd get off her back.

She glanced at the baby grand in the corner next to Daddy's office. There was no way to take anything that large with her when she moved. She'd tried to sell it—discreetly, of course—but it turned out that old pianos were a drag on the market. Her hands flexed. The Steinway was so out of tune that she could hardly bear to play it anymore, but how could anyone not love a piano?

Jase began again. "I cleaned up my father's memory as much as possible for Girl Child, but had to do some pretty fast talking when it came to her mother. I tried to keep things vague, but she added two and two and came up with five."

"Five?"

"She left a note. She's come to Bosque Bend to find you. She—she thinks you're her mother."

Laurel's eyes widened and her jaw dropped open. What? Had she heard him right?

"Me? Why? Your wife—"

His gaze held steady. "I'm not married and never have been. Lolly's mother abandoned her at birth."

Laurel felt like she was treading water. "You're a—a single father?"

He nodded.

She reached for a lifeline. "But...usually the mother takes the baby."

"She wasn't the maternal type."

The tide was rising. "But I still don't understand. Why me? Why does your daughter think *I'm* her mother?"

Jase dropped his gaze and moved his hand as if trying to back off from the question.

"I...well...it just happened. It wasn't deliberate. I think she misinterpreted some of the stories Maxie told her from when we used to live here." He cleared his throat. "You remember Maxie, don't you? Maxine Hokinson, Swede Hokinson's daughter, my mother's oldest sister? She's the one who subbed at your friend Sarah Bridges's house that summer their regular housekeeper got swarmed by Africanized bees. Anyway, you don't need to get involved—just call me if Lolly shows up on your doorstep, and I'll come fetch her."

"All right." What else could she say? She was way out of her depth.

He glanced at his watch. "I've got to go now. It's getting late, and I don't want to be gone from the old house too long, in case Lolly shows up there."

Laurel stood up to walk him out. "I'm sure you'll find her soon."

She was sure of no such thing, but at least she hoped so. A fifteen-year-old could land herself in a lot of trouble in an unfamiliar town, no matter how small. *The Retriever* had reported that a group of rowdy teenagers had been gathering in the parking lot of old Bosque Bend High School every night this summer and disturbing residents nearby. Art Sawyer had accompanied the story with a blistering editorial about underage drinking and promised more to come as the investigation continued.

Lord only knows how Art always got the inside scoop. Probably because his wife was a Hruska and her cousin's nephew was the new chief of police. That's how things worked in Bosque Bend. The old families, the ones that had been anchored there for generations, all knew each other, and—good, bad, or indifferent—the news got around.

Laurel unlocked the big front door, then held the screen open with one hand while offering the other to Jase in farewell. He enveloped it in his own for a single warm second and smiled at her—that dazzling, absolutely devastating smile that people saw so rarely, the smile that had sealed her to him for all eternity when she was just fifteen.

"Thank you, Laurel. You're kinder to me than I deserve."

Her heart thumped so loudly that he should have been able to hear it. She watched as he crossed the lawn to the long driveway on the south side of the house, waved once, and opened the door of his car—a big black Cadillac, just like Daddy used to drive.

* * *

Accustomed to Dallas's big-city traffic, Jase made his way through Bosque Bend's rush hour without even noticing it.

Where the hell was Lolly? Girl Child was quite a handful, but she'd never pulled a stunt like this before. A shiver shot through him as he glanced at the rapidly setting sun.

Relax, Jase. Everything's going to be all right. Lolly's a smart kid. She can take care of herself. In fact, she's probably sitting on the front porch of the old house right now, waiting for you to come pick her up. Where else could she be? You needn't have bothered Laurel by barging in on her like that.

He changed lanes, moving to the left.

Laurel . . . instead of working himself into a panic about Lolly, he'd think about Reverend Ed's daughter, like he always did when his life started going down the crapper. She was the only girl he'd ever loved, and remembering her kindness—her goodness—gave him peace and strength.

But this time, picturing Laurel Harlow in his mind's eye made him feel even worse. His fingers tightened on the leather-covered steering wheel. Sixteen years to learn better, and he'd still made a complete ass out of himself when he tried to talk to her—but he'd never imagined she'd be orphaned and divorced, all alone in that big, cavernous house.

His mouth twisted. He should have figured out something was going on when Information told him the Harlow number was unlisted. That was quite a change from the old days, when half the boys in Bosque Bend were on the horn to Reverend Ed—or at least the "at-risk" half.

But how could anyone be stupid enough to let Laurel Harlow get away? Driving into town earlier this afternoon, he'd thought that ol' Dave was one man who went to bed happy each night. As a teenager, Laurel had been sexy as hell—tall, with a full-breasted woman's body, soft gray eyes fringed with long black lashes, her lips sweet and tender—the princess of Bosque Bend. Now, in full woman-hood, she was in her glory.

He stomped on his brake as a traffic signal that hadn't been there sixteen years ago went from amber to red in front of him.

Time to switch on his headlights. The last of the radiant sunset had finally sunk below the horizon.

He'd better get a move on. His old neighborhood had always held a particularly prominent position on the Bosque Bend police blotter, and he didn't want Lolly out there alone after dark.

The signal turned green. He hit the accelerator and shot forward.

Crap! He'd missed his turn.

No wonder. The old Alamo Drive-in on the corner of Crocket Avenue had finally been torn down, and in its place was a Walmart, complete with a large, white marquee advertising a post–July Fourth sale in patriotic red-and-blue letters.

Which meant that Overton's Department Store, which had reigned supreme on the city square since before he was born, finally had some competition. Jase smiled grimly. At least Overton's blatant racism ended when Reverend Ed threatened Dolph Overton, this generation's CEO, with a congregational boycott. You didn't fuck around with the pastor of the biggest church in town.

Exiting at the next street, he circled back, driving through the crowded parking lot. A constant stream of customers entered the store through the sliding door on the right, slowing him down to a crawl. Another wellspring exited from the slider on the left, the adults carrying bags of merchandise and pushing grocery baskets while the children bounced red, white, and blue balloons on strings. He maneuvered carefully around a little boy dashing about in the near dark with a blue balloon tied to his wrist, U-turned, and eased out onto Crocket again.

How much time had he lost? The streetlights were glimmering now. Night was falling fast.

Chapter Two

Laurel stayed outside on her porch to watch the last of the dying sun dodge behind the English half-timber directly across the street. The early evening had dissolved into a humid, uncomfortable twilight, but she felt reborn. She'd been in a haze for six weeks, ever since she'd been laid off, but the scent of honeysuckle was on the breeze, Jase Redlander was back in town, and she was alive again.

Losing her job had been the ultimate shock after almost three years of shocks. First there was the business about Daddy, then the inevitable repudiation by their friends and neighbors, then the divorce. Through it all, Laurel continued driving across town every day to teach her music classes at Lynnwood Elementary. In fact, she had to—with Daddy unemployed, she was the family breadwinner.

She'd always enjoyed teaching, but as Mama's health declined, her students became even more important to her. No longer was she a twinkle-toed fairy who danced through life with her feet scarcely touching the ground, no longer a two-dimensional representation of her saintly father and well-bred mother, but someone who brought the joy of music into children's lives.

She sang with them, taught them rhythm instruments and recorders, explained elements of music theory, planned performances, stayed after school to teach basic piano to those who were interested. And all the time, she loved them, even the ones who didn't love her—especially the ones who didn't love her, because now she understood that they were the ones who needed her love the most.

So how in the world had she, a favorite of students and parents alike, ended up being laid off?

"The school board has chosen not to offer you another contract, Laurel," her principal had told her. "I'll give you a good reference, but I've been told there aren't any other positions open for music teachers in Bosque Bend at this time."

In other words, the Lynnwood residents, newbies to Bosque Bend, may have liked her, but the old guard wanted to sweep her under the rug. Betty Arnold knew the score. And Laurel did too—the good reference was a bribe so she wouldn't get the state teachers union involved.

"So sorry, my dear." Mrs. Arnold gave her a fake smile. "Have you considered relocating?"

Yes, darn it, she was relocating, and she hoped never to set eyes on this misbegotten little town ever again!

Now, Laurel, you're not being fair.

The truth was that Bosque Bend had given her an incredibly idyllic childhood. As the daughter of the most respected man in town and the heiress to the Kinkaid fortune, she'd been everyone's darling. Teachers had praised her scholarship and character, the city council passed a resolution every year wishing her a happy birthday, she was elected president of every school organization she belonged to, she had an escort to any function she chose to attend, and all the kids wanted to be her friend.

But now she was the town pariah.

The yard lights across the street switched on, stunning the cicadas into silence and illuminating the Bridgeses' front lawn with the sharp brightness and harsh shadows of a nighttime carnival. Laurel tensed and clutched at a porch post as a tall woman, her hair catching fire under the artificial light, walked out the front door with a preteen boy. She had a ball in one hand and a leather mitt in the other.

This must be the week that Sarah visited her mother. If it were three years ago, she'd have crossed the street the second that red Mercedes SUV pulled into the driveway. But not now.

Dear God, she missed Sarah. Sarah Bridges. Well, Sarah Bridges *Edelman* now—her best friend since they were seven years old.

Out of the corner of her eye, she caught the flicker of a light being turned on in the fourth-floor turret of the stucco Spanish-style castle next door to the Bridges. Everyone in town knew what that meant—Pendleton Swaim was hard at work on the second installment of his thinly veiled fictionalized account of the history of Bosque Bend, or, as he called it, *Garner's Crossing.* The first book had all the old-timers threatening to shoot him because of what he'd written about their great-grand-daddies—especially Coy Menefee, who told everyone he met that he was carrying concealed, which pretty much eliminated the element of surprise.

Sarah's son let out a yell as he caught a high ball.

Laurel smiled. *Good boy!* That was her godson, Eric. He had a real arm on him, and with a coach like Sarah, he'd be an all-star.

She inhaled sharply and tried to duck behind a porch post as the Pflugers' beautifully restored Bentley Flying Spur turned into their driveway next door, their headlights momentarily sweeping across her.

But what did it matter if Sarah spotted her? After three years of ignoring her, there was no way her old friend was going to acknowledge her now. Laurel edged forward to get a better view as mother and son threw the ball back and forth with smacking force.

Sarah, tall and long-limbed, had been a natural athlete from elementary on. She was a cheerleader in middle school and high school, played on the softball team, and ran cross-country. Laurel did the cheerleader thing in middle school too, but decided to concentrate on academics in high school. Academics and, of course, music. For Mama and Daddy, it began one Sunday after church when, just four years old, she'd gone to the piano and sounded out "Amazing Grace." But for her, the music had begun much earlier, maybe when she was born, maybe at the first moment her DNA was strung together.

The front door opened as Mrs. Bridges and Sarah's middle son, Luke, came out and sat on the front step to watch Sarah and Eric practice. Mrs. Bridges's aging Great Dane lay at her mistress's feet.

Laurel moved to the edge of the porch to get a better look at the toddler Mrs. Bridges was carrying in her arms.

Sarah's youngest was a firetop, just like his mother.

Luke and his grandmother yelled and hooted as Eric missed an easy lob. Nothing daunted, he ran into the darkness of the Overtons' house next door to find the ball in the deep grass, Sarah fast behind him.

Balancing her grandson on her hip, Mrs. Bridges stood up from the porch step to watch. Her short hair, more auburn now than the bright red it had been years ago, looked almost black under the night lights, but it was, as usual, perfectly styled. In fact, Laurel had never seen Sarah's mother when she hadn't been perfectly turned out. Tonight she had on jeans, mocs, and a loose peasant blouse. On anyone else, the outfit would look casual. On her, it looked haute couture. Maybe it was the bangle bracelets and hoop earrings. Maybe it was Marilyn Bridges.

Laurel had regarded Mrs. Bridges as her second mother, and she knew Sarah's house as well as she knew her own. Of course, it had been more fun across the street. Mama and Gramma, who were always hanging around when Sarah visited, preferred that she and Sarah play indoors, usually with dolls or at quiet board games, but Marilyn Bridges encouraged them to go outside and bounce on the trampoline, splash in the big backyard pool, or wave green-and-gold pompoms and shriek out Baylor football cheers.

Mrs. Bridges readjusted her grip on her grandson and raised a hand to her mouth like a megaphone. "You'll never see it in the dark! Get another one or wait till tomorrow!"

Eric reached down and lifted up the missing ball. "Found it!"

Luke cheered and Mrs. Bridges applauded from the porch steps.

After high school, Sarah went off to the University of Texas to play softball for the Longhorns while Laurel traveled just down the road to Baylor to major in music and pick up a teaching degree, but they'd stayed in touch. Sarah, who'd apparently slept with every straight guy at UT, discovered her birth control had failed her the semester before she graduated, and asked Laurel to be maid of honor at her hurry-up wedding. Four years later, Sarah, pregnant with her second son, was the honor attendant when Laurel, the world's oldest virgin, married Dave Carson.

The little redhead whimpered and began moving restlessly in his grandmother's lap. After a few minutes, Mrs. Bridges stood up and took him and Luke inside.

Sarah looked toward the door and removed her mitt, but Eric thumped the ball into his glove a couple more times. "Aw, Mom, stay out with me. We don't have to go in now."

Sarah shook her head. "Sorry, hon, but you know how cranky Baby gets at this time in the evening. It's not fair to palm him off on your grandmother."

She started toward the house, then suddenly turned around as if she'd just had an idea.

"Okay, Eric, just one more." She edged backward toward the house, which made Eric take a position nearer the street to face her.

"Think high!" She lifted her arm and hurled it forward.

Eric leapt up, but the ball sailed far above his head.

Laurel lost its arc in the darkness, then was surprised to hear something land with a plop scarcely five yards in front of her.

In a flash, Sarah, dodging a minivan that came to a screeching halt to accommodate her, ran across all four lanes of Austin Ave. She bent down to pick up the ball, gave Laurel a quick smile, breathed out a quick "Hi!" then raced back across the street and motioned to her son. "Come on, hon. Time to go in."

After hanging back for a resentful second, Eric trudged after his mother, closing the door behind him. The yard lights went out.

Laurel blinked into the darkness. What was that all about? Was Sarah losing her touch—or had she deliberately overthrown the ball as an excuse to cross the street and reestablish contact?

* * *

Jase drove slowly down the road, searching for his old home.

He knew twilight was a great equalizer, but the neighborhood sure looked a lot better than it had ten years ago when he'd come back to town after Growler fell into the Bosque River after a night of heavy drinking and drowned. In fact, it looked downright respectable—without a single junk pile, broken-down car, or scavenging dog pack in sight.

Thank God that Lolly would never know the squalor he'd grown up in. "Poor but honest" was the picture he'd always painted of his childhood—he'd told her very little about his father, sugarcoated his childhood, and said squat about why he'd left town.

His high beam cut across the front of the house as he turned into the drive, but no forlorn-looking teenager was sitting on the front steps.

His mouth went dry and his chest tightened.

What if...

No, he refused to go down that road. He was Lolly's father. He'd know if something had happened to her...wouldn't he?

He ran his eyes over the shadowed porch again.

Goddamn—where was she? If she wasn't at Kinkaid House, she *had* to be here.

He backed the Cadillac into the driveway—if there was an emergency, he needed to be able to haul ass. Easing himself out of the car, he leaned against the side of it for a long moment, gazing into the sky and trying to be logical while his heart raced like the Indianapolis 500.

Maybe she'd found a way to get into the house. Girl Child had been an expert at picking locks ever since she was two, when she'd shrieked "Me do it!" and unbuckled her own car-seat belt, which, of course, meant he had to spend half the night on the Internet, searching for a tamperproof seat belt. But, truth be told, he was proud of her willfulness, even encouraged it. As far as he was concerned, it was a survival trait.

But there was a big difference between a willful toddler unlocking her seat belt and a willful fifteen-year-old taking off down I-35 on her own.

And, oh God, I love her so much.

He shoved off the car and walked up onto the porch, took a one last quick look around the porch, unlocked the door, and flipped on the lights.

"Lolly?"

His voice echoed in the empty house.

Maybe she hadn't heard him.

"Lolly!"

No answer.

He made a swift search of every room, opening every closet, then checked out back.

Nada.

A chill crept over him. He walked into his old room at the front of the house, raised the blind on the lone window, and looked up at the evening star—the wishing star, as Aunt Maxie called it—and willed his daughter to miraculously appear.

* * *

Laurel turned off the TV and started up the stairs to prepare for bed. The sixth step produced a groan straight out of Transylvania. She glanced behind herself.

Get a grip, Laurel Elizabeth.

The sound of old wood creaking under stress had been part of her life since she was born, along with occasional noxious smells emanating from the walls, and lightweight curtains floating in sudden, inexplicable drafts.

As she reached the top of the stairs, the doorbell rang for the second time that evening.

* * *

Jase turned away from the window and picked up his mobile. Maybe Lolly had shown up at home and Maxie hadn't had a chance to call him yet.

He punched in her number. "Anything on your end?"

"Nothing. Have you checked with Pastor Harlow? Has he seen Lolly?"

"Reverend Ed's passed away. His wife too."

There was a quick gasp on the other end of the line. "Recently?"

Jase frowned. Why didn't Maxie know that Laurel's parents had died? The Harlows' obituaries should have been in the *Retriever*, which Maxie had maintained a subscription to ever since they left Bosque Bend. Not that Jase ever read the rag himself. No need to be reminded of the town that had tossed him out like rotting garbage.

"He died a while ago, but Mrs. Harlow went just last year. Laurel is living in Kinkaid House all alone now. She and Dave Carson are divorced."

"Divorced?" Another gasp. "Laurel Harlow? I wouldn't have expected that either."

"Yeah."

Maxie's voice softened. "I'm sorry, Jase."

She understood. Reverend Ed's daughter was the princess of Bosque Bend, the golden girl, the one for whom everything worked out, the one who lived happily ever after, giving hope to people like Jase and her that their lives would eventually turn out right too.

He nodded into the phone. "Well, anyway, I left one of those school photos with her in case Lolly shows up."

"Jase, what about your old house?" Maxie's voice perked up with hope. "Lolly might remember us talking about renting it out."

"That's where I am now. She's not here."

"Think we should contact the police?"

"I did, and they won't even talk to me. She left home on her own, even wrote that damn note about how she was going to Bosque Bend to find her mother and would be back later this evening. Officially she's a runaway and the police won't get involved."

"So what are you going to do?"

"I don't know, but I'll tell you this much—I'm not leaving Bosque Bend till I find her!"

He put the phone down on the floor beside the bed and lay back on the pillow. Brave words, but what should he do next? Drive every street in Bosque Bend, calling out her name like she was a lost puppy?

But maybe she hadn't even made it to Bosque Bend...

He looked out the window at the dark sky. It had been a long day, and the night would be even longer. He was exhausted, but there was no way he could sleep.

It was all his fault. He'd wanted Girl Child to have everything Laurel Harlow had—a beautiful home, financial security, the respect of the community, a stable family. But somewhere along the line, he'd screwed up. Somehow he'd done such a shitty job as a father that Lolly had taken off a hundred miles down the freeway in search of a mother who didn't give a flying fuck about her. He didn't know where Lolly's mother was now or even if she was still alive, and he doubted if anyone in Bosque Bend did either.

But what if Lolly was hiding somewhere, avoiding him because some bastard had told her why he'd been run out of town? Was it already too late? Had he lost his daughter at the same time that he was busting his butt trying to give her the world?

Even as he watched, the wishing star was beginning to fade.

His spirits sagged. He prayed that Lolly was safe, but in his heart, he'd begun to fear the worst.

Chapter Three

Laurel switched on the porch light and opened the heavy door enough to see a bedraggled teenager with tangled yellow curls and big, apprehensive eyes standing in front of her.

She looked like a fashion ad gone mad: shiny pink shorts, a bandanna halter top in a black-and-white splashy print, dangly pink plastic earrings that glowed in the dark, flip-flops glittering like Fourth of July sparklers. From one hand hung a bulging pink backpack and from the other, incongruously, a Louis Vuitton shoulder bag.

Almost certainly this was Jase's Lolly. Not the flirtatious, sexy Lolly of the school picture, but a younger, more vulnerable version. Laurel pushed the door the rest of the way open. Her visitor looked at a crumpled piece of paper in her hand, then at the numbers on the side of the door, then stepped forward to stare at Laurel just as Jase had done two hours ago.

"Are you Laurel Elizabeth Harlow?" The girl's voice came out thin and edgy.

Laurel stared back. "Yes. Who are you?"

The girl wet her lips and darted her eyes away.

Laurel tried not to smile. It *was* Jase's daughter, and she was trying to figure out what to say. What was it going to be? Magazine subscriptions? A lost dog? How does one explain landing on a total stranger's doorstep at nine o'clock at night?

The girl ducked her head a little and looked up from under her long, movie-star brows, as if unsure how Laurel would react. "I'm . . . I'm Lolly. I think you, like, used to know my dad, Jason Redlander."

Those were the magic words.

Laurel unlocked the screen, flung it wide, and greeted her visitor with a big smile. "Welcome to Bosque Bend. Your father dropped by a couple of hours ago and told me you might come by. You look as though you've had a long day."

"Dad? Is he here?" Lolly's eyes went wide with alarm, and she shifted her balance to her back foot.

Laurel caught her tongue between her teeth. *Wrong thing to say.* Would Lolly make a run for it? Obviously she was not overjoyed at the prospect of returning to the bosom of her family. The situation must be more fraught than Jase let on.

Continuing to hold the screen open, Laurel did her best to seem harmless. "No, I'm quite alone, I promise. I think your father's spending the night at the family homestead."

"Did he tell you I ran away?"

"Yes."

"Are you going to call him?"

"I can wait a while if you'd like, but your father is worried about you, and I feel obliged to let him know you're safe."

Lolly took another look down the hall, as if Jase might be lurking behind the antique umbrella stand, then let her shoulders slump in surrender. "Well, okay."

Laurel closed the door and turned the lock, just in case Lolly changed her mind, but by the looks of her, she couldn't have made it much farther, poor thing. She'd stumbled on the threshold, and her face was drawn and pale. Once inside, she sank onto one of the Victorian corner chairs just inside the door. Her eyes closed, her yellow head drooped like a wilted daisy, and her purse and backpack fell to the floor beside her.

Laurel blinked in surprise. The chairs—squat, square, and stodgy—were basically decorator pieces. She'd never seen anyone actually *sit* in one of them before, much less fall asleep on their lumpy cushions.

She jiggled Lolly's shoulder gently.

"Um, honey, would you like something to eat?" No way she was going to let Jase's daughter spend the night in the foyer.

Lolly raised her head slowly, as if it were very heavy. Her eyes were still half-shut. "Yeah, I guess so." She yawned and scooted to the edge of the chair. "I haven't had anything but Red Bull since breakfast."

"Let's get you into the kitchen. I think I can rustle something up. Here, I'll help you with your gear." She grabbed the straps of the pink backpack.

Good grief! The thing weighed a ton! No wonder Lolly was tired.

Lolly rose from the corner chair in slow motion and retrieved her purse from the floor. Glancing up at the arched entryway to the kitchen, she smiled weakly, then staggered toward the big round table in the center of the room. Laurel hurried over to pull out a chair, at the same time depositing the backpack on the one next to her.

Lolly flopped down, whispered her thanks, then rested her head on her folded arms and closed her eyes again.

Maybe some caffeine would help—at least enough to keep Lolly awake till Jase came for her. Laurel took a pitcher of sweetened tea out of the refrigerator, filled a tall glass, and added ice and a slice of lemon.

Lolly probably needed some solid food too. She glanced around the kitchen. Darn—where were Harry Potter's house elves when you needed them? She didn't have much of anything in the house, and cooking was not her strong suit. A well-paid housekeeper had presided over the kitchen when she was a child—except for the fancy baking, of course, which Mama, being a proper Southern lady, had reserved for herself. And when Laurel was married to Dave and both of them were working, they'd either gone out or ordered in.

She sighed. Some women were born to cook and some women learned how to cook, but she was neither. Thank goodness for microwaves, but right now her freezer was totally empty—she'd been putting off going to the supermarket till she pawned the Meissen clock.

She touched Lolly's shoulder. "Honey, do you like peanut butter?"

Lolly's head stayed down, but a weary voice answered her. "Yeah, but no jelly."

Laurel couldn't help but smile. "That's good, because I don't have any."

Uncapping a plastic container of Jif, she spread a smooth scoop across a piece of bread, slapped another slice on top, and cut the sandwich diagonally. A paper plate, a handful of potato chips, and a yellow napkin from the holder in the center of the table completed her presentation.

Apparently the pungent smell of peanut butter did the trick. Lolly raised up as if from the dead and pulled the plate and glass toward herself.

Laurel breathed a sigh of relief—at least Lolly wouldn't die of starvation on her watch. Now to fix herself some tea and sit down so they could get acquainted.

But Lolly's sandwich was disappearing so fast that she immediately returned to the counter to make another one. This one went down a little slower, after which Lolly delivered a hearty sigh of satisfaction and a soft burp, then beamed across the table at her hostess.

"Thanks. That was good. I didn't know I was so hungry." Her peanut-buttery smile widened.

A pang of recognition pierced Laurel. Lolly may be fair while Jase was dark, but she had the same clean bone structure across the cheeks, and, when she chose, the same brilliant smile.

Don't go maudlin, Laurel Elizabeth. Now you have to convince her to call her father and let him know she's here, safe and sound.

She glanced at the clock on the wall across the room, and her internal alarm bell rang. Grabbing her glass, she took a couple of big swallows to wet her suddenly dry throat.

Two hours was the max by car between here and Dallas, three hours—maybe four—by Greyhound. Jase had said she'd left home in the morning. That meant there was a fair amount of time unaccounted for. Maybe it would be better to get a handle on the situation before Jase arrived. Besides, what else did they have to talk about? She wasn't about to let Lolly get onto the topic of her parentage.

She schooled her tone to sound light and casual. "Did you travel by bus?"

"Well, partway. I paid the brother of a friend of mine to drive me here from Dallas, but"—Lolly's pretty face twisted—"he got, like, mad at me and drove off and left me at

a service station in the middle of nowhere. Stole my iPod too."
She shrugged carelessly, as if iPods grew on trees. "The station
didn't have much business, so it took me a couple of hours
to pick up a ride, but a lady who was heading to Grapeland
agreed to take me as far as Waxahachie—even dropped me off
at the bus station." Lolly paused to gulp down the last of her
tea. "I bought a ticket to Bosque Bend, and got off at a furniture shop downtown."

Laurel's eyebrows lifted. The roofed bench that served as
Bosque Bend's bus drop-off was attached to the side of Josie's
Muebleria Usada, a used furniture store across the street from
Ulrich's Drive-in Beer and Grocery, where the Friday-night
bad boys hung out. The way Lolly was dressed, it was a miracle
they hadn't given her a hard time. Must be a quiet week-
end. Of course, it was—everyone was recovering from the big
Fourth of July blowout.

"How did you get here from the bus drop-off?"

"I walked."

Laurel shivered. Ten blocks on a moonless night with the
streetlights few and far between? Mama and Daddy would
have grounded her for life. And what exactly had happened re-
garding the kid who took her iPod? She had the feeling Lolly
was glossing over something.

"The boy who was giving you a ride—are you all right? Did
he...try anything with you?"

Lolly made a sound of contempt. "He thought he was so
studly!" She looked at Laurel out of the corner of her eye.
"Don't tell Dad."

"Why not?"

"He wouldn't understand. He'd get all bent out of shape
and say I should have known better."

"Honey, until this morning I hadn't seen your father in sixteen years, but I don't think he's changed so much that he'd be mad at you because some sleazeball made a pass at you."

Lolly's lower lip pouted out. "He hates me."

"Your father?"

"He's always yelling at me about stuff."

"What kind of stuff?"

"Oh, my grades, my friends, boys, what I wear—that sort of thing."

Laurel couldn't help but smile. When was it she and Sarah had started viewing their parents, especially their mothers, as demanding, irritating people who didn't understand them? Who purposely embarrassed them and stood in the way of everything they wanted to do?

Sarah complained that her mother was such an old fuddy-duddy that she wouldn't let Sarah invite boys to her slumber party like the Fassbinder twins did, and her father, the county attorney by then, made her dip into her birthday money to pay her speeding ticket rather than get it dismissed, which anyone who really loved her would have done.

Laurel, in turn, insisted that Mama ruined her life when she nixed buying her a strapless dress for junior cotillion that looked exactly like the dress on the cover of one of her favorite romance novels. Then there was the battle of the shorts. Her mother absolutely refused to let her walk out of the house in shorts, and Daddy backed up Mama with a lecture about modesty and how she should set a model for other girls rather than try to be like them. But the greatest injustice of all was that Sarah received a new Thunderbird after she passed her driver's test, while Laurel's only reward for finally getting her license six months later was being allowed to share her mother's car, Grampa's old Lincoln Town Car, which was as big as a boat and looked like a hearse.

Yes, Laurel understood where Lolly was coming from. Adolescence was hard.

Putting on a bright smile, she charged into the fray as gently as she could. "Isn't that the usual thing parents and teenagers disagree on? I bet the other girls feel the same way about their parents."

"Yeah, but..."

"But what?"

"They have mothers."

It was a blow to the gut. As angry as Laurel had gotten about the car and the clothes, she always knew Mama was there for her. Daddy had been more prominent publicly, but he had his church and his parishioners and his good works to tend to. Mama's primary concern was her.

"Mothers are very special," she finally replied.

She missed her mother so much, but Mama's world had turned against her, and, almost exactly a year ago, she swallowed every pill in the house to escape. Couldn't she have stuck it out? Or put the house up for sale so they could move someplace that people didn't know them?

No way. In the same sweet voice she always used, Mama said she had been born in Kinkaid House, and she would die here. And she did, preferring to join her parents and grandparents in the cemetery along the river rather than stay in a world that had turned against her. Thank goodness the burial plot had been prepaid, but strongly Protestant Bosque Bend had a Catholic abhorrence of suicide, and Laurel had a heck of a time finding a clergyman who would perform the simple graveside rite. Finally, Mrs. January, who'd retired as their housekeeper when

Laurel was in middle school, had prevailed upon her son, who headed a small AME congregation in Waco, to lay Mama properly to rest.

"My dad doesn't want me to meet my mother," Lolly continued, building up steam. "He told me she wasn't ready to take care of a baby so she sent me to him, and that he lost track of her, but he won't even tell me her name. He says she asked him not to tell me and that he's honoring her wishes. But I think that's *bull crap*!"

Lolly spit out the last two words defiantly, her eyes blazing blue.

Laurel stifled a smile. Was "bull crap" the best Lolly could come up with? She'd heard worse from second graders. "This is all very personal, Lolly. Maybe you need to wait and discuss it with your father."

"Or with my mother." Lolly stared meaningfully across the table.

"Or with your mother," Laurel repeated, folding her arms Indian-style in warning.

Somehow she'd been lured into dangerous territory. What Lolly said was logical, but the way she said it implied a lot more. But if she launched into a denial, it would seem she was being unduly defensive, making Lolly more certain than ever that she really was her mother.

She let it pass. This was really Jase's business, not hers.

Lolly's eyes wavered and she licked her lips. "Aunt Maxie—Aunt Maxie said you were a friend of my dad's when he lived here in Bosque Bend."

A change of subject. Maybe Lolly had realized it was terminally rude to try to lay claim to someone as your mother less than an hour after meeting her.

"Yes. We would visit every Wednesday after school when he came to the house for counseling with my father."

"Do you know who my mother is?"

Back to the starting point. "Lolly, I do not know who your mother is, and I will not discuss the matter any further." She tilted her head questioningly and lowered the boom. "Do you want me to call your father to come over now and pick you up?"

Lolly half rose from the table. "No, don't call him! I don't want to go yet! I want to stay here with you tonight! Please, I won't be a bother, I promise!" Big blue eyes shimmered across the table. "I'll go with Dad tomorrow afternoon. Just let me stay here until then."

To her surprise, Laurel realized that she wanted Lolly to stay. Because she was Jase's daughter, of course, but also because her curls bobbed when she talked, her eyes signaled as much as her voice, and she was so intense and fearless—a breath of fresh air in a house that had been shut up much too long.

"Well, okay, if your father agrees. But we'll have to go to the den and call him to let him know you're here, safe and sound."

Laurel rose from the table, and Lolly reached out to clasp her hand. "Thank you." She flashed the heartbreaking Redlander smile. "This is so important to me."

* * *

Jase rolled over on the first ring and picked up his mobile from the floor beside the bed. His hand trembled as he pushed the icon.

Please, please, please . . .

"Jase, this is Laurel. Lolly's here with me, and she's okay."

A two-ton elephant lifted off his shoulders. He sat up and moved to the edge of the bed. "I'll be there in twenty minutes."

"I think it would be best if you waited a while. She's feeling a bit—well—unsettled. I'll call you when she's ready, maybe tomorrow afternoon."

Instantly he was all father. "There's a problem?"

"No, no—it's just that she's tired right now. She'll be fine tomorrow."

He frowned. Laurel's answer seemed to come a little too quickly. "Be honest with me. Is Girl Child giving you trouble? There's not much traffic at this time of night, and I bet I can cut my time to fifteen minutes."

"Trouble?" Laurel sounded surprised. "Not at all. She's charming. I'll enjoy the company, and I think I can help."

Jase relaxed. "I'll wait till tomorrow, then."

Like father, like daughter. Maybe Laurel could work the same miracles with Lolly that Reverend Ed had with him. His relationship with Girl Child had become particularly fractious lately. Maxie said it was because she was fifteen, but he'd been worried enough to consult a psychologist, who basically told him the same thing—that Lolly was testing her limits and asserting an adulthood she hadn't quite reached yet, that everything would be up and down for a while, but they'd both survive if he kept his cool. But it was damn hard for him to keep his cool when she wouldn't let him keep her safe.

* * *

Laurel was trying to gently hustle her guest up the stairs, but it was slow going. Lolly's eyes were overbright, and she'd gotten her second wind.

"Oh, wow! Awesome! That mirror in the foyer, and the chandelier! Like something out of *Phantom of the Opera!*"

Laurel couldn't help but glance up, even though she'd walked under the same light fixture every day of her life.

"And the grain of the wood!" Lolly caressed the banister. "Killer! Is it walnut?"

"I'm not sure."

"Your house is like a museum—or a royal palace! Aunt Maxie and I made a tour of European castles last summer." She did a three-sixty survey of the foyer, then looked at Laurel, two steps above her. "Everything's so old and beautiful! And these paintings…" She gestured at the ascending display of deceased Kinkaids. "You must get a total charge out of living here!" Her glance swept up the stairway. "How many bedrooms do you have?"

That one Laurel knew the answer to. "Ten in all, but the ones on the third floor have been closed off for ages. There are four on the second floor—two smaller ones and two large suites. I use one of the smaller ones, and I'm putting you in the one across the hall."

Lolly indicated the gilt-framed portrait on the wall beside her. "Are these your grandparents?"

"No, they're my parents." It was her favorite picture of Mama and Daddy. Somehow the artist had done a better job of capturing Daddy's intrinsic goodness and Mama's gentle warmth than any photographer ever had.

"Dad talks about your father a lot, you know. He says Reverend Ed was the kindest, wisest person he's ever known."

Laurel tried to smile.

Lolly moved on past Grampa Dabney and Gramma Lorena's portrait, barely glanced at the picture of Grampa and his brother as children, then stopped at a pair of large oils. "Who are these people?"

"The stern-looking woman with the four little girls is my great-grandfather's first wife, Adeline Quisenberry, and the stern-looking woman in the painting one jump up from them, the one with the two boys clinging to her skirts, is his second wife, my great-grandmother, Ida Mae Benton."

Lolly stifled a yawn, nodded, and moved up several steps to study a large, dramatic painting of four dark-haired women in low-cut gowns.

Pendleton Swaim had been interested in that picture too, Laurel remembered. He'd even made a quick sketch of it three years ago during the garden club's historic homes tour. No telling how he'd use the information.

Lolly gestured toward the painting. "Who are they? They're so pretty."

"They're the little girls all grown up. Gramma said they were wild and that the oldest, Great-Aunt Barbara, ran off to Italy with the architect who designed the house, but I don't know about the others."

Lolly squinted at the picture as if trying to bring it into better focus. "They're all wearing necklaces with animal things hanging from them."

Laurel nodded. "Their father gave them the necklaces when he was in what Gramma called his 'Chinese phase.' The animals represent the year each girl was born in."

"Cool. I'm a rabbit."

They'd almost reached second-floor landing, but there was

one more portrait to go. Laurel made a grand gesture of introduction. "Lolly, I present to you my great-grandfather, Erasmus Galileo Kinkaid." She nodded her head in his direction, and he twinkled back, the cheeky devil.

Lolly's eyes lit up with renewed interest. "Hey, he's sexy!" Her brow clouded over. "He didn't own slaves, though, did he?"

Laurel shook her head. "Not Erasmus. He didn't arrive in Texas till sometime in the late 1860s, but his wives' families had cotton plantations before the Civil War."

Truth to tell, she'd always been a little uneasy around the black kids in school whose last names were Benton or Quisenberry. Emancipated slaves often took the surnames of their former masters, and the fact that the Bentons were so light that some of them had "passed" made her want to ask her mother questions she was pretty sure Mama didn't want to answer.

Lolly turned to her with a frown. "But why isn't *your* portrait here?

Laurel raised her hands in mock despair. "There wasn't room for me in the stairway, so I was exiled to the dining room. You can see me before you leave."

She took the final step onto the landing, opened the first door on the left, and switched on the light. If Lolly liked old-fashioned, this was the mother lode: a gilt mirror over the dressing table, antique furniture, and pink-flowered dimity curtains looping over gilded Cupid hooks, then hanging down on either side of the window.

Lolly came in behind her, stood in the center of the room, and pivoted slowly to take everything in.

"It's all so beautiful—I love the Aubusson and all the pastel colors. And that pale green bed and chest and vanity table are supercool. Are they, like, French Provincial?"

"Well, yes. Not the kind you get in stores, though. My great-grandfather bought it all in France way back when."

"Awesome. And I bet this is a feather bed." Lolly dropped her purse and backpack to the floor, then carefully sat down on the edge of the mattress, bouncing a little to test it. "I always wondered how it would feel to sleep on a feather bed."

Laurel laughed. "Sorry. That bed has had several mattresses through the years. The feathers have flown the coop."

Lolly's face fell. "No feathers?"

"They tend to hatch lice. I think you'll like the inner springs better."

Lolly yawned again, nodded a reluctant acceptance, and looked over at the half-open pocket door beside the bed. "Is that an en suite?"

"Uh-huh."

"Cool."

Laurel slid the door open and stepped inside the bathroom for a quick inspection to make sure no spiders had expired in the tub recently, as they had the distressing habit of doing. Score one for modern insecticides.

"There's a clean nightgown hanging on the hook behind the door, and you can use all the towels you want," she said, returning to the bedroom. "As you'll see, we've got plenty." Although she would have sold every one of them if there'd been any sort of market for old linens.

Lolly yawned and sat down on the bed, her head drooping toward her shoulder, and smoothed the sheet with her hand.

"Thank you."

Laurel moved to the door. "You're welcome, honey."

She turned on the window unit, and Lolly jerked around as the machine wheezed into action. Laurel smiled. Let Jase be the one to explain Stone Age technology to his daughter.

"Sweet dreams. I'll leave the bathroom light on in case you wake up during the night."

Lolly nodded, yawned again, and kicked off her flip-flops. "Good night."

"Good night, honey."

Laurel closed the door and crossed the hall to her bedroom, a nest of warmth settling between her breasts.

Jase's daughter was sleeping across the hall in her house tonight.

Chapter Four

Laurel slipped off her shoes and scrunched her toes into the soft silk rug beside the bed, another vestige of Erasmus's Chinese phase.

This room would be hard to leave. It had been her own private place—her bower—since she was born. She'd store the rug and the cherrywood bedroom suite till she had a place big enough to accommodate them, but the room itself, with its high ceiling, crown molding, and wall-length closet—there was no reproducing that.

Opening the door to the connecting bathroom, she turned on the faucets of the tub. Nothing like a long, restful soak before bed. She unbuttoned her shirt and slipped it off her arms. Her bra followed next, then her slacks and panties.

What if Jase hadn't left town sixteen years ago, and if, by some miracle, they'd actually ended up getting married? He wouldn't have deserted her like Dave did.

Or would he?

She glanced at herself in the mirror and teased her nipples erect to make sure they still worked.

Get real, Laurel Elizabeth. If Jase knew what everybody else in Bosque Bend knows, he probably wouldn't even have allowed Lolly to spend the night here. Not that it mattered. Now that his daughter had turned up, he'd come pick her up, turn that Caddie around, and hightail it right back to Dallas. Just like she would hightail herself out of town the second she had a contract on the house.

She stepped into the tub and settled down into the warm, soothing water, expecting to drift into near unconsciousness, but the second she closed her eyes, her brain began rerunning a mental tape from sixteen years ago.

* * *

News of the scandal had leapt from house to house like a shake-roof fire, but Laurel first heard about it on Thursday, during her daily hour as a student aide, when she was filing absence slips in the anteroom off the main office. Sarah's mother's voice was loud and clear as she discussed the event with the school secretary.

"What do you think, Gail? I know the Redlander boy comes from bad stock. After all, his father has that horrible beer tavern, Beat Down or whatever it's called, across the county line." Mrs. Bridges's voice lowered a decibel or two, as if she were trying to be discreet. "Nyquist told the school board he heard Marguerite screaming for help when he dropped by her house to pick up some papers, but Odelle Schlossnagel said that Jase and Marguerite had been at it for months, that she saw him vaulting over Ms. Shelton's fence when she was putting out Christmas lights back in December." Her voice ratcheted up a notch again. "Nyquist's story is that Jase overpowered Marguerite, but my God, Gail, how could that boy have forced himself on that woman for four months straight without her uttering a word of complaint?"

Laurel risked a quick look toward the front desk and saw Ms. Fogarty raise a carefully penciled eyebrow and glance in the direction of Mr. Nyquist's empty office. "Well, Marilyn, all I can tell you is that we've never had any trouble with Jason. He's built like an adult man, though, six two in his stocking feet and still growing, while Marguerite's only an inch or so above five feet." She snickered through her nose. "On the other hand, she always looked *very* happy when she clocked in every morning."

Jase and Ms. Shelton? Laurel didn't believe a word of it. And apparently Ms. Fogarty and Sarah's mother didn't either—they seemed to be more amused than shocked.

A harsh buzz drowned out the women's knowing laughter. Time for lunch.

Laurel's brain whirled as she placed the rest of the absence slips on top of the filing cabinet for the next hour's aide to finish off. She walked down the hall to the lunchroom like she was in a trance, filled her tray, handed her punch card to the monitor behind the register, then went over to the table near the window where she and her best friends always sat.

Rebecca Diaz, Saundra Schlossnagel, and Jennie Lynn Pietzsch weren't there yet, but Sarah started talking before Laurel could even set her tray down.

"Did you hear what they're saying about Jase?"

Laurel sat down on the bench across from her friend. "Yes, but I don't believe it."

Sarah's dark eyes sparkled with excitement. "Well, the school board does. Last period in drama class, Amy Fassbinder—her father's a trustee, you know—told me Mr.

Nyquist called their house at seven this morning and said he'd caught Jase in the act."

Laurel ripped open her milk carton. "I still don't believe it."

"Maybe Jase—" Sarah glanced across the room. "*Shh*, here comes Rebecca. Don't say a word. You know how prissy she is."

Laurel nodded, picked up her fork, and loaded it with a chunk of meatloaf.

She had no intention of talking to Rebecca or anyone else about Jase and Ms. Shelton, but she sure was thinking about them. The whole idea was ridiculous—Ms. Shelton was far too old for him. Besides, when she'd talked to Jase yesterday, before Daddy called him into his office, he hadn't acted any different. Mr. Nyquist must have gotten it wrong—or maybe Ms. Shelton made it all up. Jenny Lynn, who had been in her class last semester, said she was a good teacher, but she spent a lot of time flirting with the football guys.

How should she act when Jase came to the house next Wednesday? What should she say to him? What *could* she say to him?

She stared at her fork. *Meatloaf?* She loathed meatloaf! She shook it off onto her plate and took a big gulp of milk straight from the carton.

Daddy would know what she should do. She'd talk to him when she got home. But how in the world do you discuss something like that with your father?

However, as usual, Daddy made it easy. As soon as she mentioned Jase's name, he nodded, took off his glasses, and gave her his full attention. "Jase is a victim and no danger to anyone but himself," he said in his usual dry, precise tone. "You should behave normally around him and not listen to gossip."

Which, Laurel decided, meant Jase was innocent, just as she'd thought. However, Mama, whom she always talked with after her evening prayers, was more cautious. "Ms. Shelton has been replaced by a permanent substitute because of health problems," she said, patting Laurel's hand. "Perhaps it would be better to avoid Jason from now on, dear."

In an instant, Jase became a tragic hero, and one whom Laurel would defend to the death.

She would be his friend, his helpmeet, his champion. With her by his side, he would be completely exonerated. Then all the petty gossipers, realizing what a terrible mistake they had made, would come to him on bended knee and beg his forgiveness for their small, dirty minds. And after she and Jase were married in the hazy distant future and had moved in with Mama and Daddy, she would be the envy of all of her friends, especially the Fassbinder twins, because Jase would tell everyone that he wouldn't be here today if it weren't for her unyielding faith in him.

And, most important of all, her father would be proud of her.

* * *

The first thing she had to do the next morning was find a way to talk to Jase. She tried the gym—that's where all the jocks hung out before classes started—but Jase wasn't there. Saundra said she'd heard he left school at lunchtime the day before, and no one had seen him since. Later in the afternoon, she looked him up in the office files and discovered the school didn't have a phone number listed for him, but there was an address.

That meant she'd have to track him down at home over the

weekend, which meant prevailing upon Sarah, with her brand-new driver's license and brand-new car.

No problem. As usual, Sarah was game for anything. Besides, Sarah knew Laurel was in love with Jase. Whenever they got tired of singing along with Mariah and Madonna, and after Sarah ran out of things to say about her latest boyfriend, Laurel would talk about Jase. Not that she would be allowed to go on a real date till she was sixteen, and not that there was the slightest chance her mother would *ever* allow her to go anywhere with Growler Red's son, but she could dream.

Her courage ebbed as Sarah turned onto Jase's street.

Talk about hardscrabble. This was the kind of neighborhood she and Mama delivered church charity baskets to at Christmas. It was farther out on the long west arm of the Bosque than she'd realized, and the overcast sky made the scene look like the set of a depressing old black-and-white movie. While Jase's house wasn't any worse off than the other two shacks staggered along the dirt road, it wasn't any better either. Something had gnawed the siding as far up as it could reach, the asphalt shingle roof was a patchwork of tan, brown, and red, and Jase had parked that old rattletrap Chevy pickup of his on what should have been the lawn.

Sarah took a long look around and wrinkled her nose. "Are you sure?"

Laurel's stomach tightened, but she reminded herself that her cause was noble, like when Joan of Arc led the troops of Charles VII at Orleans.

"I'm sure."

She opened her door, and her white flats sank immediately into the springtime gumbo. The sticky black loam was great for growing cotton, but hardened like concrete when it dried on your shoes. Mrs. Claypool, the new housekeeper, would kill her.

Sarah stuck her head out the window. "When do you want me to pick you up?"

Laurel gave her what she hoped was a confident smile. "Don't worry. I'm sure Jase will give me a ride home."

"Well, okay. If you say so."

The Thunderbird sped off and Laurel started across the yard, scraping her muddy shoes against the knee-deep knots of Johnsongrass as she went. A saucy April breeze riffled the hem of her skirt as she walked up the steps to the front porch. She'd decided to dress up, to wear her Easter outfit, a yellow skirt topped by a white blouse that had little yellow flowers embroidered around the neckline—after all, she was engaged in a worthy cause. Besides, Jase had never seen her dressed up before.

She paused at the top of the steps and looked around. A rusty metal chair sat on the right of the door, and on the left, a bone-thin hound sprawled across a sagging old davenport. The dog lifted an eyelid in inquiry, and Laurel remembered that Mama's older sister had died from rabies.

Better get herself inside quick.

She raised her hand to the doorbell. *Ew!* There was no way she was going to touch that thing! It was more grime than button! Maybe a gentle knock would do it. She gave the doorframe a light rat-a-tat-tat, stood back politely, rechecked the dog, and waited.

Why wasn't anyone answering the door? Jase's truck was parked in the yard, so he must be at home. She'd have to knock louder. Opening the rusty screen and holding it away from her dress, she prepared to pound on the door itself, but it swung open at first touch. After peeking into the morning shadows, she walked inside.

The smell hit her first—the rank, dank odor of stale cigarette smoke and unemptied trash cans. The visual was even worse—the place was a mess. Crusty paper plates, overflowing ashtrays, and herds of longnecks littered every available surface, including the floor. She'd heard that Jase's Aunt Maxie dropped by from time to time to keep things tidy, but circumstances, namely Growler Red, went against her. Laurel hadn't realized how badly.

She swallowed hard and moved forward boldly, like Joan of Arc would have. "Jase, are you there?"

A muffled groan answered her.

Jase!

Following his voice, she turned to the left and walked straight into his bedroom. A little thrill chased through her stomach. She'd never been alone in a boy's bedroom before. In fact, she'd never been in a boy's bedroom at all. And not only were she and Jase the only ones in the house, but Jase was still in bed.

Her mouth went dry as she stared at the ropy muscles of his arms and the masculine darkness that shaded the center of his chest between the small, brown, male paps.

What had happened to his pajama top?

Jase propped himself up on an elbow and peered at her as though he couldn't believe what he was seeing.

Laurel definitely couldn't believe what *she* was seeing. Jase's long, dark hair, almost the length of hers, was tousled and damp, and his eyes were slits of black. Stubble shadowed the lower half of his face. She wondered for an eerie second if she'd walked into the wrong house.

Apparently he did too. "Laurel! What are you doing here?"

It *was* Jase! "I came to tell you that I believe in you."

"What?" Shaking his head as if to clear it, he hoisted himself up a little further.

Her cheeks went red. Daddy always wore pajamas to bed—pima cotton, usually pale blue with darker blue piping—but Jase had been sleeping in his underpants. Should she look away or pretend she didn't notice?

It didn't matter. The important thing was what she had come to say, which apparently he hadn't quite comprehended. She moved forward to explain, cleared her throat, and began again. "I don't believe all the stupid stuff everyone is saying. The stuff about you and Ms. Shelton."

Her foot knocked into a beer can that clanked across the floor and banged into another can under a leg of the bed. Nude pinups and football posters papered the wall behind him. A tuna tin full of cigarette butts sat on the rickety metal table beside the bed.

"I—I just thought you'd want to know." Her voice was breaking, and she was trembling on the verge of nervous tears.

Maybe visiting Jase wasn't such a good idea after all. The whole scene had played out differently in her imagination. The house had been sparse but clean, and Jase had been wearing his football jersey. After she'd declared her faith in him, he'd clasped her knees in gratitude, like in the historical romance she'd been reading. Then she'd lifted him up and they'd embraced decorously, plighting their troth.

Instead, he was lying half-naked in a rumpled bed in a filthy house, looking at her like she was crazy. God help her—she'd made a complete fool of herself.

Suddenly the ignominy of it all crashed in on her, and she burst into tears.

Holding the sheet around himself, Jase reached for her arm and pulled her down beside him on the bed. "Don't cry," he crooned, patting her back awkwardly and putting an arm around her so she sobbed on his bare shoulder. He dropped a light kiss onto the top of her head and patted her as if she were a child. "I can't stand to see you cry."

But she was not a child, and delicious new feelings were creeping into her consciousness—a longing she'd never experienced before, impelling her to prolong her sobbing as a means of squirming closer to the wonderful warmth of Jase's bare skin.

He gave her a quick peck on the side of her face, his morning beard rasping against her sensitive cheek.

"Oh Jase, I love you so much," she whispered, turning her face up to him.

"I love you too, Laurel."

That was all the encouragement she needed, Shivering, she turned and caught his lips with her own, and sucked at them shamelessly.

It was like he caught fire. "Laurel...Laurel..."

Half rising on the bed, he pulled her closer, kissed her tears, then moved his mouth across her lips and throat. A blazing heat raced through her as he nuzzled the shells of her ears and stroked her arms and shoulders.

She could hardly bear it—the touch of his hands, the sliding of skin against skin. She'd never felt like this before—so happy, so alive. Sensuality might have been new to her, but she was ripe for it.

"I love you, I love you," she repeated, kissing him, moving against him.

He pulled away for a second and looked at her. "We shouldn't be doing this."

His voice was rough and his words so thick and slurred that it was hard to understand him, but she didn't care. The black glaze of his eyes and the flush on his cheeks were all that mattered. She moaned and swayed back into his arms, pushing against him so they sank down sideways, face-to-face, the upper half of his body covering hers.

She was in utter bliss, reveling in the feel of him—his lips, his arms, his hard body.

Her palms and the insides of her arms were prickling beyond bearing, so she rubbed them against his back, and when his hand caressed her hips through her skirt, she couldn't help but move her legs together for relief. Arching her neck backward, she rolled her head from side to side, making strange mewing sounds she couldn't suppress.

His mouth traveled down to the tops of her breasts, sensitizing her skin every inch along the way. On the return trip, he reclaimed her lips, while his hand went inside her blouse, touching and caressing.

Laurel's eyes closed, her cheeks burned, and she let her head roll back again, offering him her throat. This should never end. She wanted more.

The bed creaked as Jase shifted his weight so he was on top of her all the way down, with one of his legs between hers.

"Laurel, sweetheart," he whispered, first circling the outer edge of her lips with the tip of his tongue, then coaxing them open and tracing the inside rim of her mouth. She shuddered and moaned again, which seemed to excite him even more. His breathing was loud and ragged.

He slipped his fingers under the band of her old-fashioned cotton bra, releasing it to tease her sensitized nipples with his tongue and teeth and hand. His other hand moved up under her skirt, bunching it and her half-slip up around her waist. When his hand moved back down, her panties ended up below her knees.

Her panties! Laurel's eyes snapped open. An alarm bell rang in her brain.

"Jase—"

Immediately his tongue plunged in and out of her mouth in a sharp, swift movement that frightened her, then thrilled her. The alarm turned itself off.

Her blouse and bra disappeared, and one of his hands was at her breasts again, kneading them and manipulating the sensitive nipples. His other hand was below, stroking her stomach and the outside of her legs.

He circled and teased, approaching the juncture of her legs, then moving away, then returning—touching, teasing, exploring, and, finally, finding.

She whimpered and rotated her head in frustration. Her entire body had become a strange new creature, a wonderful new creature of sensation and delight. She moved tentatively against his hand, and he rewarded her with a low-voiced growl.

The alarm bell rang again as he moved his weight onto her more fully, and his hard erection rested against her stomach, with only the knit fabric of his briefs between them. She looked up at him. His eyes were glassy, his face flushed, barely unrecognizable. His hot hand reached down to free himself from his underwear, and she knew what would come next. He wanted to do the thing to her that her mother had warned her against, the thing that would ruin her forever in the eyes of God and her parents and all of Bosque Bend.

One of his hands continued to work her as the other eased

down his briefs. She could feel him now, his maleness, against the flesh of her body. She didn't want to do this, but she didn't know how to get out of it either. Had she promised something that he would hate her for if she didn't follow through on? Maybe it wouldn't matter, because he could tell everyone he'd done it to her anyway.

He tried to wrap her hand around himself.

"Touch me, Laurel. Feel how much I want you."

She froze in horror, and all her fine madness fled. She wasn't Juliet Capulet or Joan of Arc after all. She wasn't even a sexy heroine from one of Mrs. Bridges's paperbacks. She was plain, simple Laurel Elizabeth Harlow, the preacher's daughter, a good girl, and she wasn't ready for all this. Pulling her hand back, she tried to roll away from him.

At first he didn't seem to realize what was going on and grabbed at her hand again.

"No, Jase! Let me go!"

"I love you, Laurel. I adore you," he crooned, returning to her breasts and face, but she twisted her head to avoid his lips and willed herself not to respond to his touch.

Her voice dropped to a soft plea. "Jase, we can't don't do this. Please."

He closed his eyes for a long second, then released her hands and rolled off her to sit on the edge of the bed. His loud breath rasped in the quiet room as he stared at the far wall. "Get dressed. I'll take you home."

Then, like a naked young Hercules, he strode down the hall toward the bathroom.

Laurel didn't need a second invitation. With a wary eye on the door, she pulled her skirt and slip down to cover her naked thighs, scurried about the room to retrieve her panties, bra, and blouse, and dressed faster than she ever had before in her life. Standing on tiptoe, she checked herself out in the small mirror over the bureau next to the door. Her hair was a mess, and her face looked like she had a fever.

After running her fingers through her hair to smooth it, she pressed her cheeks with her hands to bring down their color. Her lips were swollen and her eyes were dark and hollow, but there was nothing she could do about that. She'd have to sneak in the side door and stay in her room for an hour or so before facing Mama and Daddy.

There were probably marks on her body too, maybe bruises, but she was the only one who would see them.

Jase emerged from the bathroom. He'd pulled on a pair of jeans and a shirt that he hadn't bothered to button. "You ready?" His voice was gruff and curt.

"Yes."

"I have to get some shoes."

She backed up as he entered the room, her eyes following his every move as he reached under the bed for his sneakers, but he didn't even glance at her. She might have been in Ethiopia for all he seemed to care.

She looked at the room one last time and felt sick to her stomach. It was all so sordid—the tuna tin of cigarette butts, the football posters and lurid pinups, the unmade bed.

"Let's go," he said, standing beside the doorway, his face expressionless, the color high in his cheeks.

She walked slowly toward the doorway, nervous about passing so close to him, then scuttled through it quickly, ready to fight him off at any moment. Outside the weather had turned bright and sunshiny, a beautiful, uncaring morning full of promise and delight. What irony. How could the day be so lovely when, in less than half an hour, her whole life had turned upside down?

Jase held the passenger door to the pickup open with mock courtesy, and she slid gingerly onto the torn vinyl seat, remaining as close to the door as possible. Walking around to the driver's side, he lit a defiant cigarette before he got in, and started the engine.

They rode in silence for a few minutes until he spoke.

"Everything they say about me is true." He sucked at the cigarette and floated the white smoke out through his mouth and nostrils. "I've been doing Ms. Shelton since before Christmas, and I'll do you too if you give me half a chance. You've had your warning. I'm bad news. Stay clear of me from now on."

And she had stayed clear of him, which wasn't hard since he left Bosque Bend within a week.

When Sarah asked what had happened the next day at church, she'd said Jase had thanked her for her concern, asked her to pray for him, and driven her home.

But for days after that, her nipples tingled when her breasts moved against her starched cotton bra. And in her virgin bed at night, when the whole world was dark and anything was possible, she relived that morning at Jase's house again and again. The awkward ride home was a forgotten footnote as she reveled in the memory of his passionate kisses and the touch of his body.

What would it have been like if she hadn't made him stop?

Chapter Five

J ase took a couple of deep breaths, then punched in Maxie's number.

"Lolly's safe. Laurel Harlow's taking care of her, but I'm getting the idea Girl Child's being difficult."

He could hear the exasperation mixed into Maxie's sigh of relief and knew exactly how she felt.

"You'd better come down here tomorrow morning. Call me as soon as you have a flight number and I'll pick you up at the Waco airport."

"What about Lolly? Do you need me to bring anything for her?" That was Maxie—always on top of things. God knows what he would have done sixteen years ago if she hadn't already made plans to move to Dallas for a full-time job with an insurance company when the school board got him kicked out of town.

"Why don't you bring her a change of clothes, just to be sure, and I'd appreciate you packing a suitcase for me too. I'll probably stay here a while to scout out the local scene. It looks like Bosque Bend might have some business possibilities."

"Will do. See you tomorrow."

Jase replaced the mobile on the floor beside the bed and laid his head back on the pillow.

He'd check around to see what properties were available. If Walmart had a new store here, the town must be on the upswing.

Who was he kidding? He didn't need any small-town properties. What he wanted to do was keep busy so he wouldn't make an ass out of himself knocking at Laurel's front door and demanding to see his daughter before she was ready for him.

Damn, he and Girl Child were at loggerheads all the time now, and he loved her so much. She was his life. Thank God that Laurel had taken her in last night.

Laurel...

Something must be wrong with ol' Dave. Back in high school, he'd been a lazy sonuvabitch, always looking for the main chance, and in Bosque Bend, with her mother's money and her father's reputation, Laurel Harlow would've been it.

So—what was the divorce all about? Jase himself would never have let go of Laurel, and not just because of her father. He shifted uncomfortably as he remembered the curve of her breasts against the thin fabric of her shirt when she answered the door this evening, her moist red lips opening in surprise at the sight of him, the sway of her hips as she led him to the front room.

Taking in a deep breath of air and exhaling strongly, he tried to make himself relax.

Cut it out, Redlander. You don't stand a chance.

* * *

Laurel woke up happy and lay in bed for a few minutes longer just to savor the new day. Jase Redlander had visited her yesterday, and he would visit her again today. That smile, his voice, those dark eyes that seemed to absorb her into their depths—dear God, had she ever gotten over her a crush on him? How did he feel about her? Was there...a possibility?

But why was she lying around? She shouldn't let one precious moment of this precious day go to waste. Humming a kindergarten tune about sunshiny faces, she made up her bed and laid out her clothes, tan chinos and a blue-checked shirt—simple, comfortable, and practical—one of her favorite teaching outfits. Chalk smudges, stray ballpoint marks, playground dirt, you name it—this shirt had swallowed them all and washed clean.

She stared at it for a moment. As happy as she was, she wanted to put on something new, something different, something she'd never worn before, and she knew just where to find it. Kneeling on the floor, she opened the bottom drawer of her bureau, where she stored all the tees her students had given her that Dave had considered inappropriate for the wife of a banker to wear.

Yes, there it was, right on top—an orange shirt decorated with a fat, yellow happy face. She pulled it over her head, swiped on some lipstick, inserted tiny gold hoops through her earlobes, and tied her hair up in a scraggly ponytail, then checked herself out in the long cheval mirror in the corner of the room.

Now she looked the way she should.

Stepping across the hall, she opened the door carefully and peeked into the room. Sometime during the night, Lolly had straightened herself out and pushed the sheet to the foot of the bed, but she was still sound asleep. Let her rest, poor baby. She'd had quite an adventure yesterday.

Humming again, Laurel walked downstairs and went outside to search for the *Retriever*—for once, without first making sure no one was around. Lord help her, she was downright giddy. Would Lolly want to read the paper? Probably not. She was a teenager. All she'd be interested in was food.

Food. Laurel froze in her tracks. She'd need to fix some kind of breakfast for Lolly.

"Miss Harlow? Are you okay?"

She whirled around, half expecting to get something thrown in her face, but it was Bosque Bend's least favorite author, Pendleton Swaim. Every now and then, he left his Spanish-style stucco castle on the corner and took a turn up and down the block.

Laurel stiffened.

The Kinkaids had not escaped their neighbor's sharp pen. Pen had portrayed Great-Grampa Erasmus—"Benjamin Franklin Chapman"—as the disinherited son of Quakers, who never looked back once he hit Texas. Instead, he married the daughter of a wealthy family in Waco and bought land up cheap from cotton farmers who couldn't pay labor costs for newly freed slaves. And when the first wife died, he married into an even wealthier family in "Garner's Crossing," the whole time enjoying a string of mistresses, even financing the brothel one of them set up down near the tracks of the K-T Railroad he'd helped bring through town.

Mama was indignant, but Daddy shrugged it off, saying who knew what was research, what was rumor, and what Pen Swaim had made up out of the back of his head to titillate readers. Besides, having a colorful ancestor gave Mama bragging rights.

Laurel was embarrassed. She'd learned far too much about her heritage.

"Yes, thank you. I was—was just thinking about something."

He gave her an understanding nod. "I was coming to see you anyway. I have a visitor, and I wonder if you would be kind enough to receive him."

"Receive him?"

"Allow him to come in and soak up the atmosphere in Kinkaid House."

"This has to do with the movie that's going to be made of *Garner's Crossing*, doesn't it? The one with the all-star cast?"

Art Sawyer had ballyhooed the news more than a month ago, and the town still hadn't decided whether to be thrilled or horrified. Sure, all the "fictional" characters being portrayed were long dead, but a lot of the dirty laundry that the town had rinsed out white as snow over the past hundred or so years would be hung out for everyone to see.

Swaim nodded. "Yes. And I do so want them to get it right."

"I don't know—"

"I'll send him over and you can decide at the door."

"Well, I—"

But Pendleton had moved on, leaving her talking to air.

It didn't matter. She returned to the house. Right now she had to come up with a nice breakfast for Lolly. And Pendleton's pal might never show up.

Hurrying to the kitchen, she laid the newspaper on the tile counter and went from cupboard to refrigerator to the pantry. Lolly deserved something special. But what sort of breakfast did she have the ingredients for—and know how to make?

How about French toast? On Sunday mornings, Mama would take over the kitchen and prepare it as a special treat for the family. Laurel was pretty sure she remembered the process. All it took was bread, eggs, milk, and—and cinnamon. Did she have cinnamon? She checked the far reaches of the pantry. Yes, back in the corner.

Channeling Rachael Ray, she gathered the ingredients together on the counter next to the stove and greased a pan. Then, to complete the scene, she tied on Mama's old apron, a frilly affair designed more for looks than utility. The second Lolly appeared, she'd turn on the burner.

This is what it would be like if Dave had stuck around and she were making breakfast for her own family. She turned on her coffee machine.

Easygoing, good-natured Dave. He'd been popular with Bosque Bend's social set and she'd thought he was the perfect fit. She'd have adored any children they would have had. Of course, parenthood would have complicated matters when he left her, because she had a good idea he would have abandoned the children too. Dave always was one to minimize his losses.

Shrugging off what might have been, she poured herself a cup of coffee and opened up the *Retriever* to catch up on what was happening in Bosque Bend, then paused. Why was she so excited about Lolly being here? Did she miss her parents so much? It had been two years since Daddy died and not quite a year since Mama found her own escape, but she felt like she'd been alone forever.

Today's issue was mostly ads, and, for once, Arthur Sawyer didn't have anything controversial to editorialize about. *Rats*. Just when she needed something to help pass the time.

She glanced up at the kitchen clock. When would Lolly wake up?

Laying her apron across the back of a chair, she wandered

into the den and paused in front of the big teak bookcase to pull out her favorite high school annual, the one from her sophomore year. She cradled it against herself and traipsed upstairs to her room. Curling up on her bed, she went through it page by page.

First came the photos of the school administrators, each one with a separate page. Principal Nyquist's picture, which led the pack, was the same one he'd used for years. He couldn't help the way the camera angle emphasized his broken nose, a souvenir of his coaching days, but there was something about his squinchy eyes and the grim set of his mouth that had always put her off.

She turned to the pictures of the faculty members. Marguerite Chalmers Shelton, MA, English, smiled seductively out of a cunningly lit headshot from a three-quarters angle.

Laurel tilted the book to get it in a better light. Ms. Shelton wasn't really *that* pretty, once you looked at her feature by feature. Her eyes were sort of an odd color, a light hazel, although that could just be the fading photo, while her nose was short and snubby and her mouth a bit overwide. She had gorgeous hair, though: reddish blonde, curly, and thick.

Laurel remembered that hair. Sometimes Ms. Shelton wore it up, but more often she let it flow to midway down her back. Saundra Schlossnagel had said she looked like a fashion model, but Laurel knew Saundra was way off base, because she and Sarah had made an in-depth study of models when Sarah was considering becoming the next Heidi Klum—in addition to playing softball in the Olympics, getting a law degree, and running for governor.

Anyway, Laurel knew Ms. Shelton was just too short to walk the fashion runway. Not that she didn't try to make up for it by teetering along on stilettos while every other female teacher in the school wore Keds. Sarah said she did it to make her boobs and butt stick out. Whatever, the guys liked it, and apparently Mr. Nyquist did too, judging by the expression Laurel had seen on his face when Ms. Shelton was talking to him in his office one day. He was smiling down at her like a loon, acting as infatuated as any of the boys.

Laurel looked up from the page, considering. Had it gone any further? Hadn't there been a rumor Ms. Shelton and Mr. Nyquist were having an affair? The whole school had buzzed with the thrill of it, but then Ms. Shelton's secret lover turned out to be Jase Redlander. And later that summer, Bert Nyquist created his own scandal by running out on his wife and children in the middle of the night, leaving behind a rambling note about what a total bastard he was.

Laurel leafed quickly through the book to the sports section and her own favorite page. She was surprised the book hadn't fallen open to it. Through the years, she'd made quite a study of all Jase's photographs, but this was the one she liked best.

The varsity team was pictured in a group photo on the left page, with Jase seated next to his fellow linebackers, Ray Espinoza and Ahmed Quisenberry. But on the right-hand page, the players were featured in small individual photos. Most of the guys looked like human bulldogs, no doubt as instructed by Coach Gifford. But by some quirk of fate, Jase had been caught smiling, not the full-blown Redlander dazzler, but a soft, warm, almost wistful smile. Laurel could never look at that picture without smiling back at him, without her heart turning over, without thinking of that morning in the house on the edge of town and what had almost happened.

Laurel allowed herself a cynical sniff. It may not have happened with her, but Lolly was living proof that it had certainly happened with some other girl.

She flipped back to the individual class pictures, barely skimming the seniors to concentrate on the juniors, Jase's class. Which one was Lolly's mother? Running her finger down the photos, she stopped at each fair-haired girl, trying to remember which blondes were natural. Betty Jean Powell? She stared at the picture of a towheaded girl with five earrings in one ear and eight in the other. Sarah had told her that Betty Jean had a butterfly tattoo on her behind and would do anything with anyone.

Remnants of freshman biology began to permeate Laurel's brain. It could be that Lolly had been the result of recessive genes of both sides, that her mother was just as dark as Jase.

But her finger continued its trek.

Tammy Spivak? Sarah had said she was doing it too, and her family did move out of town right after Jase left.

"Laurel?"

She nearly jumped out of her skin. The annual toppled to the floor. Lolly stood in the doorway, her hair hanging loose and her clothes rumpled, but her face bright and blooming from a full night's sleep.

"Sorry. Didn't mean to startle you, but I wanted to take a bath and couldn't figure out how to make the stopper work right."

Laurel stood up. "Of course. That one's kind of tricky. Just a minute."

She picked up the album from the floor and laid it on her bed, hoping that Lolly hadn't realized whose picture she was studying so intently. "Would you like some fresh clothes? I'm taller than you are, but you could wear some of my stuff if you'd like."

"Cool. That'd be great. This shirt feels pretty grungy."

After helping Lolly with the tub, Laurel went through her wardrobe for appropriate teenage attire. Her bottom drawer yielded up a sequined and star-spangled tee, but Lolly would have to wear the same shorts she had on yesterday.

She deposited the shirt on Lolly's bed, then rapped on the bathroom door. "Breakfast will be ready when you are."

Now to get rid of the evidence. Grabbing the annual from her bed, she hurried downstairs and dropped it in the den before returning to the kitchen to set the table with bright yellow paper plates on top of woven turquoise-colored placemats. Then, after reclaiming Mama's apron, she waited. The burner went on at the sound of the sound of Lolly's foot on the stairs.

"Hey, something smells good."

Lolly entering the room was like the sun coming out all over again. It wasn't just the color of her hair. There was something about her, a glow of energy that seemed to make the air sparkle around her.

Laurel couldn't help but smile at the twin ponytails bouncing on either sides of her face. "You've got doggie ears."

Lolly touched one of the masses of curls. "Yeah. I change my hair around a lot."

"Take a seat. I've poured you some orange juice, and breakfast will be ready in a minute. Hope you like French toast."

Lolly's face clouded. "I've never tried it. Aunt Maxie and I always have Cheerios at home." She took a seat at the big table.

Laurel was glad the old table was getting some use. It had been here since Kinkaid House was built, but it was yet another item that would be up for sale if she didn't get a buyer for the house soon. She'd never need anything that large for herself, and oak tables were scoring good prices these days.

Wielding a spatula, she lifted the eggy toast onto a serving plate and brought it to the table. Lolly eyed the concoction suspiciously. "It's sort of soggy."

"You eat it with a fork. Try it." Sitting down next to her with her own plate, Laurel demonstrated the technique.

Lolly, still looking doubtful, cut the toast and speared a small piece. She glanced at her hostess for encouragement, then grimaced as she lifted it into her mouth and chewed thoughtfully.

Her expression cleared. "Gosh, it's good!"

Laurel laughed, enjoying Lolly's surprise.

What a sweetheart—she'd been willing to try her cooking just to please her.

After cleaning up the remains of breakfast, they moved to the den again, where Lolly made a tour of the room, peering at all the photographs and reading aloud the inscriptions on all the plaques and trophies.

"This looks like the oldest picture," she said, pointing to a dingy tintype in the bookshelf. "He's the guy at the head of the stairs, isn't he?"

Laurel nodded. "You have a good eye. That's Erasmus Kinkaid again, when he first came to Texas."

"Cool. He must have really been something."

Laurel laughed. "Gramma always referred to him as 'that rascal,' and I don't think she meant it lovingly."

Lolly's eyes widened with interest. Obviously she liked rascals. Jase must really have his hands full.

Lolly reached for a picture of Erasmus and his two sons. "What about your grandfather? Was he a rascal too?"

"A little bit, or at least a sharp businessman. He diversified the family holdings, and we made it through the Great Depression so well that he could fund a major renovation on the house in the 1930s and another one in the 1960s." That one had cost almost a million dollars. Mama had planned on putting in central air and renovating the kitchen three years ago, until suddenly there was no money for anything.

"And your father? I know he was a pastor, but did he also make investments?"

Laurel managed to keep her smile in place. "Daddy wasn't interested in investments, and Mama didn't see it as her place to get involved."

Daddy thought money grew on trees, and Mama was oblivious.

Lolly replaced the picture of Erasmus and looked at a large photograph of Laurel and her parents on the shelf above them. "What sort of family did your dad come from? Was his father a preacher? Did it run in the family?"

Laurel shook her head. "I don't know. Daddy was raised in the Methodist Home in Waco. His father gave him up when he was about ten, and I got the feeling his life was a lot better at the orphanage than it had been with his parents."

Daddy had speculated once that her musical talent came from his mother, but never elaborated. She'd known from the look on his face that the subject was closed.

"Poor guy," Lolly said, sitting down on the overstuffed leather chair across from Laurel. Her eyes moved around the room in assessment.

"Why are you leaving all this? There's a FOR SALE sign in your yard."

"The upkeep on a house this large is more than I can handle by myself." It was the same pat answer she'd given the real estate agent and what she would tell any prospective buyers.

"But do you, like, *want* to leave?"

Laurel paused a minute because she wasn't sure of the answer herself. She wanted to leave Bosque Bend, yes, but did she really want to leave Kinkaid House? Jase's daughter deserved an honest answer. "I don't know. All of my life is here, which can be very comforting, but it's also very confining. I don't want to spend the rest of my life as a caretaker."

"Where will you go?"

Laurel shrugged. "Probably south, to the Rio Grande Valley."

"You could come to Dallas and live with us."

Laurel laughed to cover the heat wave which swept through her. "You'd better check with your father before you make that kind of offer."

Lolly's head tilted to one side, as if sizing up the situation. "Aunt Maxie said he loved you. She said he used to talk about you all the time."

"Lolly, you really shouldn't tell me things like that. They're personal." Her brain cautioned her not to be an idiot, to chalk anything Maxie might have said up to a few passing remarks, but the tentacles of her heart embraced Lolly's every golden word.

As if on cue, the phone rang. It was Jase. Laurel handed the phone to Lolly.

"Hi, Dad." Lolly smiled winningly into the phone. "I'm okay. Sorry I ran off like that." There was a pause, and her face began crumple as she held back tears. "I love you too, Daddy."

A few more minutes of silence, after which Lolly nodded and turned from the phone to address Laurel. "Dad's about to leave to pick up Aunt Maxie at the airport in Waco and wants to know when he should come get me." She covered the receiver with her hand. "Let me stay longer, Laurel, please, *please*."

"Well, uh, yes, okay, if you want to and it's okay with your dad."

She really would like Lolly to stay a while, although she knew that a lengthier stay would make the house seem even more empty when she was alone again. "We could invite your father and aunt over for dinner this evening."

"Dad, did you hear? Did you hear? Laurel says you and Aunt Maxie can come for dinner. Say yes, Dad! Say yes!"

She listened for a moment and turned back to Laurel. "He says that instead of causing you to all that bother, he'd like all of us, him and Aunt Maxie and me, to take *you* out to dinner somewhere. You know—so you won't be put to any more extra work and to thank you for taking care of me."

Laurel smiled thinly and took the phone from Lolly. "Let's eat here, Jase. It's been a while since I had dinner guests, and it would be so much fun," she said in her most dulcet tones. "And I think it might be easier for both you and Lolly if your reunion is here rather than in a public restaurant."

Most of what she said was true, but the real reason she didn't want to appear in a public restaurant involved her life, not theirs. *Please God, just let me have these few hours with Jase, just a short interlude without the past intruding, and I won't ask for anything more.*

"Well, okay," he agreed. "If it wouldn't be too much trouble for you."

"No trouble at all. And I'll look forward to seeing your aunt again."

"Thanks."

"Maybe you should wait until you've eaten to say that," she

returned, striving for a lighter tone. "I'm not much of a cook."

"I'm not talking about food, Laurel. I'm talking about everything. You've been a far better friend to me than I deserve."

"That's kind of you to say, Jase. See you about six? We dine early here in the boondocks."

"Whenever you say."

Laurel put down the phone with blood ringing in her ears and a faint flush spreading across her cheeks.

Chapter Six

In the meantime, she, whose height of culinary achievement was French toast, had to plan a dinner for four.

After opening up the dining room, which hadn't been used since Mama died, Laurel unlatched the French windows to let in some early morning air. Then, throwing caution to the wind, she packed Lolly in the Escort and drove down the street to the neighborhood Piggly Wiggly. While she'd never had a confrontation in the store, probably because there were so many people around, she knew she was taking a chance.

As it turned out, they caught a few gimlet stares and a couple of middle-aged sniffs, but she didn't think Lolly noticed. Teenagers were accustomed to being disapproved of. Of course, there was a possibility the check she wrote to cover the groceries might bounce, but she was relatively confident she could reach the pawnbroker and the bank in time Monday morning. One of her newly developed skills was estimating how long it would take checks to clear.

If this were three years ago, she would have used a credit card, but she'd cut up all her plastic when finally paying off the last balance after her mother died. No more living beyond her means. The interest and late fees were killing her.

With the groceries packed in the back of the Escort, she decided to pick up a late lunch at G&G Chicken. The drive-thru's speaker emitted an annoying buzz when she tried to talk into it, so she drove up to the window, where a teenage boy greeted them with a metallic smile and a tilt of G&G's trademark yellow cap emblazoned with a crowing red rooster. Laurel placed the order and sat back to wait, but the boy lingered at the window.

"You live around here?"

Startled, she stared at him, then realized she wasn't even on his radar. He was talking to Lolly, who was leaning around her and giving him the full radiance of the Redlander smile.

Lolly's doggie ears bobbed as she shook her head *no*. "I'm visiting from North Plano, near Dallas."

The teen flashed his orthodontics again and winked. "Make it a long visit."

Laurel waited till he left the window, then turned toward Lolly. "I think you've made a conquest."

"Yeah, guys usually like me. I think it's the hair." She twisted a yellow curl around her hand.

Laurel was hard put to keep her mouth shut, but didn't Lolly realize the power of that smile?

Rooster Cap returned and handed over the chicken, keeping his eyes glued on Lolly the whole time. Laurel paid him with the last of her ready cash, which he didn't bother to count.

Good grief—she could have given him Monopoly money and he'd never have noticed!

He winked at Lolly again. "Tell your mother you want to stay the rest of the summer."

Laurel's foot, which had been poised above the gas pedal, nearly shoved it to the floor. How old did that kid think she was? Somehow she managed to get the Escort down the drive without crashing into the large plastic rooster that crowed farewell as they left.

Of course, a mother was exactly what she'd been acting like for the past twelve hours, but did she really look old enough to be the mother of a fifteen-year-old? She paused at the street and angled the rearview mirror so she could make a quick check for wrinkles and sagging flesh.

Lolly was watching her every move. "Did it bother you that he thought you were my mother?"

Laurel poked at her hair. The ponytail was a real loser, but she didn't notice anything different about her face. "A little bit. I don't think of myself as old enough to be the mother of a teenager."

Lolly trained her eyes straight ahead. "A teenager with a bastard baby. It must have been hard for... for my mother."

Laurel froze. She'd accidently set Lolly off again. Putting on a schoolteacher face, she used the voice that had let rambunctious fifth graders know she meant business. "As I told you, I know nothing about your mother, but I'm sure it was difficult for her, whatever her age." Her tone grew even more brittle. "And for your father too." Ramming her foot down on the accelerator a lot harder than was necessary, she moved into the traffic flow.

A curtain of silence hung between them the rest of the way back to the house. Lolly cast several sideways glances in her direction, but Laurel kept her eyes on the car in front of her.

Maybe she was just testing the waters. Pray God that she wouldn't force the matter. She wanted her time with Lolly to be a pleasant interlude—no drama, no conflicts.

But what was it about her mother that Jase didn't want Lolly to know? It had to be some girl from school. Why didn't he at least tell Lolly her name?

* * *

The atmosphere began to thaw as they carried the groceries in from the car. Lolly seemed to realize she'd overstepped a boundary and, eager to reestablish herself in Laurel's good graces, smiled a lot, chattered nonstop, and insisted on carrying the heavier bag. After stowing the food in the refrigerator and pantry, Laurel set the kitchen table with paper plates, and they did G&G proud, then retired to the den again. Lolly, still on her best behavior, embarked on a detailed recounting of her most recent trip to Disney World.

Laurel was fascinated. Apparently the place had changed a lot since Mama and Daddy had taken her there the summer after middle school, and she'd thought it was perfect back then. In fact, she remembered, the trip was all she could talk about when she'd met Jase for the first time. Since Mama spent Wednesday afternoons at the Ladies' Aid society, and Mrs. Claypool, the new housekeeper, needed Wednesday afternoons off, she was Daddy's official greeter.

Odd. She and Jase had been only a grade apart at school, but she'd never exchanged a single word with him until he showed up at the front door. Of course, they'd run in completely different crowds. She was the daughter of the saintly Edward Harlow, revered for his good works, and Jase's father was—well—Growler Red.

Following the usual procedure with "Daddy's boys," Laurel had ushered him into the drawing room. "Pastor Harlow will call you soon," she'd said, gesturing toward the sofa. Most of the boys, cocky and full of bravado, sauntered into the room like they owned the place, but Jase didn't move. He just stood in the doorway, staring.

"We can talk while you wait." She sat down and patted the place next to her to put him at ease.

He'd walked over toward her very slowly, as if afraid she would cut and run any second. When he finally did sit down and she began to make polite conversation, as Mama had taught her to do in strained social situations, he looked at her like she'd just gotten off a shuttle from Mars.

Laurel winced at the memory of her fifteen-year-old self. He must have considered her a complete idiot—all she could think of to talk about was going round and round in the stupid teacups.

Lolly spotted Laurel's annual on the footstool and picked it up. "Oh, look, Dad has one of these. Your father sent it to him after he moved to Dallas. That's where I saw your picture." Flipping open the book, she turned immediately to the center section and gazed admiringly at Laurel's full-page photo. "You were real popular—sophomore favorite and everything. Everybody loved you. Dad said it was like you were a princess—the princess of Bosque Bend."

"Not really." Laurel glanced over Lolly's shoulder. "I think the kids voted for me because of my family."

The next year, of course, after Jase had left town, it had been different. She didn't feel much like socializing, and even being the daughter of the senior pastor of the biggest church in town hadn't been enough to maintain her popularity. Her self-isolation had been good for her grades, though—in fact, she'd ended up as class salutatorian. Then, after college, she'd returned to Bosque Bend and done all the right things—moved back in with her parents, attended the garden club with her mother, accompanied the children's choir at church, married a local boy, and signed a contract to teach at the new elementary school across the eastern arm of the Bosque.

And if her marriage didn't fulfill her, her students did.

Until her world turned upside down, and the town that she'd tried to reject had ended up rejecting her. Not that she was going to explain any of that to Lolly, who was reading all the idiotic tributes her classmates had written in her annual.

"Wow, cool! Someone wrote you a really nice letter. She made a rhyme with the letters of your name too!" Lifting the book closer to her eyes, Lolly read the verse aloud:

> L is for Listening, which you always do
> A is for Always, because you are true
> U is for Us, because we are friends
> R is for Rosy, which your future will be
> E is for Ever, which has no ends
> L is for Loving, which is our Laurel E.

Lolly looked up at Laurel. "It's signed, 'Always, Your Own *Fri-* without *-end*, Sarah.' Who's she?"

"Sarah Bridges, a rather bad poet," Laurel replied, trying to keep her smile in place. "She was my best friend since second grade, but we're out of touch now. She used to live in Bosque Bend, but then she married a doctor and moved to Austin."

"Tough luck. You must miss her."

Laurel nodded, surprised to realize she missed Sarah more than she missed Dave. But then, Sarah had more personality. "It's odd how things work out. Her family had just moved into town, and I remember the day when the elementary school principal walked her into the classroom. I didn't like her."

Flame-haired and brash, Sarah Bridges was the new girl, an outsider without a single connection to Bosque Bend, not even a second cousin three times removed.

"Her family lived across the street from us, but my grandfather told me to ignore them. He didn't like the way they'd remodeled the house, didn't approve of the red Jaguar convertible Mrs. Bridges drove, and never responded when she gave him a friendly wave while she was waiting for Sarah after school and he was waiting for me."

Lolly's eyes glowed with interest. "How did you and Sarah get to be friends, then?"

Laurel took a strengthening breath. All these years later, and the scene was still vivid in her mind.

It was the week before Halloween, and she'd run to the car to tell Grampa that she'd been chosen to narrate the class pumpkin play, but Grampa was slumped down against the door, his jaw agape, a thin line of drool oozing out if the corner of his mouth. When she'd jerked the door open, he fell to the pavement.

"Grampa had a stroke while he was waiting for me, and Mrs. Bridges called an ambulance for him, then took me home with her. My parents were at MD Anderson in Houston because my grandmother had cancer, so I stayed with Sarah and her family till they came home."

By the time Mama and Daddy came home, Laurel and Sarah had bonded for life. Or at least she'd thought so, but Sarah had proved to be as faithless as Dave.

Dave—good ol' Dave. He was a late development. She'd dated Tucker Beebe all through college. Tuck—tall, dark, handsome—another classic hero straight off a book cover—was in the ministerial program. Maybe Daddy would hire him as an assistant pastor when he got his degree, and they could marry and move into Kinkaid House. Or maybe they'd have a big wedding in Daddy's church, then go off somewhere nearby and start their own church. Independent congregations were getting to be a big thing. She'd play the organ and direct the choir while Tuck preached and counseled, but eventually they'd return to Bosque Bend and live with Mama and Daddy, just like her parents had lived with Gramma and Grampa.

But the day after they graduated, Tuck took her out to dinner, apologized, and told her he'd fallen in love with a wonderful man he met in Christian Scriptures class. Laurel was more dumbfounded than heartbroken. How had she been so blind? And here she thought he'd never made the final move on her because of his high moral values.

She'd stuck around Baylor for two more years to nurse her injured pride and pick up a master's degree before heading home.

Enter Dave. He and Karen Fassbinder had been an item ever since middle school, but she eloped with Ted Menefee three days before their wedding. Suddenly Laurel was running into Dave everywhere—at Piggly Wiggly, Overton's, and the Bosque Club. Soon he was calling her on the phone just to talk, inviting her out, sending flowers. It was a whirlwind courtship, and it worked. Laurel thought she had found her soul mate, her mother approved of Dave's family connections, and her father noted Dave was gainfully employed.

Looking back, she realized she'd been ripe for marriage. All the girls she'd grown up with were married—some of them even had a couple of kids—and she didn't want to end up like her mother, who remained single till she was in her midthirties, and then produced only one child. Besides, she wanted sex. Dave had taken her halfway there a couple of times, but never gone all the way until their wedding night—after all, she was Pastor Harlow's virgin daughter.

But that was past history, like the high school annual Lolly was poring over so intently. Laurel was amused to notice her guest had skipped to the front and begun a page-by-page critique of the faculty members' photos. Apparently her major categories were "ick," "gross," "gnarly" or "has funny hair." Looking over her shoulder, Laurel was surprised to hear that sexy Marguerite Shelton garnered a unique "sly-faced."

Tiring of her game, Lolly dropped the annual back on the footstool and turned to Laurel. "What next?"

"We'll get dinner ready. Let's start by setting the table." As soon as they entered the large dining room, she closed the French windows and turned on the window unit. The room was heating up fast.

Lolly ran her hand down the smooth wood of the table. "This is mahogany, isn't it? Our table at home is mahogany, but it's not a curvy one like this one, and the chairs are really plain—no carvings at all."

"My great-grandmother was the one who chose it." Laurel gave the table the evil eye. "It was all the fashion back then, but, to tell the truth, I prefer a simpler style."

Lolly's face lit up. "Then you'd love ours. It's real plain—straight up and down. You can see it when you visit."

Apparently Lolly had accepted the fact that Laurel was not her mother, but was now playing matchmaker. That child was desperate for a mother.

Opening the closet door, Laurel pulled out a protective pad for the table, spread a pale pink tablecloth across it, then topped everything with delicate lace. Her fingers caressed the fragile threads. "Gramma Lorena crocheted this for her hope chest." Mama had saved it for special occasions, and Laurel figured that having Jase and his daughter for dinner was as special as it could get.

Lolly eyed the tall, glass-fronted china cabinet. "Are we going to use the stuff in there?"

"Be careful. It's antique." In fact, so was everything else in the house, which could get claustrophobic. It was like there was an invisible sign on the whole lot:

DO NOT TOUCH: PLEASE KEEP TWELVE INCHES DISTANCE FROM DISPLAY.

She wiped each plate with a soft towel as she took it down, just as Mama used to do, then handed it to Lolly to carry to the table. Later this fall, if the house didn't move, the china would have to go. She'd already sold the Rosenthal, but had hoped to hang on to the Limoges Haviland. Lord only knows why—it wasn't as if she'd ever have a use for it.

Laurel watched as Lolly set the crystal and the silver in place. She weighed a knife in her hand. "This stuff is heavy."

"Erasmus bought the silverware for his first wife right after the house was finished."

"You have so much family history."

"I guess I have been sort of rattling on."

"I think it's interesting. Besides…"

Laurel froze in her tracks. Did Lolly *still* think she might be a Kinkaid? How could she handle this tactfully? "Honey—"

Casting her a panicked look, Lolly quickly altered her course. "I don't know much about my own family." Her eyes went bright, and she started talking so fast it was hard to follow her. "Dad won't tell me about my mother, and I think he's holding back about his father too. Aunt Maxie's told me all about *his* mother, though. She was her youngest sister and sorta wild."

Laurel pressed her lips together and shoved a meat platter and two bowls into Lolly's hands, then scanned the china cabinet for the butter dish. "After we decide which serving dishes to use, we'll be through in here."

Taking the hint, Lolly flashed the Redlander smile and changed the subject. She gestured toward the table setting. "Gosh, Laurel, whenever Dad throws a party, Aunt Maxie always hires a caterer. But you know how, like, to do all this yourself, don't you?"

Laurel glanced at the table settings. "I prefer a more hands-on approach," she lied, her voice gentling. But maybe it wasn't a lie. There was a warm, secret joy to preparing dinner for Jase and his family, even if she was only warming it up.

* * *

By five thirty, the roast was biding its time in the oven and the sides were simmering on the stove, all according to the instructions printed on their cans, boxes, and plastic bags. Laurel hung her mother's frilly apron on the back of a chair and breathed a sigh of relief. She might not be Cordon Bleu, but she could read.

Taking a seat at the big round table, she closed her eyes for a second and inhaled deeply. Cooking was a hassle, but it smelled wonderful. If she could bottle up that aroma and sell it, she wouldn't have to move out of Bosque Bend—she could buy the town outright.

Lolly cast a glance at her, then pulled the rack out to baste the roast again, although Piggly Wiggly's instructions didn't call for basting more than once. Since cooking was apparently as new an experience to Lolly as to her, Laurel suspected her culinary assistant was getting a kick out of playing with the juice. No harm done. She closed her eyes again.

"Laurel."

What now? Lolly was standing in front of her, frowning.

"Laurel, I can take care of everything down here, so why don't you go up and change clothes? You know"—she smiled and batted her lashes—"get into something sexy."

Laurel blinked and glanced down at her happy face shirt. Lolly was right. She did need to change—not into anything sexy, of course, but something more appropriate for company.

She rose from the chair. "Okay, and you can borrow one of my dresses if you want to. I think I have a few that would work, but they'd be ankle-length on you."

"Me? This shirt will do me just fine. Dad sees me every day, but you"—she smiled again—"you're special."

Laurel passed Lolly's comment off with a laugh, but she couldn't help but wonder. Had Jase fantasized about her over the years like she had about him? She'd thought there was an immediate reconnection on both sides when he visited her yesterday, but was it for real?

But she really should get into a nicer outfit. All the way up the stairs, her forebears agreed, especially Erasmus's first wife, who was supposed to have been something of a stickler for convention. She probably needed to be, with those four roguish-looking daughters.

Laurel anointed herself with the last of Mama's Chanel body cream, changed to fresh underwear—as if anyone would be able to tell—and slipped into a cream-colored trousers outfit she'd bought years ago on a shopping trip to Dallas. It was fairly conservative, covering everything quite well, although the fabric was somewhat clingy. Pearl drops went in her ears, and she draped a triple loop of pearls around her neck.

Now for her face. It had been a couple of years since she'd used anything more than lipstick and sunscreen, but, sorting through her dressing table drawer, she located some mascara and a compact of eye shadow. That should do the trick. Or did it? She studied herself in the mirror. She looked so—so *commonplace*. Lolly wanted her to look sexy . . . and maybe Jase did too.

She undid the two top buttons of her blouse. Her mother's soft voice immediately told her that people expected more modesty and less exposure from a minister's daughter.

Maybe she should rebutton.

On the other hand, Mama always worried about what people thought, and it killed her in the end.

Laurel moved her hand away from her neckline and released her ponytail. Another minute to fix her hair and she'd be ready. She picked up her comb and looked in the mirror.

Darn! The rubber band had crimped her up! She wet a comb and tried to repair the damage in the bathroom mirror.

Quick footsteps came down the hall and paused just outside her door. "You decent?"

Laurel moved back into the bedroom. "I'm dressed, Lolly. Come on in."

"I just thought I'd come check"—Lolly blinked in surprise—"You look *hot*!" She reached out to touch Laurel's sleeve. "I love the feel of the fabric—and the way it moves." Stepping back, she looked her hostess up and down, frowning as she focused on her hair.

"We need to do something about your—um—*coiffure*. You sit down and I'll be right back. I never go anywhere without my hair stuff."

A second later, she returned with a bathroom towel over her shoulder and her arms overflowing with salon supplies, all of which she dumped on Laurel's bed.

Laurel stared at the pile: scissors, shampoo, conditioner, a blow dryer, giant containers of styling gel, mousse and hair spray, and what looked like an industrial-sized curling iron. No wonder there wasn't any room in Lolly's backpack for a change of clothes.

"Uh, I have my own curling iron and blow dryer," she ventured in a weak voice, eying the black-and-chrome mechanism Lolly was plugging into the electrical socket on the wall. That thing looked lethal.

Lolly pinned a bathroom towel around Laurel's neck. "You just stay still and let me take care of everything." She waved the curling iron around for emphasis. "I do all my friends' hair and they love it." Combing through Laurel's hair, she lifted tresses here and there to examine them. "You've been cutting it yourself, haven't you?'

"I didn't want to bother going to the hairdresser's." She didn't want to spend the money, Besides, Saundra Schlossnagel Crosswaithe, who'd taken over Ooh La La Salon and Boutique when her mother developed Parkinson's, had sent her a registered letter telling her they would no longer welcome her patronage.

"It's uneven." Lolly reached for her scissors. "I'll, like, take care of that. Just a snip here and there."

Laurel started to protest, but Lolly was already cutting.

"There, I've fixed it," she announced. "All you needed was a little trim. Now for the fun part."

Laurel watched in the mirror as Lolly worked a glob of foamy mousse into her hair, then picked up the comb and smoothed out the bangs, blending them to the side. A few deft twists of the curling iron and Laurel's shoulder-length bob became a graceful cascade turned slightly under at the tips, with one purposefully errant strand going against the tide.

Lolly stepped back to pouf the hairdo with spray. "Check it out. Wiggle your head a little."

Laurel watched her hair ripple and fall back in place again. "This is great, Lolly. You really know what you're doing. Thank you."

"Yeah, well, I want you to look good when Dad comes to dinner."

Laurel glanced at the clock on her dressing table. "He'll be here any minute. We'd better check how the roast is doing."

There were no pauses on the stairs to study the portraits this time, but once in the kitchen, Lolly insisted Laurel's role be strictly supervisory. "You need to sit down and stay nice. I'll lift all the lids and open the oven."

Laurel couldn't help but smile. Lolly obviously had a not-so-ulterior motive, but as long as it remained unspoken, she'd go along with it. Luckily, the only casualty was the tin of rolls, which had burned because the timer had been set wrong. Lolly dumped the tiny, pitiful lumps of charcoal into the step-on trash can, and Laurel stuck their backups in the oven. All she would need to do was delay everyone at the door for a minute or two for the replacements to finish baking. Or, if Jase and his aunt were a bit late, it would be even better.

Lolly took the chair next to her. "Those pearls you have on are gorgeous. Are they for real?"

Laurel reached up to the necklace. "Yes. They were my

grandmother's. Grampa gave them to Gramma when they were married, and Mama had them restrung for my sixteenth birthday."

Lolly tilted her head in inquiry. "What was she like—your mother, I mean?"

"Mama? She was older than most of my friends' mothers and rather conservative, but very sweet."

"But what did she *look* like?" Lolly persisted, her voice quieting. "I can't tell from the painting because her hair is mostly white. Was she dark, like you?"

Laurel shook her head. "No. I take after my father. He was tall and had brown hair, but Mama was fair and rather short, more your height."

Lolly's eyes widened and she sucked in a deep breath.

Laurel could have kicked herself. Her description had given Lolly wings to another flight of fantasy, and there was no way to take it back. But it didn't matter. All she wanted was to keep the peace for what little time they had left. Jase would be here soon and Lolly would leave with him, and she'd probably never see either of them ever again.

* * *

Jase spotted a familiar intersection, signaled, and turned south, flipping down his sun visor against the relentless sunshine coming in from the right. Almost there. He'd know the way to Laurel's house blindfolded.

The scent of newly budded roses wafted across the car, and he glanced over at the sheaf of blush pink that Maxie was holding for him. A gentleman brought flowers to a lady, especially if the lady had invited him for dinner, and he was determined to make a good impression on Laurel. Attitude, behavior, and self-control were the keys to success, he reminded himself. Reverend Ed had taught him that.

They'd been in the pastor's small study off the front room, and Jase had just vented his anger at the world. "I hate my father and I hate Bosque Bend and I hate myself," he'd said, banging his hand on Reverend Ed's desk for emphasis.

He hated Marguerite too, but he wasn't going to say it.

The good man hadn't even blinked. Instead, his austere features reflected concern and sympathy. He'd laid a comforting hand on Jase's shoulder.

"You're angry, and you have a right to be, Jason—the world has dealt badly with you." He'd stopped for a second, as if searching for the right words. "But be careful. Remember that you want to take a positive viewpoint, be honorable, and not let yourself be led astray. Hate will get you nowhere. In fact, it gives that person a certain... certain *power* over you. You need to free yourself of the past in order to plan for the future." Then Reverend Ed had taken an old-fashioned fountain pen from his pocket and reached for a legal pad. "Now, let's figure out some immediate goals for you."

The future, not the past—wise advice from a wise man, advice Jase tried to live by. And not only had Reverend Ed pointed him toward a better life, but he'd also stuck by him when news of the mess with Marguerite broke. He'd even tried to persuade Charles Bridges, the district attorney, to file charges against Marguerite for statutory rape.

As if that would fly in Bosque Bend. Bert Nyquist, who had the ear of Dale Fassbinder, a school board trustee, was insisting that Jase had assaulted Marguerite. The school board's reaction was to hush everything up by putting Marguerite on leave and running him out of town.

Nevertheless, he owed Laurel's father a lot.

He glanced across at his aunt. And he owed Maxie a lot too. Not many teenage guys get saddled with newborns, and the idea of fatherhood, of being responsible for a tiny, squalling, demanding scrap of humanity, had been scary. He could never have handled the situation without Maxie.

And tonight, resplendent in a blue linen skirt and matching short jacket, she was determined to do him proud. As soon as she'd heard the plans for the evening, she'd insisted he drive her to Mister Jacques's Fashion Boutique to pick up an outfit equal to the occasion. Born and bred in Bosque Bend, she regarded an invitation to dine at Kinkaid House as a command performance.

"I remember when Laurel's mother, Dovie Kinkaid, was married," she murmured, shifting the roses in her lap and releasing another wave of fragrance. "It was the talk of the town. She was in her midthirties, Lorena and Dabney's only remaining child, and everyone thought she was going to end up an old maid until Edward Harlow came on the scene. At first all of us were scandalized. After all, she was an heiress and five years older than he was, but, in the end, it didn't matter. They were in love, and she had more than enough money for both of them. Besides, he was such a good man."

Jase nodded in agreement.

"Dovie was forty when Laurel was born—top crop. You know, the last harvest before the winter freeze sets in." Maxie adjusted the roses again. "She was older than the other mothers, of course—quite reserved and terribly old-fashioned, but a really nice lady."

"I never met her." It had always been Laurel who answered the door, Laurel who walked him down the hall and sat with him in the big front room, visiting with him until Reverend Ed came to fetch him. At first Laurel did most of the taking, and all he could do was mumble back, because he didn't know what to say to someone like her, who smelled like sweet honey and smiled like she was glad to see him.

He remembered how her eyes had glowed with excitement as she talked about a trip to Disney World she'd taken that summer, and, the whole time, he was seeing her as a fantasy fairy princess in spangles and stardust. But if Laurel was a princess, then he was a frog, a big lunkhead from the wrong side of the tracks. She was the perfect daughter of a perfect family, while he was the byproduct of a loudmouthed bully and a woman Growler had knocked up in passing and married at the point of her father's shotgun. And not all the roses in the world could make up for that.

Setting his jaw, he pulled into the gravel driveway beside the house. At least he had good timing. It was exactly ten minutes after six, allowably late—much better, one of his former lady friends had assured him, than being exactly on time.

He parked a couple of yards in front of the porte cochere, but before getting out of the car, he took a second to look up at the house, at its square turrets and ornate trim. But what were all those damn air conditioners doing sticking out of the windows? His eyebrows drew together. They'd probably been there sixteen years ago, but he'd overlooked them then because the other houses on the block hadn't been converted to central air yet. Now Kinkaid House was the Lone Ranger. Why? It was easy enough to get an old house sealed for AC, if you had the money—and Kinkaids always had money.

He helped Maxie out of the car, took the roses from her, and glanced around the yard. *Shit*. The place was downright seedy, and it used to be a showplace. With the blazing sunset behind him yesterday evening, he hadn't noticed that the azaleas had gone scraggly, the hedges needed trimming, and the lawn was browning out in the middle. Probably lack of good help. Everyone knew the Reverend Ed employed a full-time cook-housekeeper, a full-time gardener-handyman, and a part-time maid—an old house like this required a lot of up-keep.

He spotted a Realtor's sign at the corner of the yard. That was another thing he'd missed seeing yesterday. So, Laurel was serious about selling.

He took Maxie's arm to help her across the uneven ground. They stepped up onto the porch and he pushed the doorbell.

Chapter Seven

Laurel fixed a gracious smile on her face and walked at measured pace to open the door. A secret delight sang in her veins. For the second day in a row, she'd see Jase Redlander.

He looked just right—nice, but not too formal. The sand-colored slacks and charcoal jacket fit like they'd been tailored for him, which they probably had. She swallowed hard as she noticed that his tieless white shirt, open at the neck, revealed a hint of the dark masculine shadow that had so shocked and fascinated her as a teenager.

Down, girl. He's your guest, not the main course.

Jase stood on the porch and stared at her for an awkward moment, then abruptly thrust a sheaf of roses at her. "For you."

Lifting the bouquet up to her face, she inhaled deeply before extending her hand to him. "They're beautiful. Please come in."

He stepped across the threshold and reached back to close the door behind himself, but a small woman in blue edged in beside him.

"Miss Harlow, I'm Maxine Hokinson," she said, holding out her hand.

Laurel quickly changed the roses to her left arm so she could take Jase's aunt's hand. "How nice to see you again, Miss Hokinson, but please call me Laurel."

"And I'm Maxie."

She'd forgotten how tiny Maxine Hokinson was, maybe five feet at the most—short and scrawny—but her bright blue eyes sparkled with energy. This was a woman who could move mountains, and Lolly bore a striking resemblance to her—watch out, world!

The dining room door opened and Lolly, wrapped in Mama's frilly white apron, came down the hall toward them. "Dinner is served," she announced in a mock-unctuous voice.

"Lolly!" Maxie rushed forward to embrace her niece. "We were so worried about you!"

Lolly threw her arms around her. "I'm sorry, Aunt Maxie. Truly I am. I didn't mean to upset you." She reached out her hand to her father. "I'm sorry, Dad, but this was something I had to do."

He joined in the family embrace, but his voice was gruff. "Well, now that you've done it, young lady, we can take you home."

Lolly pulled away from him, her eyes blazing.

Laurel caught her breath. This must be the "yelling" Lolly had complained about. Jase's comment was tactless, but typically male. Couldn't Lolly tell the effort it took for her father to control his emotions, how relieved he was that she was safe? *Time to intervene.* She moved forward with a big smile and held the rose bouquet out to Lolly.

"Honey, I know you and your dad have a lot to discuss, but would you mind taking these lovely flowers to the kitchen and putting them in water for me? The vases are in the upper cupboard next to the pantry."

Recognizing an out when it was offered, Lolly grabbed at the bouquet. "Sure thing, Laurel. It'll just take a sec. I have to get the rolls out anyway." She gave her father a dark look and fled down the hall.

"We'll be at the table," Laurel called after her. Then, just as Mama used to, she led the parade into the dining room. Jase held her chair and Maxie's before taking his seat directly across from her. Maxie was to her left, and Lolly, after setting the rolls on the table and the roses on the buffet, took the remaining chair.

Looking around the table, Laurel was pleased to note that Lolly had done an exemplary job of arranging the serving dishes. Apparently Maxie's caterers had made a lasting impression on her.

She unfolded her napkin. Daddy always offered up a short grace before a meal, but since she usually ate standing up at the kitchen counter nowadays, she'd gotten lax. Tonight, however, as she placed her napkin in her lap and lifted a fork to signal the meal had begun, a panic raced through her, and she sent up her own desperate supplication.

Please, God, let the food be edible.

Then, with what she hoped was a confident smile on her face, she sampled her fare and relaxed back into her chair. Piggly Wiggly had fulfilled its promise. The candied carrots tasted just like the ones Mrs. January used to make as a special treat, the roast beef lived up to its aroma and was as tender as the package promised, the French-cut green beans were delicious, and the mashed potatoes were smooth and buttery—although it would be hard to mess up mashed potatoes.

Lolly put down her fork, raised her glass, and smiled in a way that made Laurel nervous. *What now?*

"Let's drink to Laurel," she announced. "She spent all afternoon preparing this delicious meal for us. Made everything from scratch."

Jase and Maxie clinked their glasses together with Lolly's.

Laurel had no choice but to say "thank you," though she couldn't help but wonder if toasts made with water were legitimate. Wine, of course, had been out of the question. It might be de rigueur at sophisticated dinner parties now that the county had gone wet, but all she was aiming at was adequacy. Besides, if anyone had seen her studying labels in Piggly Wiggly's wine-beer-mixers aisle, it would have been all around town that the preacher's daughter was drowning her sorrows in drink.

Directing the conversation toward her guests, she asked Jase about his career and hung on to his every word as he briefly outlined his climb up the ladder from parking attendant to lot manager, from employee to employer to investor. Laurel couldn't be anything but impressed. Jase had worked hard. He was so different from Dave, who'd ducked out of work every opportunity he could to try out a new putter or play a couple of rounds of golf with his buddies.

"The turning point was when Jase bought his second lot," Maxie interjected. "I could retire then and stay at home with Lolly. We thought that was important."

Lolly grinned at her great-aunt. "I don't know why. I had everything under control." She turned to Laurel to explain. "We were living in a condo then, and the service people all knew me."

Jase laughed. "You mean you had them all wound around your little finger. You were a spoiled brat."

She gave him a look of mock innocence. "So?"

Laurel enjoyed watching the interplay between father and daughter. All was well in Redlander country—at least for the time being. Fifteen was a mercurial age, as she well remembered.

* * *

Jase could have kicked himself. He'd made a total ass of himself, as usual, when Laurel Harlow was concerned.

That white pants thing she was wearing clung in all the right places, which meant his dick immediately expressed interest, which also meant he hadn't heard a word that came out of her mouth when she opened the door. Her lips were moving, so she must have been saying something, but the blood roaring in his ears drowned her out. Must have flooded his brain too, because he completely forgot about Maxie.

Damn. When he'd taken her hand, he'd wanted to hold it forever. What would she have done if he'd brought it to his lips and touched her palm with the tip of his tongue?

Sixteen years ago, Laurel had said she loved him, but what does a fifteen-year-old know about love? It shook him to realize that Lolly was now exactly the same age as Laurel had been then. If any boy tried to do to Lolly what he'd tried to do to Laurel, he'd beat him within an inch of his life. And Laurel had never told her father, which made Jase feel twice as guilty. Reverend Ed had been his lone supporter, and look how he'd repaid him—by rutting after his virgin daughter as though she were the same kind of slut as Marguerite.

He'd known the gig was up at midmorning when Mr. Nyquist announced over the intercom that a substitute would be taking over Ms. Shelton's classes for the rest of the semester.

The kids sitting around him glanced at him, smirked, and gave each other knowing looks, which meant the word had gotten around.

He'd sat through the rest of the period class with a glazed smile on his face—then headed for the parking lot. His school days were over.

Friday evening, Bert Nyquist appeared.

He'd been out front, working on his truck, when the school district car drove up.

Growler hoisted his longneck in greeting and gestured his visitor toward the rusty lawn chair. "Come to see me about something, Bert?"

Nyquist remained standing. "Mr. Redlander, I am here representing the Bosque Bend School Board. Your son has sexually assaulted one of his teachers, but she will not press charges if you make arrangements for Jason to leave town immediately."

Jase's heart stopped beating for a moment, then went into overdrive. *Make me leave town? Could they do that?*

Growler grunted, glugged his beer, and heaved himself to his feet—all six feet, six inches, three hundred pounds of him. His arms hung loose from his shoulders, ready for action.

"I already heard about it at the tavern, Bert, an' the way I see it, it's all a part of growin' up, an' that old cow was lucky to have had a young bull like my Jase servicin' her for as long as he did." He took a step forward, and his voice deepened past its trademark rasp into an even lower, more menacing tone. "Now, get off my property before I dunk you in the Bosque!"

Nyquist raised his hands, palms out, as if fending Growler off. "Now...now, Mr. Redlander...let's not get carried away!"

Growler took another step forward, and the floorboards

creaked as his weight shifted. Nyquist turned tail and scurried down the steps to his car.

Later that evening, Growler, pumped with adrenaline from the confrontation he thought he'd won, took Jase off to Beat Down, slapped him on the back, and called him a chip off the old block. "Been porkin' that cute little number down at the high school the kids talk about," he'd bragged to the Friday night crowd.

Every man jack in the place wanted to buy Jase a drink, and he'd been so miserable that he'd taken them up on it. He'd had occasional beers since he'd been in elementary school—even when the water was cut off, the beer kept flowing—but that night he went overboard. A turbulent stomach had awakened him soon after he went to bed, and he'd made it to the bathroom just in time.

The next morning, Laurel appeared.

* * *

Jase finished off his serving of roast and looked around the room. It was large and well-lit, with French windows behind him opening onto a small terrace under the porte cochere. He'd never been in this room before. In fact, the only parts of the house he'd ever seen were the hall, front room, and Reverend Ed's study. He'd never even had the nerve to ask to use the bathroom.

The whole situation was surreal—that he, Jason Redlander, his aunt, and his child, were guests in Kinkaid House, actually eating dinner here.

He played with his carrots—because he sure as hell wasn't going to eat them—and studied the portrait of Laurel on the wall behind her. The artist had captured not only her likeness, but also her nature: Posed in a pinkish dress and sitting in a rose arbor, which must be somewhere on the property, she was serenity itself, a lady, as she had always been and still was. Laurel had grown up with tradition and taste and elegance. He, on the other hand—well, everyone knew how he'd grown up. Sure, he'd fought his way to the top of the dung heap, but she'd been born on a plane far above him.

He forced himself to take a polite bite of carrots, then put down his fork. Next came dessert—cheesecake—which, strangely enough, tasted exactly like Sara Lee. Then Laurel moved everyone to the comfortable den for coffee and conversation. Laurel and Maxie took the couch, leaving the big recliner to him.

He half closed his eyes and studied Laurel as she talked with Maxie.

As Laurel leaned forward to look at picture of Sir Frederick, Maxie's long-haired dachshund, her blouse fell open, revealing shadowed cleavage. He took an audible breath and she looked up to meet his eyes, blushed, then licked her upper lip nervously.

The air conditioner was grinding away, but the room suddenly seemed too hot for comfort.

*   *   *

It was sixteen years ago, but he still remembered the warm weight of those pink-crested adolescent breasts in his hands.

He'd been groggy with sleep, when he heard someone call out his name. At first he'd thought she was his father finally coming in or maybe Aunt Maxie stopping by to check on him. Then Laurel had said something he was too sleepy to understand, and started to cry. He'd tried to give her brotherly comfort, patting her and making soothing noises, all the time aware that he had a boner the size of the Texas Panhandle.

"I love you so. Please kiss me, Jase," she'd whispered, her eyes bright with tears, her soft breath fanning across his bare chest.

It was the request of a child, he'd thought, a child concerned about the welfare of a good friend, because he was sure everyone in Bosque Bend knew by then that he was in a shit-load of trouble.

He aimed for her cheek, but somehow her lips were under his and her full breasts flattened against him. She was Reverend Ed's daughter, but she was also young, soft, and female, and he was not only male, but totally aroused as well. His body demanded action. He moved his mouth over hers slowly, lingeringly, as Marguerite had taught him, all the time trying to control the wildfire that was raging through him.

He'd tried to maintain the pure, Knight-of-the-Round-Table sort of love he thought he felt toward her, all the time knowing he was fighting a losing battle. He'd been awakened by a seasoned voluptuary to far more sexual awareness than any sixteen-year-old could control, no matter how good his intentions. He also had more sexual skills than other sixteen-year-olds, even the sexually active ones, because Marguerite was a very good teacher.

But somehow, with Laurel, it was all new and wonderful. For the first time, he was making love to a girl he really cared about, not performing like a trained seal for Marguerite. Laurel's skin was tender and firm, her mouth sweet and generous. He kissed her warm young breasts, tipped with dusky pink rosettes, so different from Marguerite's large orangish nipples.

And Laurel was passionate, even without knowing, her face flushed from his kisses and her wide gray eyes dilated with desire. Unpracticed she may have been, but her ardor more than made up for it.

Then he went too far and she froze up on him.

He also remembered the aftermath. He'd been a real asshole, lighting up and trying to act like a tough guy, but he'd been embarrassed and ashamed and—well—frustrated. He loved her, but knew she was too young and innocent, too good for him.

And he still loved her, and she was still too good for him—so good that despite everything, she'd admitted him to her house yesterday, taken care of his daughter, and was now hosting him and his family for dinner.

Maxie's voice cut through his reverie.

"Look at the time! Lolly and I have to be at the airport in thirty minutes! Our flight leaves at nine, and Pastor Richter expects us to help with early communion tomorrow morning!"

Lolly sprang up and headed for the front hall. "I'll be just a second, Aunt Maxie. My backpack and purse are upstairs."

Laurel started after her. "I'll help."

* * *

Lolly reached under the bed for her Luis Vuitton handbag while Laurel grabbed Lolly's pink backpack from the side chair. It lifted far too easily.

"Your hair equipment is still in my room!"

They dashed across the hall. Lolly stuffed her portable salon in her backpack, which Laurel held open. They gave each other a congratulatory high five, then paused. Laurel could feel a fluttering panic rising in her breast. This was good-bye, and she didn't know what to say. She didn't want Jase's daughter to leave. She didn't want to be all alone again.

Lolly glanced down at herself. "Hey, I've still got your shirt on."

"Take it as a gift." On impulse, before she could second-guess herself, Laurel unwound her necklace and lifted it over Lolly's head. "And take this too, to remember me by." The pearls had been given to her in love and deserved a better fate than the pawnbroker's window.

Lolly stood stock-still in the middle of the carpet, lifted the pearl rope in both hands and looked down at it, then up at Laurel. Her voice was soft, her eyes compassionate. "Was it, like, because of your parents that you couldn't keep me?"

"What?"

"I mean, when I was born. It must have been hard, you being a preacher's daughter and all. Did your parents make you give me up, turn me over to Dad?"

Laurel's knees buckled. She sat down on the edge of her bed, stared up at Lolly. She'd put it off too long, but it was time to end this fantasy—for both of them.

"Honey, I'm not your mother. You're a lovely girl and I wish I were your mother, but I'm not."

Lolly sat down beside her. "I understand that you don't want to admit you had a baby out of wedlock," she insisted, "but you must be my mother. I can tell from the way Dad acts around you—and Aunt Maxie said he's always been in love with you. Besides, I'm named after you."

"Named after me?"

"*Lolly* is just what they call me. My real name is Laurel Elizabeth, like yours."

Laurel looked at her in surprise. Lolly was a Laurel Elizabeth? Jase had given his daughter her name? No wonder Lolly thought she was her mother. If only.

She took Lolly's hands in hers. Gray eyes met blue. "Lolly, listen to me. I like you a lot. You're a charming girl, and if I had a daughter, I'd want her to be just like you. But you aren't mine. Your father and I have never been, well, *intimate*. I've never had a child."

And probably never will.

Suddenly the years of desolation stretched in front of her like an endless, empty tunnel. The last twenty-four hours had been a magical respite, but tonight Lolly would leave her and Jase would leave her and she'd be by herself again.

She couldn't hold it in any longer. There were just too many sorrows stored up, too many tears she'd suppressed. Great, painful sobs tore from her throat, and tears cascaded down her cheeks. Tears for her father, her mother, her botched marriage, her dreams of love, her doubtful future.

All the while she was vaguely aware that someone was patting her arm and babbling at her. "I'm sorry! I take it all back! I didn't mean to make you cry! I'm sorry! Please stop crying—Dad will kill me!"

But there was no way she could stop.

Chapter Eight

Jase leaned against the newel post, waiting for Lolly to collect her gear.

This was taking too long. Was Girl Child trying to wheedle a couple of days' more hospitality out of Laurel? He gave Maxie a telling glance. She rolled her eyes.

A sound came from the second floor, like someone choking. Jase moved to the bottom of the steps and put a hand on the newel post, ready for action.

Suddenly Lolly, big-eyed and white-faced, appeared on the landing. "Dad, you've got to come! She won't stop crying! Laurel won't stop crying!"

He vaulted the steps two at a time, Maxie right behind him.

Lolly hurled herself into his arms. "I'm so sorry! It's all my fault! I didn't mean to!"

Jase held her tight and patted her shoulder soothingly. "That's okay, baby. It'll be okay." He walked her back into the room.

Laurel was slumped on the edge of her bed, a hand to her face, shaking like a leaf and sobbing uncontrollably.

Jase looked from one to the other. God, Laurel was crying her eyes out, and Girl Child was coming on hysterical. He had to separate these two. Still holding Lolly with one arm, he nodded at Maxie and felt in his pocket for his keys. "I think it would be best if you and Lolly left," he said, handing the keys over to his aunt. "Just park the Caddie in the overnight lot at the airport. I'll take care of Laurel. I was going to stay in town another day anyway."

He gave Lolly a quick hug and a reassuring smile. "Laurel will be fine, baby. You take care of Aunt Maxie."

She wiped her nose and smiled weakly. "I will, Dad. I promise." Still snuffling, Lolly picked up her backpack and purse, then followed her aunt out of the room, a rope of pearls dangling incongruously from her neck.

Jase frowned. Wasn't that the necklace Laurel had on at dinner? The one she'd told Maxie was actually a single long strand? Oh well, it was the least of his worries.

In less than a minute, the big front door thudded shut, leaving him alone in the house with Laurel.

A trickle of sweat rolled down the back of his neck. *Goddamn. The room is hot as Hades.* He doffed his jacket and slipped it over the back of the dressing room chair, then turned on the window unit. Taking a deep breath, he picked up the tissue box, took one, and sat down beside Laurel, patting her arm so she'd know someone was there.

Weeping women were not his area of expertise, and his first impulse was to make a run for it. But, no, he'd said he'd stay, that he'd take care of her, but the rampant femininity of the room made him uncomfortable. All that pinky color. And it was Laurel's room, her *bedroom*, for God's sake, and he was sitting on her *bed*.

What the hell had Lolly done—or said? She must've brought up the mother thing.

Damn it, he'd tried to cut her off at the pass with that soap-opera nonsense about her mother entrusting her to him because she thought he could give her the best home, then making him promise to not to reveal her name. Couldn't she be satisfied with that? Girl Child wasn't old enough to hear that her mother hadn't wanted her. He'd tell her more when she was older, when it would mean less to her.

He patted Laurel's arm and handed her a tissue.

God, where did all that water come from? Females must be born with extra storage tanks behind their eyes. Lolly wept like that too. He'd even seen Maxie cut loose a couple of times.

Quieter now but still sobbing, Laurel wiped her cheeks. Then, as if too weak to sit up on her own, she leaned against his side, her breast pressing against his arm. He looped the other arm loosely around her shoulders and gently rocked her. The bed creaked in a suggestive rhythm that he tried not to think about.

"That's okay. It'll be okay," he said in a singsong voice, the same assurance he had given Lolly.

Maybe *she* was going to be okay, but he wasn't so sure about himself. He'd wanted to comfort Laurel, but he'd been stiff as a stovepipe ever since he sat down beside her, and his idea of comfort was rapidly expanding its scope. God, she was so damn female! He kissed her silky hair and let his lips wander across her forehead.

He'd always thought Laurel looked very Southern—the dark hair and pale eyes, the graceful slenderness of her body. She was made for plantations dripping with Spanish moss, for mint juleps and long, hot nights with all the windows open, for mosquito netting floating over sweaty beds in the night-time breeze. But right now his bayou babe was gulping back tears and making strange snorting noises. She grabbed a couple more tissues, blew her nose loudly, and rested against him again.

He shifted closer and brushed her forehead with his lips.

She looked up at him in surprise, then touched his face—hesitantly—as if to make sure he was real.

He tracked a teardrop across her cheekbone with his finger. "Why were you crying? What did Lolly say?"

Her mouth was tremulous, her eyes heavy-lidded and wet. "No, Jase. It wasn't Lolly. It's you—because you're leaving."

He was leaving and taking all her silly dreams with him, the romantic stories she'd woven around him ever since she was fifteen. He'd go back to Dallas and she'd move out of Kinkaid House, leaving her childhood behind. This was the end, the last time she would see him.

Her eyes widened in appeal and their depths darkened to slate. "Kiss me, Jase, kiss me," she whispered.

At first he thought he wasn't hearing right, because what she said was so much what he wanted to hear. But then she turned her face up to him and closed her eyes.

His mouth tasted her—gently, sweetly. He didn't want to come on too strong, but she melted against him. He buried his face in the side of her neck to inhale her fragrance, then adjusted her against his chest and moved his lips toward her ear. "Laurel, I've waited so long."

"I've waited too. Love me, Jase. Make love to me."

"Yes." His voice caught in his throat so he said it again, louder. "Yes."

She wanted him. The princess of Bosque Bend wanted *him*, Jase Redlander. And he'd always wanted her. His first impulse was to rip that slinky pantsuit off her and grind himself into her so hard that the whole town would hear her come. But Marguerite, may she burn in hell, had taught him better. And Reverend Ed's daughter deserved better. Laurel was different from the women he'd been in the habit of casually hooking up with over the years.

Go slow, you big ape. Make this good for her. Stretch it out as long as you can.

His lips traced the tender skin behind her ear. She whimpered and moved her hand down his back. *Good.* He kicked off his shoes and sank her down on the bed, their heads twisting in kiss after kiss; the bed's wooden slats protested loudly all the while.

Ghosts of dead Kinkaids? *Tough shit.* If those old dudes and dames on the staircase hadn't had sex at least once in their lives, Laurel wouldn't be here today.

He rocked his forehead against hers, smushing their noses together. She moaned and rubbed the undersides of her arms against his shoulders as the tip of his tongue outlined her mouth, then sought entry to explore the inner rims of her lips and the sensitive flesh above her teeth. He couldn't get enough of her.

He caressed her arms and hips—barely touching her skin to sensitize her, then using longer, stronger strokes for his own satisfaction. He dropped kisses on her nose, her eyelids, her cheeks, then licked at the circles of her ears.

She shuddered and clutched his head to bring him close for deep soul kisses. His sleepy Southern belle was demanding her just due. Her legs moved restlessly as her tongue twined with his.

He stroked her arms again, lightly touching the sides of her breasts at the same time. She opened her eyes and breathed in hard.

Undoing the cloth-covered buttons on her blouse, he played with the tops of her breasts, then sucked her nipples through her lacy, barely there bra.

Was he rushing her? He skimmed his mouth across her fevered cheeks and let his breath whisper in her ear. "You okay? We can slow down."

"No. Don't slow down." Her voice was husky. She ran her hand up under his loosened shirt and buried her fingers in his chest hair.

His brain rocketed into outer space, and he took her mouth again, releasing the back hooks of her bra at the same time. Her sweet breasts tumbled free, and his finger circled one dusky pink tip before he tested it with his tongue.

She moaned and her eyelids closed. When he mouthed her other nipple, she uttered a short, sharp cry.

"That's it, baby," he breathed in her ear. "I want to know what you like."

She stroked his arms. "*You*, Jase. I like *you*."

His heart thumped in his chest so hard it hurt. He nipped at her neck and lowered his mouth to her breasts again, sucking first one crest, then the other, until they glowed like twin rubies.

She ran her hand along his jaw. He'd shaved before he came over, but probably had fresh stubble by now. The beard didn't seem to faze her, though. In fact, from the way she was writhing against him, it seemed to turn her on.

Remember that, Jason.

He trailed his hand down her throat to the juncture of her breasts, then farther down, to the front closure of her slacks. The buttons, hook, and zipper opened easily, and he slid the slacks off her to the side of the bed, then pulled down her panties. She arched her breasts and gave him a come-hither smile.

Oh God, she was an erotic fantasy, her dark hair fanned behind her head, her blouse spread beneath her shoulders, her face flushed with passion, her mouth swollen with desire—desire for him.

"You're beautiful." His voice was so thick she probably couldn't understand a word he was saying, but she was more than beautiful. She was glorious, his own goddess of delight. Her breasts, tipped by dusky pink rosebuds, were full and firm; her belly was flat, her hips rounded, her legs long and curvy, and her pale skin incandescent in the evening glow.

He tore off his shirt and ran a hand along the curve of her hip, tantalizing himself with the feel of her, then followed with a trail of wet kisses down to the spread of dark curls at the juncture of her thighs.

Lifting himself just enough to unfasten his belt, he used one well-practiced motion to push his slacks and briefs off to the bottom of the bed, jackknifing his butt backward so she wouldn't get the full visual of his erection yet.

You could hang a flag on that guy.

Laurel felt a thrill pass through her as Jase shucked his pants. They were both naked now—skin to skin, body to body. This was a time for truth between them. There were no subterfuges, no places to hide. He was man, she was woman, and tonight they would merge their bodies and become one.

She reached a hand up to caress his stubbled jaw again, the slight irritation of her palm sending a ripple of heat racing through her veins. All in all, she was reacting with an ardor that would have astounded her ex-husband, an ardor she'd given up on ever experiencing.

Sex with Dave hadn't been the rhapsody she expected after her experience with Jase, and certainly nothing like the love scenes in her favorite novels. In fact, it had been surprisingly dull, starting with a painful wedding night in which she'd bled through to the mattress. Dave had strutted around the hotel like a spread-tailed peacock afterward, but she'd been so embarrassed, she'd hidden out in their room for the rest of the week.

Apparently her well-guarded virginity was all she had to offer Dave, because after they got home, he complained about her lack of response. "It's like you're not even there," he'd said. "I could get the same satisfaction from one of those inflatable dolls."

Determined to make a go of her marriage, she'd supplemented her white cotton underwear with sexy little nothings from the specialty boutique Saundra Schlossnagel's mother had added to Ooh La La, then borrowed a couple of X-rated videos from Amy Fassbinder, but nothing seemed to work. What had Dave wanted that she couldn't give him?

Jase didn't seem to find her lacking. In fact, he was as hungry for her as she was for him. She moved her hands down to Jase's shoulders as his shaft nudged her leg.

Slowly, inexorably, he bent her back on the four-poster till they were lying crossways to the headboard, his leg between her thighs, his shoulders pinning her beneath him.

She raised up to claim his mouth, and he gave her a quick kiss as he shifted himself so he was totally over her. A fountain of flame erupted behind her breasts and flowed to the female core of her being.

This was it. She guided his manhood into position. This is where he belonged.

He smoothed her hair and bent down to kiss her once

more. Then, reaching down to slick her with saliva, he touched her in just the right spot.

She threw back her head and gasped as a bolt of lightning shot through her and Jase thrust home. Then, encircling his body with her legs, she drew him as close as she could, trying to suck his whole body inside herself.

His dark eyes glittered as he rose above her and began his rhythm.

Now it would be fast.

She met his every stroke, clutching at him with her inner muscles.

She was panting now, little intakes of air accompanied by wispy moans. The window air conditioner was rumbling at top speed, but she was so hot that she felt as if she was going to burst into flames. The bed might break beneath them, but there was no way she could stop. Everything feminine in her was hell-bent on speeding her to the ultimate conclusion.

Suddenly she was soaring beyond the room, beyond the earth, beyond the moon. They were as one being now—she was him and he was her. The waves of release seemed to roll on forever.

Afterward, she lay in his arms, her eyes shut, her fingers trailing down his thigh, her voice a seductive whisper.

"Stay the night."

Jase lifted her hand and carried it to his mouth to taste the tender palm, just as he'd wanted to do when he'd given her the roses. "Forever."

The air-conditioning hit their glistening bodies and Laurel began to shiver, so Jase pulled the sheet up over them.

Then he turned off the overhead and returned to bed.

Because total darkness is also an aphrodisiac.

Chapter Nine

Laurel awoke to late morning sunlight streaming through the slits of the blinds. Startled to find herself naked in bed with an equally naked man, she relaxed when she realized he was not just any man, but the man of her dreams.

She sat up against her pillow and rested her arms on her knees to think everything over. She'd made love all night long outside the legal bonds of matrimony, which meant, according to every precept she had grown up with, she was a fallen woman—a slut. She looked toward the window. Maybe she would become the latest town scandal. Who was sleeping with whom might not matter in Hollywood, or even in Dallas, but it did in Bosque Bend, where everybody was into everyone else's business. If her parents were still alive, they'd be mortified.

Her lips tightened in defiance. But they *weren't* alive, and they both had sins of their own to answer for.

She settled back in the bed. Did she herself have any regrets? She looked over at the big man slumbering beside her.

None at all.

Her eyes studied her lover, memorizing him for when he

wouldn't be around anymore. The sheet had slipped down past his waist while he slept, revealing his brawny torso, every inch of which she'd explored last night. She'd licked and kissed the large cicatrix on his shoulder as if to heal it, run her fingers along his muscled arms. Jase was an adult now, nicked and scarred, powerfully built and sexually demanding, and everything that was woman in her responded to him.

His jaw had darkened considerably overnight, making him look almost villainous. Dave had always seemed younger when he slept, more boyish and vulnerable, but Jase looked harder and more dangerous. The taut planes and hard angles of his face took on something of a satanic cast, and his unsmiling mouth seem unforgiving and cruel.

Laurel shivered. Last night he was hers, but how long would that last? How would he react when he learned the truth about Daddy? Would he reject her like Dave had? Would he shun her like everybody else in Bosque Bend?

Suddenly afraid, she leaned closer to him, wondering, searching his face for mercy. As if sensing her scrutiny, he opened his eyes and smiled. "So, you're here. It was real."

Relief surging through her, and she leaned over to kiss him lightly on the forehead, her breasts teasing his mouth.

He pulled her closer, then brought her imprisoned hand down between their bodies for his own purposes. He was turgid and ready, which sent her hormones into overdrive.

He came into her carefully, as if mindful that he'd been rough a couple of times during the night, but she was wet and eager, arching up to receive him. Whatever Jase wanted from her, she would give.

Afterward, he kissed the palm of her hand again, which seemed to be a thing with him, and told her he loved her again. She wondered if he meant it or if that was just his way of expressing gratitude for the use of her body.

They spent what little remained of the morning in bed, playing and experimenting with each other, laughing and talking. Even a day before, Laurel could never have believed she'd feel so much at ease with a man. It was as if they'd been together forever.

"Your hair is soft as silk," Jase said, weaving his fingers slowly through the sable strands and watching them fall back in place. She'd worn it the same way as a teenager, he remembered. Sixteen years ago, the style had looked sweet and wholesome, but now it looked incredibly sexy.

He moved his hand along the nape of her neck and traced the curve of her ear, enjoying the way she trembled in response.

"I thought you hated me." His voice was a low-pitched whisper. In fact, he'd spent his last few days in Bosque Bend expecting to be thrown in jail before finally realizing Laurel hadn't told anyone about their encounter.

Cold comfort. The shame of everyone knowing she'd been touched by Growler Red's lunkhead son probably would have been even worse than what actually happened.

She looked at him in surprise. "I never hated you. I was in love with you, but I was too young for what you wanted back then." She rolled over on her stomach and looked at him through coyly lowered lashes. "But I'm all grown up now."

"So I've noticed," he said, flashing her a wide grin, his mood completely changing. "Hey, this is Sunday morning, and you've missed church!" He gave her a playful slap on the rump. "What would your father say? And how will you explain this lapse to the church council?"

Laurel had a sudden vision of herself, wrapped in her fringed bedspread, standing in front of that august assemblage and solemnly explaining that she hadn't attended services because she'd been rollicking in bed with the historically notorious Jase Redlander all morning. Not that she went to church any more, of course. That avenue of comfort had been rather definitely closed to her. God might be merciful, but his earthly representatives were more circumspect.

Jase leaned back against his pillow, folding his hands behind his head. "You were old enough for love, but not for sex." He shook his head in disbelief. "Damn, that's something I talk to Lolly about all the time. I guess all of a father's past sins come back to haunt him when he has his own children." He turned toward Laurel. "Except for *your* father, of course."

Her eyelids widened slightly, but she didn't flinch. She even managed a slight smile. "*My* father—of course."

"He gave Maxie and me twenty-five hundred dollars to get a start in Dallas," Jase continued, looking into space. "It was a godsend, enough to support Lolly when she arrived."

"I'm glad." Generosity was one of Daddy's best traits. Unfortunately not all the people to whom he gave money put it to such good use as Jase and Maxie.

His brows drew together at the memory. "Taking care of a baby was hard at first, and neither of us could give her a lot of time. Maybe that's the reason Lolly's so headstrong now. Maxie says first we neglected her, then we spoiled her, but we did the best we could."

"I think she's darling," Laurel protested, reaching out to twist a clump of his chest hair into a ringlet. "And most teenagers are headstrong. They're trying their wings, and sometimes they fly, sometimes they flop."

He claimed her hand and took it to his mouth for a kiss. "I remember how you were, and I always wanted her to be just like you."

"Was that the reason you gave her my name?"

Jase looked embarrassed. "So, she told you about that." He moved his hands in a gesture of apology. "I guess I shouldn't have hijacked your name, but I never thought you and Lolly would meet." His eyebrows went up in question. "Are you...offended?"

She couldn't help but smile. "Of course not. I'm honored. But you know that's one of the reasons she thought I was her mother."

"Yeah. She went through that damn annual and found your picture."

Laurel drew a circle on his shoulder with her finger, wondering how far she could explore the subject of Lolly's maternity. "I'm—I'm not sure it's any of my business, but did her birth mother name her?"

Jase's mouth twisted and his voice hardened. "She never bothered to give her a name. And she didn't use her own name on the birth certificate either, although she had no compunctions about giving *my* name out. The midwife tracked me down in Dallas, presented me with the baby, and disappeared. We had to get a DNA test to be sure Girl Child was mine." He turned to Laurel again. "Lolly didn't have a very good start in life, so I wanted her to have the very best name I could think of, sort of like a magic amulet."

Laurel sat up, pulling the sheet up around her breasts. It was hard to have a serious discussion with her nipples on high alert. "Wouldn't it be easier to tell Lolly the truth about her mother, whatever she did?"

He sighed, rolled to the side of the bed, and sat up. "It would be easier for me, but harder for her. I've got to wait till she's older."

She decided to push it a little further. "Jase, who was Lolly's mother? Did I know her? Was it...Betty Jean Powell?"

Betty Jean, who always sat in the back of the class and tried to copy other people's tests. Laurel's crowd ignored her like she was wallpaper, but, looking back, Laurel had a dim memory of a small, narrow-faced girl, thin as a rail, who never had enough lunch money and frequently came to school with purple bruises on her arms.

A pang of guilt swept through her. If she'd seen marks like that on any of her students, she would have suspected parental abuse. Maybe there was a reason Betty Jean was an easy mark for every guy who bought her a burger.

Jase swung his head around. "Betty Jean? Hell, no!" His eyes drilled into hers. "Haven't you guessed?" His voice turned ugly and grating. "It was Marguerite Shelton! Who else? Apparently in her never-ending quest for new and different experiences, she decided to try motherhood—until after the baby was born!"

"I never—I mean—" She wasn't sure what she meant. No wonder Ms. Shelton had disappeared so quickly.

Jase stood up and stalked to the window, opened the blinds, and looked out on the side yard below. Laurel deserved an explanation, the full, sordid story, but he didn't want to see the expression on her face when he told it.

"It all started when I was mowing her lawn." He frowned and corrected himself. "No, actually, it began the first day she walked into school and I wound up in her class. By the end of the week, she was all the guys talked about in the locker room—the way her boobs moved every time she took a breath, how she smiled with her eyelids half-closed, how she talked in a throaty purr that made you uncomfortable if you were sitting down and embarrassed if you had to stand up."

Laurel dropped the sheet and joined him at the window, putting her arm around his waist.

In for a penny, in for a pound. She hoped Pendleton Swaim wasn't out walking today. A naked Laurel Harlow embracing her equally naked lover in full view of anyone passing by would really spice up his next book.

Jase stared out the window, into the past.

"All the guys speculated about what she'd be like in the hay, but none of us would've made a move on her. She was off limits, an adult, a teacher."

He might not want to get up from his desk after she'd swayed down the row to hand out papers, but Marguerite had to be the one to make the first overture. And she did.

She called it "special help," just the two of them sitting close together in the deserted classroom during lunch period, the warmth of her breasts or thighs "accidentally" rubbing against him, the "friendly" touching, her scent wafting into his consciousness. Hell, the smell of gardenias still gave him an instant erection. Her conversation was witty, sophisticated, and just a tad naughty. And her eyes—those sherry eyes...

Then came the compliments. "You're so mature for your age, Jase," she would purr, running the edge of her fingernail down his arm. "You've really got a build on you—I noticed it the first day you walked into my class. I bet half the girls in school are crazy about you. They must keep you busy. I'm surprised you even have the strength left to come to school in the morning."

Damn, he'd loved it. He'd laughed nervously and been embarrassed and flattered and confused and excited, but he loved it. In reality, the girls avoided him, at least the nice girls. He was too tall, too muscular, too dark. His father always claimed Indian blood, but Jase doubted if he really knew. Ol' Growler's parentage had probably been as haphazard as his own.

Marguerite was the perfect seductress. Attentive and available, she praised him for his triumphs and commiserated with him over his disappointments. Growler had never asked him about his classes or even attended one of his football games.

He tried to explain. "Marguerite seemed to care, and there weren't many adults in my life who gave a damn. Maxie tried to help, but she was working full-time and taking care of her mother too, so that didn't leave much time for me. Granny hated my dad—and me. Probably because of my mother." He shrugged as if it didn't matter. "Anyway, she died the year before I was run out of town."

He paused for a moment before continuing. This was the hard part, and he didn't know how Laurel would take it.

"Marguerite knew I was pretty much on my own, so she started hiring me to do chores around her house. At first it was just on weekends because football practice was right after school. Coach had waived the fees for me so I didn't dare skip a practice." He snorted. "Not many six-foot-two guys around Bosque Bend High School at the time."

Laurel nodded. Jase had been the tallest boy in the junior class, and he'd had the musculature to go with it.

"Anyway, all that fall, I spent Saturday afternoons at that little stone cottage she'd rented, mowing the lawn or trimming the bushes or cleaning out the gutters, sometimes washing her car. She'd invite me inside afterward and she'd give me a glass of lemonade, which changed to hot chocolate in November. It became a ritual—she called it 'our time.'" He glanced at Laurel. Would she understand? After all, she'd grown up with *real* parents.

"She never had much on—short shorts and a tank top or a halter thing, even when it got colder." He stopped for a moment to consider what he should say next, then stated it straight-out.

"She took me into her bed in December. I didn't catch on at first."

The first Saturday of the month, Marguerite told him she was going to take a shower while he raked up the leaves. His imagination had gone into overdrive on that one, and when he came into the kitchen for "our time," there she was, clothed in a lightweight kimono that clung to her damp, naked body like Saran Wrap.

An erection had started nudging against his fly, and he'd tried to look everywhere else but at her, then downed his drink in one scalding gulp and bolted out the back door, without even waiting to be paid. The rest of the weekend had been misery, and he'd dreaded seeing her again at school on Monday, but she'd been as friendly as ever, paid him for his yard work as if nothing unusual had happened, and he convinced himself he'd overreacted.

The next weekend was really hot, a freak throwback to the dog days of August. After he finished raking the leaves again and giving her grass a needless winter trim, his tee was virtually plastered to his body.

Dressed in shorts, a blouse loosely tied under her breasts, Marguerite had come out on the back step to invite him in. As soon as they were through the door, she swayed toward him and ran her hand down his chest.

"Jase, we must get this shirt off," she'd said with a throaty laugh, plucking at the shirt and lifting it up. He'd obliged, of course, pulling his tee over his head and draping it on the back of a kitchen chair.

Then she strolled casually over to the back door and locked it, turned to smile at him, and, just as casually, untied the front of her blouse and dropped it on top of his shirt. Her full, tight-nippled breasts lifted with the motion, a mouthwatering feast to his hungry eyes.

He was frozen to the spot as she raised herself onto her toes, ground herself into him, and pulled his head down for a full-tongue kiss.

The rest of the afternoon was spent in her big bed in the attic bedroom. Afterward she'd told him how mature he was, what a terrific lover, what a man, that she had known from the first moment she set eyes on him that it would be like this. But it was "our secret" of course, because "ignorant people with small minds" wouldn't understand the "sophisticated relationship" they had.

She paid him for the lawn mowing. Overpaid, in fact. He'd protested, embarrassed, and tried to return the money, but she'd insisted he keep it. "Don't be silly, darling. You're worth it." She tapped his bare chest. "You mow a great lawn."

"I was an easy mark for her," he admitted to Laurel. "She knew what she was doing. By January, I was in her bed on a regular schedule—Monday, Wednesday, and Saturday, to be exact."

Laurel looked up at him. "She should have been the one who had to leave town, not you."

His voice grew softer. "I know what the man on the street would say, that I hit it lucky when an older woman, a looker like Marguerite, took me on as her lover." He shook his head. "Maybe for some other guy, but I was already damaged goods. Growler resented me from day one, and the kids at school had all been warned by their parents to steer clear of me."

Of course, when adolescence hit and he suddenly stood a full head taller than the rest of the seventh grade, the coaches came a-courting. Sports had served as an outlet for his anger and ensured him passing his courses, but didn't help him much socially. He established casual friendships with a few of the guys on the team, but no decent girl wanted to be seen with him, whether he was on the team or not. And he wasn't interested in the other kind.

No, he hadn't hit it lucky with Marguerite Shelton. He wouldn't wish her on anyone.

"I was no more ready for sex than you were back then, at least not the sort of sex Marguerite introduced me to." He reached for Laurel's hand. "I was just sixteen. I didn't belong in the big time. Oh sure, I'd had some experience with the girls who hung around the tavern, but they were amateurs compared to Marguerite. I should have been stealing kisses in parked cars, trying to get inside my date's bra, not functioning as Marguerite Shelton's prize stud. That woman had me so well trained I could have won a gold medal at the Indoor Olympics."

His mouth tightened to a bitter line. "She had total control over me—I couldn't escape. I felt dirty—used—but I was addicted. I couldn't break it off. If Nyquist hadn't busted us, I might still be swinging myself over her fence three times a week for a fix."

"I'm so sorry, Jase." Laurel leaned her head against his shoulder, then stepped to the side, out of his arms. Standing naked in a side window was one thing, but having sex in the window was another. "Let's go down and have some lunch first. I'm starving."

"Well, now I know how I rate with you." He pulled up his slacks and shrugged his shirt on, not bothering to button it. "One step below pizza."

Laurel drew on a light summer robe, and the two of them grandly descended the elaborately carved staircase, arm in arm.

Since there wasn't much left over from last night's dinner, they made themselves peanut butter sandwiches and washed them down with a pitcher of iced tea. Jase was surprised at how bare Laurel's pantry was. Even for just one person, she should keep up her supplies better. And the kitchen seemed to be in retro mode, the counter occupied by a few bins and a disheartened-looking microwave. He spotted a dishwasher under the counter next to the sink, but its controls seemed strangely askew.

"It's broken," Laurel explained airily, following the direction of his glance. "I haven't had the time to get it fixed." The heck she was going to let him know how dire her circumstances were.

He rose from the table to drop their paper plates and cups in the trash can. "We'll have to do last night's dishes by hand, then."

Her eyes went wide with shock. "The dishes—I totally forgot about them!" The dining room had been closed for so long that she hadn't given it a thought. Good grief—the mess might have stayed there until the house sold if Jase had left last night like he'd planned.

She hurried to the dining room to look the situation over,

but no good fairy had cleaned up the table overnight. Everything was exactly as they had left it. And even though the drapes were closed and the air conditioner was still chugging away like a trouper, the room was beginning to heat up.

She sighed. If it was this hot at noon, the afternoon would be a real scorcher, maybe up to a hundred ten. Usually she just toughed it out, but today she'd have to turn on all the air conditioners if she wanted Jase to be even moderately comfortable. It would send her electric bill into the stratosphere, but she'd rather have her utilities turned off than let Jase know how broke she was.

He came in behind her and started stacking plates. "You go back to the kitchen and start running the water while I bring everything in. I've got plenty of experience in this area. Used to moonlight in a restaurant for my supper."

She gathered the silver and returned to the kitchen to turn on the hot water. Jase arrived with the plates, cups, and saucers, setting them down next to her, then went back for more. Thirty minutes later, everything was washed, dried, and returned to the china cabinet.

Laurel gave him a coquettish glance. "You're very handy to have around."

He grinned at her. "Maybe you should keep me."

Her heart fluttered. Was he sincere? Or was it as meaningless as saying "I love you" after they'd had sex?

While she tucked away the protective pads in the bottom drawer of the buffet, Jase took the linens to soak. He came back from the laundry room with a light sheen of perspiration on his face.

"Whew. That place is hot!"

"There's no window."

"Have you ever considered central air?"

"Mama and Daddy were going to put AC in a couple of years ago, but it didn't work out." Let him make whatever he wanted to out of that.

He nodded. "It'd cost a bundle with a house this big. Might as well let the next owner do it."

"Exactly."

As if she were that much of a skinflint. The house would have central air in a New York minute if she had the money. "Let's go to the den." Insulated by being at the center of the house, it stayed cool in the summer and warm in winter.

Jase settled down on the leather couch and pulled out his phone. "I need to report in to Maxie and check up on Lolly."

Okay—so maybe he was going to stick around for a few more days, but Laurel knew there was no use bargaining with God for any extra favors. She'd already been given more than the few hours she'd asked for.

She picked up a romance novel she'd been reading and made herself comfortable in the recliner as Jase called home.

"Yeah, Maxie, Laurel's okay now, but I'm gonna camp out in Bosque Bend for a while to be keep an eye on her." He grinned from across the room and winked. "Scouting out some real estate too, the usual thing...Is Girl Child there?...May I talk to her?"

"Hi, sweetheart. Hope you're doin' okay...Tennis? I didn't know you were interested in tennis...How much will it cost?...Who else is taking the class?...Where is it being held?...Well, okay...Love you too, baby."

He put his phone down and looked at Laurel. "I think Lolly's put the mother business behind her. She's enrolling in a class 'a real hottie' is teaching at the country club. Let's just hope this roots crap has been postponed for a while."

Laurel made herself relax back in the chair. Judging by what Jase had told Maxie, the length of time Jase would stay in town would depend on how long it took him to check out the local real estate market. But sooner or later, he'd return to his home in North Plano. After all, that's where his home was.

She took a deep breath, determined to embrace the inevitable, and gave him a bright smile. "It must be hard for you, even with Maxie helping. I mean being a single father—the bottom-line decisions are all up to you."

"Yeah, there've been times that were worse than others, but all in all, it's worked out. Lolly's a really great kid."

He held out his hands to Laurel and pulled her up to him, front to front. His chin rested comfortably on the top of her head.

"Com'ere, woman," he growled, smiling broadly and joining his hands behind her back to mold her against himself. "I helped with the dishes, and surely the laborer is worthy of his hire." Grinning wolfishly, he cupped her breasts, then circled the rising crests with his thumbs. "And you know what I desire in payment." He raised her up a little and butted himself against her hips.

Bending her head back to see her lover better, Laurel was hit by a wave of desire so scorching that her eyes closed and her body went limp. Jase quickly transferred her to one arm and used his other hand to release his slacks. They fell to his ankles and he stepped out of them, ready for action.

Before she could even begin to protest, he'd peeled her out of her robe.

Her ego flared with indignation. Did he take her so much for granted already? Well, she had other ideas! Her cheeks flamed with excitement, and her gray eyes sparkled black.

Twisting away from his embrace, she grabbed her robe and backed toward the doorway, her eyes shining with challenge. "But I did more cleanup than you did. I washed—you just carried!" With a roar of frustration, Jase leapt after her.

Giggling with delight, she danced out of reach and flapped her robe at him as if it were matador's cape, daring and taunting him.

"Toro! Toro!"

Jase stood still for a moment, the shirt hanging loose from his shoulders. Relaxing onto one hip, he pretended he'd lost interest in the game, but Laurel could tell that his eyes were tracking her every move.

Closer and closer she came, flirting with him, watching him, brandishing her robe, teasing him to action, but he knew to bide his time.

Finally she moved close enough that he thought he had a chance. He lunged for her, but she laughed and eluded him easily, scampering down the wide front hall just out of reach of his fingertips.

Jase roared and ran after her. He hadn't played strong-side linebacker for nothing.

Laurel liked this titillating new game, sort of a remake of Daphne and Apollo, but unlike the stupid wood nymph, she wanted to get caught—eventually.

She glanced back at Jase, enjoyed the sight of his nudity in action. The furniture was fully clothed, but Jase was naked, naked, naked.

And so was she. Her full breasts jiggled against her chest as she ran, and her thighs rubbed against each other. She had never done anything like this before, and part of her was aghast at her daring. The other part of her was stimulated beyond belief.

Panting with exertion and excitement, she ran into the dining room, where Jase almost cornered her behind the mahogany table at which they had dined just the night before.

They dodged back and forth twice. She feinted to the right but ran to the left, past the tall china cabinet and down the hall to the drawing room. There at last, in the jungle of Victorian furniture, Jase caught one of her arms and hauled her against himself, bearing her down to the thick oriental carpet, half under the piano.

Laurel wound herself around his neck and kissed him as if the world was coming to an end.

"You vixen." He nibbled at her ear and tossed her robe out of reach. "I'll fix you so you never try to get away from me again."

She gave him a challenging look. "How?"

His eyes glowed with wickedness and his voice was a dark, hoarse whisper. "By fucking you so thoroughly that you never want to get up from this floor again."

Chapter Ten

Fuck—when Sarah had first discovered the silly-sounding word and told her what it meant, they'd snickered about it for weeks. By the time they hit high school, it had become a casual adjective Laurel heard every day, but Dave had been surprisingly squeamish about using "dirty words," so this was the first time she'd ever heard the word used in context. It was delicious, shocking—and exciting.

Jase held her in place with his big body and lowered his head to her lips. When his tongue snaked into her mouth, she drew back with a scowl. "Ummph—you taste like peanut butter!"

"I thought you liked peanut butter."

"To *eat*, not to—to—"

He raised his head, and his black eyes glittered at her in wicked amusement. "Then let's just try it the other way around." He reversed himself on her.

Laurel was startled. "No, Jase, I—I..."

His mouth claimed her body as it had her lips, and she caught fire. Her flesh didn't exist anymore, and neither did her mind. The only thing left was a burning, shimmering heat consuming all that lay in its path.

"Jase, Jase," she chanted mindlessly. "I want—I want—"
But she didn't even have the words for what she wanted, because there were no words.

But he knew, Jase knew.

Then it was her turn. She opened her mouth to his male flesh.

* * *

An hour later, Jase lay exhausted on the floor, watching the dust motes dance in a sunbeam. It was a good that those lacy curtain things were drawn, but he wasn't sure it would have mattered one way or another. He wasn't acting sanely as far as Laurel was concerned.

What was it about her? He rolled onto his side and studied her as she slept, curled up on the jewel-toned carpet, the afternoon sun dappling her skin.

Her eyes were gray, he knew, her nose straight, and her mouth soft and inviting. She was pretty, but in a quiet, subtle way, not like the brassy, come-hither looks that dominated beauty pageant runways. And she was—well—*nice*, that much-overused word that covered everything from her loyalty to him sixteen years ago to her kindness to Lolly this weekend. There was a certain aura about her too—almost a regal air. That came from her heritage, of course. She was a lady, from the top of her head down to the tips of her toes, but she was also sexy as hell. And she was all his. He smiled in satisfaction, stretched a little, and sat up partway, leaning back on his elbows.

Damn. This was a first—the front room floor.

What if Laurel had after-church visitors? He snorted to

himself, picturing a mad scramble as they ran upstairs to get some clothes on. Or maybe he'd saunter down the hall and answer the bell with a pillow strategically placed and inform Mr. and Mrs. Hoity-toity that the notorious Jase Redlander was back in town, thank you, so they'd better lock up their wives and daughters.

He bent his legs and leaned forward to rest his arms across his knees. The sad fact was that, at one time, a warning like that would have been accurate. Marguerite had awakened an appetite in him that, in the beginning, needed constant appeasement. The second he hit Dallas, he took every female he could get, with a decided preference for older women. It started out as a winning combination on both sides, but the relationships were never more than physical—and fleeting.

He was damn lucky that one of the women he'd had a fling with not only told him off good and proper, but also gave him the name of a top-notch therapist. Otherwise he might have been on the town forever, perpetuating Marguerite's legacy. He'd tried to be more selective of his bed partners from then on, more considerate, but he'd never developed deep feelings for any of them.

The only woman he'd ever loved was Laurel Harlow, the most popular girl in the sophomore class.

So why wasn't her doorbell ringing? Why weren't people calling on her after church?

He looked over at her. She'd pulled her robe across herself in a belated attempt at modesty before she fell asleep, but one rose-tipped breast had escaped its cover. He considered the possibilities. Tempting, but he was thirty-two, not sixteen. Enough was enough—for now.

His eyes roamed the room. It looked different somehow.

Those creepy naked statues, the ones that always made him uneasy, were missing from the entrance to Reverend Ed's study. Had she sold them? He was more convinced than ever that Laurel was having money troubles. The economy had been down lately, and maybe her father had lost a bundle in the stock market or gotten sucked into a Ponzi scheme. Life could be hard without money, he knew, but at least he'd never had to keep up appearances.

He glanced around the big room again. In the bright light of day, he could see details he'd missed before. The place looked downright shabby.

Maybe he could help her out, loan her money to get the house back in shape. Hell—he'd *give* her the money. But she wouldn't take it, he knew, not after last night. It would seem like payment for services rendered.

He recovered his trousers from the den and returned to the front room to awaken Laurel by running his hand down her shoulder. "Rise and shine, sweetheart. We need to do some serious grocery shopping."

She yawned, and sat up. Taking both her hands, he helped her to her feet, growled, and nipped at her neck.

"If I'm not fed at regular intervals, I get ver-r-r-y hungr-r-r-y."

She yipped appropriately and drew her robe on the rest of the way. He draped his arm over her shoulder as they walked up the stairs.

* * *

Laurel looked at the family portraits along the way, wondering what her forebears would have said about their naked romp.

The girls were smiling at her, but their mother seemed disapproving. Why? Even Victorians had sex. In fact, from what she'd read, they were obsessed with it.

Upstairs, she slipped into a wide-necked tee and a colorful cotton skirt while Jase buttoned his shirt and rolled up the sleeves to accommodate the weather, but he didn't bother to tuck in the tail.

With the day as hot as it was, Laurel wished she could get up the nerve to wear shorts to the store. There were a few pairs stuck in the back of her bottom drawer, leftovers from high school physical education classes that might still fit, but not wearing them had somehow become a way of honoring her mother's memory.

On the other hand, Mama used to pull on pantyhose whenever she went out, which Laurel could never imagine doing. Times change. Maybe someday she'd try wearing shorts in public and see if the world would come to an end. But not today.

She sat down at her dressing table. Sunscreen, lipstick, her favorite gold hoops in her ears, and she was ready. As she gave herself a final check, posing in front of the cheval mirror in the corner, Jase moved behind her and rested his hands on her shoulders. She smiled at their reflection.

Was it true that some mirrors could retain images forever?

* * *

Fifteen minutes and one long shopping list later, they were in the car. Jase backed Laurel's Escort out of the garage, turned it around in the brick-paved parking area, and drove to the edge of the street to ease his way into the traffic.

A redheaded woman in white capris and a yellow tank top was playing three-sided catch with two boys in the front yard across the street, while an even younger boy, a carrottop like she was, clung to her leg. She looked vaguely familiar. Damn. What was her name?

He nodded in the mystery woman's direction. "That woman over there—she looks like someone I used to know, but I can't place her."

Laurel froze and her voice turned brittle. "Sarah Edelman. She used to be Sarah Bridges. She was All-District in softball."

"Yeah, now I remember." Sarah Bridges was also a cheerleader and played the lead in the class play. In fact, she did pretty much everything in Bosque Bend High School that Laurel didn't do. Between the two of them, they had the school all sewn up. He made the turn and gave Laurel a questioning glance. "You two hung out together all the time. Wasn't she your best friend?"

"I guess so." Laurel stared down at her hands, refusing to meet his eyes.

"Well, what happened? I mean, she stared at us for a second there, then looked away. Y'all have a fight or something?"

Laurel tossed her hair in an I-don't-care gesture.

"I guess we grew apart. She married a doctor and lives in Austin now. They have three children. Eric, the eldest, is my godson. Then there's Luke and—and...I don't know the name of the youngest." She smiled—a little too brightly. "It's hard to keep up with everyone."

Jase frowned. What was going on here? Another mystery? He mentally shrugged his shoulders. It was none of his business who Laurel chose for her friends.

He drove down the street for several blocks and turned left

into the Piggly Wiggly parking lot. The little Escort fit easily into a space that a bigger car could never have managed, which reminded him that he needed to pick up his Cadillac at the airport tomorrow. He wasn't going to let himself run into anybody he used to know without the luxury car somewhere in the background. Let them all see what Jason Redlander had made of himself.

As they walked toward the store, Laurel seemed to hesitate, to hang back. Jase was instantly suspicious. Gossip systems function quite effectively in towns the size of Bosque Bend. Was she ashamed of being seen with Growler Redlander's spawn?

But she wasn't like that, he told himself. Laurel had been willing to stand up for him sixteen years ago, and she wouldn't let him down today. Besides, it'd been a long time since he'd been in Bosque Bend. No one would recognize him. Probably she was just shy, embarrassed that people might guess he'd spent the night in her bed.

His protective instincts caught fire. No one was going to make any snide remarks about Laurel Harlow while he was around! Maybe it would be a good idea to be more discreet, to minimize the time they'd be seen together in the store.

As soon as they went through the door, he grabbed a plastic grocery basket and slid its handles over his arm. "Why don't you take the cart and go get the groceries while I pick up a few things for myself. Meet me in the bakery when you're through."

"Sure." She ran her eyes down the list they'd made. "Give me thirty minutes. I'll try to be quick."

He watched her head off in the direction of the produce department, checked his watch, and started wandering around the store, accumulating random items he might possibly have a use for.

He caught sight of a few faces he thought he recognized, but no one showed any particular interest in him. Instead, people smiled and nodded at him along the way, saying "excuse me" or "*con permiso*" when they crossed in front of him—or when he inadvertently cut in front of them—which startled him at first until he remembered this was standard operating procedure in small towns. People had enough time to be courteous to each other.

Half an hour later, he started walking slowly toward the bakery by way of the pharmacy. Laurel was probably on some kind of birth control, but he'd better grab a package of condoms, just in case.

He paused for a moment. If he could have had Laurel all to himself without sex, would he have claimed her? Would he have accepted her as the eternal virgin princess? Was that the way he saw her? Maybe back then, but not now. That was one thing the shrink had cleared up in therapy. Sex did not have to be a dirty secret leading to guilt or anger. Good sex was a tender, joyful fulfillment of an honest relationship.

He arrived at the bakery area and looked around. Laurel wasn't in sight yet, which gave him the opportunity to check out the display cases and pick up some brownies and a loaf of fresh bread. The solidly built woman behind the counter looked him up and down as she started bagging his purchases.

"You usually shop here?"

"No. I'm from around Dallas."

Her face brightened. "My cousin lives in Dallas. LuAnn Ramirez. Used to be LuAnn Stout. You ever run into her? She drives a school bus."

He shook his head. "I don't think so. Dallas is a big place, and, actually, I live outside it, the North Plano area."

She nodded slowly, as if he'd said something profound. "How long you gonna be in town?"

"Not sure."

"Well, you have a good visit, y'hear?" She gave him the bakery bags and dismissed him with a valedictory smile, at the same time signaling another customer that she'd be right with her.

Turning away from the counter, he spotted Laurel pushing the loaded cart in his direction and moved toward her. He put a hand on the cart. "I'll take everything through checkout. You go on out to the car and turn on the air."

Her back went ramrod straight and she tightened her grip on the cart's handle, looking at him as if she was the queen of England and he had offended her majesty. "These are *my* groceries. You're not paying for them."

Damn, he hadn't counted on her making a scene.

The bakery lady and her customer stopped talking and looked their way. He nodded at the two women, then smiled at Laurel and lowered his voice so that she was the only one who could hear. "Tell you what. I'll bill you later. Now, how about you hustling your cute little fanny outside to the car and getting the AC running?"

She looked at him for one long second, her face drawn white with rage, before releasing the cart handle like it was a red-hot iron and marching out of the store, her chin held high.

After giving one last nod to the bakery lady to apologize for the disturbance, he pushed the cart toward the checkouts. When he got to the car, Laurel was sitting in the driver's seat, stiff as a poker, her profile set in stone. Not saying a word, he stowed the groceries in the hatch, adjusted the passenger seat to accommodate his length, and got in the car.

She switched on the ignition, backing out so quickly she almost hit a motorized train of grocery carts, and pulled onto the street without looking at him even once.

Jase sucked in his cheeks. Why the hell was she being so difficult about him footing the bill? Whatever the problem was, someone had to break the ice, and it didn't look like she was going to be the one to do it. He cleared his throat.

"Um, mad at me?"

What a jackass thing to say. Of course she was mad at him, but he had to get her to start talking somehow. At least he'd learned something for the small fortune he'd forked over to the shrink every week for four years.

Barely moving her lips, Laurel answered him in a flat, clipped tone. "I don't like you paying for the groceries. You're my guest. It was the principle of the thing. Guests do not pay for food."

Jase reached over and touched her arm lightly in apology. "I'm sorry I offended you, Laurel, but I didn't think it would look good for us to go through the line together. You have to live with these people, at least until the house sells, and I thought...I thought it would be easier on you if they didn't know that you...that you had a male guest...that you and I..." He floundered to a stop. "Damn it, Laurel, you have a reputation to keep up!"

After a pause, he saw her shoulders relax, She gave him a quick, penitent smile. "I'm the one who should apologize, Jase. I overreacted. Thank you for buying the groceries."

He heaved a sigh of relief. Their first quarrel. It was bound to happen. At least now he knew for sure she was human.

* * *

Laurel could still feel the color washing into her face. Jase had been trying to protect *her*. God help her, but he didn't know how far her star had fallen. She doubted if anyone cared if she had a live-in lover. She wasn't Pastor Harlow's virgin daughter anymore. She was the divorced daughter of the man who'd betrayed the town's trust.

At least she'd been lucky in the store. She'd actually been relieved when Jase suggested they separate to shop. That way, there would be less chance of anyone seeing her and Jase together and spilling the beans to him about Daddy. But as she was putting milk and chicken and frozen pizza in her wheeled basket, she became more and more anxious about the possibility of some old acquaintance cornering Jase when he was alone and bringing him up-to-date on the goings-on in Bosque Bend. The only thing to do was move him out of the supermarket quickly and take the groceries through checkout by herself. But he beat her to it, and paid for the groceries besides.

Principle was important, but it was even more important to extend Jase's visit as long as possible. She was more in love with him than ever.

* * *

Jase rolled his sleeves down. "Would you mind if we drive over to the old place after we get the groceries put away? I need to pick up my clothes. I really do own more than one shirt."

"No problem. I'll even throw in a guided tour so you can see all the changes that have taken place around here since you left."

"And don't make anything for dinner. I'll take you out."

"Out? I-I'm not dressed to go out anywhere." And she didn't want to go out to eat anywhere. They might run into someone who knew her.

Jase laid his hand on her knee. "Relax, babe. Just for a hamburger."

She let herself start breathing again. Fast food. That should be safe. Most of the chain restaurants were on the new side of town, and no one would recognize her over there.

Twenty minutes later they were in the car again, with Jase behind the wheel this time. To her surprise, he kept on going north instead of cutting over to the east.

"Where are we going? I can't think of anything out that way."

"How about Hardy Joe's? I spotted it on the way into town. Couldn't believe it was still there."

"Sounds great. I used to go there a lot when I was in high school."

Jase nodded. Of course, she'd gone to Hardy Joe's. It had been where all the popular kids gathered, which had pretty much cut him out of the picture. He liked the idea of buying Laurel a hamburger there to make up for all the ones he hadn't bought her sixteen years ago.

A low-slung building came into sight. On its roof, a neon fisherman was reeling in a giant neon swordfish. Jase laughed. "More than twenty years, and that damn fish still hasn't been landed."

It was a miracle the drive-in was still in operation, but times moved slower in small towns. In Dallas, ol' Hardy Joe's would've long since been knocked down for a parking lot—maybe one of his.

He swung Laurel's Escort into the drive-in and ordered for them from the speaker.

Laurel took off her dark glasses and glanced around. "It looks like this is still a high school hangout. We must be the only adults here."

"Not all the teenagers are customers," Jase said, indicating a girl carrying a red tray and heading their way. She looked something like Lolly, blond, eyes of blue, five foot two—except that Lolly was barely five feet, much to her chagrin. He pulled out his wallet and extracted a credit card as the girl placed the tray on the stand beside the car.

She gave him the tired smile of someone who'd been toting trays in the hot sun all afternoon.

"Hardy Joe's, home of the SuperBurger, hopes you enjoy your meal, sir. That'll be twelve ninety-five."

He signed the tab and handed her a fiver for herself. Having served his time in low-paying service jobs, he made it a point to overtip. And always in cash so the manager wouldn't claim a cut.

Her smile perked up and her eyes sparkled. "Gee, thanks, Mister. Have a great day!"

"You too."

He watched her as she walked back to the restaurant, then reached for their drinks and lifted the hamburger bags off the tray, passing Laurel her SuperBurger Special.

Mmm. Smelled good.

A teasing smile crossed Laurel's face as she unwrapped her burger. "Did you ever bring a date here after a school dance?"

"I never went to a school dance."

She looked shocked. "Why not?"

"I didn't think anyone would go with me, at least anyone I

was interested in." God knows, he'd never allow Lolly to associate with the sort of bottom-feeder he'd been.

"Is this the first time you've been in Bosque Bend since high school?"

He eased around to face her. "I came back when my father died and a couple of other times to set up the house for rental. There wasn't much reason to visit while he was still alive. Growler was never much of a family man." He bit into his hamburger, chewing slowly to savor the taste. What was the big deal about the burger? It was okay, but didn't match up to its aromatic promise—nothing really "super" about it. Must be the frustrated fisherman that drew in the customers.

Laurel took a sip of her drink. "What happened to your mother? She was Maxie's sister, wasn't she?"

"Yeah, there were five girls. Hanna was the youngest, the black sheep. Lolly looks something like her. Hanna and Growler were quite a couple for a while, I've heard. I've seen old pictures, and my father was fairly presentable before the booze got to him. He was still on the wrestling circuit back then. Anyway, my mother was killed in a car accident when I was three, and Growler went even further downhill after that."

She reached her hand out to his arm. "I'm sorry, Jase."

"I survived."

There didn't seem to be much more to say after that. They finished their supper in silence and hit the road again. Laurel took over navigation, guiding him back south, toward town. Her first point of interest was the new Walmart. Jase didn't have the heart to tell her he'd already noticed it the day before.

"They built it four years ago. You should have seen the grand opening. Daddy gave the invocation, the mayor cut the ribbon, and the chamber of commerce provided hot dogs and soft drinks. It was a big party. Everyone in town was there."

"What's the mayor's name?" Getting acquainted with local officials was vital if he decided to invest in the area. Some places didn't like new blood, and he wasn't about to fight that battle.

"Larry Traylor."

"He was one of your father's pals, wasn't he? I think I met him once, at a football dinner."

"Um—yes." Her gaze immediately switched to the other side of the street, as if she was trying to change the subject. "And look—here's the Dairy Queen. The Mayfields have remodeled it again."

"What's that beside it?" He nodded toward a squat cinderblock building with a dog-shaped sign in the window. "Old Man Sawyer's moved the *Retriever* over here? That used to be a doughnut shop."

"His headquarters over on Washington Avenue burned down a while back. Half the town thinks he torched it for the insurance to keep the newspaper going."

Jase laughed. "Wouldn't put it past him. I liked the old goat, but he was tough as nails. Hired me to throw papers for him, and he kept me on till Growler got drunk and tossed my delivery in the river one time too many."

They stopped at a red light, and he looked over at her as the light turned green. "Which way?"

"Still south, but we've got a lot of one-way streets now, so you'll have to zigzag. I want to show you the courthouse. It's been completely restored."

He turned to the right and moved over to Bowie Avenue, then drove straight south, toward the river. This was the main commercial district, he remembered. Might as well check it out. Bosque Bend could be a real find. Ordinarily he didn't get involved with small-town properties, but it was advantageous to get in on growth areas, places on their way up but not yet at their peak.

Everything looked good so far. The copper roof of the courthouse gleamed in the harsh evening sun, and its buff-colored brick had been sandblasted within an inch of its life. They'd removed those tacky green-and-white-striped aluminum window awnings too—and landscaped the grounds. Only two storefronts on the square around it seemed to be vacant, he noticed, and there wasn't an overabundance of those silly gift shops small towns tended to load their squares with.

The data was adding up. If Bosque Bend had the money to spend on prettying up its courthouse square, it was on the move.

Laurel was obviously relishing her job as tour guide. "Now, I want you to see what's happening down at the river."

He glanced at her, his eyebrows raised in surprise. "The Shallows?"

She eyes sparkled. "You'll see. Just get to First Street—but don't turn here!"

The warning came too late. *Damn.* The street was one-way now, but he was halfway through the intersection and couldn't retreat. He'd just have to circle the block and try again. Exhaling in frustration, he swung to the left at the next intersection and stopped dead.

Smack-dab in front of him stood the setting for many a recurring nightmare: Bosque Bend High School. Tall antebellum columns marched across the front of the structure, and the slanting sun transformed the yellow brick into slabs of pure, cruel gold. The parking lot was chained shut, and the windows were boarded up with plywood.

"It's being used as a storehouse for administration records and old equipment now," Laurel explained. "There's a new consolidated high school outside of town to pull in the country kids. It's good for football. Brought us up to 4-A in Inter-scholastic League."

Jase didn't say anything, just sat at the stop sign in silence, staring at the gilded building in front of him.

This had been his school, his sanctuary. Maybe he hadn't been the most popular guy on campus, but no one cuffed him around, the football coaches valued him, and he could fool himself that he blended into the crowd—until he got kicked out because Marguerite Shelton had a yen for teenage boys.

Laurel reached over and put her hand on his arm. "It's all in the past."

He didn't reply, just squeezed her hand, flipped the turn signal, and pressed his foot on the accelerator. Then, with his jaw set so tight it hurt, he made his way toward First Street and the Bosque River just beyond.

Chapter Eleven

Why was Laurel so intent on his seeing the Shallows? The best thing that could be done for that eyesore was pave it over with cement.

Mrs. Johnson, his fourth-grade teacher, had dedicated a fair amount of her Texas history unit to the origins of Bosque Bend, so Jase knew that after the early settlers had driven out the Huacos, a peaceful tribe that had been cultivating crops on the fertile bottom land for decades, the town had been laid out in an unrelenting grid that started about a half mile above the ever-changing riverbank. That left a swampy no-man's-land about two miles long between First Street and the Bosque to accommodate the inevitable flooding. The Shallows, as the area was called, always had a reputation for dark dealings. Its further reaches harbored a semipermanent homeless encampment, and all sorts of debris littered its shores—mattresses, condoms, broken syringes, and the occasional bloated corpse. Every spring, Jase recalled, the Methodist Sunday school would spend a couple of weekends cleaning up the area, but, come the next flood, the Shallows would be business as usual.

The aura of danger, of course, was a surefire lure to any

teenage boy worth his escalating testosterone. Jase's teammates used to talk about driving across the county line to Beat Down and loading their trunks full of Growler's booze for weekend beer busts in the Shallows. It was even more exciting if the cops showed up and everyone had to make a run for it.

He'd never been invited to one of the get-togethers—the guest list was limited to the upper social stratum and their dates—but it didn't matter. There was always beer in the refrigerator at home, and getting shit-faced and playing hide-and-seek with the law was not his idea of fun.

He glanced at Laurel. "You ever go to a party at the Shallows?"

She looked at him as if he were crazy. "Me? Heavens, no. But Sarah did—once. She said it was gross. The guys got drunk, took off their shirts, and danced around the fire like lunatics, then went off into the bushes and hurled their guts out. She called her dad to come pick her up."

"Mr. Bridges. I remember him."

Charles Lehman Bridges, the district attorney. The man Reverend Ed had talked to about going after Marguerite for statutory rape, for what little good it did. Sarah's father had obviously thought Growler Redlander's son was as irredeemable as the Shallows. Jase smiled to himself. With a little luck and a lot of hard work, he'd been able to make something of himself, but the Shallows were hopeless. Whatever the Methodists had done this time, it wouldn't last.

He turned onto First Street and nearly ended up in the oncoming lane as his eyes took in a graceful rock-walled concrete walkway winding next to the river.

Damn! Someone must have finally gotten a flood control engineer involved.

Driving slowly, he rubbernecked the entrance to the park, where a large fountain sparkled in the setting sun. Gone were the knee-high weeds and scraggly underbrush, replaced by a carpet of green grass and scattered groupings of redbuds and mountain laurels. A line of frothy pink crepe myrtles bordered the wall.

Jase signaled for a right, entered the gravel parking area, and took a space two down from a dark blue minivan with a car seat in the back. Turning off the ignition, he rested his arms on the wheel and stared.

"I don't believe it."

Laurel grinned like a chessy cat. "The city council went after a federal grant to channel the river all the way through town and build up its banks. Then the garden club got into the act and planted the trees and shrubs. You should see the place in the spring. They seeded the whole area with bluebonnets and red poppies."

Jase took a quick glance at the blaze across the western horizon and opened his door. "Let's go for a walk while there's still light enough to see anything. I want to check this thing out up close."

They headed toward the self-latching gate at the entryway. Yellow lantanas crowded the path inside the park, and just beyond, surrounding the fountain, was a cobblestone plaza edged with clumps of purple verbenas.

Jase paused, absorbing the moment. Paved paths branched off from the plaza toward the east and west. Taking Laurel's hand, he started down the path to the left, putting their backs to the brilliant sun. "We'd better get a move on. Wouldn't want to get caught out here after dark."

A frisky little dog, its pink tongue hanging out and its tail rotating with glee, scrabbled up the path toward them, two boys hurrying after it. The taller one held a leash with a red collar still attached.

"Petey, come back here! Stop! Stop!"

Jase laughed as the pup ran at them, but the escapee, obviously assuming Laurel was more sympathetic to his cause, made a beeline for her and leapt up on her legs. To Jase's astonishment, she screamed and started flailing at the puppy as if she were being attacked by a pack of wolves.

Laurel was afraid of dogs? And this one was supersmall—probably a toy breed.

Jase reached down, encircled the dog's middle, and lifted it up to his chest. The pup squirmed upward and licked at his chin as the boys rushed forward to claim their pet. The older one reached out as Jase handed the dog over.

"Thanks, Mister. Petey's figured out how to slip his collar. He's real smart." He petted the pup's head and regarded Laurel warily. "Sorry he scared you, ma'am. He just likes to make new friends."

The younger boy nodded in solemn agreement. "Petey won't bite."

"Try to keep him on the leash from now on," Jase advised. "Some people aren't used to dogs." He watched the boys as they carried their charge toward the gate.

"I guess I overreacted," Laurel ventured, pushing her hair back into place. "I feel like a fool." She glanced at Jase. "You probably grew up with dogs."

"There were always a couple of mongrels hanging around, though God only knows why," he said, still staring after the boys. "Growler never so much as put out a water bowl for them."

Refusing to succumb to melancholy, he took Laurel's hand, swinging it as they continued down the winding path. They walked in silence for a while, their shoulders and hips touching frequently. Just being around her soothed him. Somehow she healed a pain so deep within him that he couldn't even name it.

A redbird flew across the trail in front of them, and a bushy-tailed squirrel sat up on its haunches to chitter at them for invading its territory. Gentle breezes rustled through the live oaks along the eastern boundary of the park. Except for a couple of runners who'd thundered past, they were alone on the path.

Was that a doe and her dappled fawns in the shadows? Jase wasn't sure. One thing he did know—as long as Laurel was with him, he could walk down this trail forever.

He pulled her against himself for a long, tender kiss.

* * *

The light had dimmed considerably by the time they reached the turnaround at the end of the trail. Jase looked around. The trees were gathering too much darkness under their low, spreading branches to suit him, and he'd bet there was still a homeless camp somewhere in the woods. Glancing at his watch, he was surprised to see they'd been strolling for almost an hour.

"Time to go back."

She nodded and huddled closer to him as a sudden gust of night wind chilled the air. He couldn't help but seek her lips, then reach up to mold a breast with his hand. What he really wanted to do was lay her down on the soft grass and make sweet love till dawn, but his brain told him that sex in a public park was not a good idea. Besides, he'd noted a couple of suspicious-looking exchanges between some of the guys on the trail. Never a good idea to be in the vicinity when anything like that was going down.

"Tonight," he breathed, moving against her so she could feel his arousal.

"Tonight," she repeated in a dreamy voice, lifting up to fit herself to him, then jerking back as one final bare-chested runner came toward them at a fast clip. Jase stepped in front of her as the man ran by, and watched as he turned at the end of the path and started back up the trail into the dying sun, passing them again. The guy looked harmless enough, but there was no telling. If bad stuff was gonna go down, the Shallows would probably be the place for it, and he didn't want any part of it.

The sunset had faded to a golden memory reflected in the Bosque's placid waters when they arrived back at the plaza. Jase scouted the parking lot with his eyes as they walked past the fountain toward the gate. Only one other vehicle, the minivan, was still in place.

Probably belonged to that last runner. He must be doing the western path too—which reminded Jase that he needed to get a good run in soon. It'd been three days since he had a chance to hit the pavement. He let his hand trail across Laurel's hip.

Not that he wasn't getting plenty of another kind of exercise.

The runner came into view again, waving his arm. "Redlander! Wait!"

Jase went rigid and handed his car keys to Laurel. "Get in

the car and lock yourself in. If there's any trouble, drive off and don't worry about me. I can take care of myself."

He turned to face the newcomer, every muscle in his body primed for action. The man was tall and muscular, but he'd be winded from a long run. There'd be no problem taking him down, even if he pulled a knife, but a gun would be real trouble. Not many people out running would carry a firearm, but this was Texas.

The man slowed, stopping a couple of feet away and bending over with his hands on his knees to get his breath. "Took me...a while to figure...out who you were."

Relief flooded through Jase as he recognized the voice. "Ray Espinoza, you fuckin' dawg!"

Still panting a little, the runner stood up, a big grin spreading across his face. "Long time, no see, *hombre*."

Jase seized his old teammate's extended hand, slapped him on the back, and lifted his clenched fist for a knuckle thump. "Linebackers rule!"

Ray stepped back and wiped his forehead again. "Coach was really pissed about losin' you senior year, dude. Tried movin' me into your spot, but all I did was get my front teeth smashed in." He grinned at Jase, thrusting his upper jaw forward. "Like my implants?"

"Sorry about that, dawg. You shoulda chomped down harder on the mouth guard."

Ray shrugged. "Water under the bridge." He reached through the half-open window of the minivan for a T-shirt and pulled it on. "You still playin' football?"

"A little tennis and a lot of gym workouts, but no football. I'm into real estate now. In town from Dallas looking at a few properties. What about you?"

"Buildin' houses with *mi padre* out east of town. Can you believe it? Bosque Bend actually has a suburb." He patted his haunch as if looking for a pocket, then smiled ruefully. "Sorry, don't carry any cards in my runnin' shorts."

Jase laughed. "I think I'll remember the name."

Ray was one of the few teammates he'd developed a friendship with strong enough to extend past the football season. All fall, Jase had played strong-side linebacker, the human tank the team depended on to obliterate any running backs or tight ends who were dumb enough to crash through the line, but come Thanksgiving, he became the scummy spawn of the Meanest Man in Texas again.

Ray moved closer to the car. "Hey, who you got with you? That your wife?" He peered in the window, then reared back as if he'd been bitten. "Reverend Ed's daughter!"

Jase positioned himself in front of the window and smiled broadly and firmly. "Ms. Harlow's been kind enough to give me a tour of the changes in town, but I guess I'd better get her home now."

Ray seemed uncomfortable. "Yeah." He backed off toward his own vehicle. "Uh, well, gotta scram-o. *Mi esposa* expected me about fifteen minutes ago." Clicking his door open, he climbed in, waved at Jase, backed around in a spray of gravel, and was gone.

* * *

Laurel braced herself for questions about his friend's reaction to her when Jase got back in the car, but all he did was start the car and turn to pull out.

"That was Ray Espinoza," he said, driving slowly to the exit.

"He was telling me Bosque Bend has some new construction east of town."

"Yeah. I recognized him once he got up close."

Of course she did. Ray's younger brother had been one of the boys paid off to keep his mouth shut. Sarah's father had arranged it all. He'd visited the house almost daily back then, keeping Daddy up-to-date on negotiations and picking up more big settlement checks. Whenever Mama spotted Mr. Bridges crossing the street, briefcase in hand, she'd flee to her bedroom, now separate from Daddy's, which meant Laurel had to be the one to usher him into her father's study.

Jase glanced out his window at the pale twilight, criss-crossed by garish streamers of pink and purple clouds. "It's going to be semilight for at least an hour yet—I'd like to check the area out."

"What area?" She'd lost track of what they were talking about.

"Ray's subdivision. Is it across the river?"

She nodded. "Yeah, it's called Lynnwood, after his sister. Lots of new families with little kids. I used to teach at their elementary school."

* * *

The sodium vapor lights were coming on, one by one, as Jase turned onto Lynnwood Drive and entered the subdivision. The heat of the day had died down, and the neighborhood residents had moved outside for the evening, the adults sitting in lawn chairs and quaffing iced tea while their children yelled back and forth and raced from lawn to lawn.

Laurel stared out the window. How many of those children

had been in her classes last year? Did they miss her? Was their new teacher keeping up the after-school piano lessons she had offered?

Finally they ran out of streets. Jase leaned back and exhaled slowly, apparently having satisfied his curiosity about Ray Espinoza's development.

He turned to her, his dark eyes smiling. "Okay, Sacagawea, how the hell do I get to my old house from here?"

* * *

The night had gone totally dark by the time they pulled into the driveway.

He knew this house by heart. He'd hated it when he lived here, but for some reason, he hadn't sold it when he got rid of Beat Down after Growler died. Maybe because it was his last link with Bosque Bend and Laurel Harlow. Or maybe because he needed a sense of his own origin, his life path. This was his home.

He paused at the door. *Home*—an interesting concept. Somewhere deep inside, he still thought of this little house, where the worst of his life had been lived, as his home. His brow wrinkled. Perhaps everyone yearns for that kind of underpinning, to know one's origins. Was that what Lolly was trying to find in her search for her mother? Was she looking for an extended family, a heritage? Not that he knew anything about Marguerite in regard to her family. She never talked about anything personal. Even in bed, their relationship was instructor-student.

He turned his key in the lock. "I decided to keep it for income after Growler died. Hired a crew to update everything and replace the porch steps, then got the drive paved and the lawn sodded. Of course, the Bosque River still runs thirty yards behind the house, but some people see that as a plus."

Laurel nodded. Sixteen years ago, she'd walked right in a door that opened at a push. What if the house had been locked up that Saturday morning? Would they still be here together right now? How much had that fateful day determined their current relationship?

Jase flicked the switch beside the door. Laurel blinked as a sudden flood of light ricocheted off the stark white walls. The air in the house was fresh and the temperature comfortably cool, which meant not only had the place been cleaned up and repainted, but central air had been installed somewhere along the line as well.

He turned toward the front bedroom. "I'll just be a few minutes. Have to grab my gear."

So, he'd automatically taken his old room.

Not sure what to do while Jase gathered his clothes, Laurel went exploring. The dining area, an ell to the right off the small living room, connected to the left with a tiny, modernized kitchen more up-to-date than the one at Kinkaid House, then led to the back bedroom, which contained a double bed stripped down to its mattress. The hall took her past the bathroom, where Jase was busy packing his toiletries into a leather bag. She moved on to his room, taking a seat on the single bed.

With a clarity etched on her brain for all eternity, she could picture every item that had been in this room sixteen years ago—the football posters and sexy pinups on the wall, the tall bureau with the small mirror above it, the beer cans littering the floor, the tuna tin overflowing with cigarette butts.

Jase came in and took a suitcase from the closet, "Maxie packed everything but the kitchen sink," he commented as he pulled a vinyl garment bag off the wooden rod. "She even stuck in my old boots. They'll come in handy when I'm walking property lines."

Laurel studied his face as he gathered his luggage. He looked different in the brightly lit nighttime room, almost like a stranger. She remembered that she'd had the same apprehension when she'd walked into this room sixteen years ago. Suddenly nervous, she said the first thing that popped into her head.

"Do you still smoke?"

She hadn't smelled any tobacco on his breath, and she'd certainly been close enough to tell, but for some reason, she wanted him to say something, as if to confirm his identity.

He wedged his Dopp kit into an outer pocket of the suitcase and zipped the bag shut. "No, not for years. Too expensive a habit for a young father, and one I didn't want my daughter to pick up." He set his gear next to the door. "Why?"

"Just wondering." In a strange, unnamable mood, she changed position, languorously stretching out on the bed and leaning back on her elbows, her knees bent, her head flung back. There was a hot running fever in her that had to be appeased, a molten river of desire.

Jase looked over at her, and his eyes narrowed as he remembered the last time she had seen him smoke and the last time she had been in this room. He walked over to the bed slowly, purposefully.

"I don't usually drink much either," he said in a deeper voice, anticipating her next question and sitting down beside her on the bed. "Now or then."

He sat beside her and leaned over to drop little half kisses on her forehead and nose and cheeks. "But, I can't say the same thing about sex," he added in a hoarse whisper. "That's a bad habit I haven't been able to break."

She looped her arms around his neck to pull him down to her mouth and kiss him, moving her lips to his mouth and cheeks, tracing his ears with her darting tongue. Her hands slid under his shirt for access to his warm, solid flesh, and she fumbled at his slacks, which he hadn't bothered to belt.

God, she is dynamite, this sleepy-eyed Southern honey! The back of his mind cycled back to that other time when they had been together in this room, when he had wanted her because she was clean and decent and because he loved her more than anybody else in this world. Now it was her turn to take the lead.

She managed to unbutton the tab of the pants to get them unzipped, but was stymied by his body weight when she tried to move them off him.

"Let me take care of that," he muttered, rising and turning enough to slide his slacks and briefs off at once.

She fumbled with her own jeans but was too disoriented to figure out how to unfasten them. Jase pushed aside her hands and opened her jeans himself, then pushed them down to her knees.

She was on him like a fury. Her eyes were closed, her color was high, and her moist, searching mouth was half-open. God, she was hungry! He rolled her beneath him, entering hard and fast. She thrashed and moved her head back and forth, arching up against him for deeper penetration.

This was going to be quick. He was already up to warp speed.

Her fingernails clawed his back, and his brain cut out on him. This was it!

She hit first, cutting loose with a long, quivery cry as she bucked up against him.

He arched back in response and groaned as his tension reached its zenith, then released him into shudders of unbearable ecstasy.

They lay in the narrow bed afterward, cuddling and talking. "I want us to sleep here tonight," Jase said, holding her against him. "In my house, in my bed. This is where it all began."

* * *

The next morning Laurel awoke to the world of reality. With Jase's luggage in the back of the Escort, they returned to Kinkaid House. After dropping his suitcase and garment bag off in the bedroom across the hall, they showered—separately—changed clothes, and enjoyed a leisurely breakfast of what Laurel now considered to be her specialty, French toast.

She added a little nutmeg to the recipe to spice it up, then congratulated herself on her cleverness. There was nothing to this cooking business. People made too big a fuss about something that was basically pretty simple.

The first thing on her agenda for the day was a trip to the Waco airport for Jase to pick up his car. Before they left, she placed a carefully packed Meissen clock in the Escort's backseat.

"I'll drop it off at the repair shop on the way back," she explained. "It's not keeping the right time."

But after letting Jase off at the airport parking lot, she sped over to her favorite Waco pawnshop and scored three hundred dollars. It could have brought ten times that if she had left it with an antique dealer on consignment, but she needed the cash immediately. Back in Bosque Bend, she deposited the check in First National and heaved a sigh of relief.

* * *

Jase was surprised to see that he'd beaten Laurel back to the house, and even more surprised to see Sarah coming across the street toward him as he was getting out of the car.

He walked down the drive to meet her. "You're taking your life in your hands, crossing Austin Avenue like that."

She glanced back at the street and shrugged. "It's not really that bad, if you're careful. I've been doing it since I was a kid. There are always lulls." Pausing for a moment, she looked at him as if trying to decide what to say. "You're Jase Redlander, aren't you?"

He nodded, suddenly wary. Bosque Bend could be quick on the trigger. Was he going to get run out of town again? He'd couldn't help but take a quick glance toward Laurel's house. At least this time they'd have cause.

"I'm Sarah Edelman." She extended her hand. "I used to be Laurel's best friend, but we've sort of lost contact lately." She held on to the handshake, her dark eyes dancing as she smiled up at him in shrewd assessment. "Lord, you're a hunk. I remember back in high school, when Laurel had such a terrible crush on you. She thought you hung the moon."

Jase grinned. What else could he do when a pretty woman complimented him? "I felt the same way about her. I still do."

Sarah's playfulness faded and she dropped his hand. "I just wondered... How's she doing. I mean, is she okay?"

Jase was baffled at the strange turn of the conversation. Did Sarah think he'd killed her old friend and stowed the body in the attic? "She's just fine. Uh—would you like to come inside and wait for her? I'm expecting her any minute."

"No, no, that's okay. My mother would wonder where I'd gotten off to." She flashed a quick, meaningless smile. "You know, she'd think I'd ditched the boys on her and run off to join a circus or something."

There was a message unspoken that he didn't understand. "Do you want me to have Laurel call you when she gets home?"

"*No!*" Sarah caught a quick breath and stepped back in denial. "I mean, I'd better be getting back now. Uh—nice to see you again." She raised her hand in a brisk farewell, walked quickly to the curb, and made her way across the street without looking back.

Chapter Twelve

Jase watched to be sure Sarah made it across the street.

What the hell was that all about?

He shrugged. Oh well, he had other things to tend to, and first on his list was the dishwasher. He walked to the den and picked up the phone, offering an extra twenty if the repairman got to the house within fifteen minutes.

The guy made it in ten.

* * *

Laurel paused for a second after entering her driveway. She'd given Jase a key in case he got back first, but she hadn't expected him to have company. There, in the parking area in front of the garage, angled beside Jase's Cadillac, sat an appliance company van.

She entered through the kitchen door. What now?

God help her. Jase, Mr. Cool, was leaning against a kitchen counter, his long legs crossed at the ankles, as he carried on a conversation about the Baylor Bears' upcoming season with a uniformed repairman who was down on the floor doing something to the innards of her dishwasher.

A twinge of anger zinged through her. Now she'd have to pay for something else she couldn't afford.

Jase came over to her, encircled her waist with one arm, and kissed her cheek in greeting. "I didn't think you'd let me put in central air, honey, but I'm going to insist on this thing being fixed."

Slipping out of his embrace, she affected an air of indifference. "I've been meaning to have it taken care of, but it just didn't seem worthwhile with me being the only one in the house."

Moving to the pantry, she began to prepare sandwiches for their lunch, which gave her an excuse to stay in the kitchen and keep an eye on developments.

How much would the work cost? Could she ask to be billed?

But when the repairman started to present her with an invoice, Jase hauled out his wallet, peeled off a couple of large bills, and handed them over. It was a relief, but it also made her uncomfortable.

Guests don't pay for food, and they don't pay for dishwasher repairs either.

After lunch, they retired to the den. Jase had some calls he needed to make, and she wanted to read a little—not that she could concentrate on Georgette Heyer's historical with all the talk of CPDs, LOIs, and Phase I Reports going on. None of the terms meant a thing to her, but Jase's way of handling things was an eye-opener.

The business side of him was *all* business. His voice became clipped, his face hardened into granite, and he brooked no nonsense. Want and hardship had forged him. He'd gone through fire and come out steel.

Maybe she should have been repulsed, but actually this

hard-as-nails aspect fascinated her. If Daddy had possessed even half of Jase's business acumen, she wouldn't be pawning clocks on the sly. Laurel winced in sudden sorrow—Daddy had had more weaknesses than letting money flow through his fingers like water.

The phone rang again, but with the opening bars of "Five Foot Two." Jase's voice changed, becoming more humanoid.

"Hi, sweetheart. Good to hear from you."

Laurel smiled. He'd switched into father mode.

"You want how much money for *what*?...Lolly, don't you think the one you have is good enough? It's not as if you'll be playing tennis at school this fall. You've already committed to the volleyball team...My permission?...Okay, give me the guy's name and where I send it..."

Jase was gesturing at her now, making a wiggling motion with his hand. Laurel stared at him, trying to understand. Did he want her to write something down? There was a tablet in the desk. She stood up and rolled back the top.

He turned away from the mobile for a second.

"My pen, Laurel!" he hissed. "I left it in the kitchen when we were making the grocery list! I need my pen!"

"Gotcha." She raced down the hall, picked up his Mont Blanc, and was back within seconds, grabbing a notepad on the way.

Jase seized the pad and uncapped his pen. "Thanks, babe. I was about to write on my palm."

Still holding his phone to his ear, he scribbled an address on the pad. "Uhm-hmm...uhm-hmm...well, okay, but I want to see some follow-through...okay...yeah, uh, okay, I'll tell Laurel you said that...I love you too, sweetheart. 'Bye now. Take care of Aunt Maxie for me."

He ended the call, looked at Laurel, and breathed deep. "I never know what she'll be into next."

"The tennis camp?"

He smiled in paternal resignation. "Lolly's usual idea of an emergency. Her instructor mentioned a particular racket he liked, and she wanted permission to go out and buy it immediately—two hundred and fifty dollars on the hoof, and she's just been playing for three days."

"Was that all? The conversation sounded a little odd toward the end." She'd heard her name mentioned.

Jase came around and captured her waist from the back. "That was because she caught on that I'm still at your house."

"Was she upset?" Lolly was no dummy. She knew what it meant that her father was staying at her house, and teenagers could be real prigs as far as the sexual behavior of their parents was concerned.

Jase kissed the back of Laurel's neck and smoothed his hands down her hips. "She wants you to come back to North Plano with me."

"She doesn't still think I'm her mother, does she?"

"No, you pretty much cleared that up, but she's got a crush on you—just like I do."

Laurel smiled and snuggled her buttocks against him, but before they could get anything going, the phone rang again. Jase released her and morphed back into Mr. Tycoon.

Half an hour later, he glanced at his watch and announced he needed to visit the bank before it closed. "I assume First Bosque Bend National is still downtown?"

She nodded. "It'll be there forever."

"I need to talk to a banker, someone who knows the local

scene." He stood up. "Gotta go grab a sports jacket and head over there."

Laurel bit her lip. "Dave is a vice president at First. He moved up when Consolidated bought it. His new wife's father is a big stockholder."

Jase's nostrils flared. "This is about business and growth potential, not about old times."

And not, she prayed, *about me.*

Or Daddy.

*   *   *

His head buzzing with speculation, Jase swung into traffic and headed to town, which translated to six blocks farther down Austin Avenue.

Laurel had seemed worried about him running into her ex. Was she afraid Dave would say something derogatory about her? Maybe tell Jase why they'd divorced?

Why *had* the marriage gone bad? Laurel wasn't the type to play around—but neither was Dave. More likely, the money had run out. In fact, maybe Dave had somehow caused the money to run out. Maybe he'd spent all of Laurel's inheritance, then ditched her. But that didn't make sense—Dave was an opportunist, not a high roller.

The light in front of him turned red and Jase braked to an easy stop. Looking around, he noticed that a medical facility was being constructed on the big corner lot where the farmers' market used to be. Yeah, Bosque Bend was definitely on the move.

A redheaded child in the car next to him caught his eye, reminding him of Sarah Bridges's visit earlier in the day, just before Laurel got back to the house.

No, not Sarah *Bridges* anymore—Sarah *Edelman*. It was hard to imagine her settled down and with children. She'd always been a real live wire.

He mulled over their strange conversation. Why had Sarah acted so oddly, asking about Laurel's welfare, yet not wanting him to tell Laurel? Did it have anything to do with that constant shadow that seemed to be lurking behind Laurel's calm gray gaze? With that odd reticence whenever he brought up her father's name? What was the big secret? He'd told Laurel everything there was to know about himself—his father, Lolly, Marguerite—yet she didn't trust him enough to tell him what was bugging her. What was so horrible that she had to hide it from him?

He snorted. Goddamn. Given his background, there wasn't anything he couldn't accept. Had she killed someone? Robbed a bank? He exhaled on a slight laugh.

Nope. Given the obvious state of her finances, that one was out.

The pickup behind him honked, and Jase realized the light had changed. Stepping on the accelerator, he cleared the intersection and settled into a sedate thirty miles per hour.

His mind focused on the business at hand as he neared First National. He hoped he'd be able to deal with Dave in a straightforward way. They'd never had much of a relationship off the field, but he'd always seemed genial enough—sort of low-key, actually.

He circled the block to scope out the lay of the land, parking in a suddenly available space right out front. First National was no longer the only show in town, he knew, but it was the biggest, and thus the one best suited to his purposes. He remained in the car a few minutes longer, studying the scene.

Apparently the hookup with Consolidated had been benefi-
cial. First National's marble-columned facade had expanded to
take in what used to be a hardware store next door, and, from
what he could tell, the building's two upper floors now housed
bank offices instead of law firms and insurance agencies.

He grabbed his white Stetson from the seat beside him.
Did he dare invade the sanctum sanctorum of Bosque Bend
enterprise? Times change, and memories fade, he reminded
himself. Besides, money talks, and that's one thing he had
plenty of. He caressed the soft leather upholstery of his top-of-
the-line Cadillac as he slid out of the car and affected an easy,
confident stride as he walked up the steps into the bank.

Never let 'em see you sweat.

The lobby was a far cry from the dark, cramped stronghold
where he used to cash checks from his lawn-mowing customers. Sunshine poured in through a skylight in the center of
the room, and loan applicants now awaited their turns in the
comfort of deep-cushioned couches instead of a row of penitent, straight-backed wooden chairs. Old Mrs. Maguire, who
used to reign supreme over the information desk and would
watch him like a hawk when he walked through the revolving
door, had been replaced by a thirtyish blonde who looked at
his business card and told him how to get to the appropriate
office.

"Welcome to Bosque Bend," she added in a throaty tone
that reminded him of Marguerite. "If you'd like to see what
the town has to offer, I'm free for the evening."

"I think my wife has other plans," he responded, smiling
broadly. It was his standard line to warn off women on the
make. He'd do his own choosing.

The bank officers were housed in the bowels of the building, the old section down a dark hall. Jase half wondered if there was a dungeon waiting for him at the end of it. But no, the hall opened into an airy room presided over by a middle-aged woman who smiled and told him that Mr. Carson had signed out for the day, but Mr. Freiberg, vice president in charge of investments, would be happy to see him.

Craig Freiberg turned out to be an eager up-and-comer with a brand-spanking-new MBA. Jase, who'd squeezed in a couple of years of business classes after he'd gotten his GED, liked MBAs. He hired a lot of them.

"My wife and I are both from Houston, but we didn't want our kids to grow up in a big city," Craig explained, handing Jase his card. "So when I got the offer here at First, we jumped on it."

Jase pretended to relax back into his chair, but his mind was working at the speed of light. Craig seemed a lot sharper than ol' Dave had ever been, which meant, although there was no chance of playing detective about Laurel's failed marriage, he had lucked out businesswise.

He handed over one of his own cards to introduce himself.

Craig's eyes opened wide as he read it. "Jason Redlander. I've heard of you."

Jase nodded and started to relax for real. He liked the positive name recognition. It made up for his first sixteen years of the opposite.

Craig leaned forward, the very picture of an eager puppy. "What can First National do for you?"

"You can orient me to what's going on locally. I'm interested in undeveloped properties, initially for parking lots. My company has investments up and down the I-35 corridor, and from what I've seen, Bosque Bend's good to go."

Smiling like Foxy Loxy, Craig folded his hands on his desk. "No problem. You made the right choice coming here. Bosque Bend used to be your typical moribund Texas small town, but within the past ten years, it's had a change in attitude and decided to let the rest of the world in. The population has doubled, and we have lots of new businesses—Walmart, Office Depot, Home Depot, Starbucks, G&G Chicken, you name it. A couple of small manufacturers have set up shop here too, and we've got a big hotel chain coming in. Sometimes we have problems with the Old Guard, but the mayor and city council are very proactive. They've even swung a couple of big government grants for beautification and flood control. Drive down by the river and you'll see what I mean." Craig gestured in invitation. "I've seen pictures of what the area used to look like, and you wouldn't believe the change."

"You mean the Shallows?" Jase nodded in agreement. "I can believe it. I grew up around here."

Craig's face lit up with interest. "You're visiting relatives?"

"Staying with an old friend."

Craig reached into his desk drawer and pulled out a beige postcard-sized pasteboard. "Well, if you're going to be here for a few of days, let me give you this." He signed the card with a grand flourish and handed it over to Jase. "It's is a guest pass for two to the Bosque Club, good for an evening out on the bank. You'll enjoy it—and might run into some people you used to know."

Jase looked at him in surprise. "The Bosque Club? It's still in existence?"

When he was growing up, the 1880s limestone block building on Crocket Avenue had acted as the second home for the high-and-mighty families of the town, with Reverend Ed frequently serving as president. Laurel probably knew every brick of the building by its first name.

"Alive and well. I hear it used to be sort of dull, but it's picked up steam lately. Good place to do networking—Mayor Traylor's a longtime member. Great guy, very forward-looking."

Jase looked at the card, a plan formulating in his mind. "Thanks." He smiled. "I'll be sure and take advantage of this." Rising from his chair, he held out his hand. "And, remember, if you get wind of any land you think I'd be interested in, give me a call."

Craig walked Jase to the door of his office, shaking hands with him again. "I'm your guy."

Jase headed for the car, his step buoyant. The prodigal son had come home, not with slop on his face, but with his head held high.

The bank visit had been his first official public appearance, and he'd half wondered if the armed guard would check him out on some sort of Bosque Bend shit list and throw him out on his ear. So far he hadn't run into anyone who recognized him except Ray and Sarah, but he was bound to run into old acquaintances at some point. He looked a lot like Growler, he knew, which irritated him, but he'd learned to live with it.

He pulled away from the curb. Now to find a place to get a cartridge for that ink-jet printer he'd discovered under a dust cover in Laurel's den. He thought he'd spotted an Office Depot down Fourth Street. Might as well buy a cheap fax machine for good measure. Laurel's computer needed replacing too, but that could wait for now. She'd probably insist on paying for it herself, and he wasn't about to rouse that sleeping dog again.

He turned right and picked up a parking space in front of

the store. As he got out of his car, a huge pickup with an extended cab and four wheels on the rear came to a sudden stop on the street behind him. The driver lowered his window, and a deep voice rumbled at him.

"Jase, Jase Redlander!"

Jase grinned in recognition. Damned if it wasn't Rafe McAllister.

Rafe had been a junior partner in the Dallas architectural firm that designed Jase's house in North Plano. The two of them had hit it off right from the start, but he'd lost track of the genial redhead after the house was finished.

What the hell was he doing in Bosque Bend?

Rafe glanced behind him at the oncoming traffic. "If you got a couple of minutes, I'll treat you to coffee at Starbucks. It's a block down, on the corner."

Jase widened his smile. "You go get parked and I'll be waiting for you."

* * *

The barista brought their coffee to the table, a service Jase had never before enjoyed at Starbucks. The woman, a pretty brunette about thirty, kept her gaze trained on Rafe as she set their coffee down and provided them with napkins.

Jase snorted. Rafe usually had that effect on women—he'd seen it before. Probably had to do with the redhead's eyes, which were actually a little unnerving. His irises sparkled like they were composed of shards of multicolored glass.

Rafe gave her a lazy grin. "Thanks, honey."

She blushed, stared at him one last time, and scurried back behind the counter.

Rafe took a healthy gulp of his coffee and looked across the table at Jase. "How's it goin'? Still buyin' and sellin'?"

Jase grinned. That lazy-talking cowpoke accent got him every time. "That's my life."

"Anythin' local?"

"A few possibilities, but Ray Espinoza's subdivision has made everyone all too aware of property values."

"Yeah—taxes been goin' up like crazy on account of all the activity in the area."

"Sorta lost track of you in Dallas, Rafe. What happened?"

"I had to come home and take over the ranch. My dad passed on a while back."

"Sorry about that, man." His brow clouded. "You're one of the McAllisters from C Bar M Ranch? What about the architecture?"

Rafe nodded and gave him an easy smile. "I keep my architecture iron in the fire too. Ol' Ray's hired me to design homes for the new section of Lynnwood, and Art Sawyer wants me to submit a plan to the city council to repurpose old Bosque Bend High as a city museum."

"Think the museum idea will pan out?"

"Why not? You remember what Sawyer's like. He'll ride that cayuse till it drops."

"How's Beth like living in this area?"

Rafe's smile vanished. "Beth died last New Year's." He glanced at the gold band on his left ring finger, and his face turned somber. "We'd been together since we were eighteen, then one day she's gone. And it was so damn random—a stray shot from some cowboy across the road celebrating New Year's Eve."

Jase shuddered as a cold chill passed through him. What if something like that happened to Laurel, something he couldn't control? What if the only time they had left was right now? He glanced at Rafe's wedding ring. *Maybe I should move up my timetable.*

"The only thing that keeps me going is our little girl," Rafe continued. "She's about to turn two. Delilah won't even remember her mother. I never thought——"

Rafe's shirt pocket rang with "The Eyes of Texas."

"That's my brother. Must be trouble at the ranch."

Jase finished off his coffee as Rafe exchanged a series of terse "yeps" and "nopes," ending with, "That cow's crazy. Leave her be till I get there."

Rising from the table, Rafe handed him a card. "Gotta go now, but call me if you get any spare time, and I'll take you out to my uncle's honky-tonk for some good ribs and great music."

Jase slipped the card in his pocket. If he stayed in town long enough, he'd take Rafe up on his invitation. *Wonder if Laurel would like honky-tonk.*

But in the meantime, he'd better hotfoot it over to Office Depot.

* * *

Twenty minutes later, he walked out of the store with his purchases under his arm and was immediately accosted by a snaggletoothed little girl about eight years old with her hair plaited in tight corn rows. The bright yellow sundress she had on reminded him of a dress Lolly had loved so much that she'd insisted on keeping it in her closet long after she'd outgrown it. Might be there still, for all he knew. Lolly did tend to hang on to things.

"Mister, you want to buy some cookies? We're having a bake sale to raise money for new playground equipment for Westside Elementary."

Westside Elementary? That was his old alma mater.

Going into the store, he'd noticed a card table set up against the storefront but hadn't registered what it was for. Sure enough, taped to the front of the table was a hand-printed sign: SUMMER BAKE SALE, WESTSIDE PTA.

"I'm feeling really hungry for cookies," he announced, walking over to look at the display. He had warm memories of the Westside PTA. Those kind women had fed and clothed him all through elementary school. He owed them.

The table was heavily laden with cakes, specialty breads, and bags of cookies. While one of the women behind the table made change for a customer, the other was keeping an anxious eye on their little salesperson. The child danced around him as he approached the table, pointing proudly at a pile of bags labeled *oatmeal cookies*.

"My mom made those. They're real good."

Jase smiled. "I'll take two bags, and—let's see—how about that marble pound cake too."

The mothers thanked him profusely, especially when he gave them a hundred-dollar donation. It was the least he could do.

After stowing the Office Depot bags in the trunk of the car, he put the cookies and cake on the seat beside him. The cake, he'd take back to Laurel for dessert this evening, but the cookies, he'd unload on the first street beggar he saw. However, despite slowing down at every intersection and looking up and down the cross streets, he couldn't spot anyone displaying a GOD BLESS sign. Bosque Bend must still be too small a town for panhandlers as of yet.

He cast a darkling glance at the cookies. Looked like he was stuck with them. Oh well—maybe Laurel liked oatmeal.

Laurel...just one more block and he'd be with her again. He smiled as his mind wandered idly over the past few days. It was going to be hard to leave when he had to go back to Dallas.

He slowed down to turn into Laurel's driveway, then caught sight of Sarah throwing a ball back and forth with the older boy in the front yard again. On impulse, he turned the big Cadillac into the Bridgeses' drive.

Sarah, softball in hand, walked over to him with a welcoming smile. Rolling down his window, he proffered the offending bags of cookies.

"I got my arm twisted by some nice PTA ladies outside Office Depot and thought your kids might like these." He jiggled the bags. "They're oatmeal."

Sarah took the cookies from him. "Thanks. The boys will love them." She positively glowed at him, which made him feel guilty.

"Well, actually, I'm just trying to get rid of them," he confessed. "I can't stand oatmeal."

She laughed and winked. "Jase Redlander, you are a sly dog, but I like your style. Just keep plying me with cookies, and Laurel will have some competition."

"I should be so lucky," he said, waving good-bye. Backing out, he zipped across the street, where he belonged.

This was getting to be quite a day. He'd been welcomed with open arms at First Bosque Bend National, been given a guest card for the Bosque Club, run into an old friend, and been winked at by Sarah Bridges, head cheerleader. She was talking to him too—just light, harmless banter, but it was more conversation than he'd ever had with her in high school.

* * *

As soon as Jase was out the door, Laurel started leafing through the vintage cookbook she'd found in the pantry. This afternoon she would learn how to cook. She couldn't depend on being treated to a SuperBurger again tonight, especially now that the refrigerator and pantry were stuffed with groceries, but Chicken Maryland looked easy enough, and she did have a bird in the refrigerator, though God only knows why she'd bought it.

After tying on Mama's apron, she laid the slippery fowl on a towel and lopped off its wings and legs the best she could, then hacked at the rest of the carcass until she'd separated it into four somewhat equal pieces. They'd probably look okay with breading on them.

The dipping and shaking were sort of fun, but making bread crumbs to roll the chicken pieces in seemed too labor-intensive, so she used crushed crackers instead.

She paused to clean up the counter. All of this would have been a lot easier if she'd seen anyone cooking when she was growing up, but the kitchen had always been the private domain of the housekeeper, first Mrs. January, then Mrs. Claypool.

Mrs. January retired when Laurel was twelve, and Mrs. Claypool left right after Mama died. Loyalty could only stretch so far when there wasn't any money left for paychecks.

Now the pieces of chicken had to dry for more than half an hour. The recipe implied they would be safe sitting out, but the temperature in the kitchen must be over eighty now. It was the hottest room in the house, whether the oven was on or not, and, while she may not know anything about cooking, she did know one shouldn't leave raw meat out for any length of time.

It would probably be safer to "dry" the chicken in the oven on low heat for a while, then "brown" it at what—maybe 400 degrees?

The doorbell rang. Who now? Lolly was in Dallas and Jase had a key. This couldn't be good. Laurel washed her hands and hurried down the hall. She opened the door cautiously, prepared to slam it shut at the first sign of trouble, but the stranger on the porch stepped back a pace, smiled, and ducked his head deferentially.

"Ms. Harlow? My name's Kel. K-E-L. Pendleton Swaim thought you might be able to help me."

So this was Pen's house guest. He was younger than she'd thought he would be and seemed somewhat unsure of himself. Her brows drew together. He didn't look like showbiz—no flashy clothes, no big-toothed smile, no leathery tan, no overenunciated bell-like tones. Instead, his jeans were worn, his white tee looked like a Walmart special, his voice was soft, his tone deferential, and he had the clearest blue eyes, the longest eyelashes, and the sweetest smile she'd ever seen.

But she had dinner in the oven and needed to tend to it.

"I can't talk now. I'll probably be free tomorrow morning, but call me first. Pen has my number." Although Lord only knows how he got it.

Kel nodded his head and smiled again. "Thanks. That would be just fine." He looked back for a second and lifted hand as he stepped off the porch. "See ya."

Laurel stood in the entryway for a moment before closing the door and hurrying back to the kitchen. *What a lamb.* Was he Pendleton's latest lover? Seemed awfully young for him. She'd never been able to tell gay from straight, but the gentlemen who'd lodged with Pen over the years were usually older and more dapper.

She opened the oven door to check on the chicken.

Rats. It had cooked a lot faster than she'd thought. She'd better reduce the heat. If all went well, it should be ready in thirty or forty minutes, which meant she'd better stick in the potatoes to bake. Then just before they sat down, she'd warm up a can of French-cut green beans. Jase had taken a big helping of them at dinner Saturday, which seemed a century ago.

But what about dessert? She wasn't about to attempt a pie, and they hadn't bought any cake mixes at the store.

Jell-O! She'd make lime Jell-O for Jase! She'd better start it now so it would be set by dinnertime.

Satisfied that the meal was under control and she wouldn't make a liar out of Lolly's extravagant boast about her cooking skills, Laurel decided to check on the plants in the drawing room, but instead she ended up pulling the drapes aside to watch Sarah and Eric play ball in the Bridgeses' front yard again.

A big black Cadillac turned into Sarah's driveway.

It was Jase—and Sarah, she noted, was acting very friendly, walking over to the car right away like she and Jase were old friends. After a couple of minutes of conversation, Jase waved, backed out of the driveway, and turned around. Laurel raced to the kitchen, arriving just seconds before he came in the door.

Had Sarah told him about Daddy? The past three days had

been a magic interlude—but was this when they would end, when he would storm out and she'd ever see him again?

Her conscience hammered her with guilt. Maybe it would have been better if she'd told Jase about Daddy's downfall the first day he came to town, or the evening he and Maxie came to dinner, or after their first wonderful night together. But the longer she'd put off saying anything, the harder it became to figure out just what to say. How could she work a topic like that into a lunchtime conversation? How could she bear to look at Jase's face when she told him Daddy had toppled off his pedestal and she was part of the peripheral damage?

Dear God, Jase had said he loved her, but was his love strong enough to hear the truth about his mentor?

She fixed a bright smile on her face as he walked in and deposited a Saran-wrapped pound cake in her hand. "For you, from the good mothers of Westside Elementary."

Then, before she could even put the cake down, he took her in his arms and kissed her as if they'd been separated for years rather than hours.

Sarah hadn't given her away. Why not? She and her mother had shunned Kinkaid House the same as everyone else.

Laurel looked down at the cake. "I don't understand."

"Got lassoed into a PTA bake sale, though I was able to ditch the oatmeal cookies with your friend Sarah."

She laughed in relief. "Is that what you two were talking about? Oatmeal cookies?"

Jase's eyebrows went up. "You were watching? Peeking through the front curtains?" He gave her a teasing smile. "Are you...jealous?"

She tried to look embarrassed. "I'm sorry, Jase. I guess living here alone has made me a little paranoid." *But not about what you think.*

She ran her hand down his thigh. "You can give Sarah all the oatmeal cookies you want, as long as *I'm* the one with *benefits.*"

His eyes glittered as he seized her wrist and brought her palm up to his mouth. "Only you, Laurel. Only you."

She took her hand back, but gave him a wicked smile. "We eat at six."

* * *

Dinner wasn't exactly a fiasco, but it wasn't a raving success either.

The table settings—colorfully painted plates Mrs. Claypool had used for casual serving platters—may have been charming, but they didn't make up for the chicken being leathery, and, at the last minute, her having to replace the nearly raw baked potatoes with mashed potatoes made from a box. The beans turned out well, and the Jell-O was okay, thank goodness—although she later realized she'd left the marble pound cake in the refrigerator. But at least that meant she already had a dessert on hand for tomorrow night.

She might as well face it—cooking was harder than she'd thought. There was nothing to do but clear the table and retire to the den. If Jase was still hungry, he could snack on some of the fruit they'd bought at the store.

But apparently he had other things in mind. Laurel savored each golden moment as he hooked up his fax machine and installed the new ink cartridge.

Bit by bit, he was moving in. Could she keep him?

* * *

The next morning, Laurel decided to take the plunge and try on her old PE shorts.

Whaddaya know? She could still get into them, although they fit more snugly than when she was in high school.

Somewhat self-conscious, she topped her outfit with a long, loose tee, as though obscuring more of her upper body made up for her naked legs. Pretending a confidence she didn't feel, she strode downstairs. Jase didn't seem to notice the shorts, but then, he'd seen her in a lot less. However, he did compliment the oversized shirt.

"Gives me easier access," he said, running his hand up under it and snapping her bra, then drawing her close for a good-morning kiss.

He released her to pick up a manila folder from the table. "I'll be out most of the day looking at properties Craig Freiberg has located for me. Probably won't be in till about six, but put on your glad rags. We'll be dining with the elite tonight."

Laurel nearly choked. The elite were exactly whom she didn't want to meet.

"No way, guy," she said, trying for sultry. Standing tall and swaying against him, she moved her hand over a very sensitive part of his anatomy. "I have a special evening planned for you here at the house tonight, and I don't think we want an audience."

"I'll take a preview," he said, bending her backward over his arm and kissing her so thoroughly that she started wondering about the possibilities of the kitchen table.

He released her abruptly and stepped back. "If I didn't already have a hot date with old Mrs. Anderson..."

He winked and was out the door before her passion-addled brain could register what was happening. Weak at the knees, she sat back down at the table. Gradually her last words to him permeated her brain.

"A special evening"—where had that line come from? What was she going to do? She'd implied some sort of outrageous sexual escapade, but what could she think of that would even begin to top what had already happened on the drawing room floor? Sarah had told her about a movie she saw in which a woman painted herself with chocolate sauce for her lover to lick off, but Laurel didn't think she was up to anything like that.

And she'd never get the chocolate out of the sheets.

Let the sex take care of itself, she decided. Everything had worked out fine in that department so far. She felt the heat rise in her cheeks.

More to the point, what could she feed him? Judging from last night, there was more to cooking than literacy. She stared around the kitchen, hoping inspiration would strike, but none obliged. Only one recourse: She grabbed her keys and headed off to Piggly Wiggly to throw herself on the mercy of the pre-cooked foods aisle again.

Various menus ran through her head as she drove down the street. She'd already served beef, and she was obviously no good with chicken. Barbecue was too messy, and fish scared her. Pork? Didn't seem sexy enough. Maybe a vegetarian feast—but somehow she didn't think Jase was the type of man who'd appreciate a meatless meal.

She raced into the store at full throttle, not caring who might see Reverend Ed's daughter in shorts. The important thing was to get in and out in enough time to make preparations for the erotic evening she'd promised. She'd open up the dining room again and set out candles. The Limoges wouldn't work, though—the Haviland pattern was too old-fashioned. Nor would Mrs. Claypool's brightly painted crockery. How about glass plates? They were cheap enough, and sort of sexy, especially dressed up with a white tablecloth, white napkins, the heavy silver, and good crystal.

What did it matter? She'd probably screw it up. The only thing she could handle was frozen dinners.

Frozen dinners... *Gourmet* frozen dinners!

She trundled her cart out of the precooked food area and over to the refrigerated displays.

Shrimp! She bet he'd like shrimp—and she could get three of the dinners to be sure there was enough food for him.

With a sigh of relief, she tossed the dinners in her cart, picking up a set of four glass plates as she headed toward the checkouts. Right in front of her stood an artistic display of wines. She couldn't tell one vintage from another—that wasn't something one learned in the household of a small-town central Texas Bible Belt preacher—but that deep red was a pretty color.

Why not? Without even looking around to see who might be watching, she seized a bottle and stuck it in her cart.

Chapter Thirteen

I stink like hell," Jase said, wiping the sweat off his forehead as he came through the back door. "Been checking out available land from here to Waco and back." He slapped his hat down on the table and glanced around the kitchen, then at the table, innocent of all but a napkin holder. "What about dinner?"

Laurel never would have guessed she'd be so turned on by the stench of honest labor. Her first impulse was to yell "catch me, catch me," then take off up the stairs with Jase in hot pursuit. Instead, she pulled the cloth belt of her terry cloth robe tighter and frowned at him.

"Go take a shower in the bedroom across the hall, then give me twenty minutes. We're eating in the dining room tonight."

He paused, looking her terry cloth robe up and down. His voice lowered to a growl. "I hope you don't have anything on under that."

She smiled like a woman with a secret. "You'll never find out."

He wrapped her in his arms. "Until later, then."

She lifted her face for a his kiss.

"Yee-ha!" He reached down, grabbed one end of her belt, and jerked it off so her robe fell open.

"Jase!" She quickly clutched the edges of the robe together, more embarrassed that she was wearing plain white cotton panties, a leftover from her pre-Dave days, than if she hadn't been wearing anything at all.

He shook his head in disappointment. "We'll have to get rid of those undies after we eat."

Before she could react, he was on his way up the stairs.

That was her cue. Now to retrieve the gourmet dinners from the freezer and stick them into the preheated oven. And she'd better check to be sure the dining room was cool enough that she could turn off the noisy air conditioner. With the oven timer set and her clothes laid out, she could take her time getting ready, although it was vital to make it down to the dining room before Jase did.

The eyes of the four Kinkaid sisters sparkled with interest as she ascended the stairs. Laurel grinned back at them. She must find out more about her great-aunts sometime. Pen Swaim would probably have the lowdown on them—he knew everything about the families of everybody else in Bosque Bend. His parents, Baylor professors, had retired to the castle on the corner when Laurel was a child, and after they died, Pendleton inherited the house and the copious research his father had compiled on the town's history.

Sitting down at her dressing table, she opened the wide center drawer and selected her makeup—a light base, smoky eye shadow, mascara, and blush. Her lipstick would be a vibrant red to match her gown. Next came the gold earrings—heirlooms, like almost everything else she owned. She checked out the Spanish-style dress. A winning combination.

She draped her robe over the back of the chair and picked up the jumble of scarlet and black spread out on the bed. Off the hanger, the dress looked shapeless and bulky, but it was actually the sexiest thing she'd ever owned. Also one of the most uncomfortable. The first time she'd worn it to a formal tie event with Dave, she thought she was going to die. Every breath was a Herculean labor against the ever-tightening black bustier—but, with any luck, she wouldn't have it on for very long.

She picked up the boned corset, which boosted her breasts to heights previously unknown. It attached to a black under-skirt of starched tulle. Over the black went the scarlet, which clung on top and swelled out below.

She wished she didn't have to wear the bustier, but other-wise...

Otherwise?

Otherwise the scarlet plunged into free fall between her breasts and dipped four inches below her waist in back. She held the sleek, soft dress fabric her cheek. *Mmmm.* It was heaven to touch. Maybe...did she dare?

Slipping the scarlet over her head, she slithered across to the standing mirror—what else could one do in a dress like this but slither? The fabric clung to her like a second skin, the skirt draping and redraping against her each time she moved. Her mother's voice protested dimly in the background, but the im-age in the cheval mirror drowned her out.

She looked hot. Not only hot, but indecent.

Good. She struck a pose and ran her hand down her hip and discovered a panty line. She'd have to change to hose.

Or...

She slid off her panties and studied herself in the mirror

again. No panty line, but her breasts were peaking from the friction of the fabric across them.

So much the better.

Before she could censor herself, she slipped into black stilettos to compensate for the length the dress had gained from the loss of the stiff tulle, rechecked the clock on her dressing table, and headed out the door. Now she was ready for their "special evening."

Jase wasn't downstairs yet, which meant she could set out the dinner without him being any the wiser about her nonexistent cooking skills. The situation was ridiculous, but Lolly had established expectations, and she was just too proud to admit that she was thirty-one years old and didn't know how to cook.

She removed the dinners from the oven and distributed the food to the two glass plates, giving Jase the lion's share of the shrimp. The scarlet fabric shifted wickedly against her bare skin as she carried the plates into the dining room. Would Jase be able to tell she didn't have anything on under it?

She hoped so.

Hearing him on the stairs, she posed beside the table with her shoulders back, one hand reaching down to rest on the top of a chair.

He stopped just inside the room, his mouth dropping open as he focused in on the dip between her breasts. Raising his gaze to her face, he cocked a wicked eyebrow and gave her The Smile.

"Special, huh?" His coal-black eyes burned with a hunger that went beyond food.

Her earrings swayed, and she felt a warm blush creeping up her face. Dressed in dark slacks and a long-sleeved white shirt open at the throat, Jase looked like nothing so much as an eighteenth-century buccaneer. All he needed was a sash, a sword, and a parrot.

"Light the candles and pour the wine, will you?" she said, edging sideways so he couldn't see her rear exposure yet. "I'll switch off the overhead."

She took her chair quickly, to avoid his playing the gentleman and seating her. Her half-bare bottom was the dessert, not the appetizer.

The candlelight flickered between them, blurring her vision, and she had a split-second fantasy of him sweeping everything off onto the floor, candles and all, then lunging across the table for her. But her saner brain hoped he wouldn't. The house would catch on fire, they'd end up huddling naked under blankets on the lawn with the volunteer fire department gawking at them, and she wouldn't be able to collect insurance on the house because the policy probably had a sexual frenzy exclusion.

She picked up her fork to indicate Jase could begin eating. He was quite punctilious about manners, she'd noticed. Some woman must have schooled him along the way. He'd certainly never learned table etiquette from Growler Red.

Laurel sampled each item on her plate, but was too keyed up to finish anything. The rice was a little sticky but the broccoli was good, and the sauced shrimp had turned out surprisingly well. If she could work a few gourmet dinners into her budget, she'd buy this brand again. Not that the food mattered. This dinner was more about seduction than sustenance. The real meal would be when they went upstairs—or maybe into the den or the drawing room.

She took a sip of the wine to clear her palate and couldn't

help making a face. She didn't know how wine was supposed to taste, but this Merlot thing made her want to scrub her tongue.

She let her neckline fall to one shoulder, then the other, so he got a different view with every breath she took—but never more than a glimpse. Her nipples tightened with every pass of the scarlet fabric across her breasts.

Neither of them spoke, but Jase's eyes followed her every move. Did he realize she was testing his endurance, daring him to action?

Jase speared his last shrimp and lifted it toward his mouth. Upping the ante, Laurel slipped off a shoe and nudged his ankle under the table.

The fork slipped from his hand, and she made a moue of distress, as if apologizing, and withdrew her foot.

He crossed his fork on his plate and stared at her.

A heady thrill shot through her. She licked her lips in excitement, but the look she gave him was pure, wide-eyed innocence.

He poured himself a second glass of wine, lounged back, and sipped at it slowly, never taking his eyes off her.

She'd never realized how loud silence could be, how fraught. The very air seemed electrified. She shivered, but not from the cold. Instead, a wild heat spiraled along her nerves, and moisture pooled exactly where it needed to. Maybe she should have worn panties after all. It was going to be hard to explain to the nice Vietnamese woman at the dry cleaners in Waco exactly what sort of stain she'd gotten on her scarlet dress.

Now for the coup de grace. She stood up and turned her back to him so he could see her back was bare halfway down her butt. "I'll go get dessert."

Jase shoved his chair back so hard it crashed to the floor. "You—you minx!"

Before she knew what was happening, he'd crossed the room, his eyes dark with desire, and pressed her against her until she felt the wall at her bare back.

A *minx*? She, Laurel Elizabeth Harlow, the preacher's daughter, the nicest girl in Bosque Bend High School, the class salutatorian, was being called a *minx*?

It was the sexiest thing anyone had ever said to her, and there was only one way to respond—she clung to his shoulders and ground her mouth into his. She wanted his arms around her, wanted his hard chest pressed against her, his erection teasing her thighs. She wanted him inside her as deep as he could go.

He pushed the slippery scarlet fabric away from her hips, opened his fly, and entered her. She buried her head in his neck and met him, thrust for thrust, then screamed in ecstasy and went limp.

Jase guided her with one hand as she slid down the wall, while his other hand hitched his trousers together. "If that didn't bring the cops down on us, nothing will," he muttered, swinging her up in his arms.

Laurel waved her arm weakly toward the table. "My shoes..."

"Get 'em tomorrow."

Then, just like Rhett Butler, he carried her up the wide stairs to her room, and the night was all she could have ever dreamed of. Afterward, she slept with her head on his heart.

* * *

Jase put his arm around Laurel, who was curled up against his side. For once, she'd fallen asleep before he did, but he'd pretty well worn her out. And he'd fulfilled his ambition—the whole town must have heard her come.

He'd half wondered if her insistence on a "special" evening was just a put-off, another example of her strange reclusiveness, but excuse or not, it worked for him. The food was passable—although he'd suspected she'd ordered in—the atmosphere was sexy as hell, and Laurel was a goddess of sensuality.

That dress—he couldn't believe Reverend Ed's daughter had something as hot as that in her closet. The color was like a flame against her ivory skin, and every time she moved, it clung to her in a different way, now outlining a breast, now the thrust of her hip. She'd really gotten him going with her peek-a-boo performance during dinner, but when she'd turned her back to him...

He ran his hand absently down the groove of her spine, and she shifted against him.

It was amazing how quickly he'd gotten accustomed to sleeping in the same bed with her—all night, not just for an hour after sex.

He liked sleeping with her. He liked waking up with her. He liked walking through the Shallows with her and having meals with her, even when they were as bad as that chicken, and having her sit in the den with him while he worked out business details. He wanted to put off returning to Dallas forever.

But he had responsibilities—the business, his employees, his family. If only he could take Laurel with him.

He rolled over on his back and folded an arm under his head.

Well, why not? Apparently she didn't want to stay in Bosque Bend any longer. Why not ask her if she'd come back to Dallas with him? Permanently, like in marriage. The idea had been playing around in his mind ever since he'd talked with Rafe McAllister, but he'd been afraid to voice it, even to himself.

Lolly had voiced it, of course. Just this afternoon, in fact. "If you marry her, Dad, she really would be my mother."

Marriage.

He pictured Laurel seeing his house for the first time. All her life, she'd lived in a century-old mansion on the busy main street of a small town in which everyone knew everyone else. What would she think of the sprawling contemporary retreat Rafe McAllister had designed for his eight wooded acres just on the fringes of North Plano? He wasn't even sure he'd recognize his neighbors on sight.

Maybe she'd be ready for a change of scene, but would she want to live with *him*? She liked him as a sex partner, but would she be willing to formally unite her august heritage with the son of the Meanest Man in Texas?

He supported his head on a bent arm as he studied her face.

He was moving too fast. Five days did not a courtship make. He knew he was good in bed—Marguerite had made damn sure of that—but good sex didn't necessarily make for a good marriage. Laurel had said she loved him, but that just might be a leftover teenage fantasy speaking. She might not be ready for another legal commitment so soon after whatever had gone wrong with her first marriage. And when he thought of it, their lives were vastly different: She was a schoolteacher—a music teacher no less, the gentlest profession of all—and he was a real estate speculator—a shark who ate other sharks.

Yep, a marriage proposal this soon would probably scare the pants off her. He smiled and caressed her hip. Maybe he'd better reword that—the pants were long gone.

On the other hand, he didn't want to lose her.

He leaned back in bed and closed his eyes. This one he'd have to play by ear.

* * *

Ray Espinoza was Jase's first appointment of the day. After they ran the Shallows down and back, he followed Ray to the Lynnwood area to look over the new section that Espinoza and Son was opening up.

"I ran into Rafe McAllister, and he said he's working on house plans for you."

"Yeah. We're buildin' for the high-end trade here, dude," Ray explained. "More upper-middle than the first section of Lynnwood. Media rooms, three-car garages, larger lots, optional pools—all the trappin's. Thinkin' of putting in a country club and an eighteen-hole golf course. People in Bosque Bend are makin' money now, and they wanna move up. We got a lot of wealthy retirees comin' to town too. Overflow from Sun City down in Georgetown."

Jase pulled the brim of his Stetson lower against the morning sun. "How are you gonna get this off the ground, man? Who's financing you?"

"First National has faith in us."

"First National? But I thought—"

Ray laughed. "You thought they wouldn't loan to anybody named Espinoza, right?"

"No offense, man, but that's the way it was when I lived

here." He shook his head. "Gotta admit, they wouldn't have loaned to Growler Red's son either, and now they're almost watering at the mouth to hand over the cash."

Ray looked out over his kingdom. "Dad and I built the first section of Lynnwood with private financin', and it sold so well the bank couldn't turn us down. Besides, we got an attorney who knows our rights better'n we do."

Jase nodded, understanding perfectly. "And success is sweet, especially when you're sticking it to The Man, right?"

The two men looked at each other, grinned, thumped fists, and knocked elbows.

* * *

Laurel woke up late and took her time getting dressed, pairing a lime green tee with yesterday's shorts. The world hadn't exploded yet, so she thought she'd risk baring her legs again. Maybe she'd even get herself a couple more pairs of shorts, which would certainly be a lot cheaper than turning up the air-conditioning.

She posed in the standing mirror, twisting from one side to the other to study herself. Her legs looked okay—slender but not skinny, and her ankles were narrow. Her knees were nice too, their bones well-defined, with no extra flesh alongside. She hoped Jase had noticed.

A rush of heat suffused her. Last night he'd noticed everything.

She pulled up the sheet and topped it with a light summer spread. Why did she even bother? It seemed a futile, given the amount of time they spent rumpling the covers.

Going downstairs, she made herself some coffee and read

the latest *Retriever*. Sawyer was on a new campaign, this time to have Bosque Bend High School resurrected as a museum housing memorabilia from the town's past, going as far back as the Huaco Indians. Laurel didn't hold out much hope for this particular project succeeding, but, on the other hand, she hadn't thought the Shallows would ever be turned into a riverside park either—and the *Retriever* had been the first to propose the idea.

Art had also written a long diatribe on the indolence of Bosque Bend youth, one of his favorite topics.

Where did the drive come from to publish what was basically a personal-opinion tabloid? Everyone knew advertising was tight and that Sawyer operated on a shoestring budget, but, for as long as she could remember, the *Retriever* had appeared on the doorsteps of Bosque Bend every Wednesday and Saturday. Arthur Sawyer could be cranky, but he was also an idealist, and Bosque Bend needed his voice. Besides, he'd been kind when Daddy fell into disgrace, not mentioning a word about it in print. He hadn't run obituaries for Mama or Daddy either, which would have riled up the populace all over again.

She finished the paper and laid it aside for Jase when he returned from his meeting with Ray Espinoza.

Taking another sip of her coffee, she leaned back against the counter. Would this be the day when her idyll came to an end? She was becoming more and more fatalistic. If Ray said something to Jase about Daddy, there was nothing she could do about it. The truth was bound to come out sooner or later.

The phone rang. Her Realtor? She put down her cup and raced to the den.

"Ms. Harlow? This is Kel. Do you have time for me this morning?"

"Oh—I stood you up yesterday, didn't I?" How rude of her. She'd dashed out of the house and spent the best part of the morning in Piggly Wiggly, trying to put together a decent meal for Jase.

She glanced at the wall clock. "Um, how about now? I should be free for a while yet."

"Thanks. I'll be right over."

* * *

He was wearing a faded UCLA tee with his jeans today.

How in the world had this sweetheart ended up in Hollywood? Sure, he was tall, probably over six feet, but he didn't *look* tall, maybe because she had gotten used to Jase's six five. Or maybe because of his soft voice and sweet smile. If she'd had a brother, she would have wanted him to be just like Kel.

He smiled a greeting, wiped his feet on the doormat, and stepped over the threshold. "I really appreciate you letting me see Kinkaid House. I'm trying to get a feel for Garner's Crossing and Benjamin Franklin Chapman."

They walked down the hall to the drawing room. "You're a set designer?"

He paused and gave her another one of his soft smiles. "Didn't Pendleton tell you? I'm an actor. I'll be playing Benjamin."

"Erasmus? But he..." She'd read Swaim's book too, and how could she tell this nice young man that he was the wrong type to play her great-grandfather? Erasmus was not just a rascal, but a strong-willed opportunist, even a bit of a villain.

Kel looked around the room slowly, as if soaking in the antique atmosphere, then turned to her, still smiling.

"Pen said there was some bad feeling in town about the book, but I promise you I'll try to portray Benjamin—*Erasmus*—in a positive light. He was quite multifaceted, from what I've read, and I'll try to show all sides of him."

"I'm sure you will." *Including the quadroon mistress and the brothel down near the railroad tracks?*

He studied the dark rectangles on the wall. "You've removed several paintings recently."

"Yes, I'll probably relocate to South Texas, so I've put them in storage while I sell the house." Actually, she'd sold them last year to pay for the cost of Mama's interment.

"Do you have any family pictures?"

"They're in the den. I'll show you." She led him across the hall and, probably trying to make up for yesterday, gave him an extensive guided tour of the old tintypes and photographs set around on the bookshelves.

"So these are Benjamin's wives," he said, picking up their framed photos. "Annabel and Caroline."

"Adeline and Ida Mae," Laurel corrected.

Kel nodded. "I wonder which one he liked best?"

Laurel edged away from him.

As if sensing her discomfort, Kel replaced the photos in the bookcase and gave her a guileless look and another of his sweet smiles. "May I see the kitchen with the round oak table?"

"Yes, of—of course." She led him quickly through the kitchen, then to the dining room, where he gazed at her portrait and smiled.

As they moved back into the hall, he looked at his watch. "I'd better go now. I expect your boyfriend will be back for lunch soon."

Heat rushed to her face. "How did you know?"

"Pendleton. He's got a telescope in that upstairs room and keeps track of the comings and goings in the neighborhood. Did you know that Dolph Overton Jr. visits Phyllis Pfluger first thing in the morning after her husband leaves for the office?"

* * *

Laurel returned to the kitchen and poured the remains of her cold coffee into the sink.

So now she'd met a movie actor. She didn't know his last name, though, and his first name didn't ring any bells. He seemed vaguely familiar, but she didn't keep up with show folks.

Jase entered just as she turned on the water to rinse out her mug.

He didn't seem as beat as yesterday, but it was obvious the hundred-degree weather had taken its toll. His face was grimy, and there were damp rings under his arms of his short-sleeved knit shirt.

"Hiya, hon. Cold water in the fridge?"

"Do we live south of the Mason-Dixon Line?" She took the plastic container from the refrigerator and poured him a paper cup of water.

"*Mmmmm.*" His eyes closed as the cool liquid ran down his throat. "Nectar of the gods."

"More like product of Town Lake." She shoved the *Retriever* across the counter toward him. "You might be interested in this. Sawyer is calling for the old high school to be turned into a history museum."

"Yeah, I heard about it from Rafe McAllister." He picked

up the paper and carried it to the table. "I haven't read a *Retriever* in years."

Laurel sat down across from him. "Rafe McAllister? How do you know Rafe? He was homeschooled and didn't attend Bosque Bend High until just before it was closed down. The only time I met him was when he and his brother needed an accompanist for a talent show they were putting together for a Fourth of July celebration."

"He designed my house while he was working for his uncle's architectural firm in Dallas. I'd lost track of him until I ran into him in town this morning, but he's running the C Bar M now."

She nodded. "I've heard that the inheritance always goes to the oldest son."

He thumbed through the paper as he finished his water. "Hey, there's a story on Ray and his father in here."

"Art's been running profiles of important people around town lately. The Espinozas are a big deal."

Jase gave a short, grunting laugh. "Must be really chapping some local hides. Ray was almost as far down the social totem pole as I was back in high school. Espinoza Construction used to be penny ante." He looked up at her in question. "What happened? It couldn't all have been an equal opportunity push. There must have been big money involved somewhere, some kind of financial backer."

"In a way," she said, trying to sound like she found the topic boring. She'd long suspected that her father's cash settlement had been the breakthrough for the Espinozas. Ironically, Daddy would have been pleased that the money had been put to good use.

Jase finished the paper and disposed of it in the step-on trash can. "What are we having for lunch?"

"I haven't even thought about it. Probably frozen pizza."
Even Rachael Ray must take a vacation every now and then.

* * *

At midafternoon, Jase turned off his mobile to get a little
respite. All hell had broken loose earlier in the day. The sale of
one of his North Texas holdings had fallen through, San Antonio was going berserk, and half of Bosque Bend wanted to
show him their back forty acres.

Needing a change of scenery, he wandered into the front
room and looked around. As if drawn by a magnet, he
walked to the door of Reverend Ed's study. To his surprise,
the knob wouldn't turn, but on second thought, it made
sense that Laurel might want to keep the room sealed off,
like a holy temple.

Placing his hand against the door for a moment, he let
the vibes of comfort roll. Reverend Ed's study had been his
refuge, where he could talk about everything that was bothering him—everything but Marguerite, of course. He'd like to
visit the little room again, just once, to look around and remember the kind, wise man whose counseling had influenced
his life so profoundly.

Laurel popped her head into the front room. "There you
are. I'm going upstairs to get my laundry, and I wondered if
you need anything washed." She balanced a latticed plastic
basket on her hip.

"No, I'm cool right now. Would it be okay with you if I
looked into your father's study, for old times' sake?"

Her head jerked and she stared at him blankly, as if she
hadn't heard what he'd said, then curved her lips into a faint

smile. "No prob. I'll take care of that as soon as I put my clothes in the washer."

Several minutes later, she returned with a large, old-fashioned key and joined him at the study door.

"I'm glad those two cheesy Greek guys are gone," he commented. "I'd never seen sculptures like that in person before." That *naked*, at least, but he wasn't going to say that. His artistic tastes had become more sophisticated in the past sixteen years, but he had yet to furnish his house with life-sized nude statues.

Laurel looked away and shifted her shoulders carelessly. "I never thought much about them. They were original with the house. My great-grandfather bought them on a trip to England and had them shipped over." She moved her foot in a vain attempt to smooth out the depression in the carpet where one of the youths' pedestals had stood for more than a century. "I think they were leftovers from the Elgin Marbles craze in the early 1800s."

Odd how Mama was so prudish about women wearing shorts, but didn't seem to notice the naked statues in her own drawing room. Maybe because they were cold, dead stone, and she'd grown up with them.

Truth to tell, they'd always seemed just part of the scenery to her too, until she was ten and had walked in on her father running his hand lovingly down the smooth flank of one of the fig-leafed youths. "They're so classic and graceful," he'd explained to her. "I can't resist touching them." From then on, the statues embarrassed her.

Willing her hand not to tremble, she turned the key in the lock, then pushed open the door and stood aside for Jase to enter. This would be the first time she had been in Daddy's office in almost two years. Two years, in which she'd tried to forget it was even there. It represented so much of him—the good and the bad. Her ears felt hot and her knees weakened. She leaned against the wall for support.

If she closed her eyes, she could imagine him still working at his desk with the door always open in case his daughter needed him—except, of course, when he was counseling.

Her eyelids prickled at the memory—for herself and for Daddy.

* * *

The air in the small room was musty and close, but as soon as Jase walked in, a feeling of peace came over him. His eyes swept across the collection of recognitions, awards, and plaques on the far wall, then focused on the adjacent wall, its tall bookcases crammed full to overflowing. Over the desk hung a large photo of the family wearing their best smiles—Reverend Ed, Mrs. Harlow, and Laurel.

Everything was the same as it had always been. In fact, he had the eerie feeling that any second now his mentor would come walking through the door. As if in a trance, he took the chair opposite the desk to wait for him.

There was a sound behind him, a stifled sob. He whirled the chair around and stood up.

Silent tears were running down Laurel's cheeks.

She wiped her face with her hand. "I—I loved him so much."

He went to her immediately. What a jerk he was, getting her to let him in the study just so he could indulge himself with a trip down memory lane. Putting an arm around her waist, he walked her out of the room and closed the door behind them, as if he could shut away the sorrow.

"It's exactly how he left it," she said in between sniffles. "His reading glasses are still there on the desk, ready for when he needs them. Mama and I didn't have the heart to go through his drawers, so Mr. Bridges did it for us before we locked up the room."

Jase looked back at the closed door in silent tribute. "He was my hero."

* * *

Laurel strolled out into the backyard to be alone for a while, finally taking a seat in the rose arbor, the one she'd posed in so many years ago. The roses still climbed riotously all over the arched wooden trellis, just like they had ever since she could remember.

Of course, Daddy was Jase's hero. He was everybody's hero—the Reverend Edward Harlow didn't leap tall buildings in a single bound, but he did advocate equal rights for all, feed the poor, promote education, and participate in whatever other good cause came along. No wonder Jase admired Daddy so much that he even drove the same kind of car.

She rested back against the slatted swing.

She'd thought she had come to peace with her father's death, but being in his study brought all the old pain back to her. That little room, which had always been the private retreat of the man of the house, was the only room that had been totally and entirely Daddy's. She wasn't sure what Erasmus had used it for, but Grampa had stored his liquor in it to escape Gramma's Baptist eagle eye. After his father-in-law's death, Daddy had claimed the room and fitted it out to his own specifications. In hindsight, Laurel wished all he had been doing in there was swilling Jack Daniel's.

She closed her eyes and inhaled the sweet scent of the rich red blossoms twining around the white-painted slats surrounding her.

She'd never been able to reconcile the two sides of her father's personality—the patient, caring man of God and the man with the dark appetites he kept hidden from everyone. How could he have done it? Daddy was so sensitive to people's feelings—hers, her mother's, everyone's—how could he have taken advantage of those boys who came to him for guidance, who trusted him to help them?

He did help most of them, she knew. That was the only thing that saved him from being hauled off to jail. Of all the youths her father had had access to through the years, he'd abused only six of them. But that was six too many.

None of the boys had told on him. Apparently, Daddy himself had decided enough was enough, and, one fine summer day, he'd crossed the street and confessed all to his best friend, the district attorney. Arrangements for the various settlements were already under way when Daddy called Laurel and her mother into his study to explain what was happening.

She remembered how he sat them down on the two chairs while he remained standing, his hands clasped behind his back. They'd just come back from church where, at the end of the service, he'd shocked everyone by announcing that he was leaving the pulpit. Sitting with her mother and Dave in the front pew, she'd been gripped by an ice-cold fear that her father had terminal cancer.

But it was worse.

Once Mama and she were seated, Daddy had cleared his throat several times before beginning. He was nervous, Laurel realized, which made her nervous too.

"Dovie, Laurel," he'd begun, as if taking roll of those present—Dave had a one o'clock tee time and couldn't make it. "I have committed grievous wrongs, and you, unfortunately, will be the ones to suffer for them." He swallowed, cleared his throat yet again, and, in the same carefully articulated accents in which he'd delivered a sermon on God's unfailing love that morning, her wonderful daddy began confessing his sins of the flesh.

"I have long had an attraction to young men, which I never indulged. Marriage to my wonderful Dovie fulfilled me completely." He dipped his head toward his wife. "However, in the past several years, this unwanted—uh—*desire* has grown stronger, sometimes so overwhelming that I acted on it. My victims were six young men whom I was counseling in my study."

Her mother's face went white. "No, no! Those nasty boys..."

"It wasn't the boys, Dovie." Daddy compressed his lips as if he was in pain and lowered his head.

Laurel's ears rang with disbelief, and her brain was running riot. *My father sexually involved with boys?* She shook her head in denial. "Daddy, perhaps you don't understand what—"

His eyes squeezed shut, he swallowed hard, and his mouth turned into a grim, down-turned line. "I knew what I was doing and I knew it was wrong. I am so sorry. I cannot apologize enough to you, your mother, the boys, and their families."

Mama started sobbing quietly into the antique lace-edged handkerchief she carried just for show.

Daddy wiped his eyes and regained the same dry, crisp, matter-of-fact tone he used when discussing the comparative merits of altar flowers.

"Charles Bridges is making financial arrangements that will protect the boys from having to testify in open court and preclude my incarceration, but, in the meantime, I have resigned not only from the pastorate, but also from all my clubs and committees. My public life is over."

Laurel remembered staring at the large family photo over the desk, the photo which had witnessed her father doing—whatever he did—to six teenage boys.

No, this wasn't real. It was a bizarre nightmare. She'd wake up any second now, Sunday would start all over again, and she'd laugh at her ridiculous dream.

But it wasn't a dream.

The next month was a whirlwind of negotiations. Daddy was allowed to resign without public censure, but without any retirement pay, and he had to make the church the beneficiary of his life insurance policy. Kinkaid money paid for immediate settlements with the boys and their families, but the counseling costs were an ongoing expense. Erasmus's fortune, which had shrunk considerably in recent years, was almost entirely depleted.

Of course, Dave had bailed as soon as he realized being married to Laurel Harlow was no longer an asset.

It was still hard for her to think about that day in Daddy's office. She leaned against the arbor, careful not to crush the roses. She'd always been so proud of her father, proud to be identified as his daughter, secretly glad she looked so much like him—tall, gray-eyed, and dark-haired.

From then on, everything changed.

They were all under a strain, and within a year, Daddy had been rushed to the hospital for his first heart attack. The second one apparently gave no warning—he'd just walked into the backyard, sat down in one of the lawn chairs, and fallen asleep. Laurel couldn't help but wonder if he'd recognized the symptoms and decided he didn't want to be resuscitated this time. Then her mother had taken the pills—Laurel wasn't quite sure which ones did the job, because Mama had emptied every one of Daddy's leftovers that were still in the medicine cabinet and added all of her own to the mix.

Strangely, Laurel realized, her parents' deaths didn't affect her as much as they would have before Daddy's revelation. She grieved for Mama and Daddy, but from a weird sort of emotional distance, as if she were a distant observer rather than their only child, like she was floating on a cloud and looking down, seeing, but not participating.

She'd had to move on, to forge her own identity. Not as Dave Carson's wife or Pastor Harlow's daughter or Dovie Kinkaid Harlow's heir, but as herself—independent, resourceful, and self-sufficient.

That fateful day in Daddy's study had been the worst day of her life, but she had the feeling there was an even darker reckoning to come.

Chapter Fourteen

Jase took himself off to the den after lunch to make a long, involved conference call about a San Antonio parcel he wanted to buy, then received and returned several faxes from his Dallas office, followed by a strategic communication with a particularly garrulous state representative he'd been courting.

After resting his ear for a few moments, he decided to make his daily call home to check up on Lolly. She'd been unreachable yesterday, which bothered him. Was she avoiding him on purpose?

Maybe he should talk to Maxie first.

"I doubt if Lolly even looked at her cell yesterday," she reassured him. "There was some sort of cheerleader camp, and she came home exhausted. I sent her to bed right after supper."

"Cheerleader camp? What about tennis?"

"That's where she is today, out playing tennis with Chloe Ginsberg. The cheerleader camp was just one day long. She's thinking of trying out next year."

"I'll call again this evening, then. Take care."

Jase drew a long, deep breath after he placed the phone back in its cradle. He never knew what Girl Child would be into next, and it was all-or-nothing with her—once she'd decided on something, there was no changing her mind. She'd always been headstrong, even as a toddler. Maybe she got her persistence from his own mother who, according to Maxie, was as stubborn as a mule.

He leaned back in the recliner and tented his fingers. Lolly...Every time he talked to her now, she hammered at him about marrying Laurel. For years he'd done his best to instill in her the idea that love meant more than sex, and now she was tossing it right back at him.

And she had a good point.

He'd planned to give Laurel more time, but, on the other hand, time was a commodity he didn't have much of—he'd already overstayed the two days he'd allotted for his visit to Bosque Bend. Trying to run his business long-distance was a bummer. He needed to get back to Dallas.

He heaved himself out of the recliner, stretched a little, and glanced at his watch. Better get a move on so he could make it to the bank before it closed. Craig, who'd proved to be a real find, was negotiating the purchase of a prime piece of acreage for him a mile to the north of Lynnwood, near the McAllister ranch. It was a test. If the young banker handled it well, he'd hire him away from First. If he dropped the ball, it was no big loss—Jase never let too much hinge on a single deal.

He walked down the hall and opened the front room doors into an extravaganza of melody. Laurel was playing the piano. She'd said it was out of tune, but he couldn't hear any sour notes, which didn't mean anything. Last year's lover, an aspiring country-western singer, had told him that he had a hard heart and a tin ear. Of course, that was after he'd refused to bankroll her planned takeover of Nashville.

Walking quietly into the front room, he waited till the last chord had died away, and rested his hands on her shoulders.

"It was beautiful, like sparkling colors." He bent down to kiss the side of her neck.

She leaned her head back against him and reached up to clasp his hand. "Thank you. And Ludwig thanks you too. It's 'Gertrude's Dream Waltz.' Beethoven wrote it for one of his students. It was my recital piece when I was seven." She smiled and ran a couple of arpeggios up the scale. "I had to roll the chords back then."

Jase nodded, but didn't understand. He enjoyed music, but only as a listener, like a restaurant patron who likes what he eats, but has no comprehension of all the slicing and dicing that went on in the kitchen. To him, Laurel's playing was sheer magic, wonderful and unexplainable.

Most of the kids he'd gone to high school with had been into music big-time. A few of them even played the guitar or sang, which he thought was great, but not for him. His activities had to put money in his pocket. Football had been the only exception, and he figured the physical competition had been what made him sign up year after year. That, and the attention the coaches gave him. It was nice to be valued. Who knows? Maybe he even saw them as father figures.

His stomach rumbled and Laurel laughed, removing her hand and standing up to face him. "Sounds like someone needs a snack."

"No time now. But what's for dinner?"

She went rigid, and her eyes widened with alarm. "I—I really haven't thought about it yet."

He tried not to smile. She looked like Lolly when he was

confronting her about some harebrained escapade she'd tried to keep secret from him.

"Com'ere, hon." His voice softened with tender amusement as he drew her out from behind the piano bench and into his arms. "You don't have to pretend anymore. I spotted the shrimp boxes in the trash can when I threw away the newspaper this morning." He massaged her shoulders gently. "Tell you what. We'll go out to eat tonight. I'll be back about six to change clothes so I won't disgrace you. I've got a guest card for the Bosque Club."

He kissed her hard on the mouth, and, before she'd registered what he'd said, he was out the back door.

Laurel's knees buckled and she sat down hard on the bench. Her eyes wandered sightlessly around the room. If ever in her life she was going to have a stroke, this was it. She'd known Jase's visit had to end sometime. Dear God, she'd had much more time with him than she'd asked for, but she'd hoped...well, she'd hoped for a miracle, maybe that he'd tell her he'd known about Daddy all along, but didn't want to distress her by discussing the situation. Or maybe that he'd take her back to Dallas with him, at least for a visit.

She braced her hands on the piano bench. His escorting her to the Bosque Club would be like throwing herself to the wolves—and him too. How could she get out of it? She'd already played the sex card.

With a sudden rush of energy, she rose and began prowling the room, touching a lampshade here and the back of a couch there, as if searching for advice from the furniture. She even peeked out to see if Sarah was in the front yard with one of her kids.

No Sarah. And it wasn't as if her former friend would have cared anyway.

Letting the curtain drop, she walked back to the piano and played a restless one-handed scale to the top of the keyboard, then glanced over at the door to her father's study. The key was still in the lock. She walked over to the door and, on sudden impulse, pushed it open and went inside the room.

She didn't know what she'd expected—the study looked the same as it had yesterday, which was the same as always. Sinking into her father's swivel chair, she glanced up at the family portrait above the desk.

"What should I do, Daddy?"

But no dry, kindly tones echoed answered her from the great beyond. She was all alone and talking to a stupid photograph. She pushed herself up from the chair and walked out, locking the door behind her. Nothing to do but retreat to her bedroom.

The afternoon heat was gathering, but she didn't turn on the window unit—she didn't deserve to be comfortable. Picking up an old paperback, she sprawled across the bed and tried to read, but couldn't make herself care about the beautiful blond heroine's problems with her handsome rapscallion of an Italian *conte*.

Blondie would have a happy ending, but Laurel wouldn't. She'd made her bed and now she had to lie in it, but it would be a bed of nails rather than the one she wanted to be in. Resigned to her fate, Laurel laid her head on the pillow, turned off her brain, and slept.

Hours later she heard a masculine voice calling her name. Still half dreaming of an Italian *conte* who inexplicably preferred so-so brunettes to drop-dead-gorgeous blondes, she managed to sit up on the side of the bed as Jase came rushing into the room.

"Wake up, sleepyhead. You've got half an hour to get ready for the Bosque Club."

"I'm not going," she heard herself say as she stood up to confront him.

She hadn't planned to say that, but that's what came out, without excuse or explanation. Maybe it was her subconscious taking over and fighting to prolong Jase's visit. Maybe it was heroine's voice from the romance she'd been reading. Whatever the source or intent, she was standing by it.

He gave her a long, level look, and she knew he was going to ask her the question she didn't want to hear.

"Why?"

Refusing even to try to answer, she stared back at him, her lips pressed together.

His face hardened, and his left eyebrow lifted. "Don't tell me you don't have anything to wear, because I've seen your closet. If you want, you can even wear that sexy red number again—if you put something on under it."

"I have a headache." It was true. She did have a headache, but she always got one when she took an afternoon nap in the heat of the day.

"So? Take an aspirin."

She could feel her defiance crumbling under his steady gaze and tried wheedling. "I don't like the Bosque Club. It's too crowded. Couldn't we go somewhere else where we could be more private?"

Jase's eyes narrowed to slits of jet. "Somewhere people won't recognize me?" He spoke slowly, enunciating each word with care, like a death sentence.

Laurel was startled at his misinterpretation. "No, no, that isn't it at all! I'm proud to be seen with you—anywhere!" Her words tumbled over each other into a near incoherency. "It's not you...that was sixteen years ago...even Bosque Bend doesn't have that long a memory—oh, maybe a few old fuddy-duddies...but it wouldn't matter if everyone did. I love you...I always have—"

"Then, what's the problem?"

Her shoulders slumped as she suddenly understood the unrelenting tenacity and determination that had enabled Jase to rise in the business world. Did she actually think she could withhold Daddy's downfall from him in perpetuity? She probably should have told him when he first appeared at her front door, but now she'd waited too long. Besides, what would she have said? She didn't have the words. She'd never discussed it before, not even with her mother.

The end of her idyll was in sight, but maybe she could delay it one day longer.

"Okay, I'll go, but not tonight." She tossed her head. "Tomorrow night."

Jase studied her face for a moment, then nodded his assent and held out his hand. "Promise?"

She clasped his hand and even managed a smile. "Promise."

He sealed their bargain with a long kiss before relaxing his embrace so they could talk. "I'll cancel the reservations, then. And about dinner—don't worry about it. I put in a stint as a short-order cook and can rustle up edible grub in two shakes of a lamb's tail."

After a dinner of chicken tenders and fries, they watched an old Michael Douglas movie and made love on the leather couch in the den before trailing upstairs to bed.

Her last night with him. She tried to absorb every moment of it to warm herself during the cold, lonely nights to come.

* * *

Thursday morning dawned bright and clear, auguring another sweltering afternoon. Laurel's dreams had been troubled, but she decided to suck it up and think positively.

Maybe everything would turn out just fine. Maybe the club would be stuffed to the gills with new members, people who'd moved into town so recently that they wouldn't know who she was. And maybe the old-timers would keep their mouths shut, as Ray apparently had.

The other side of the bed was empty, but she could hear Jase's heavy tread on the stairs, accompanied by a rhythmic clinking. She sat up in bed to greet him as he came through the door, holding a small tray.

He put it down on the edge of her nightstand. Coffee and toast.

"Breakfast in bed, milady, but you'll have to take care of yourself for lunch." He pulled up a chair to sit with her while she ate. "I'll be out till later in the afternoon. Got a hot deal I need to handle personally."

"It sounds like you're buying up the whole town."

He laughed. "It's a numbers game. Most of the prospects don't pan out, so I've got to keep a lot of them coming in. Perseverance is what it's all about."

Perseverance. Laurel rolled the word around in her head. *Perseverance*—that was the key. Her spine straightened. *Perseverance.* She'd make it through tonight, come hell or high water.

* * *

It was cleaning day. After Jase left, she dressed in her old gym shorts and a Lynnwood Elementary tee, then went through the whole house, room by room.

If Mama could see her now, bucket and mop in hand, she'd be horrified, but Laurel wasn't leading her mother's untroubled, leisurely existence. Dovie Elizabeth Kinkaid Harlow had lived all but the last two years of her life in a cocoon, insulated from anything the least bit unpleasant. Would she have been strong enough to handle bad times if she'd had more challenges earlier in her life?

By noon, she needed a break and some fresh air. Boldly opening the front door without first checking if someone was waiting in ambush, she walked out onto the sidewalk and took several deep, cleansing breaths.

She looked up and down Austin Avenue. She'd always been proud of where she lived. All six houses on this block had been built in the late 1800s, when cotton was king of the blackland prairie. Most of them had changed hands through the years as old-time fortunes ebbed or their owners aged. The house next door had been sold four years ago when old Colonel Kraft, whose family had been in residence there since the place was built, had to be hauled off to a nursing home when he began flashing the housekeeper. The Carrolls—a young couple who drove off to their jobs in Waco at six every morning and returned at eight every evening—lived there now. Laurel had never met them and doubted anyone else on the block had either.

Kinkaid House, though, had stayed in the family, and Laurel had grown up assuming she would inherit it and fill it with a brood of noisy, happy children, enough to keep the Kinkaid heritage going for generations to come.

When she and Sarah contemplated their future families—they both considered being only children a tragedy of monumental proportions that they'd never impose on their own children—Sarah limited herself to one boy and one girl, while she'd decided on three boys and three girls, enough to fill the third-floor bedrooms.

She caressed the top of the old-fashioned hitching post at the curb and glanced back at the house. Well, she'd inherited it, all right, but now the house would pass into the hands of someone else. If it would ever sell, that is.

Feeling the darkness gathering again, she went back inside. Maybe music would cheer her up. She sat down at the piano and tried to play some Schubert, then crashed the keyboard, stood up, and closed the lid like a coffin. The dissonances were more than she could bear.

A peanut butter sandwich served for lunch, after which she armed herself with a duster, polish, and vacuum cleaner, and climbed up to the third floor again.

Good thing Kel hadn't rung the doorbell today. She didn't want him to see her with a dish-towel apron, her hair bound up in a kerchief, toting cleaning supplies around.

The rooms went fast, and, in less than two hours, she'd closed the windows again and hauled the vacuum down to the second floor.

By late afternoon, the whole house was clean, but she herself was filthy. After a quick shower, she gave herself an iced tea break and retreated to the cool den.

Exhaustion felt good—she'd earned it. Leaning back in the overstuffed leather chair, she took a long, slow swallow from her glass, then jerked to attention as the phone beside her rang.

It was Jase.

"I won't be back till later, hon, but plan on leaving by about six thirty. Okay?"

"Six thirty? I'll be ready."

What should she wear? The way she saw it, she could either dress for her funeral or dress to conquer, and she wasn't planning to die anytime soon.

She sorted through her evening dresses. The pale pink was pretty, but far too subtle, and the black looked more stately than sinful. The fuchsia strapless—yes!

She hauled the dress out of her closet and held it up to herself in front of the mirror. The deep pinky-purple matte satin looked great on her. The Bosque Club would never know what hit it.

* * *

Jase came through the door at full speed, vaulted up the stairs, burst into her room, and rapped on her bathroom door. "Sorry to be late. I'll dress in the room across the hall and meet you downstairs."

He'd finished up on the real estate deal early but then had a devil of a time finding a decent place to get his car washed. He wanted the Caddie to look great, to be worthy of Laurel. In fact, he wanted everything about the evening to be perfect, because he was planning to ask her to marry him. Sure, it was too soon, but it wasn't as if they'd just met. She'd been his dream girl since he was sixteen, and now that he had a chance with her, he was going to take it.

He removed his suit from its vinyl bag and hung it on the closet rod, then showered and shaved. It was an Armani, his armor, his proof of success. He had a whole wardrobe of them at home, and sometimes he'd slide open the closet door and count them just to be sure they were all still there.

After carefully knotting his deep maroon silk tie, he ran a comb through his wet hair. The cut cost big bucks, but it was worth it. Grabbing his jacket, he went downstairs to wait for Laurel.

Was the ring still in his pocket? He felt for the velvet box. It might be the wrong size, but they could always get that fixed.

Of course, she might reject him. A lot of women preferred to remain single these days, especially after a divorce. Look at Maxie. She'd been married for six years, caught her husband cheating on her, divorced his sorry ass, and never looked back.

He glanced up at the landing again. When the hell would Laurel be ready? He checked his watch, jiggled the ring box, and felt for his mobile, then remembered that he'd decided to leave it at the house this evening.

"Jase?"

He swung around and looked up at her as she came down the stairs step-by-step.

God, she was gorgeous.

It wasn't just the dress, although that was spectacular—a purplish sort of thing which left her shoulders bare and looked like a waterfall from the waist down to her knees. It wasn't just the sparkles at her ears and throat. It wasn't just her face or her hair, which was pinned up in some kind of twist. It was Laurel herself—her grace, the slow curve of her smile, the glow in her eyes.

"You are so beautiful," he intoned huskily.

He would make this the most wonderful night of her life, and before it was over, she'd have a three-carat diamond ring to match her necklace and earrings. They might not be real, judging by the obvious state of her finances, but the ring was. And his love was real too.

Chapter Fifteen

Jase escorted Laurel to his car as gallantly, he hoped, as any of her forebears ever walked their ladies to a waiting carriage, although it was hard to live up to dead people. Opening the car door, he watched as she slid across the leather seat in one fluid motion.

She looked up at him through her lashes. Her "thank you" was soft and sweet-voiced.

"You're welcome," he returned, tucking her ruffly skirt in and shutting the door like a proper gentleman should, when what he really wanted to do was push her down on the car seat, shove up that bubbly skirt, and bury himself in her in her sweet, welcoming body.

Later, Redlander, later.

Circling around the car, he caught his foot on the kickplate as he got in.

Shit! She was still the princess and he was still a frog. Couldn't he even get into his own car without tripping?

After turning around in the parking area, he guided the car down the driveway and out onto the street. The ring was burning a hole in his pocket. When exactly should he pop the question? He was usually good at strategizing, but he didn't have any experience asking a woman to marry him.

He'd thought about doing it while they were at the club, but that was too public. Some idiot might interrupt them at the wrong moment, or he might spill a drink on her. Or, worse yet, she might turn him down, which would pretty much kill the evening.

At the house afterward would be better. Should he go the old bended-knee routine? It was all over television. Seemed to be the style right now. But she might be tired from the evening out. Maybe after lovemaking? That was it—catch her when she was mellow.

Laurel motioned with her hand. "Make a left turn here."

He swung the wheel toward the setting sun and yanked the visor down when he was momentarily blinded. What if he'd had an accident? He could see Art Sawyer's headlines now: *Redlander son kills Harlow daughter in car wreck.*

Pulling the Cadillac to a stop at the valet stand in front of the club, he walked around the car to open the door for his lady fair. Her dress edged up as she angled onto the sidewalk, giving him a good view of the curve of her legs in those nose-bleed heels.

Down, big boy!

"This is something new," Laurel said, looking around. "We used to park our cars ourselves. Daddy always tried to get a space under a streetlight."

Jase handed his key over to a teenager in a black T-shirt with "Bosque Club" printed on it in silver curlicues, then offered Laurel his arm. "Big-city ways, sweetheart. Bosque Bend is growing up."

To his surprise, she clung to him like she was on the *Titanic* and the deck was beginning to tilt. Searching her face for clues, he noticed her jaw was set for battle. Did she expect them to get tossed out? Craig Freiberg's ass would fry in a pan if that happened.

He glanced up at the front of the two-story building as they neared the front door and noted that, unlike First National, the Bosque Club hadn't changed in the least. Fluted bas relief columns still rose on either side of the entrance, and two hitching posts were permanently embedded in the sidewalk next to the curb. As a kid, he used to imagine he was a cowboy tying his horse to one of the wrought iron rings before sauntering off to the nearest saloon for a sarsaparilla, which sounded a lot more interesting to a nine-year-old than the beer Growler stocked in the fridge.

Maxie had told him the shotgun-style building started out as a bank and later housed a dry goods store, but stood vacant for several years until the Bosque Club, which had been meeting in its members' homes, moved in and got it a state historical medallion.

His eyes swept the brass plaque at the entrance. "The Rev. Edward Harlow" was listed as one of the club's founders, but someone had drawn a line through his name with what looked like red lipstick. Jase frowned in confusion and disapproval.

A tall, thickset black man, dressed in a uniform that reminded Jase of a naval captain's, stood under the short canopy, guarding the door. Knowing hired muscle when he saw it, Jase produced his guest card. The doorman examined it for several long seconds before looking up at Jase and handing the card back.

"Welcome to the Bosque Club, Mr. Redlander," he intoned. His face was deadpan. "We hope you enjoy your evening with us. If you have a cell phone, please turn it off it at this time."

Jase patted his pockets. "No phone. It's a social evening."

As he opened the door for them to enter, the doorman's eyes registered Laurel's identity and flicked wide for a split second. "Miss Harlow!"

He should have bowed, Jase thought, walking the princess of Bosque Bend through the town's most sacred secular portals.

* * *

Entwining his hand with hers, Laurel guided Jase down the hall toward the collection of rooms beyond.

So far, so good. Jasper had recognized her as they came in, of course, but at least he hadn't barred the door. Maybe Bosque Bend was too engrossed in whatever new scandal had erupted to pay attention to her anymore.

She could feel herself relaxing as they moved into the first room. It was all so familiar—the piano music coming from the dining room beyond, the gold-toned bamboo wallpaper above the dark wainscoting, the squat, deep-cushioned couches and chairs upholstered in bold persimmon and saffron prints, the collection of original oils on the walls—mostly by members of the Bosque Bend Art Guild—all depicting bluebonnets, live oaks, broken-down windmills, or picturesque outhouses.

But if the decor was relaxing, the family throng occupying most of the room rang all her alarm bells—Dave's two sisters-in-law and their families.

Laurel tugged at Jase's hand. "It's so crowded here. Let's try the next room."

Persevere, Laurel Elizabeth.

Four middle-aged black men who looked only vaguely familiar were the only people in the next room. Hunched around a coffee table and talking in low, intense voices, they didn't even look up as she and Jase came in. Probably working out some kind of business deal. A lot of deals went down over drinks and appetizers in the Bosque Club.

Jase sat them down on a comfortable plush couch with a garish hill country landscape of prickly pears and mountain laurels on the wall behind it. A white-haired waiter approached for their drink order. Laurel shook her head in negation.

"Cutty and water for me," Jase said, producing his guest card. "The lady won't be having anything."

The old man's eyes twinkled. "No ginger ale, Miss Laurel?"

She couldn't help but respond to the warmth in his voice. "Thank you, Grover. Ginger ale would be fine."

Jase took a handful of popcorn from the wooden bowl on the low table in front of him and glanced at the huddle of men across the room. One of them looked familiar, but he couldn't place him. Maybe he was an old schoolmate, maybe someone he'd talked to earlier this week.

The drinks arrived. He tasted his whiskey, set it down on the side table, and smiled at Laurel. "As I said, I'm not much of a drinker."

Laurel nodded and sipped at her ginger ale. "Neither am I. I used to have a Vodka Collins now and then when I was in college, but I'm afraid Grover would have been scandalized if I'd ordered one. Everyone around here thinks I'm still eight years old."

Jase leaned back into the comfort of the couch and moved

his arm around her shoulders, enjoying the touch of her magnolia-soft skin all along the way. "Not everyone, sweetheart, and certainly not when you're wearing this dress." He snuggled closer and touched her cheek with his lips.

Watch it, Redlander. You'll get yourself thrown out of the joint if you keep this up. He removed his arm and, picking up his drink again, took a calming swallow.

What the hell—was that Ray Espinoza coming out of the dining room with the pregnant woman in the red dress on his arm?

Jase stood up. "Hey, Ray! Over here."

"Jase, dude! Good to see you again, bud!"

The men across the room looked around for a brief moment as Jase and Ray greeted each other with a smacking high five. Jase gave Ray's date a slight bow. Snapping black eyes and curly black hair—he was pretty sure he recognized her, even though he couldn't call her by name. "And this must be your wife, Ray."

Ray laughed. "Damn tootin'. You remember Rebecca Diaz." He drew her forward.

"Of course. Bosque Bend's football queen." Jase gave her a big smile. "Ray's a lucky man."

Rebecca was even prettier now than she'd been in high school, but he'd always heard pregnancy gave women a special glow. "You know Ray threatened us all with fire ants in our jock straps if we didn't vote for you."

She laughed. "And then he told me I had to date him because he was the one who rounded up the votes." Her gaze moved behind Jase to Laurel, still seated on the couch, and she turned to her husband with a shocked expression on her face.

Ray jerked her arm slightly, and she started smiling again, somewhat unevenly, but only at Jase.

Jase frowned. What was going on? Rebecca and Laurel used to run in the same crowd.

A strong hand grabbed his arm from behind, and he heard a familiar voice. "Jason Redlander! Just the man I wanted to see!"

The last person Jase had expected to run into in the Bosque Club was Art Sawyer. The curmudgeonly newshound had antagonized so many people with his journalistic rants that it was a wonder he was still allowed in the door.

Thank God he'd decided against proposing to Laurel onsite. It would have been a headline story.

"Mr. Sawyer, sir," he acknowledged.

Damn. The guy's grip was like iron, and he must be in his seventies by now.

Sawyer released him and slapped Ray Espinoza on the back. "And Raymond. Good to see you too. Glad you guys have reconnected. I remember when you two held the line against the Jarrell team in the play-offs."

"Ahmed Quisenberry was there too," Jase reminded him. "Greatest middle linebacker ever." Ahmed was the strategist, Ray the runner, and he the rough-and-stumble.

"You still in touch with him?"

"Ahmed? No sir, not really."

Ray moved forward. "He's a DC lawyer now."

"Well, if you ever get wind of him coming back to town, do me a favor and let me know. I'd like to interview him." He turned to Jase, who was flexing his hand to make sure it wasn't broken.

"From what I hear, young man, you've been causing quite a stir around town the past couple of days yourself."

"Checking out a little real estate, sir."

"Like to run a story on you, Jason, if you have the time to talk to me. Local-boy-makes-good sort of thing. Maybe it'll inspire some of these lazy bums we've got around here to get off their rumps and do some honest work for a change."

"Yessir." What a turnabout, to be a hometown hero, when sixteen years ago Bosque Bend did everything but tar and feather him. *Take that, Bert Nyquist.*

"Tomorrow morning about ten at the Dairy Queen? I'll treat you to some frozen custard."

"I'll be there." Jase smiled as he glanced over at Laurel, who seemed be trying to make herself invisible. "I'm planning to stay in town for a while yet."

Sawyer edged back. "Oh, Miss Harlow! Didn't notice you sitting back there. Nice to see you again. I remember when you would come here with your parents." He looked at her sternly, as if trying to convey an editorial message. "It's been too long. You ought to get out more often."

Out of the corner of his eye, Jase saw Ray's wife cast a pleading look at her husband and pull at his hand.

Ray spread his face into a big, false smile. "Uh, Jase, Mr. Sawyer, guess we gotta be gettin' along. On a tight schedule, ya know. Rebecca's sister is babysittin', and we promised her we'd be back early."

Jase gave him a nod. "See ya later, man."

What was going on? There was more to their hurried departure than babysitting—Rebecca was purposely avoiding eye contact with Laurel. Why?

Sawyer watched Ray leave. "That's another young man on the way up. Ray and his father have done great things for themselves and this community. Wouldn't be surprised to see him mayor one of these days."

Grover reappeared and approached the tabloid editor. "Sir, you have a phone call in the office upstairs."

"Thanks. I'll be there in a second." He shook hands with Jase. "See you tomorrow, boy." He looked at Laurel and dipped his head formally. "Miss Harlow."

Jase sat back down with on the couch, a bemused smile on his face. "I think I've just gotten a promotion. From throwing the *Retriever* to being featured in it. How ironic can it get?"

Laurel laughed. "All this and dinner too."

"Speaking of dinner, do I need to reserve a table?" He looked toward what seemed to be the dining area.

"Not unless there's a crowd." She glanced around at the half-empty room. "Doesn't look like it will be a problem tonight."

"Then, are you ready to dine, milady?" He stood up and offered her his arm.

Fluttering her lashes at him, she played along. "I'm looking forward to it, kind sir."

An impressively impassive maître d'hôtel took charge of them as they entered the dining room, and showed them to a white-clothed table in a secluded corner. Laurel recognized him immediately. Augustus had been with the club ever since she could remember, but not by so much as a blink of an eye did he acknowledge that he knew her now. Apparently it had slipped his mind that Daddy had been the one to recommend him for the job because he was some kind of relative of Mrs. January's.

Before they could open the menus, a slight, bright-haired man waved at Jase from across the room, then left his table to come join them, pulling out a chair for himself.

"Jase, didn't realize you were here!"

"Good to see you, Craig. Laurel, this is Craig Freiberg. He's been helping me set up some local operations."

Freiberg nodded at her politely. "Mrs. Redlander."

Laurel's heart jumped a beat, but she didn't correct him.

Jase didn't either, which made her heart beat double.

The maître d' approached the table again. One of Augustus's duties, Laurel remembered, was to discourage table-hopping.

"Mr. Freiberg, please return to your table. Your dinner will be served presently."

Freiberg stood up. "Oops, guess I'd better get back where I belong. Jase, I'll check in with you tomorrow." He pushed his chair back under the table and nodded at Laurel, all his teeth gleaming. "So nice to meet you, Mrs. Redlander."

Laurel watched him hurry back across the room. Craig Freiberg was one of those people who seemed to have speed built into their DNA.

Jase lifted her left hand and touched her ring finger. "Mrs. Redlander," he repeated. "It sounded good. Maybe we should consider it."

"Maybe," Laurel echoed, smiling at him, all the time knowing it was impossible. Their relationship was living on borrowed time. If only things were different, if she weren't her father's daughter, she'd marry Jase in an instant, leave Bosque Bend behind, and start a new life. But that wasn't about to happen. If Jase did actually want to "make it legal," she'd have to tell him everything, which she absolutely could not do. Not only would it destroy their relationship, but it would destroy him. He'd built his life on Daddy.

No, better to let this affair run its course and have Jase ride off into the sunset when it was over.

In the far corner of the room, the pianist serenaded the diners with a random mix of slow, soulful blues. Sometimes Mrs. Atherton, who'd been Laurel's piano teacher from when Laurel was four till when she went off to college, would present a whole program of ragtime, but tonight was apparently one of her more contemplative evenings.

After Jase gave their dinner orders to the waiter, he led Laurel from the table to join another couple on the small parquet dance square. The club had always featured live music, but only in the past couple of years, since the year before Daddy's fall from grace, had a few tables been cleared for dancing. The Baptists and Church of Christers had protested, of course, so out of respect for his fellow clergy, Daddy had asked Laurel to limit her dancing to other venues, but she figured his death made her promise moot.

She laid her head against Jase's shoulder and closed her eyes. It didn't matter whether he was a good dancer or not. All she wanted was an excuse to be close to him. And, with her head buried in his shoulder, no one would recognize her.

At some point Augustus discreetly informed them that their dinner was served, and they returned to their table. For all Laurel knew, she could have eaten meatloaf—she was with Jase, and that was all that mattered. Afterward they meandered back into yet another one of the club rooms, this one decorated in oyster and aqua, and Grover brought them coffee.

A wave of crazy exhilaration swept through her. *Wow!* Nobody had said anything about Daddy—not Art Sawyer, not even Ray Espinoza. Everything would be okay after all. Just a few minutes more and they'd be out of here. What had she gotten herself so worked up about?

"Ready to go back to the house?" Jase asked, running his

hand lightly down her arm. "I think I've signed for everything, and we're free to go."

She gave him a radiant smile and started to rise, then sat back down again as Craig Freiberg burst into the room with two older men in his wake.

"Jase! I hoped you hadn't left yet! Here are some guys you really need to meet!"

Laurel cowered back into the sofa and willed the floor to open up and swallow her whole.

No, not now, when all her defenses were down—Uncle Larry and Uncle Ricky. They weren't her uncles by blood, but that's what she had grown up calling them.

Freiberg presented his finds like a proud parent. "Richard Simcek has a finger in every pie in town, and Larry Traylor is our mayor."

Laurel suppressed a shudder. Uncle Larry, a member of her father's congregation, had refused to let Daddy remove his personal mementoes from the church office. Uncle Ricky had turned his back on Mama in the produce section of Piggly Wiggly three days before she killed herself.

Larry Traylor stretched his face into a jolly-fatman smile that didn't quite reach his eyes as he stepped forward with his hand outstretched toward Jase.

No one had noticed her yet, Laurel realized. All their attention was focused on Jase, who was in fine form, pumping hands and introducing himself as "Jason Redlander, Redlander Properties out of Dallas."

Dear God, her gentle, considerate lover had automatically gone into shark-hunter mode.

The men's wives were surging forward now too.

"My wife, Betsy," Uncle Ricky said, presenting her to Jase.

"So nice to meet you." She gave Jase her hand and, as usual, glanced at her husband to make sure she'd said the right thing.

Aunt Betsy had aged a lot in three years, Laurel noted. Had Uncle Ricky been playing around on her again?

As soon as Betsy Simcek backed off, standing beside her husband again but keeping anxious eyes focused on Jase, Uncle Larry's wife stepped forward to introduce herself.

"I'm Isabelle Traylor, but everyone calls me 'Izzy.' Just plain ol' Izzy, that's me." She tossed her mink stole behind her shoulders for emphasis.

In contrast to Betsy Simcek, Aunt Izzy didn't seem to have changed in the least—still pleasantly plump, still wearing her purple-tinted hair in rolls and puffs, still jovial. At least on the surface. Everyone in town knew her as a hard-boiled businesswoman whose money sense was the only thing that, time after time, had saved her showboating husband from financial disaster.

Suddenly Laurel realized Jase was tugging on her hand. When she tried to resist, he exerted even more pressure, forcing her to stand up.

"And this is Mrs. Redlander," Craig announced.

Jase corrected him with an easy smile. "Not quite yet, but we're working on it." He dropped his arm around her shoulders. "I think you all know Laurel Harlow. I understand her father was one of the founders of the club."

Laurel tried to smile, but could feel the room closing in on her. The foursome's faces looked like he had just introduced them to Lady Dracula.

Uncle Ricky and Uncle Larry were the first to recover, closing their jaws and blinking their eyes back into their heads simultaneously. She'd seen them in action before—nothing caught those two by surprise for very long.

A drawing of the lips that passed for a smile spread across the mayor's face. "Well, isn't that just great!" he said in a hearty tone. "Jase Redlander and little Laurel Harlow. How about a congratulatory kiss for your ol' Uncle Larry?"

Advancing on Laurel, he enclosed her in a hearty hug, then planted a smacking buss on her cheek. Laurel smiled stiffly and lifted an arm as if to welcome his embrace. Maybe they could all play this off, and she could hurry Jase out to the car.

Uncle Ricky took over where Uncle Larry left off. In his day, he'd been quite handsome, and she'd had a short-lived crush on him in her early teens. That was when she learned about his tendency to grope, which had been going on for so long that she doubted if he was even conscious of it anymore. Sure enough, one of his hands managed to brush her hip as he gave her a quick hug.

Jase frowned as he watched the men greet Laurel. This was awkward. What the hell was going on? Something was wrong. Traylor and Simcek wanted to reject Laurel, just like Rebecca Diaz had, but they had to accept her because she was with him. Their wives were still hanging back, though.

Then the big one, Izzy Traylor, lifted the slack sides of her mouth into a beaming smile, and stepped forward to grasp Laurel's hand, murmuring how nice it was to see her again.

But Simcek's wife was a different kettle of fish. She shook off her husband's grip and backed off from Laurel. "No, no, Ricky! I won't shake hands with her! You can't make me!"

Her jaw sawed back and forth in indignation, and her eyes were rolling with rage and anger. "I won't do it, no matter what! Not after what Ed did! Maybe you don't remember, Ricky, but I do! My own nephew too! Maybe it didn't come to court, but it should have! That dirty old man—and he bought his way out of it!"

Jase's jaw dropped. What was she talking about? Reverend Ed, a dirty old man? Was the woman insane? And, of course, everyone in the place was coming into the room to check out the train wreck.

Fuck, he didn't need this.

He took Laurel's arm. "I think we'd better leave." Maneuvering her through the gathering crowd, he headed down the wide hall to the entryway.

The doorman, ignorant of the commotion within, tipped his hat politely as they left and wished them a good night.

* * *

Laurel was wooden with fear. Now Jase would have to know. Had she thought she could keep it from him forever? *You knew it wouldn't last. Just be grateful for what time you had with him and let him go.*

Neither of them spoke as they returned to the house. He parked under the porte cochere again and helped her out of the car. They let themselves in by the same side entrance they'd left from a century earlier in the day.

He walked her into the front room. They took seats across from each other.

"Tell me," he commanded.

These were the words she had been anticipating and dreading all the way home, and she still didn't know what to say. How could she explain about Daddy? But she was tired of running and hiding and pretending everything was all right, so she just blurted it all out.

"My father sexually molested six of the boys who came to him for counseling." She'd never said the words aloud before, and could feel a flush rising in her cheeks. "Betsy Simcek's nephew was one of them. Apparently it had been going on for a couple of years."

Jase stared at her as if he hadn't heard her right. "Are you sure?"

She nodded, not trusting herself to speak.

Jase shook his head in denial. "I don't understand."

Laurel sighed, closed her eyes for a second, and tried to remember how her father had explained himself. "Daddy said he'd always had...an attraction...to teenage boys, but he was able to keep it in check. Apparently as he got older, his control...slipped. At first it was inappropriate touching, but when it escalated, Daddy turned himself in to Mr. Bridges, who worked out a way to protect my mother and me by keeping it out of the courts. Daddy promised to pay damages to all the families and for psychotherapy for all the boys like—like Betsy Simcek's nephew and...and Ray's brother, Carlos. After Daddy died, Mama and I inherited his financial obligations—and the town's ill will. People felt deceived, I think, because they'd thought Daddy was so perfect, but he wasn't. Mama—Mama couldn't take it and...committed suicide...about a year ago, so now I'm the only one left to hate."

She didn't cry. She was long past that, and it had never helped. Anyway, she was merely peripheral damage, not one of the real victims. Those boys, even Betsy Simcek's smarmy nephew—they were the ones who deserved the sympathy.

Jase drew a deep, shuddering breath. "Is that why Carson divorced you?"

"Yes. He didn't think he could get anywhere anymore in Bosque Bend if he was connected with my family." Her neck felt so tight. She rolled it on the back of the chair. *No more questions, please.*

"And that's why you didn't want to go the club tonight?"

"Yes, yes," she answered, impatient with him now. She had a headache and she wanted to go to bed. She needed to sleep. To sleep and forget.

"And that's why you were worried about me talking to Sarah, because you were afraid she would tell me about Reverend Ed?"

"Yes, everything you say! I didn't want you to know!" She knew she was getting snappish, but she couldn't help it.

He pierced her with his eyes. "Don't you think it would have been better to warn me? To level with me beforehand?"

"Yes—no—I don't know." She twisted her hands together in her lap. "I've never talked about it to anyone before. I didn't know how to tell you, what to say. And...I guess I was protecting myself too, because then I'd have to admit...the reality."

He stared at her with cold, dark eyes. "I despise sexual predators." His voice sounded like God's judgment.

"I know."

"I despise adults who seduce children under the guise of helping them. I think they should be shot on sight."

She nodded, weary of it all, but understanding she'd have to hear him out.

He stood up and walked the room, then smacked his fist into his hand.

"God! How could he do it! I respected him more than anyone else in the world! He was the only one who stood by me!"

He turned on Laurel. "He even gave me money. Did he expect some kind of return on it?"

Laurel sat there with her head down, trying to ward off his voice. She knew all the questions. She'd wondered about some of them herself.

Jase started pacing again. She could almost see the energy pouring off him.

"What a sham! Edward Harlow, the *Reverend* Edward Harlow—" he repeated. "I've built my life around a sham! Ever since I was sixteen, I've tried to live up to the standards he taught me—to work hard, to live honestly, to look forward rather than backward, to respect other people! And all the time he was..."

He looked toward the office door and shook his head in disbelief.

Laurel continued to sit silently, helplessly, waiting for the final blow to fall.

"This is too much. I'm sorry, Laurel, but I can't handle it. I've got to get out of here." He reached for his jacket. Something fell out of a pocket and rolled across the floor, but he snatched it up and stuffed it back in his pants pocket before she could see what it was.

Chapter Sixteen

So, it was over.

Just like that, she was alone again. Sure, Jase's belongings were strewn all over the house, but that was only temporary. Maybe he'd take back the dishwasher repair too.

She trudged upstairs and exchanged the sexy fuchsia dress for a chaste white cotton nightgown, then returned to the den. There was no way she could sleep in the bed tonight that she and Jase had shared. Instead, tucking her feet under herself, she curled up in a chair and pulled an afghan over her shoulders to keep herself warm, then flicked the remote at the TV.

The programs seemed even more banal than usual, but the real performance was in her brain as it continuously reran the Betsy Simcek show. And she hadn't been the only audience. By the time Betsy finished, everyone in the building must have crowded into the room to find out what the ruckus was about—the waiters, Dave's new wife's family, Art Sawyer, Mrs. Atherton, Kel, Pendleton Swaim (where had those two come from?)—people she knew and people she didn't. Everyone.

Dear God, she'd almost made it, almost gotten out of the

club scot-free, and then Jase's minion appeared with Larry Traylor and Rick Simcek right behind him.

She understood Aunt Betsy's reaction to seeing Edward Harlow's daughter all dressed up and enjoying an evening out. The Simceks didn't have any children, so Betsy lavished all her attention on her sister's only son. Laurel was still writing monthly checks for his psychotherapy, although she suspected his problems went far beyond her father. Still, she didn't begrudge him. How could she? What Daddy had done was unforgivable.

There was no getting around the fact that she was her father's daughter, and, as far as Betsy Simcek was concerned, if Daddy wasn't what he should have been, his daughter wasn't either. Apparently Jase felt the same way.

The glare from the television screen began to bother her, and she closed her eyes for a moment's rest. This was absolutely the worst day of her life, even worse than when Daddy had made his confession.

* * *

Jase had no particular destination in mind when he left Laurel's house. He just needed to get away. Everything was too much—a bad dream, a nightmare. If only the world would reverse course and go back to the way it was sixteen years ago, when Laurel was princess of Bosque Bend, and Reverend Ed its virtual king.

Sexual abuse—molestation, probably other things he didn't want to think about. He couldn't believe it.

Damn. How many times had he daydreamed about Growler dying and Reverend Ed adopting him?

The psychologist had told him that sexual predators seemed to have an instinct for children deprived of affection. That's why Marguerite Shelton had zeroed in on him, because he'd been vulnerable. Was that what Reverend Ed had seen in him too, his vulnerability? What might have happened if he had stayed around town another year or two?

Halfway through an intersection, he realized he'd run a red light. Who cared? It was night, there weren't any other cars around, and he could buy his way out—just pay the ticket and be done with it. In fact, he could buy almost anything he wanted. Not like Laurel, who apparently was stone-cold broke.

Well, at least now he knew where the Kinkaid fortune had gone. And why she hid herself away in that big house all the time. And why she wanted to leave Bosque Bend. All his questions had been answered, just as he'd wanted, but the answers hadn't been anywhere near what he'd expected. If only he'd left well enough alone. Maybe he and Laurel could have slipped out of town, flown up to Nevada and married quietly, then appeared in Dallas as man and wife, and no one would be the wiser—least of all him.

But ignorance is *not* bliss. He would have learned about Reverend Ed sooner or later, and if he couldn't deal with learning the truth now, how would he have felt learning about it after he'd brought her into his house as his wife?

He hit the wheel with his hand in frustration. Damn! He'd governed everything he did by Edward Harlow's precepts, and so much of his feeling for Laurel was bound up with his admiration for her father...

He was careful to stop at the next light. Bosque Bend didn't have that many traffic signals, but he was hitting them all wrong. Fuck! Must be bad timing. Just like with Laurel.

The ring felt heavy as lead in his pocket.

Maybe they could still do Vegas. He could make a U-turn right now, pick Laurel up, and whisk her out of town to a new life. They'd lock all this—this *sordidness* in a closet and never talk about it again.

But would it be that easy to forget? Every time he looked at Laurel, he saw her father in her—her gray eyes and dark hair, something in the shape of her face, the way she carried herself. She even sounded like him—calm, soothing, concerned. He snorted. Maybe her concern was as false as Reverend Ed's must have been.

No, he knew better than that—didn't he? Oh God, what *did* he know? His whole world had just been blasted to smithereens.

He deliberately ignored a stop sign.

Would he ever be able to make love to her again without thinking of what her father had done?

Fuck, what was he doing at the Shallows? He'd thought he was driving aimlessly, but maybe this was an appropriate destination. For all its beautification, the place was just river bottom. And, for all his money and closetful of Armani suits, he was just Jase Redlander, son of the Meanest Man in Texas.

He parked in the lot, rolled down his window, and stared up into the night. Holy shit, the cicadas were wailing like banshees on crack.

Had Traylor and Simcek recognized his name? He certainly knew theirs. Those canny old buzzards had been wheeling and dealing around Bosque Bend since he'd been in grade school. But then, the way he figured it, if there was a buck to be made, they'd remember him as the angel Gabriel. And apparently, for his sake, they were even willing to make nice to Reverend Ed's daughter too—all except Mrs. Simcek, that is.

He uttered a brief, sharp laugh. What a switch. Laurel Harlow, the princess of Bosque Bend, being tolerated only because she was with Jase Redlander, despoiler of innocent schoolteachers.

The stars were high now, and the moon was a distant disc of white. His world had been knocked out of orbit, but the heavens kept revolving as usual. He stared out the windshield into the dark night and wondered what would happen if he married Laurel, and they had children. Could he protect them from learning about Reverend Ed? Hell—what if they found out about Growler? He was having a hard enough time trying to protect Lolly from learning about Marguerite.

God didn't send him any answers, so finally he put in a CD of Charlie Pride oldies and leaned back on the seat to rest, awakening occasionally through the night to fight off images of two fig-leafed Greek statues closing in on him.

The next thing he knew, a cruelly bright sun was glaring through the windshield as it rose over the placid Bosque. He glanced around at his surroundings, trying to orient himself.

Damn, sleeping out here all night—that was a stupid thing to do. There was no way to fence the park off, and he'd bet bad boys still congregated in hidden places when the sun went down. He was lucky he hadn't been mugged.

Putting the Caddie in gear, he backed out of the parking space and headed home, home to the old house on the west arm of the Bosque for a morning shower and a good cup of coffee. He was sticky with sweat and his mouth tasted fuzzy.

Besides, he didn't want to face Laurel yet.

She'd understand.

* * *

There was an insistent ringing in Laurel's ear. If the phone hadn't been on the desk next to her, she never would have picked it up in time.

"Hullo?" Was it Jase? Her brain hustled itself into wakefulness.

"Good morning, Ms. Harlow. This is Craig—Craig Freiberg. I, uh, want to apologize for the incident at the club last night. I'm so sorry about Mrs. Simcek. I hope you won't hold it against me. Her husband said she'd been having nervous problems lately. I had no idea she would fly off the handle like that."

"That's okay." What else could she say? Nothing was Craig Freiberg's fault. He was trying to help Jase by introducing him to the mayor and his business crony.

"Uh, may I speak with Jase, please?"

"He's not here." She tried to sound nonchalant. "Have you tried his cell?"

"It seems to be turned off, but he gave me this number as a backup. I assumed..."

Glancing at the century-old photo of Erasmus in the bookcase across from her, Laurel straightened her shoulders, put on her best schoolteacher voice, and took control of the conversation. "Mr. Redlander's visit was limited in duration, and I do not know when he will be returning."

"But I thought..." Craig stopped dead, finally realizing something was wrong. "Uh...okay...thank you. I'll try him again."

Laurel replaced the phone on its cradle, switched off an irritatingly cheery morning TV host, made her way up the stairs, and started running her bath.

Brazening it out hadn't worked. She was defeated, kayoed,

out for the count. There was no other way their relationship could end. She'd known from the beginning that Jase wouldn't be able to handle the scandal.

She stripped off her gown and stepped into the warm water. Her affair with Jase had been a wonderful interlude, a magic bubble, one she would always hold in her heart. Now she had to continue with the rest of her life, which meant there was nothing left to do but clean up the leftovers and erase all evidence of Jase's habitation. She'd pack up his stuff and put everything in the coat closet next to the front door. No reason to waste time hunting and gathering when he sent someone to pick up his belongings.

In a way, it was a relief that Jase was out of the picture. Now she could follow up on that job offer from Brownsville. Betty Arnold had been as good as her word in supplying her with a good reference.

Game plan decided, she dried herself and dressed in shorts and the blue-checked shirt, the tough one, the one that could absorb anything and wash out clean.

The phone rang while she was filling out her information form for Brownsville. Should she just ignore it? Maybe it was Craig Freiberg again, and she absolutely didn't want to talk to him. But maybe it was the Realtor with a hot prospect.

"Laurel? Is this Laurel?"

It was Jase. Her silly heart leapt up.

"Yes."

"You didn't sound like yourself at first."

She laughed. "It's me." Was he coming back?

"I just called to say I'm sorry I left like that. I'm heading off to Dallas in a bit, but I'll be in touch."

Her heart landed with a thud. "Oh. Well, have a good trip."

"Are you—are you okay? You sound odd again."

"Just fine." *Except that my heart is broken.*

"I'm sorry, Laurel, but I need time to get my head around this. Reverend Ed..."

"I understand."

"People like Betsy Simcek...you've had a hard time of it, haven't you? Will you be safe? I could get you a bodyguard or something."

"I can call the police if anything happens. Mervin Hruska doesn't look the other way like his predecessor did."

"Well, call me if you change your mind about the protection. You've got my number."

"Thanks."

Her eyes began to smart as soon as she hung up the phone, but she refused to allow herself to cry. She'd cried a week ago when he was about to leave, and look how that had ended up—now she was more alone than ever.

Instead, she made herself a strong cup of coffee, sat down at the kitchen table, and checked in with her Realtor again.

Good news. He'd talked to an out-of-town couple, the Cokers, about Kinkaid House, and they'd be coming to town next week to visit the property. She hoped it would work out. The way things looked right now, she would need to be in Brownsville by mid-August, and she'd prefer to sell the house before then.

Now to drink her coffee and brood awhile. She could indulge herself that much.

What was that? Someone was knocking on the door.

She started to get up, but sat back down. She didn't feel like talking to anyone. Maybe her visitor would cease and desist if she pretended she wasn't at home.

The bell started ringing and a loud, familiar voice called out her name.

"Laurel! Laurel Elizabeth Harlow! Answer the door! I know you're in there!"

It was Sarah.

Laurel put down her coffee, walked slowly to the door, and opened it a hand's width. "Go away."

"Let me in right now, or I'll call the cops and have them break down the door!"

"You can't do that!"

"The hell I can't! I'll tell them you're suicidal! Besides, you know that Mervin Hruska always did whatever I asked him to!"

Laurel opened the door. Sarah threw her arms around her the second she stepped across the threshold.

"Sweetie, I've missed you so much, and I just had to come over when I heard about what happened at the Bosque Club. Besides, Mother told me that black Cadillac wasn't in your driveway last night."

Laurel drooped her head to Sarah's shoulder. She needed her so much right now. "Betsy Simcek—"

"Betsy Simcek should be institutionalized. And Jase Redlander should be hung from a yardarm, whatever that is. Now, let's go into the kitchen and talk everything over."

* * *

Jase gave Craig Freiberg instructions about finishing up the two deals he'd committed himself to in Bosque Bend, then drove over to Dairy Queen for his meeting with Arthur Sawyer.

Sawyer hailed him from a table near the door. "You're right on time, Jason. I like that. Dependable."

"I try." Jase looked around. The store wasn't even recognizable from the last time he'd been there. Laurel had told him the Mayfields had redone the restaurant, but he hadn't expected the place to look quite so upscale.

Sawyer started to rise. "Let's go order. I'll buy you a frozen custard to soften you up before I begin third-degreeing you."

Jase laughed. "Sure thing. Lead the way."

A heavyset man wearing a badge identifying him as the store manager greeted them with a big smile. "A Blizzard, as usual, Mr. Sawyer?"

"Of course, Juan. It's Cookie Dough this month, isn't it?" He turned to Jase. "And what's your poison, young Redlander?"

"A dipped cone, I guess." That's what Maxie always ordered for him when he was a kid.

As soon as they got their treats, his host led him to a booth in the back of the side room, several tables distant from the herd of exuberant Cub Scouts who had taken over the front area.

Sawyer sucked in several spoonfuls of Blizzard before he started in on him. "Now, Jason, tell me about yourself. I understand you've accumulated considerable real estate holdings up and down the I-35 corridor."

"Yessir. I started out with one parking lot, and it just grew from there." He decapitated the custard's curly top.

Sawyer produced a small notebook and a ballpoint pen. "Actually, I've googled most of your official information. What I really want to know are what your plans are for our fair city."

"You don't use a recorder?"

Sawyer shook his head. "Makes people too nervous, like they're being interrogated."

Jase paused to recapture a large piece of the frozen chocolate shell that had broken loose. "I know the feeling."

He liked Art Sawyer as an adult even more than he'd liked him as a kid. The old guy was a straight shooter.

Sawyer enjoyed several more spoonfuls of his Blizzard, then started in again. "Now, about your plans…"

"I'm not holding back on you, sir, but I'm unsure yet what my plans are. I bought the old Anderson tract east of the river, and I'm negotiating on a smaller lot, but that's all I can say."

"The Anderson tract. That's within spitting distance of the Espinoza addition, isn't it?"

"Fairly near. They'll probably tie in eventually, but I'm not assuming anything right now. It's an investment, that's all." He'd reached the cone, the crisp, crunchy, sweet cone.

"Do you think you and Raymond might get together businesswise at some time?"

"Maybe." Crunch, crunch. "Who knows? I've always dealt in land, but I might go into homebuilding at some point."

"Even in this economy?"

Jase wiped his hands on a paper napkin and shrugged. "There's always opportunity."

Sawyer's eyes lit up. "There's always opportunity! I like that!" He scribbled in his notebook, then made a big show of replacing it in his pocket.

"Strictly off the record, what about Laurel Harlow?"

Jase was caught completely off guard. "I, uh, we're friends, close friends."

Sawyer glanced at his rumpled shirt, the same one that Jase

had worn at the Bosque Club, and raised his eyebrows. "And where did you spend the night?"

"Not where you think," Jase countered. Not where I would have liked to. "I slept in my car."

Sawyer nodded like a wise old owl. "She kicked you out?"

"No, I . . . yeah, she kicked me out." He couldn't say he'd left Laurel because he was mad at her father. It didn't make sense even to him.

Sawyer looked at him as if reading his mind.

"Now, listen to me, young Jason. Every person on this planet, no matter how good, has feet of clay. People are a mixed bag, and Edward Harlow was no exception. He did some terrible things, but he also did some good things too, some *very* good things. This doesn't excuse him, but it's important to recognize both sides of the man. People around here have not only vilified Edward Harlow, but they've also extended their anger to his family. Dovie Kinkaid was one of the sweetest, gentlest women I've ever known, and they drove her to suicide. Laurel is stronger than her mother, and I think she'll make it, but she's got to get the hell out of Bosque Bend."

Sawyer tilted his cup up to get a last swallow of his Blizzard, put the cup down, and looked Jase in the eyes. "I came in on the end of Betsy Simcek's tantrum last night and saw Laurel's face. And yours. I can't tell you what to do except that you can never go wrong by doing the right thing. You said there's always an opportunity, and I'll add to it: There's always an *opportunity* to do the right thing."

Jase nodded. "Don't worry about my relationship with Laurel, sir. I'll be back in Bosque Bend in a day or two. I just have to—to figure everything out."

* * *

Sarah poured herself a cup of coffee and sat down at the table across from Laurel. "Okay, spill. What's been going on over here?'

"Nothing much. I've been answering the phone all morning. First there was a guy who wanted to contact Jase, then Jase, then my Realtor—it looks like the house might sell."

"What about the call from Jase?"

Laurel shrugged. "He said he'd stay in touch, whatever that means—I'm not holding out any hope."

"What I'm asking for is that you tell me what the heck's been going on this past week?"

Laurel shrugged. "I think it's fairly obvious. I've been having an affair with Jase Redlander, and now it's over."

"Bullshit. And don't get that mulish expression on your face, Miss Priss. He adores you, and you've been in love with him since you were fifteen."

"He left me."

"He left you because Betsy Wetsy made a spectacle out of herself?" Sarah frowned at her. "Wait a minute—are you telling me Jase didn't know about—about your father? You never told him?"

"How could I? All he could talk about was how great Daddy was, how much he'd influenced his life. I was afraid once he found out, he'd leave me. And he did."

Sarah's face hardened. "Then he isn't worthy of you. Hold your head high. You didn't do anything wrong. My father was a lawyer, and, as far as I know, children are not accountable for their parents' crimes."

"Maybe not legally, but the whole town hates me for what

Daddy did, and when Mama was alive, they hated her too. You and your mother acted like we were dead."

"That's not true. My mother tried to be supportive of you and your mother, but your mama turned her away at the door, then sent us a letter saying our attentions were not welcome. Mother decided to give you all some private time, but the last straw was when Dad died last year and neither of you attended his funeral."

Laurel hung her head. "She didn't want to embarrass you." Also, Mama had begun blaming Charles Bridges for the situation, as if his arrangements had caused them to have to withdraw from public life, not what Daddy had done.

Sarah sighed. "As I see it, there's been a lot of rejection on both sides. But as to the town, sure, there are some people who are always going to be whispering behind your back, but people's memories fade, and there are a lot of new people in Bosque Bend now."

"I lost my job."

"I know. Mom said that ol' Betsy talked to the school board. But you can't let people like her get to you. Move on with your life. Get a new job and find another tall, dark, handsome guy."

"I'm not sure about a new guy, but—don't laugh—I am thinking about getting a dog. The house seems so lonely now that Jase is gone."

"A dog? What kind?"

"I don't know. Just so it's had all its shots." She'd didn't want to end up with rabies like her great-aunt.

Sarah took her arm and guided her to the stairs. "Then go get dressed and I'll drive you to the pound and I'll treat you to a nice dog with all its vaccinations up-to-date."

* * *

Inwardly quaking, Laurel followed Sarah as she walked down the rows of cages. It was so noisy she could hardly think.

The dogs were throwing themselves against their wire doors as if they wanted to tear her to shreds, and the smaller the dog, the more desperate it seemed, barking and jumping like its life depended on it, and maybe it did. On the way to the facility, Sarah had described in graphic detail what happened to dogs that weren't adopted.

They walked into the next room, which housed the larger cages. The dogs were quieter here, more despondent, as if resigned to their fates.

"You'll probably want to start small," Sarah said, moving quickly past the cages.

"Maybe not." She'd always liked the Great Danes that Mrs. Bridges favored. She moved closer to read the index card taped to a cage: WALDO, MALE, LAB-RIDGEBACK MIX, APPROX. 6 YRS., NEUTERED, HOUSEBROKEN.

The dog limped slowly over to the front of the cage to look up at her. His leg was in a cast. Had he been hit by a car?

Waldo continued to stare at her. Without thinking, Laurel stuck her hand through the wire. Waldo regarded it for a moment before cautiously extending a long, pink tongue to lick her fingers. Then he backed off, sat down, and gazed at her, his heart in his eyes.

Laurel's own heart answered him. "Sarah, this is the one."

Sarah joined her in front of the cage. "Are you sure?" She read Waldo's information card aloud and frowned. "He's six now, so he won't live more than four or five years longer."

Laurel tightened her jaw. "I like him. But his name isn't Waldo. It's Hugo."

Sarah shrugged. "Okay, then. Hugo it is. Get his number, and we'll tell the lady out front."

The attendant who helped Laurel fill out the forms told her "Waldo" had been deserted by his first family when they moved out of state, and the neighbors called the dogcatcher when he started begging up and down the street. Hugo's second owner, a college student, had kicked him down two flights of stairs when he was drunk.

Sarah stepped in with her credit card when the woman added up Hugo's adoption fees.

"Thank of it as a late birthday present," she said as they loaded Hugo into the backseat of her Mercedes. "I've missed a couple of years in there."

Their next stop was at Walmart, where Laurel walked Hugo in the grass margin while Sarah went in "to pick up a few things you'll need." Twenty minutes later she was back with a full cart.

"This is my late Christmas present," she announced breezily, extracting a red leather collar with manly studs on it from the pile, slipping it around Hugo's neck, and attaching a matching leash. Then, as Laurel held the big dog in check, Sarah hefted a heavy bag of dog food and a luxurious-looking dog bed into the back of her car. Bowls, a chew toy, and a jar of dog treats completed her perception of canine necessities.

Laurel got in the car and looked back at Hugo, and he moved forward to nuzzle her neck. "Thank you, Sarah. This is the best Christmas and birthday I've ever had."

* * *

Jase told himself he really had meant to get in touch with Laurel again in a day or two, but somehow a whole week slipped by without his calling. He wanted to explain everything to her, but he didn't know what to say, because he was still in a mental turmoil. And then he didn't know how to explain his delay.

He loved her, but he still couldn't put his head around her father and who he really was—the saintly pastor or the man who...who did what he did?

And then Lolly came home from a three-day tennis camp with a sunburn, her expensive racket, and a lot of questions about his relationship with Laurel that he couldn't answer even if he wanted to. He'd always encouraged her spunk, but didn't like it when she directed it at him.

Right now she was standing in front of his desk, her hands fisted at her waist like the Jolly Green Giant, but she wasn't in the least jolly.

"So that's it. Just like that, you left Laurel high and dry? Here you've been dreaming about her all your life, and you've got her at last, and you're letting her go?"

Jase looked up from behind his desktop computer and a barricade of work papers. Damn it, couldn't she see he was busy? "Don't speak to me in that tone of voice, young lady! Laurel Harlow is my business, not yours!"

Had he really deserted Laurel? He hadn't thought of it that way. He'd told her he'd be in touch. And he would, as soon as he sorted her out from her father.

Lolly's eyes flashed. "If she's going to be a part of the family, she's my business too! She'd be my stepmother, so it's important whether I like her or not!"

"Well, do you?"

She gave him the "duh" look. "What do you think? Yes, I

like her very much. I want you to marry her. Now, are you going to?"

Jase glared at his daughter, but she didn't back down. She never did. He studied her militant stance, her bouncing curls and sparkling eyes, the cute summer outfit designed to show off her precocious figure.

She narrowed her eyes and tightened her mouth. "Well, are you?"

Jase ran his fingers through his hair and shook his head as if to clear it. "I don't know."

Exhaling in disgust, Lolly turned on her heel and stalked off. He felt like a fool.

Maxie attacked him next, but she was more subtle. "Laurel Harlow is such a lovely girl," she mentioned in a casual voice as they sat together on the patio that evening. "And you did spend a lot of time with her. I do hope we'll be seeing her again, Jason. Perhaps she could visit us for a week or so."

He didn't answer. Everybody was on his case, damn it. When Craig Freiberg called from Bosque Bend to report on the latest with the Anderson tract, he artlessly let it fall that Laurel had said Jase would be staying in Dallas from now on. Obviously Craig was fishing for more information about their breakup, but Jase left him dangling.

God, is that what he had done to Laurel—exposed her to still more speculation and gossip?

He should go right back to Bosque Bend today and assure her that he still loved her. But at the moment he had a lot to catch up on with the business. As soon as all that was settled, he and Laurel could straighten everything out. Yeah, once he got his mind in gear, he could figure out exactly how to handle the situation with Laurel.

* * *

But there was no relief in sight. Bright and early the next morning, Lolly continued her campaign. "If Laurel Harlow isn't my mother, who is?" she demanded, hauling out the old annual and opening it to a marked page. "Is it that one?" She pointed to a blond, bubbly cheerleader whom she vaguely resembled.

"God, no! She wouldn't have given me the time of day."

Maxie took Jase aside later. "You've got to tell her, Jase. She's driving me crazy."

"I will," he sighed. "When she's old enough."

Four days later, Lolly had flown the coop.

Chapter Seventeen

Lolly's off on another wild-goose chase," Maxie said, calling him at the office. "It's the mother thing again. She left a note on her pillow, and the maid saw her getting into Chloe Ginsburg's little red car half an hour ago, about three o'clock."

Jase closed down his computer with fingers that had turned stone-cold.

"Where to?"

"According to the note, she's off to San Antonio to meet her mother and we shouldn't worry about her."

"San Antone? Lolly doesn't know a damn soul in San Antonio. She's only been there twice in her life—that seventh-grade tour of the Spanish missions, which she couldn't care less about, and last summer, when we did the River Walk and the Alamo. Remember that creep of a bellhop who tried to chat her up?" He rubbed his forehead to relieve a sudden ache over his eyebrows. "Why does she think her mother is in San Antonio?"

"Your guess is as good as mine."

"I'm leaving as soon as I can. Call me if there's any news." He stuck his laptop in its carry case, grabbed a jacket, and strode out of his office.

His administrative assistant looked up from her desktop computer. "Problem?"

"Yeah. I don't know how long this will take. If there's anything I haven't seen yet, I'll take it with me."

"Lolly?"

"Yep."

Connie slid a couple of pages into a folder and handed it to him. "Girl Child's run away again?"

"You got it." Opening his case, he stuffed the folder in on top of his laptop.

"Bosque Bend?"

"San Antone." He clicked the case shut and looked at his assistant. "And when I find her, I'll bring her home and lock her in her room till she turns forty or signs up to be a nun."

Connie gave him a disbelieving look. "Sure you will."

Damn Connie, but she was right. He'd never had it in him to discipline Lolly like he should have. Maybe if he'd been tougher on her, made her toe the line instead of being so fucking proud of her spirit, she'd be home whacking tennis balls against the side of the garage right now.

Bypassing the elevator, he headed for the stairs. His adrenaline was demanding action.

The Cadillac was parked right next to the door, a perk of being the head honcho. He opened the windows, turned the AC on high, made a few quick, futile calls to some of Lolly's friends, and headed for I-35. *Damn and double damn!* He had six hours of hard driving ahead to reach San Antonio by dark. A lot could happen to two girls alone in a strange city in six hours.

As soon as he hit the highway, a semi roared up behind him, swerved to pass him on the right, swung back in front of him, then abruptly slowed down so that he had to slam on his brakes to avoid a rear-end collision.

Fucking son of a bitch! What if Chloe had to deal with a crazy driver like Mr. Big Rig? She hadn't been driving very long. In fact, she'd just gotten her license a couple of months ago. Visions of Lolly's bloody corpse being featured on San Antonio's notoriously lurid news stations flashed through his brain.

He turned the radio up louder to drown out his imagination and raised his speed another five miles, which at least kept him up with that damn truck.

Shit! What the hell did he think he was accomplishing by driving to San Antonio? It had made sense for him to check out Bosque Bend last time because Reverend Ed's house was a slam dunk—but where was Lolly headed in San Antonio? He was clueless about how to even begin looking. But he had to try. He had to be on the scene. No way he could sit on his hands and expect Girl Child to come home on her own. And Laurel couldn't help him this time.

Laurel. Everything kept circling back to Laurel.

Maybe, if he found Lolly and chained her to the Cadillac doorframe, he could stop in to see Laurel on his way back to Dallas. But what would he say? *I love you, but I don't know how to handle it? I can't separate the person you are from the person your father turned out to be?*

Lolly and Laurel. His daughter kept running away from him, and—let's face it—he'd run away from Laurel. Lolly's situation was the more pressing right now, but after he found her, he'd see to Laurel. Maybe then he could get rid of this depression, this sense of unreality, of hovering in space, that had been with him since that evening in the Bosque Club.

Ignoring the exit to Bosque Bend, he hit Waco during five o'clock traffic, which slowed him down a little, but wasn't too bad. He glanced at the cars on either side of him. Had he already passed Chloe on the highway? He had no idea of what her car looked like except that it was little and red, which meant it could be anything from a smart car to a BMW coupe.

Well, at least Lolly had learned her lesson about riding with somebody's dicey brother. He was fit to be tied when she'd confessed that escapade to him.

A narrow crescent moon was climbing the inky night sky when he finally reached the sprawling outskirts of San Antonio. He lowered his speed and turned off the radio. Maybe his first stop should be the police station, wherever that was. But the situation was like before—Lolly was a runaway, not a kidnap victim. Maybe he wouldn't have had to say anything at all if he'd brought Laurel back to Dallas with him. Would a stepmother have satisfied her? His mind showed him a quick snapshot of Laurel flapping her light robe at him as she raced around the house, and he snorted to himself—*as if Lolly would be his primary reason for marrying Laurel!*

It didn't matter anyway. Whatever he could have done, he hadn't done it, and Lolly was all alone somewhere in San Antonio, searching for someone whom he hoped to hell didn't even exist anymore.

* * *

Hugo rose from his usual place at Laurel's feet, raised his hackles, and barked a warning just before the doorbell rang.

Thank goodness his leg cast was off.

Laurel still wasn't sure Hugo had become an indoor dog.

The backyard was fully fenced, originally to keep dogs out rather than in, but he'd looked so lonely out there that she kept inviting him inside—or maybe she was the lonely one.

The big dog accompanied her to the door and stood back politely as she opened it further than she used to, but not all the way. Betsy Simcek's outburst might have reminded someone else of how her father had betrayed the town's trust.

It was Lolly again, weeping and clinging to the arm of a tall, dark-haired girl.

The girl gave Lolly a beseeching look. "I'm Chloe, and I—I just wanted to help Lolly find her roots. I drove her to San Antonio to meet her mother and everything turned out wrong. She said to bring her here. She wants to be with you. Is—is it all right?"

"It's just fine," Laurel said as Lolly continued to weep and Hugo began to whimper in sympathy. "Come in, ladies." She used her most soothing voice, holding the screen open all the way. "We'll all sit down in the kitchen and I'll fix you some tea."

Chloe glanced toward the red MINI Cooper at the curb. "I can't stay. I have to be home by ten. Here's her purse." She handed a pink leather concoction to Laurel, and moved Lolly gently forward so that she slumped against the doorframe.

Laurel reached out to support Lolly, at the same time giving Chloe a quick smile of farewell. "Don't worry, honey. I'll take care of Lolly."

She put an arm around Lolly's waist, walked her inside, and guided her back to the kitchen, making what she hoped were comforting noises the whole way.

As soon as Lolly sat down at the big table, Hugo moved in to snuffle at the back of her knees, then moved around to lick her hand.

Lolly wiped her nose with a sodden tissue and looked him. "You—you got a dog."

"His name is Hugo, and he's very gentle."

The big dog rested his head in Lolly's lap while Laurel plopped her purse—a cute little novelty clutch ruffled like a rose—down on the table in front of her.

Lolly stroked his high-domed head. "Good boy."

He gazed up at her with soulful eyes. Laurel was becoming more and more convinced Hugo was a born therapy dog. He'd certainly been a comfort to her, and now he was trying to take care of Lolly too.

Lolly ran her hand through his thick fur and began talking. "It was so b-bad when I'd thought it would be so great, that maybe she and Dad had been in love and maybe her parents...you know, like I thought for you...but she was *old*—way older than Dad—and ugly and nasty, and sex was all she could talk about. Her name is Marguerite, and she said she'd been Dad's teacher at Bosque Bend High School...and she talked about him like he was an—an *animal*."

The tears gushed again. Hugo moved his head in Lolly's lap, reminding her of his presence while Laurel patted her shoulder. How could anyone be this cruel—and to her own child?

"She sort of cackled and said she didn't know that I would look exactly like her. Then she started talking about how she'd always been popular with the boys, especially when she started teaching, because she was so sexy. Her husband tried to change the subject, but she couldn't stop talking about sex...and Dad." Lolly looked down at herself and her face crinkled. "She was so...*awful*...and here I spent a whole day shopping for this outfit just to look nice for her."

Laurel nodded. That explained the pearl-luster one-inch

heels and the fitted pink sundress with the stylish shortie jacket. Lolly had accessorized conservatively, with a simple pearl necklace and matching pearl studs, and her Shirley Temple curls were contained behind an Alice band. It was the perfect look when meeting a long-lost mother, if that mother had any decency in her.

Lolly clenched a handful of Hugo's coat. "Her husband said she didn't mean it, that she'd taken too much medicine, but I don't care! I never want to see her again!"

The big dog gazed up at her questioningly. Laurel unfastened Lolly's hand from his fur finger by finger. "Um, how did you find her?"

Lolly grabbed a paper napkin from the holder in the center of the table and blew her nose loudly. "Her husband called me, some old guy named Bart or something. He said my—my mother wanted to see me, but I shouldn't tell Daddy because he wouldn't let me come." She sniffed. "And now I wish I *had* told Daddy, and he'd locked me in a dungeon rather than let me go meet her!"

Laurel pulled more napkins out of the holder and stacked them in front of Lolly. This might be a long evening.

"She was awful, so awful! I wish I never had a mother—I wish I'd never been born!" She looked up at Laurel. "I don't want to go home. Daddy—she said . . . she said that Daddy . . ." She reached for another napkin. "It's all so nasty!" Long, wracking shudders ran through her. She moved her head back and forth, then clutched at Laurel's arm. "I want you to be my mother, Laurel! Please let me stay with you!"

Laurel took her full in her arms. "Lolly, Lolly baby, that's okay. Hugo and I will take care of you. But let's get you upstairs."

Laurel supplied Lolly with a nightgown and sat by her bedside as she cried herself to sleep, then left Hugo on watch as she went down to the den to call Jase's home number.

"Maxie? This is Laurel Harlow. Lolly's with me. I've bedded her down for the night, but she's in bad shape. Marguerite got her to come to San Antonio and told her more than she ever wanted to know about Jase and their relationship—very explicitly. I can't understand how anyone could do something like that—and to her own child."

Maxie snorted. "It goes with the territory. But thanks for letting us know. I'll call Jase right away."

Laurel replaced the phone and wandered upstairs, soaked in her bath, checked on Lolly, and went to bed. But she couldn't sleep.

Why had Marguerite Shelton lured Lolly to her bedside, then—well—*attacked* her? She should have been happy that her daughter had come at all.

She fluffed her pillow and turned over. Odd how hard it had been to get accustomed to sleeping alone again after Jase left. She hadn't felt that way when Dave vamoosed.

She shut her eyes, but her mind refused to close down for the night. Would Maxie be the one to come for Lolly, or would it be Jase? She pictured herself opening the front door to him. She'd wear one of her nicer dresses, maybe the pale blue with the stiff pleats down the front. And heels, yes, definitely, heels. And she'd be a perfect lady, gracious and cool.

Ice-cold cool.

* * *

Jase's phone sounded off with Maxie's ringtone. He nosed to the side of the road and parked, fear and hope clutching at his heart. His finger hesitated for a second before pushing the icon.

"Jase, she's safe. She's with Laurel again."

His mind shuddered with relief. *Thank you, God. Again.*

"But I've got to warn you. Laurel said the meeting with Marguerite—it wasn't pretty. More like traumatic."

"Marguerite? Lolly actually found Marguerite?"

"Apparently Marguerite was the one who found *her.*"

"Damn that woman! What sort of game is she playing?"

"Who knows? Laurel said Lolly's sleeping now, but Marguerite really did a number on her. Apparently told her all about the your relationship with her, in detail and living color."

"Damn that woman to hell! That's why I didn't want Lolly to have anything to do with her!" Jase inhaled deeply. "I'll pick Lolly up in the morning. Right now I'm a traffic accident waiting to happen."

"Take care."

He nodded as if she could see him and signed off. After the wave of relief came the tsunami of frustration. His forehead dropped to the steering wheel. Bosque Bend? What happened to San Antonio? What the hell was Lolly doing with Laurel again? Probably giving her a hard time. That seemed to be the Redlander family's main purpose in life lately—giving Laurel Harlow a hard time.

He was exhausted. His brain felt like a worn-out sponge. Girl Child was aging him before his time. He'd better find a motel while he could still keep his eyes open.

Merging back into traffic, he stayed in the slow lane and turned in at the first neon blue VACANCY sign he saw. After a quick registration, he parked in front of his first-floor room, opened his car door, and checked out the parking lot. Mostly pickups and semis in the parking lot.

A shrill squeal of laughter cut through the dark night, and he looked around. Someone was holding a party on a balcony across the courtyard, and there was a familiar musty odor on the breeze. He grabbed his computer case and locked his car door. It had been a long time since he'd stayed in a dump like this. Definitely second-rate—not quite sleazy, but getting there. He took another look around and headed to his room, wondering if the Caddie would still be there in the morning.

With his door locked and a chair propped under the knob, he unwrapped the sandwich he'd gotten from the vending machine in the motel office and wolfed it down, hoping it wouldn't give him ptomaine poisoning. Then he stripped down to his briefs, turned on the TV, and lay back on the bedspread. The next thing he knew, the big rigs were heaving and groaning with the effort of gearing up, and a brilliant dawn was forcing its way through a broken slat of the metal blinds. Damn, he was still on top of the spread.

Not only that, but his mouth tasted like shit, and his body was slimy with sweat. Apparently the AC had conked out during the night. A quick shower would take care of the sweat, but freshening up his taste buds would have to wait till he was on the road. He wasn't going to trust his luck with one of those sandwiches again.

After drying off with one of the thinnest towels in existence, he pulled on yesterday's shirt and slacks. He hated wearing the same clothes two days in a row—it reminded him too much of when he was a kid and didn't have a choice. Fifteen minutes later he was out the door.

Whaddaya know? The car was still there—hubcaps, tires, fucking hood ornament and all. He reached for his Ray-Bans. Early morning and the sun was already blazing bright, with not a cloud in the sky. Today would be another scorcher.

Once he hit the highway, he began feeling better. Yeah, he was Jason Redlander of Redlander Properties, and he drove a Cadillac DTS and had a five-thousand-square-foot home on eight wooded acres outside of Dallas.

He looked around at the landscape on either side of the highway as he drove. I-35 had built up a lot from when he'd first come down this way. Not many cornfields anymore. Great American enterprise had taken over. And, for good or bad, some of it had been his doing.

What was he going to do with the tracts he'd just bought in Bosque Bend? They weren't very important as far as his operations went, but their development would mean a lot to the town. And to Ray Espinoza.

Ray—why hadn't Ray told him about Reverend Ed? Was he embarrassed that his brother had been molested? Maybe he was trying to be considerate of Laurel. Art Sawyer had delivered a message along that line, the old sermonizer.

He switched on the radio, but kept the sound down low. Carrie Underwood was singing about how life was short and love was sweet, and how time goes by really fast.

"Sorry, Carrie, you're hitting too close to home." He changed to another station.

Life is short and love is sweet, and look what he'd done to Laurel. Used her and discarded her, deserted her because of her father, just like Dave Carson had done. Only Dave did it because having a pederast as a father-in-law hurt his chances to get ahead, while he himself couldn't deal with the fact that Edward Harlow had deceived him, had betrayed the high ideals he himself had preached.

He settled back against his seat. Lucky for him, it was a straight shot up I-35 to Bosque Bend. The way his life was going these days, he'd probably get lost with any added complications. God, he'd tried so hard, but he'd made such a mess of it all.

How was he going to deal with whatever Marguerite had told Lolly? How would it affect their relationship? How does a fifteen-year-old deal with hearing her father was her mother's boy toy? His stomach gnawed at him as he bypassed a McDonald's. Lolly might not want to see him right now, but he wanted to be in the same town with her as soon as possible.

He'd never known Marguerite's exact age, but in retrospect, he guessed she must have been about forty, more than twice his own age. She kept herself in great shape, but then she had to—she'd been on the prowl for years, and she was her own bait. No wonder she'd changed schools so often, probably just one step ahead of discovery. Either that or the schools had decided to keep mum and moved her on. Pass the trash, as he'd heard the practice called.

He remembered how angry he'd gotten the day he caught her sitting on the tufted divan in her bedroom, adding his picture to a photo album of other guys who looked to be about his own age. There must have been twenty of them in there.

"Don't be childish, darling," she'd said, swishing her negligee to the side and looking at him slantwise. Amusement rippled in her voice. "Just think of it as my hobby, initiating promising young men into adulthood. I'm really quite good at it, you'll admit. In the future, you'll look back on me with gratitude. Now, come here and show me all you've learned."

She'd leaned back on the divan, opened her legs like a pair of scissors, and smiled invitingly, expecting the slow, skilled lovemaking she had painstakingly taught him. Instead, he'd taken her quickly and roughly, with all the anger and pain that was in him, which ultimately pleased her even more.

"God, you have passion!" she murmured, running a sharp nail down the inside of his thigh.

Marguerite obviously felt great, but he felt like a sexbot—which didn't stop him from visiting her every Monday, Wednesday, and Saturday.

His mouth tightened in anger. And now every moment of their relationship was coming back to haunt him through Lolly.

* * *

The next morning, Laurel, with Hugo right behind her, took a tray up to Lolly. After setting it on the nightstand, she drew up a chair to sit with her guest.

Lolly smiled her thanks and drank the orange juice in slow sips, but only nibbled at the toast, replacing most of it on the tray. "I'm sorry, Laurel, but I'm just not hungry."

"I understand." Hugo eyed the remains of Lolly's breakfast speculatively, but Laurel, who had become wise to the insatiable canine appetite, picked up the tray and placed it on top of the tallboy bureau. "You've had quite a shock. Would you like to come downstairs and watch a little television?"

"No, thanks."

"How about fixing your hair? You can use my equipment." The Alice band was gone, and Lolly's yellow curls were scrunched into what looked like a volcanic eruption on one side of her head.

"I don't feel like it."

Lolly didn't want to play with her hair? Things really were bad. Laurel sat down next to the bed again. "I called Dallas last night to let your dad know where you are."

"Oh."

"He'll probably come for you today."

Lolly turned her head into the pillow. "I don't want to see him."

Laurel wasn't quite sure what to say next. Actually, she had no idea whatsoever what to say next, but she wanted to keep the conversation going.

"Uh, are you cool enough? The temperature is supposed to reach a hundred ten today. You could move downstairs to the den if it gets too warm up here."

Lolly moved her hand on the sheet, actually pulling it up further, as if she was cold. "I'm fine."

"How about some lemonade? I could bring up a pitcher." Lemonade was something she could handle. Just dump the powder in water, mix it, and add ice cubes.

"No. Don't bother."

Hugo stuck his head up over the side of the bed, and Lolly reached over to scratch his ears.

"Do you have a dog at home, Lolly?"

"Maxie's dachshund."

"Tell me about him."

"He's old."

"What else?"

Lolly gave Hugo a final pat, closed her eyes, and turned over. "Too tired."

Laurel bit her lip. It had been better when Lolly was hysterical. At least then there had been some life to her.

Hugo started pacing back and forth, looking at Laurel meaningfully, so she took him downstairs and let him into the yard. Before she went upstairs to play nurse again, she equipped herself with a couple of books and a glass of lemonade. Lolly might not need anything to drink, but she did.

But after two chapters of Jane Austen, her eyelids started drooping.

* * *

The ringing doorbell sliced through the rumble of the air conditioner. Lolly muttered in her sleep, and Laurel rose slowly, trying to clear her mind.

The bell chimed again as she shut Hugo in the room with Lolly and hurried down the stairs. Probably Jase come to fetch his daughter. He, of course, would look like a model out of *GQ*, while here she was, still in the divided skirt and sleeveless white top she'd thrown on when she got up.

She opened the door.

It was Jase all right, but he looked more like an FBI wanted poster than a *GQ* model. His shirt was stained, his slacks were rumpled, and his hair was lying flat on his head. Maybe it was the stubbly jaw, but, all and all, but he looked like one of the lowlifes who hung out around Josie's Muebleria Usada.

She managed a polite semismile. "Come in."

He nodded and followed her into the drawing room, sitting on the sofa across from her, just as he had a month ago when he first stopped by. Laurel's mouth went dry. Right over there, by the piano, was where he had cornered her and taken her down to the floor after their naked chase through the house. She'd better get this visit over quick, while she could still breathe.

"Lolly is upstairs in the guest room," she began. "She went to see Marguerite in San Antonio yesterday, and Marguerite told her everything."

"That's what Maxie said." Jase's face went dark and his hand tightened on the arm of the sofa. "The worst-case scenario."

"Lolly can't face it. I think she views me as some sort of refuge."

His went grim. "Don't we all."

Was he mad at her? She edged forward and smoothed her skirt, then plunged on. "Well, anyway, Lolly's spent most of the morning sleeping and staring at the wall, and she doesn't want to come downstairs and talk to you."

"Why not?"

Laurel looked down at her hands. "She's embarrassed. Apparently Marguerite was quite complimentary and specific in expounding on your—uh—your sexual prowess."

Jase winced. "So now she's turned my daughter against me."

Laurel raised her eyes in astonishment. "Lolly's not against you. After all, Lolly's *your* daughter, not Marguerite's. She's a smart girl. Just give her a little time to sort things out."

"You sound like your father."

Laurel felt the blood leave her face. "I'm sorry."

"No, no—I meant it as a compliment." He inhaled on a shudder and stood up. "Oh hell, Laurel, Lolly and I are in the same boat: I'm trying to sort everything out too. I can't figure out how to deal with—with—" He moved his hands apart, palms up, and looked around the room as if searching for the words to finish his sentence. His eyes ended up at the door to Reverend Ed's study.

She followed his gaze. "I know. Believe me, I know."

He looked straight at her then, his eyes dark as coals. "I love you, Laurel. I always will. But we're all so much a part of everything else in our lives—Marguerite, my father, your father. Is love enough?"

"That's up to you."

His eyes searched her face. "You're always so calm about everything, so serene."

She gave a half laugh. "Do I seem that way to you?" Just because she wasn't screaming at him didn't mean she wasn't dying inside. Somewhere inside her, she'd hoped Jase wouldn't care about what Daddy had done.

"Have I hurt you?"

"Yes." What did her expect her to say?

"I'm sorry."

She affected a shrug "Like Lolly, I'll recover." No way she'd beg him to stay if he didn't want to on his own.

He glanced toward the stairs. "How long do you think it will take for Lolly to be ready to go home?"

"Maybe a couple of days. "If you want to go back to Dallas, I'll call you when she's ready." *That way, you don't even have to remain in the same town with me.*

"I think I'll stay here—at the old house. You have my phone number."

He stared at her. It was an awkward moment, as if he wanted to say something more but didn't have the nerve. Finally he stood up.

"I guess I'd better go make arrangements to stay in town."

Laurel rose from the chair to walk him out. "I'll call if there are any changes."

This whole scene was just a postscript. Lolly would leave, and Jase would too. Maybe they'd send her a Christmas card, but if so, it wouldn't reach her—she was going to be long gone. The Cokers had made an offer on the house yesterday, and her Realtor was drawing up the papers.

She gestured toward the hall closet as they proceeded down the hall. "Your suitcase and garment bag are in the closet. You probably want to pick them up."

Jase turned and his eyes met hers.

"I'll leave them here for the time being."

Chapter Eighteen

Jase stopped by Hardy Joe's for a lunchtime SuperBurger, then opened up the old house again. Damn, at this rate, they'd never get tenants.

He sat down on the edge of the bed and looked around the room, which was almost as empty as his life seemed to be. He wished Laurel were with him, but that issue had to wait till he got Lolly settled.

After reporting in to Maxie, he contacted Connie to find out what dire emergencies had come up the minute he left town. Not that Connie, who'd been with him for six years now, couldn't handle most of them blindfolded. Like Maxie, she answered immediately.

"You found Lolly?"

He nodded as if she could see him. "She's in Bosque Bend again."

"Is she all right?"

"Yeah, she's staying with a family friend for a few days, so I'll bunk down here at the old house till she's ready to leave."

Jase heard the pause on the other end of the line and realized Connie was debating whether or not to press him for more information. She knew almost everything there was to know about his family life and wasn't shy about keeping up.

"Mmmm...uh, glad to hear Lolly's okay."

He snorted to himself. Connie had decided to wait till he got back in the office so she could grill him in person. "Anything I need to be aware of in the office right now?"

"Just routine stuff, but there are a couple of proposals you need to look at. Where should I fax them to? Same address as before?"

He'd forgotten about the machine at Laurel's. "Uh, no. Send them to Craig Freiberg. His contact information is in my email. I'll pick them up from him."

"Sure thing. I'll get right to it."

Jase put his mobile on the floor beside the bed and lay back, cushioning his head on his arm.

Damn Marguerite to hell. She'd messed him up from the start. His conscience had bothered him so much after their first encounter that he couldn't sleep that night. He'd fucked a teacher. He almost confessed to Reverend Ed the next day, but couldn't bring himself to talk about anything so vile to that good man.

Jase snorted.

Yeah. *That good man.* What a crock.

He heard a cackle outside his window and levered himself up on his elbow. An iridescent grackle was playing in the neighbor's sprinkler. Now, that was a change. When he was a kid, nobody in the neighborhood—all three houses of it—gave a shit about his lawn. Now there was a parade of houses up and down the street and their yards were regularly watered, mowed, and edged. The area had become respectable—just like he had, judging by the number of people in Bosque Bend who wanted to sell him land or loan him money.

He stared at the black bird preening and flapping in the water and smiled. *Strut your stuff, buddy!* He'd risen in the town's esteem while Reverend Ed had hit rock bottom. But did Laurel have to go down with him? It wasn't fair. She hadn't known what Reverend Ed was doing behind closed doors.

Relaxing his arm, he studied the shadows on the ceiling and rubbed his jaw. He'd better stop by Walmart for a razor and shaving cream. Laurel—she'd been so cold this morning, so wary, as if she was afraid of him. Of course, he'd looked like Growler on his worst day. He probably wouldn't hear from her again until Lolly decided to come home.

But within the hour, she called and asked him to pick up a list of groceries. "I would go myself, but I don't want to leave Lolly alone. She's depressed and very confused."

He was instantly alert. "Should I come over?"

"Not yet. Give her time to think everything out. Marguerite..."

"Marguerite's a bitch."

Laurel's voice relaxed a little. "I think Lolly was expecting a more motherly type—like June Cleaver or Carol Brady. It'll take a day or so for her to handle the situation, but she will."

"I hope so. Listen, I've got to make a flyby to Walmart so, if it's okay with you, I'll get your stuff there too." He'd make his own purchases, change clothes and shave in the restroom, then fill Laurel's grocery list.

* * *

An hour later he was at her door, grocery bags in hand. "I brought a few things you didn't have written down." He hoisted the bags up for her inspection. Actually, in a frenzy of guilt, he'd doubled her order too, but he'd bet she could use the extras. At least she wouldn't starve for a while.

A large-headed mongrel poked his head out of the door to look him over. Laurel put her hand on the dog's head, which topped near her waist.

"That's okay, Hugo. This is Jase. We'll let him come in for a minute."

Laurel had a dog now? A dog the size of a small pony?

As he entered the house, Laurel took hold of the dog's collar, stepping aside so there was no chance Jase would brush against her as he crossed the threshold. Guess he deserved that. And she'd changed clothes too, into heels and a pale blue touch-me-not dress. Was she going somewhere?

"You know where the kitchen is," she said, walking back up the stairs. "Be sure to turn the lock when you leave."

He unloaded the grocery bags on the kitchen table and put everything away in the cupboards, pantry, and refrigerator as best he could.

Stonewalled. She'd frozen him out.

Well, Redlander, what did you expect? And now you're going to have a boring day working on tax statements and a lonely night sleeping on the same bed in which you made rowdy love to her just a month ago.

* * *

The next morning, after checking in with Laurel, Maxie, and Connie, he called to see if Craig Freiberg was free for lunch.

Might as well get a little business done while he was in town. And if nothing came up this evening, he might give Rafe McAllister a call.

Craig leapt at the invitation. "And I'll tell ya what, Jase—how's about I invite Rick Simcek to join us? He's overextended, and I bet you could get that property out to the west for a song if you worked him right."

"Sure." Why not? Just so Simcek kept his mouth shut about what had happened at the Bosque Club. "Where's a good place to eat?"

"How about Six-Shooter Junction? It's a new steak house that just opened up last month—Wild West theme. It's on the other side of the Shallows. Lots of branding irons, barbed wire, and old saddles. They must've emptied out every barn and tack room in the county to furnish the place."

An hour later, Jase shrugged into a light wool jacket he always kept in the backseat of his car, which gave just the right touch of class to his Walmart jeans and cotton shirt, and drove across town toward the river.

Bosque Bend was definitely on the move. A lot of trendy restaurants had set up on the far side of the river, but Six-Shooter Junction stood head and shoulders above the rest—literally. On top of its two tall stories, a big automated marquee advertised specials of the day, and on either side of the menu was an electronic pistol with electronic smoke coming out of its barrel.

Jase snorted. The Old West never had it so good. And never had Bosque Bend. "Six-Shooter Junction," as he remembered from Mrs. Johnson's fourth-grade Texas history unit, was what *Waco* was called, not Bosque Bend.

Passing under an archway of intertwined cattle horns, he

entered the restaurant and looked around. Overdone to the hilt—huge reproductions of 1800s wanted posters on the walls intermingled with leather chaps, ten-gallon hats, canteens, spurs, holsters, collections of old guns, and even a couple of bullwhips.

He stepped up to the high desk, presided over by a pretty girl in a dance hall costume. A row of well-worn saddles hung over the half wall behind her.

"I'm supposed to be meeting someone here. Craig Freiberg."

Miss Kitty scanned her list. "Oh yes, Mr. Freiberg is already here. He's at the Wild Bill Hickok table. It's a booth at the back."

Jase made his way through the crowded tables, dodging servers and busboys who looked like extras for *True Grit.*

Craig stood up to greet him. "We can be more private here, and it's not quite as noisy. The Navajos give us a little sound baffling." He nodded toward the Indian-style blankets on the wall behind him.

Jase sat down. "The Wild Bill Hickok table, huh?" He glanced at the portrait above the table. "Guess that's why we have our backs to something solid."

Craig looked at him blankly.

"Sorry. I read about it in one of Paula Marks's Western history books. Hickok was shot in the back from behind while he was sitting at an open table away from the wall."

Craig nodded and grinned. "I'll remember that." His eyes scanned the room. "No firearms allowed in the restaurant, but there are plenty of guys in here who are just as deadly."

A buxom girl with a sheriff's badge pinned to her vest introduced herself incongruously as Belle Starr, outlaw queen, and asked if they were ready to order.

Jase glanced at the menu in front of him. "It will be a few minutes. We're waiting for someone."

Belle twirled her Roy Rogers special, blew an imaginary puff of smoke off the barrel, and reholstered it. "Just fine, pod-nuh. I'll keep an eye on you."

Jase looked at Craig across the table. "I don't think I can take much more of this."

"I'll admit it's a bit over the top, but the food is good and—" His eyes lit up and he started to stand. "Hey, there's Rick!"

Simcek fit right into the setting. In fact, he looked like the Hollywood stereotype of an Old West gambler, with his three-piece suit and black boots. Jase knew vests were coming back into style, but in high summer? The guy must have ice water coursing through his veins.

He cut through a band of waitpersons gathering around a big table in the middle of the room, where a boisterous group of men wearing pastel-colored cardboard cowboy hats were launching into "Happy Birthday." Jase stood up for the ritual handshake, remembering that the psychologist had told him it originated as a means of proving to a stranger that one was unarmed.

"Redlander. Good to see you again."

Simcek may not have anything in his hand, but his teeth gleamed like daggers. His jacket parted as he sat down, revealing a belt chased in silver. Jase was surprised that a Colt .45 wasn't hanging from it.

Belle Starr reappeared to take their drink orders. Craig went for Bud Light, Jase asked for Shiner, and Simcek inquired about wine.

He would.

Leaning back against the booth partition, Simcek favored Jase with a smile. "Craig tells me you're interested in local real estate."

"It's my business." Jase handed him one of his cards, as if ol' Rick hadn't already looked him up on the Internet and checked him out with everyone he knew.

An apprentice cowgirl, Annie Oakley, delivered the drinks. Simcek took a quick swig of red wine and continued his spiel. "I've done a fair share of real estate investment myself."

Jase knew that was supposed to elicit an inquiry from him, but he wasn't biting. Not yet. He took a long, slow swallow of beer. Let Simcek sweat a little. He'd checked Rick out too, and knew his financial affairs were even more precarious than Craig had indicated.

"Yeah. Seems that lots of people are buying land. Guess it's a national pastime." He opened his menu. "Hey, this T-bone looks great!"

Simcek took the hint and picked up his own menu.

Jase kept the conversation light, contributing an anecdote about going hunting with his best friend, making sure to casually let it drop that Doug was a state senator. It was a funny story, mostly true, and Jase would have sworn Simcek was drooling.

This fish was hooking himself.

At last the meal was finished, and Annie Oakley had hauled away the dishes. Jase looked at his watch, making sure Rick could see it was a Rolex.

"Hey, didn't realize it was so late." He moved as if to stand up. *That should set Rick off.*

It did. In fact, Jase had the impression the man would have

leapt across the table to keep him there. "Before you go, Red-lander, I've got a piece of property you might want to consider. I'll give you a real good price on it."

There it was, out in the open. Jase relaxed back into his chair. "I don't know. I've already bought the Anderson tract."

"This is even bigger. Lots of potential."

"Where?" As if he didn't know.

"West of town. It's an up-and-coming area."

Yeah, it was, but Simcek didn't know quite how up-and-coming.

"Well, Craig showed it to me last month, and I suppose I could consider it...if the price is right."

Simcek's relief was obvious. "I'll get some figures to you this afternoon."

Jase shrugged.

Play it cool, Redlander. It's not in the bag yet.

"Just drop them off with Craig, and I'll look at them when I have time." Actually, he wanted to ice the deal as quickly as possible, before the news got out about the retirement community Ray wanted to build in the area.

He moved the conversation onto the Baylor Bears' chances at winning the conference this year, his stock topic for Bosque Bend. Within a few minutes, Simcek announced he was late for an appointment and had to leave.

Jase watched him thread his way through the tables and gave Craig a one-sided smile. "Probably running off to get those numbers down on paper while he still has me willing to look at them."

* * *

Jase stayed at the table for another round of drinks.

Three beers with lunch. He hadn't done that in a long time, but he was courting Craig for a job with Redlander Properties. It would mean a fair amount of travel up and down I-35, but it would also mean a lot more money than First National was paying him.

Finally he stuck a tip under the ersatz oil lamp and rose to go. The restaurant was emptying out now, but the birthday boys were still celebrating under a giant chandelier made of deer antlers. Jase thought he recognized a couple of his old high school teammates as he and Craig passed by the table.

Kevin Short, wide receiver, was apparently the honoree, but where was Kev's old partner in crime, Gordie Gilliam, quarterback extraordinaire? Gordie was a nasty piece of work. Probably skipped town years ago.

Jase spotted a door labeled GENTS on the near wall and realized the beer was getting to him.

"Wait a second, Craig. Gotta make a pit stop."

* * *

The restroom was strictly utilitarian, a white-tiled relief from all the kitsch outside the door. At the sink, a slender, vaguely familiar-looking man was washing his hands, his lime-green party hat on the counter beside him.

Damn. Wouldn't you know it—number one on Jase's do-not-call list—Gordie Gilliam.

Ol' Gordie had grown up in the west end, just like he had, but somehow he'd made himself everybody's favorite, in part by his constant jibes at Growler Red's oafish son.

Gordie glanced at Jase, wiped his hands on a paper towel, and walked unsteadily toward him.

He hadn't aged well, Jase noted. Gordie's bright blond hair had thinned, retreating several inches from his high forehead, and his skin seemed blotchy. He'd gained weight too, mainly in his belly. Golden Boy had been a heavy drinker back then, and apparently still was.

Gordie gave him a halfway smile. "Jase." He slurred the *s*.

Great. Gordie was soused. Should he ignore him or walk out?

"Kev told me you were in t-town. Heard you've been doing Dave Carson's ex-wife." He balanced himself against the wall. "What's she like? Always—always had a fancy for that p-piece of honey myself. All lah-di-dah on the—the outside—but I bet she's a real tiger once you get her in the sack." He winked at Jase. "With a father like hers was, you know she's no better than sh-she needs to be."

Jase gave Gordie a stare that should have turned him to stone.

"Miss Harlow is a friend," he replied in a soft, controlled voice. "I have a great deal of respect for her. In fact, my daughter is staying with her at present."

Turning his back on the most popular boy at Bosque Bend High School, he began to push the restroom door open. He could wait till he got back to the house to relieve his bladder.

Gordie snarled and came after him, clutching at his arm.

"Damn you, Redlander, don't you s-snub me! You think you're s-so high and mighty, with Rick Simcek and that new guy at the bank sucking up to you! But I remember you when you were in the free lunch line at Westside Elementary because your father drank up every cent he made! And I remember when they ran you out of town because you did the job on the best English t-teacher that Bosque Bend High School ever had!"

Jase paused at the open door and looked back. "Watch it, Gilliam. I could head drop you so hard your skull would crack open and what's left of your brain would leak out."

Bosque Bend's favorite son retreated toward the far corner of the restroom, but not without getting in his final volley.

"You're trash, Redlander! And as far as I'm c-concerned, you can have that Harlow bitch! You belong together! Two of a kind!"

Red flames erupted in Jase's skull and he started walking toward Gordie, his arms hanging loose like Growler's did when he was planning to take somebody down.

At the same time, the restroom door banged open and Craig Freiberg rushed in. "Let me handle this, Jase! He's drunk!"

Jase watched in surprise as Craig grabbed Gordie's arm, twisted it behind his back, and frog-marched him out the door. Then, breathing deeply for a minute, Jase willed himself to relax.

Who would have ever guessed Craig, the stereotypical ninety-seven-pound weakling, had it in him?

After using the urinal, he walked over to the sinks and looked in the mirror at his flushed face, realizing, not for the first time, that he looked like his father. He lifted his hands and looked at his palms. He, who'd played it so cool when swimming in Richard Simcek's shark tank, had nearly gone ballistic when dealing with a prawn like Gordie Gilliam. God, he'd wanted to grind Gordie into the concrete floor, but even if Craig hadn't appeared on the scene, he knew he wouldn't have done it.

And that's what made the difference between him and Growler.

* * *

Laurel settled Lolly on the davenport in the den, moved an ottoman between them, and shuffled the cards. Blackjack was a great way to pass the time—short, fast, and easy to learn. It was surprising Lolly hadn't encountered it before, but she attended an exclusive girls' school and, judging by what she'd casually let drop, had learned plenty of other things she shouldn't have.

Lolly cut the deck and gave her hostess an apologetic glance. "I'm really sorry to be such a bother, Laurel."

"That's okay, honey," Laurel said. She dealt a card to Lolly, facedown, then to herself, faceup. "Hey, I've got a ten, and I already feel lucky."

"Don't trash-talk me, Laurel Harlow. You're just trying to get me rattled."

Laurel placed a second card on the table in front of her. "Darn, the novice catches on quick. And here I had you pegged for an easy mark." She slid a card off the top of the deck, a deuce, as Lolly picked up her cards and scrutinized them.

"Give me another card. I mean, *hit me.*"

"You lose ten points if you don't get the lingo right."

"Yeah, sure."

Laurel gave Lolly a second card and drew a five for herself. It was iffy, but she'd hold pat. The deck was fresh, and it was anybody's guess what would come up next.

Lolly's forehead creased as she studied her hand. Laurel figured that meant her cards added up to somewhere around fifteen, so she was surprised when Lolly asked for another card.

"Hit me."

"Are you sure?"

Lolly nodded.

Laurel handed her a third card, confident that her opponent would go bust.

Instead, Lolly spread her hand on the table—a six, a nine, a three, and another three. "Twenty-one!"

Laurel gaped at her. "Talk about beginner's luck. I want a rematch."

"Sure thing, sucker."

Lolly's eyes sparkled, and her color was high. Laurel smiled to herself. Who would guess that blackjack would do the trick? She picked up the deck and dealt Lolly a card, herself a card, Lolly a card, herself a card.

Looked good. She had a deuce on the table and a jack in her hand.

Lolly looked at her hand, then at Laurel. "How in the world did you ever, like, learn to play blackjack? I mean, your dad was a preacher and all."

"You might say I fell in with low company. My friend Sarah taught me."

"Sarah. She's the one who wrote you that poem. I thought you said you'd lost track of her. Hit me."

Laurel gave Lolly her third card and picked one up for herself too, a five. "I found her again. In fact, she's the one who helped me get Hugo."

The big dog looked up from his nap at the sound of his

name. Lolly smiled at him and reached out a bare foot to massage his back.

"Dad has a big dog at the ranch."

"What kind?"

"Doberman—well, sort of. He always gets his dogs from shelters."

"Do you miss him?"

"The dog?"

Laurel laughed. "Your dad. Hit me again."

"Yes." Lolly picked up her card. "Oh, damn, an eight. That makes me twenty-five. What do you have?"

"Seventeen again. Would you like me to call him? You could talk to him on the phone."

"No. I want to talk in person, but I'm not ready yet. I need to think things out." She gathered the loose cards and handed them to Laurel. "I mean, let's face it—my mother is a pervert. She's like those pathetic women you see on TV all the time who get sent to jail for having sex with kids." Lolly shuddered. "It's so disgusting. How am I supposed to live with something like that?"

Laurel took a deep breath and put the deck on the side table. Playtime was over. "The same way I do. You just keep going."

Lolly's head whipped around. "What do you mean? Did your mother...?"

Laurel shut her eyes for a moment, trying to summon the courage. Could she say it? She'd told Jase. Maybe it would be easier this time around. "Not my mother. My father."

Lolly nearly came off the couch, bumping into the table in the process and scattering the cards across the floor.

"But your father was a pastor!"

"And Marguerite Shelton was a teacher." Laurel shrugged. "Pastors can do all sorts of horrible things. So can teachers. They're just like everyone else."

"Laurel, what—what did your dad do?"

"He took advantage of some of the teenage boys who came to him for counseling. He—he molested them."

"My dad?"

"No. It happened later, after your father left town."

"But...your father was good. Dad called him his moral compass."

Laurel started picking up the cards. "Daddy was a good person in many ways, but he was bad in other ways."

"I don't understand."

"I don't either." She stacked the cards and put them on the table again.

"Did you love him?"

She looked Lolly in the face. "I idolized him. I wanted to be exactly like him."

"Do you still love him?"

"Most of him." She covered her eyes with her hand.

Lolly touched her arm in sympathy. "I'm sorry I brought it all up, Laurel. You've been so kind, putting up with me. I don't want to upset you."

"You needed to know." And maybe she needed to hear herself say it too. Her father had been two people, and she had the same dilemma Jase did—how could she separate the good that was in her father from the bad?

* * *

Lolly returned to the den after lunch and lay on the couch, listening to her iPod, watching TV, and making notes on a tablet Laurel had supplied.

Laurel popped in and out of the room between cleaning up the kitchen and tending to laundry, then settled down in the big leather armchair with Jane Austen.

Lolly looked up. "I want to talk to Dad."

"When do you want him to come over?"

"Tomorrow morning." She looked at her notes. "That'll give me time to decide what I want to say."

Laurel held the phone out to Lolly, but she drew back.

"Couldn't you talk to him for me, Laurel?"

"No, honey. You need to do this yourself."

Lolly swallowed as though it hurt and reached for the phone. "Okay."

She pushed the buttons carefully and out the phone to her ear. "Dad? I'm ready to see you... No, not tonight... How about tomorrow morning, maybe about ten?"

Chapter Nineteen

Laurel's nerves tightened like piano wires as she and Lolly walked down the stairs to wait for Jase.

A vision flitted through her mind of Jase throwing himself at her feet, begging forgiveness for abandoning her, and promising they would never part again. She gripped the newel post to steady herself. Why was she torturing herself with fantasies like this?

Lolly glanced over at her. "Laurel, you okay? You looked sorta funny there for a second."

"No problem. I'm just fine." Not really. She was more uptight about Jase coming to the house than Lolly was.

God help her, how could she make herself stop loving him?

"Well, I like the way that dress fits you, and peach is your color."

Laurel glanced down a herself. "This old thing?"

She knew the sleeveless shift looked good on her, and she hoped it would remind Jase of what he was missing, but she didn't want to be too obvious about it. "I've had it for ages."

They walked into the drawing room and took seats across

from each other, Laurel on the ribbon-back chair that should have long since been hauled off to the antiques man, and Lolly on the sofa.

Lolly glanced down at her tie-dyed tee. "Thanks for loaning me the clothes."

"Sorry the hem and waist had to be safety-pinned." Lolly not only had the tiny waist of an hourglass figure, but she was also a good eight inches shorter than the skirt was designed for.

"I'm just glad you have stuff I can wear. I hope you burned that awful pink dress."

"It was really rather pretty, honey. I'll get it cleaned and send it to Dallas for you, if you want."

Lolly shuddered, causing her curly doggie ears to bounce. "No. Donate it to Goodwill or something. I usually never wear things like that anyway. It's just that I thought..."

"I understand."

"I'm keeping the necklace and earrings, though. Aunt Maxie gave them to me last Christmas."

Laurel nodded, rising as she heard a car in the driveway. "I think your dad's here. Are you ready?"

Lolly caught a quick breath. "Maybe."

"You'll do fine." One thing was for sure: It was hard for her to face her father, but she wasn't backing out.

Laurel walked into the hall, opening the front door as Jase stepped onto the porch. Her heart fluttered. In jeans and long-sleeved shirt, he looked like the quintessential western hero. And judging by the mud he was scraping off his boots, he must have been checking out properties in the morning sun again. How Texas could you get?

He swept his hat into his hand and took off his dark glasses as he stepped into the foyer. His eyes checked out the shadowy hall. "Where's the canine?"

"Hugo? I thought it would be better for him to stay outside while you and Lolly talk." Laurel closed the door, but didn't bother to lock it.

His voice dropped to a near whisper. "How's she doing?"

"A lot better."

They entered the drawing room. Back straight, hands folded, feet together on the floor, Lolly was the picture of a prim, well-mannered schoolgirl. She moved over to give Laurel room beside her on the sofa, pointedly leaving the ribbon-back chair across from them for her father.

Laurel sat down and nervously ran hand across the wale of the sofa. This was where she and Jase had sat and talked before his appointments with Daddy and, more recently, where he had sat when he came to the house looking for Lolly. Every time she looked at the sofa, she thought of Jase. For her own peace of mind, she'd better ship it out on consignment quick.

Jase didn't say a word, just gazed at his daughter with an easy smile on his face.

Laurel gave him points. He was playing it smart, waiting for Lolly to take the lead. It was hard for any child to be slapped in the face with a parent's sexuality—as she very well knew—but Lolly should know that her father was a lot more than Marguerite Shelton's prize stud.

Lolly swallowed hard and leaned forward.

"Dad, I have something I want to tell you." Her eyes were glued on her father's face, and her voice was strong and determined.

"First of all, I want to apologize. I will never, *never*, question your judgment again. You tried to warn me off looking for my mother, and you were right. I should've listened to you. And I shouldn't have gone to...to San Antonio." Her chin quivered, but she recovered quickly. "I thought it would be wonderful, like on TV. You know...the reunion specials." Lolly moved her hands in demonstration. "But it was horrible, and I don't...I don't ever want to see that woman ever again."

The backyard resounded with barks.

Lolly raised her voice to be heard over the noise. "Second. I know I should feel sorry for her because she's sick or something, but she's mean and nasty, and I didn't like the way she talked about you."

Hugo cut loose with a second fusillade of barking.

Jase waited for the tumult to die down before he spoke, his voice calm and cadenced. "I love you very much, Lolly, and I wish things had been different for you." He opened his hands in a gesture of inadequacy. "I wish you'd been welcomed by Marguerite and that she'd told you what a lovely young lady you are. I wish she'd told you that she regretted not seeing you grow up and would keep up with you from now on. But things don't always work out the way they should, and you have to move on and forge ahead."

Lolly's shoulders hunched, and her voice became very small. "But I'm afraid, Dad...I'm afraid I'm going to be just like her—like Marguerite."

"No way, baby. You're not like her and you're not going to become like her—ever."

Lolly's face squeezed up into itself. "You don't understand, Dad! It's in my DNA! She said I was like...like her clone! It's—it's as if I were bitten by a vampire! I don't have a choice!"

"No, honey." Jase's voice went even softer. "We all inherit physical traits from our parents, maybe some psychological traits, but it's up to us to decide the way we live our lives. You're someone new and wonderful—not your mother and not me either. Marguerite may have given birth to you, but you're your own person, just like we all are."

"You're just saying that!"

He looked down for a second, then right at her. "I *know* so." He inhaled deeply. "I've never told you much about my father, have I? Maybe I should have."

"Well, you said that after he got out of the navy, he became a pro wrestler, then he retired and ran a tavern called Beat Down. His name was Roland, but everyone called him Growler because his larynx had been injured when he was in the ring. I wrote that into my roots report. The other girls thought he was, like, supercool."

Jase's grimaced at the idea of teenagers finding Growler Redlander cool.

"There's more to it than that, honey—a lot I didn't tell you."

His eyes wandered aimlessly around the room. He'd buried Growler Red years ago, and he didn't like having to dig him up again, but Lolly needed to have a more balanced picture of him.

"Growler was kicked out of the navy for brawling. When he was on the wrestling circuit, they billed him as the Meanest Man in Texas—and he was. He ran a rough bar, sold liquor to underage kids, and knocked me around when he was drunk. I went to school hungry more days than not and started working odd jobs when I was nine to support myself. If it wasn't for your Aunt Maxie, he probably would have drowned me in the Bosque." He grimaced. "I didn't want to be anything like him, and, God help me, I'm not."

No, he hadn't wanted to be like his father. He'd modeled himself on Reverend Ed, but he wasn't going to say that. "Children don't have to be like their parents. Everyone has a choice."

Lolly's eyes went big and round. "He didn't *feed* you? He *hit* you?"

Jase nodded. "Beat me within an inch of my life more than once." He touched his chest. "You remember that big scar I've got here?"

"The one that goes all sorts of directions? You told me you got it from falling off your bike when you were in middle school."

"Honey, Growler had long since tossed my bicycle in the Bosque. I got this little souvenir when he came home drunk one night and couldn't get in because I'd locked the door." He grimaced at the memory. "Let's just say he wasn't happy with me."

Lolly leapt up from the sofa and rushed over to throw her arms around his neck. "Oh, Daddy. I'm so sorry! I love you so much! I'll never leave you again!"

He hugged her with one arm, gently, because he knew she would be shy about physical contact with him for a while. "Well, not for a long time, I hope."

"I wish I'd never found out about Marguerite. I just want things to be like they were—you and me and Aunt Maxie." She glanced back at the couch. "And Laurel, of course."

"We can't turn back time, Lolly. What's done is done. Now, let's sit back down and talk about where we're going to go from here, so Laurel doesn't feel like she's got a couple of raving lunatics on her hands."

Lolly returned to the sofa. "Was Marguerite really your teacher, Dad?"

"Yeah. English lit—*Oedipus Rex, Romeo and Juliet,* all of that."

"How did it happen—I mean, you and her?"

He wanted to be truthful, but only to a point. Lolly didn't need to know the unsavory details he'd confessed to Laurel. "I think she filled a gap for me. Marguerite gave me a lot of attention, but it was the wrong kind of attention. I was too young to be carrying on that intense a relationship with anybody, especially a woman more than twice my age."

"Was she pretty back then, Dad? Her picture in the annual looks kinda sneaky."

Jase laughed, remembering the sensuously seductive woman Marguerite had been. "She was dazzling, sweetheart. All the boys at Bosque Bend High School were crazy about her."

Lolly cocked her head to one side. "And she, like, chose you over all of them?"

He didn't like the direction this conversation was taking. "She shouldn't have chosen any of us, Lolly. What happened between her and me was wrong. Adults shouldn't be sexually involved with kids. I was seduced—not forced—but it was still wrong."

Lolly's voice turned soft. "Dad, do you hate me because I wanted to find my mother, because I met Marguerite? Are you sorry I was born?"

He'd always known she'd ask that question eventually, and the answer came easy. He risked lifting his hand to smooth her tumbled curls.

"No, baby. I love you and I'll always love you." His voice choked. "You're the best thing that ever happened to me."

* * *

The phone rang and Laurel hurried off to answer it. The Realtor had told her he might be calling today.

"Hello? Hello? Is this the Harlow residence?" Not her Realtor's friendly chirp. It was an old man's voice, breaking with agitation.

"Yes," she answered, ready to slam down the receiver at the first obscene word.

"I need to speak to Jason Redlander. His aunt gave me this number."

"May I say who's calling?"

"An—an old acquaintance. Please, get him for me. It's very important. Please, Laurel."

How did he know her name?

She replaced the receiver and returned to the drawing room. "Someone wants you on the phone. He sounds odd. And he knows my name."

Jase sighed. "Probably someone with another farm to sell. Sorry, but that's it for Bosque Bend."

He rose and headed to the den.

Lolly looked toward the hall. "Who do you think is calling Dad?" she asked Laurel.

"I don't know. I know I've heard the voice before, but—"

Hugo started barking again.

"Lolly, we can't talk over that racket. Would you mind if I let Hugo in the house?"

"Of course not. I love Hugo."

Laurel headed toward the kitchen door, picking up a doggie treat on the way. Jase would probably return to Lolly in the drawing room before she got back, but that was okay. Father and daughter could use a little private time together.

It took a few minutes, but Hugo finally allowed a rawhide

bone to lure him away from the albino squirrel who was running across the yard. As Laurel led him down the hall, he pushed open the door to the den, and she had to pull him back by his collar before he could bother Jase, who was apparently engaged in a deep conversation about a woman who was sick—Maxie? Maybe the caller was a doctor.

Then why did he identify himself as an old acquaintance?

Suddenly she remembered the voice—school bells and Friday morning announcements, the pugnacious twang of the principal listing deeds and misdeeds of the previous week.

Bert Nyquist. Come to think of it, Lolly had said Marguerite's husband was named "Bart or something," and she knew Bert Nyquist had left town soon after Marguerite Shelton. Who would have ever guessed they'd end up together?

Footsteps sounded in the hall. One look at Jase confirmed Laurel's worst fears.

He took a seat on the sofa beside his daughter and lifted her hand. "Lolly, we need to discuss something very serious. I just talked to Marguerite's husband. He says she won't last more than a day and she wants to see you one last time."

Lolly backed away into the corner of the sofa, her eyes opened wide in alarm. "I don't want to go, Dad! I don't even care if she's dying! She might say something even worse to me this time!"

Hugo rose from his place by Laurel's side, stretched, and ambled over to lay his head in Lolly's lap. She massaged his ears, then looked deep into his comforting eyes.

"Her husband was nice, though. He apologized all over the place and said she was overmedicated, that the doctor had upped her oxycodone the day before and she wasn't thinking straight, that she was talking wild." She cocked her head. "He's sort of sad, I think. He must love her a lot."

The immensity of death hovered over the room.

Hugo licked her hands. Lolly stroked his back, then returned to his ears again. "If she's dying, this would be my last time to see her." She looked into the dog's eyes. "Maybe..." She turned toward her father. "Dad, if I go, will you go with me?"

"Of course, honey. I'll be with you all the way."

"I don't mean you'll just take me there. I mean will you go inside the house with me and stay with me the whole time I'm in the room with her?"

"Yes."

She turned to Laurel. "And you'll go too?"

"If it's all right with your father."

Jase gave her a look that could have jump-started a three-day corpse. "I'd like to have you there."

Lolly continued to stroke Hugo. "And if she starts saying ugly things to me again, I can leave, right?"

Jase nodded. "If she starts saying ugly things to you, we'll *all* leave."

Lolly took a deep breath and stood up. "Okay. I'll go, then."

* * *

Ten minutes later, Jase had them all in the car and they were on the road.

God only knew what awaited them, but he wanted Lolly to have closure—as his shrink would have said—so here he was, driving hell for leather down I-35 again, taking Lolly to the very person he'd tried to protect her from her whole life. And he'd thought he was through with Marguerite Shelton once and for all sixteen years ago, when they got caught. The scene had played out like an X-rated soap opera.

He'd finished up his job at the car wash Wednesday night and driven over to her neighborhood, parking his car in an alley a block away from the little stone house.

He usually came in about eight and left around midnight, but Wednesdays were difficult to manage because of school the day before and the day after. So instead of enjoying a light doze before leaving, he fell heavily asleep.

The bulldozer roar of a familiar voice had cut through his dreams. Had he conked out in American history again? Struggling to consciousness, he realized the overhead light had been turned on and he was lying in bed bare-ass naked with his English teacher while his high school principal was standing in the doorway, jabbing his finger at him and yelling himself red-faced.

"You son of a bitch! You'll pay for this!"

Gloriously nude, Marguerite, her full, buoyant breasts swaying, rose from her side of the bed and walked nonchalantly to the chair to reclaim her negligee. "Keep your voice down, Bert. Let's not give the neighbors any more to talk about than they already do. Remember your position."

"Damn my position! What's that snot-nose kid doing here?"

Marguerite smiled. "What's he doing here?" she repeated in her husky, sexy voice. "The same thing you do, Bert, but he does it better."

Nyquist stopped dead, his mouth flapping, his angry eyes popping fire.

Jase swung to the side of the bed and Marguerite looked over at him. "I think you'd better go now, Jase. I'll take care of this."

He'd stumbled out of bed, grabbed his jeans and jerked them on, Mr. Nyquist glaring at him the whole time. His shirt and shoes were somewhere around the room, and there was no telling what had happened to his underwear and socks. He'd pushed his feet into his sneakers without tying them and poked his arms through the sleeves of his T-shirt as he headed out the back door, feeling like a kid who'd been kicked out of the house once the adults came home.

To top it off, his fucking truck wouldn't start. Some jerkface had stolen his distributor cap, and he'd had to leave the pickup in the alley and hike home in the dark.

Chapter Twenty

Laurel watched the familiar scenery roll by. They'd passed the San Marcos outlet malls already. Next would come Wonder World, then on to New Braunfels—Schlitterbahn and Landa Park, where she and her college friends would go tubing during spring break.

Soon the gravel pits lined up against the Balcones Escarpment were in sight. Not much longer.

Jase glanced at her in his rearview mirror. "Laurel, you okay back there?"

"Just fine." *Not really.* When she was a child, the drive to Alamo City seemed interminable. Today it was taking no time at all. Of course, back then, the zoo was their goal—lions and tigers and bears. This time, there was no telling what awaited them at the end of the line. Marguerite could lash out at Lolly again, and Jase's reunion with her wasn't going to be any picnic either.

Jase swerved off the highway toward Broadway Street, then turned onto a residential street south of Brackenridge Park, near the old stable at the west gate of Fort Sam Houston.

Lolly played nervously with a loose curl. "Dad, do you know how to get there? Do you know the address?"

"Nyquist gave me directions."

Laurel looked around as he turned onto a cross street. As long as she remembered, this neighborhood had been a mixture of grand old homes interspersed with more modest ones, but the last time she'd visited San Antonio, most of the mansions had been cut up into apartments, and the smaller houses were going downhill. Now the area seemed to be on an upward trajectory. Several of the larger homes had been refitted as single-family homes and were sporting fresh paint, new roofs, and well-tended lawns.

Jase turned again, and Lolly pointed to a small stucco house with a browned-out lawn centered by a dead palm tree. "That's it."

Laurel's eyebrows went up. She would have expected the glamorous Marguerite Shelton to have ended up in one of the mansions. This house, with its railed porch, reminded her of Jase's house from sixteen years ago. A rusty old glider sat to the left of the door, and a dead plant in a black plastic nursery pot was on the right. No dog, though.

The car eased to a stop. After a moment's awkwardness while the three of them got their land legs under them, Lolly glared at the house, took a deep breath, lifted her chin, and marched up the buckling, broken sidewalk. Laurel caught up with her, and Jase fell in behind. They walked up the steps onto the porch. Venetian blinds were drawn tight against the summer sun, and a dingy hand-lettered sign instructed visitors to knock rather than ring.

Jase took the lead and rapped lightly on the sagging screen door, waited a minute, then knocked so hard that the door reverberated against its frame.

Maybe Nyquist had taken Marguerite to the hospital for

her last hours. No—someone was working the lock. A bald, sallow-faced man Jase would never have recognized as Bert Nyquist in a thousand years held the screen open for them. The man must be in his sixties, but he looked more like eighty. The Bert Nyquist he remembered had been a typical ex-coach—big and beefy. This Bert Nyquist seemed to have lost several inches in height and about fifty pounds in muscle.

"Come in, Jason. Do come in. I didn't realize you would get here so soon. Come in, come in." His pale eyes darted back and forth as if he was having trouble counting his visitors. "It's so good of all of you to come." He smiled nervously at Lolly. "And Miss Redlander—thank you for returning. Marguerite wants to see you again so much, so very much."

Laurel extended her hand. "I'm Laurel Harlow, Mr. Nyquist. Lolly asked me to accompany her."

"Yes, yes. Laurel Harlow. Such a nice girl. I recognized you immediately. You look just the same."

Jase studied his former principal as he shook Laurel's hand. Somewhere along the line, Bert Nyquist had lost his belligerent edge. Life with Marguerite Shelton must have been pure hell. Why had he stayed?

"Margo's awake," Nyquist cautioned, "but she's very weak, very weak. She may not be able to open her eyes, and she probably won't say anything, but she'll know you're here."

He led them past the bathroom, toward the rear of the house. Jase recognized the layout as a standard reversal of his old homestead in Bosque Bend, with the bedrooms and bath on the right instead of the left.

Laurel seemed to hang back as they entered Marguerite's room, deferring to him and Lolly, but Girl Child grabbed her arm and urged her forward. "You promised you'd stay with me."

In contrast to the rest of the house, Marguerite's bedroom was well lit and airy. Big, old-fashioned windows opened onto the backyard and driveway, and a mat of vines draped over the chain-link fence next to the house filled the air with the scent of honeysuckle.

This room—bright, cheerful, and immaculately clean—was obviously where all of Bert Nyquist's attention was concentrated. Prints of paintings by van Gogh and Renoir—rented from the public library according to the discreet gold tags affixed to their frames—hung on the walls, and an arrangement of glads and daisies had been placed on the bureau. In the center of the far wall, a motionless figure lay on an adjustable hospital bed.

Nyquist walked over to the bed and, despite the warning thump in his chest, Jase followed.

He studied the woman in the bed for some resemblance to the sexy siren he remembered from sixteen years ago, but if Bert Nyquist looked eighty, Marguerite looked at least a hundred. Her frail head, propped up on two plump pillows, seemed transparent to the skull, her hair was white and wispy, and the sockets around her eyes were deep as death.

Nyquist scurried to his wife's side and leaned across the folding table laden with pill bottles and medical supplies.

"Margo, honey. Margo, she's here. Just like you wanted, Lolly is here. Your daughter came back."

He motioned for Lolly to come forward. "Take her hand and tell her who you are."

Lolly walked to the bed step-by-step, obviously ready to bolt at the least provocation.

"Her hand, her hand," Nyquist prompted.

Lolly lifted the frail hand on top of the bedsheet.

"Tell her who you are."

"I'm Lolly, Lolly Redlander."

The sherry-colored eyes opened. A slight frown creased Marguerite's forehead. She wet her lips in slow motion and tried to speak.

Jase tensed. *If a single foul word comes out of that woman's mouth...*

Marguerite finally found her voice, and, in the silence of the room, her hoarse, labored words were audible to everyone. "I'm sorry..." Her sunken eyes seemed to be trying to memorize Lolly's face. "Forgive me."

Jase relaxed. Marguerite was trying to make amends.

Lolly's voice was barely audible. "It's—it's okay."

Marguerite nodded and released Lolly's hand, but those beautiful, horrible eyes were searching the room now.

"Jase," she whispered, fastening him in her gaze.

He moved forward like an automaton.

Nyquist gave him a look of appeal. "Take her hand. Remember to take her hand."

Jase looked at the flesh-covered talon, clenching and unclenching in agitation.

"Please, Jase...," Marguerite forced out, struggling to articulate. "Forgive..."

A knot inside his chest dissolved and he warmed her cold, skeletal hand between both of his. "You gave me a wonderful daughter. That's all that matters now."

Marguerite attempted a smile, and her eyelids closed. Lolly started forward, but Bert Nyquist was in front of her. He adjusted the sheet around his wife's shoulders and caressed her cheek.

Lolly raised a hand to her mouth. "Is she—?"

Nyquist shook his head. "No, just very tired. She needs to rest now."

He led them back to the living room and shook Jase's hand.

"Thank you, Jason. And thank you for bringing Lolly. Marguerite didn't know what she was saying when Lolly came before, and she wanted to set things right." Nyquist's chin trembled. "Margo and I—we wronged you, Jason. You've been better to us than we deserved."

"Is it cancer?" Laurel asked quietly.

Nyquist nodded. "Marguerite taught until two years ago, when she started going downhill fast. She's been through it all—chemo, radiation, surgery, acupuncture—everything. There's nothing for her now but painkillers. The doctor said she'll probably go within the next twenty-four hours."

Jase frowned, trying to understand. "And you've taken care of her all this time?"

Nyquist looked at him in surprise. "What else could I do? I love her."

Jase's his mouth opened, but he couldn't think of anything to say. Marguerite Shelton must have led Bert Nyquist on a merry chase. Apparently he'd quit his job and deserted his family for her, but Jase doubted she'd ever given up a thing for him, least of all her string of young lovers. Yet none of that mattered to Nyquist.

He loved Marguerite whether she was faithful or not, in sickness and in health, till death did them part. There was no getting around it. For all his sins, Bert Nyquist was a better man than he.

Grabbing a card out of his billfold, he scribbled his cell phone number on the back of it, and handed it to Nyquist.

"Call me if you need anything. *Anything*. I mean it."

* * *

The three of them walked to the car in silence. Lolly slid into the back and lay down on the seat, so Laurel sat up front with Jase. The air was thick with melancholy. The past had caught up with the present, Laurel realized, and they all had a lot to think about.

Jase was like a carving in stone, occasional movements of his arms and head being the only indicators that he was more than part of the car's driving mechanism, while Lolly had wedged herself in the corner next to the door, wrapped her arms around herself, and closed her eyes. Maybe she slept, maybe not.

A few miles out of San Antonio, thunder began to roll around the sunny sky. Laurel searched the horizon and saw that a row of clouds was bunched up to the south, their bottoms darkening. As she watched, a few tentative rain drops descended, dancing delicately on the windshield. Minutes later, the wind picked up and the clouds darkened to purple.

Jase switched on his wipers as the storm hit.

Laurel tried to stay alert, but she felt totally depleted. The tension that had been building ever since Lolly appeared on her doorstep a second time had dissipated, and she was exhausted. The last thing she remembered was the Selma town hall, the old Spanish-style one that was a Hooters now, its bright pink stucco overpainted with blue-gray.

She woke up when Jase turned off I-35 at the familiar Bosque Bend exit.

After pulling into her driveway, Jase retrieved a collapsible umbrella from his center console and walked her to the porch. "We have to talk, Laurel," he said, then glanced back at the car as a long bolt of lightning lit up the sky. "But not right now. I've got to get Lolly home."

* * *

The flowers arrived the next day—a dozen red roses. The accompanying card read *Love, Jase.*

What did that mean? Was he apologizing for leaving or thanking her for taking care of his daughter? Or did it mean that... *no*, she refused to go there. Her future was built on reality, not romantic daydreams. She arranged the roses in a vase and left it on the kitchen counter.

* * *

Four days later there was still no follow-up from Jase. It was as if Jase had disappeared off the face of the earth. Despite herself, Laurel tried to call him, but a steely-voiced woman who declined to identify herself said that the ladies of the household were indisposed and Mr. Redlander was unavailable.

She replaced the phone in its cradle and moved into the kitchen for a cup of coffee. This was going to be her last day in Kinkaid House. She'd consigned her bedroom suite, the portraits, and the family mementoes in storage, and her personal belongings were either stuffed in her luggage or on their way to Brownsville. The only things she'd saved out were her traveling outfit for tomorrow and the clothes she had on—an old pair of jeans and a loose Mexican-style blouse.

The doorbell rang. Probably her Realtor with yet another paper to sign. Luckily she'd just put Hugo, who didn't like the man, in the backyard to enjoy one last day of squirrel chasing.

She threw the door open and stepped back in surprise. "Kel!"

He smiled. "May I come in?"

She stepped aside. "Of course."

Why did this polite young man make her so nervous, so self-conscious? It wasn't as though she was attracted to him—or was she? For all his soft voice and innocent eyes, there was something seductive about him. He wasn't as tall as Jase, of course, and had a lighter build, but there were real muscles beneath that thin T-shirt.

Stepping inside, he glanced at the luggage heaped by the door. "Pen told me you've sold the house and you're leaving town tomorrow."

Laurel edged over to the stairs and anchored her hand to the newel post. "Yes, I've got a new teaching job in Brownsville. That's in South Texas."

He gave her an amused smile. "I know where Brownsville is. I'm Texas born and bred. That's the reason I got the part in *Garner's Crossing*. Benjamin is a role I can really sink my teeth into."

He walked slowly over to her, stopping just close enough to make her feel uncomfortable. Was he coming on to her?

"Do you have to leave tomorrow? As I remember, school doesn't start till the last week of August."

"I thought I'd get an early start."

He picked up her hand and stroked a slow, gentle line down her index finger from knuckle to nail, watching her all the while. "From what I saw at the Bosque Club, you need a vacation."

Laurel sucked in her breath. His voice was a love song, and her whole body was tingling with the melody.

His sank into a hypnotizing whisper. "You're a beautiful woman, Laurel. How about spending a couple of days with me in California? I'd take good care of you, and the job will still be there when you get back."

She drew back. She'd been wrong—he'd be perfect for the part of Erasmus—a heartless charmer who'd sold his soul to the devil.

She gave him a stiff smile and withdrew her hand. "Thanks for the offer, but I don't think I'm cut out to be a California girl. Now, if you'll excuse me, I still have a few more things to pack."

She walked to the door and opened it.

* * *

Early the next morning, she made her final trip out to search the bushes near the door for the *Retriever*.

A loud, carrying voice called her name from across the way—Sarah's mother. Mrs. Bridges waved a large tan envelope at her, and, without even scuffing her white espadrilles, stepped into the street, walked to the center line, waited for a car to pass, and proceeded to the curb.

Laurel focused on the familiar face, surprised at how happy she was to see her. Wearing a black-and-white print boatneck blouse over white slacks, Marilyn Bridges looked as sleek and stylish as always. Her wide ivory bracelet matched the flat hoops dangling from her ears, and her auburn hair must have been sprayed within an inch of its life.

Sarah's mother hadn't changed much in the past few years. Maybe her hair had a more metallic glint to it, but her skin, in contrast, seemed much smoother than Laurel remembered—almost rejuvenated. Botox? An acid peel? From what she'd seen on TV, everyone was doing it.

She gave Laurel a one-armed hug. "I noticed the FOR SALE sign is down. Hope you got a good price."

What a relief to be able to talk honestly with someone. "Enough to pay off the last of Daddy's obligations and have some left over. The new people are buying most of the furniture too, but I've put my bedroom suite and a few other things in storage." Things like Jase's clothes, which he never did pick up. "The rest of it, when you get right down to it, is just wood, paint, and fabric."

"Who bought it? The Cokers?"

Laurel regarded her with in awe. "How did you know?"

"I saw some people in the yard one day last month when you were gone, and went over to get acquainted with them. You won't believe this, but Clovia and I were both Delta Gams at University of Texas."

Laurel smiled. Typical. Sarah's mother knew the universe.

Mrs. Bridges lifted the envelope against the morning sunlight. "Could we go inside, Laurel? I have something for you."

"Sure." Laurel opened the door and led her guest into the kitchen so they could sit at the big round table and visit.

Mrs. Bridges glanced around the room. "It must be hard on you—to sell the house, I mean. You've lived here your whole life."

Laurel shrugged. "Actually, Kinkaid House has become somewhat confining. Besides, I have a new job."

"Yes, I've heard. Brownsville."

"What about the dog?"

"Hugo is going with me. I'm hoping for a house, so he can have a yard." It was strange how attached she'd become to the big guy. She wasn't sure she'd ever be comfortable around small, yappy dogs that wanted to jump on her, but her stolid, well-behaved Hugo had become an essential part of her life.

"Well, you're leaving at a good time. It's going to be pretty dull around here now that Johnny Blue has left town and the Fassbinder twins—Karen's divorced again—can't make fools out of themselves chasing after him anymore. I guess we'll all have to be satisfied with watching Dolph Jr. sneak across the street every morning for his rendezvous with Phyllis Pfluger."

Laurel looked at her in surprise. "Johnny Blue? The one who starred in that outer-space doctor show a while back, *Quark Kent, MD*? He was in Bosque Bend?"

"Didn't you know? He was the good-looking young man staying with Pendleton Swaim. I thought I saw him at your house. You didn't recognize him?"

"He told me his name was Kel." And he hadn't been at all like the brash young ensign who healed any and every malady with what looked like an oversized TV tuner, and, on the side, protected the universe from an increasingly preposterous parade of invading baddies.

Mrs. Bridge's brow tried to pucker. "I think Kel is his nickname. I heard Pen Swaim calling him that once when they were out in the yard."

Laurel nodded to herself. Kel was a total chameleon—and predatory, to boot.

Mrs. Bridges lowered her volume as if someone might overhear. "Sweetie, I know it's none of my business, but what about Jason Redlander?"

Laurel shrugged. "Jase is gone. Every time he looked at me, he saw Daddy."

"But Laurel, your father was more than just the worst part

of himself. I'm not excusing what he did to those boys—it was unforgivable. But we should also remember all the good things he did."

"Jase didn't feel that way."

Mrs. Bridges opened the tan envelope. "I have a little gift for you before you leave. It's a collection of photographs from when you and Sarah were little. Our families had such a good time together." She pulled out a picture. "Here you two are at the third-grade Christmas program. Remember?"

Laurel nodded. "Sarah and I wore dresses exactly alike and told everyone we were identical twins. We didn't understand that meant we had to look alike too."

Mrs. Bridges laughed. "Our little princesses," she said, spreading the photos out on the table. "I had copies made of all our pictures that have you or your parents in them." She pulled a larger photograph out of the pile. "Look at this one. We're in our backyard for Fourth of July."

Laurel's heart lurched as she picked up the photo Mrs. Bridges had laid in front of her. How happy Mama looked. And Daddy, usually so serious, had a wide smile on his face.

The two families always celebrated the Fourth with a barbecue in the Bridgeses' backyard. Sarah's father tended to the cooking while Daddy set up the fireworks. One year a Roman candle had landed on the Bridgeses' roof. Mama and Mrs. Bridges screamed, and then Daddy carried the garden hose up a ladder to put out the fire.

It was the best Fourth of July ever.

"I'll take them with me, Mrs. Bridges," she said, sweeping the photos back into the envelope. "And thank you."

Marilyn Bridges had given her father back to her—the best of him.

* * *

Laurel turned off the last air conditioner. The taxi she'd ordered from Waco would be here at two o'clock to take her to the airport.

Too bad she couldn't drive to Brownsville, but her little Escort needed extensive engine work before she could have driven it all the way to the Valley, so she'd donated it to a charity for children with terminal illnesses.

She'd emptied the refrigerator, the pantry, and the cupboards yesterday afternoon and cleaned the kitchen too, then visited every room in the house for the last time, even the storage area on the third floor behind the bedrooms. She'd expected to give just a quick look-see to her own room, bare to the floorboards now, but the second she'd stepped inside, memories of Jase flooded her mind.

Jase, sprawled naked on her bed and looking up at her with his dazzling smile and wicked eyes. Would she ever get over him?

She glanced at the bulging carry-on and the two wheeled suitcases she'd placed beside the front door. Hugo's travel kennel, the biggest one Walmart had in stock, rested beside them. Everything else—her books, the rest of her clothes—should have reached Brownsville yesterday.

Looking around the foyer, she suppressed a shiver. The house had become a stranger to her. Even the piano, which she'd had tuned last week, seemed to have developed an eerie echo.

Did she hear a car turn into the driveway? Looking out a front window, she saw a red Mercedes come to a halt halfway up the drive. A flame-haired woman got out of it.

Sarah!

Laurel raced to the door with an excited Hugo right behind her. "Your mother didn't tell me you were coming!"

"She didn't know. I wanted it to be a surprise, and Mom tells all. Now call off your monster dog, unlock the frickin' screen, and let me in."

"Drama queen! As if you're afraid of Hugo!"

Sarah patted the big dog's head as she entered, and received a frantic tail wag in response. "I would be if I were up to no good. I think he's twice as big as when you got him."

"He eats like a horse."

"Good thing you've got a new job, then." She caught Laurel in a quick embrace. "Nearly didn't make it. The maid ran late, Keith got called in for emergency surgery, and the traffic was hell. Had to get these to you, though." She handed Laurel a tinfoil package. "They're chocolate chip cookies. The airlines don't serve anything but peanuts anymore."

Laurel laughed and unrolled the tinfoil enough to peek at the cookies.

"I'm not sure they'll last until I board." Delivering herself from temptation, she stuffed the package in the top of her carry-on. "Come into the kitchen and sit down. I can't feed you anything, but the refrigerator still makes ice cubes."

"Cold water sounds perfect." Sarah led the way down the hall and took a seat at the oak table while Laurel filled two paper cups from the faucet, then added ice.

Sarah guzzled her water, sighed, and leaned back against the chair. "How have things been going lately? Like with the good citizens of Bosque Bend?"

"You wouldn't believe it, but my relationship with the town seems to be a lot better now that they all know I'm leaving. On the other hand, Pendleton Swaim keeps trying to get in touch with me about the Kinkaid genealogy, probably for his new book about Garner's Crossing—as if I'd help with that—and I seem to have acquired a shadow." Laurel swirled her ice in the cup and took another sip. "His name is Craig Freiberg, and he shows up wherever I go."

"Mom's never mentioned him."

"He's a banker, one of Jase's contacts. I even ran into him yesterday in the hallway of the title company when I went in to sign the final papers. I tried to laugh it off by saying something stupid about a man on the move having to get around, but all I did was make him nervous. He has one of those really pale complexions, and he turned red as a beet, blurted out that he came to the title company all the time for First National, then made a run for it." She laughed. "It was funny, Sarah. He acted like he'd been caught spying on me."

"Well, just so he doesn't follow you into the ladies' room." Sarah went to the sink to refill her cup with water. "Hey, what's with the roses?"

"I haven't figured them out, but they're from Jase."

"Was there a card enclosed?"

"Just *Love, Jase.*"

"That's pretty powerful, Laurel. Sounds like somebody's trying to get a message across to you."

Laurel shrugged. "Too late. I've got a one-year contract with Brownsville. Anyway, I think he got his message across pretty darn well when he left town after he learned about Daddy." She glanced at the wall clock. "I'd better get a move on. The cab should be here right about now. I'm supposed to be at the airport by four to go through security."

"Relax. Taxis are always late."

A honk sounded from the driveway.

"Oops. My bad." Sarah rose from the table. "I'll go tell him you're coming."

Laurel looked around the foyer one last time. The stairwell seemed naked with the family portraits gone—and they'd been the very devil to get down too, as if they didn't want to leave the house.

Sarah came back in. "I moved my car into the parking area and told the cabbie you'd be out in a minute. Anything I can help with?"

"Would you ask him to carry the kennel to the cab for me?" Laurel snapped a leash onto Hugo's collar.

Sarah nodded. "Yeah. I'll go tell him you need help." She raced out of the house and returned immediately, followed by an older man wearing a shirt with the cab company logo embroidered above the pocket.

He made a motion as if tipping his hat at Laurel, but backed off at the sight of Hugo. "That dog bite?"

"I'll be handling him. Just put the kennel in the cab, and I'll get him in it. There won't be any problems." At least she hoped there wouldn't be any. She'd had Hugo sleeping in the thing for a week.

"Whatever you say, lady." He hefted the big cage and was out the door.

Laurel picked up Hugo's leash and grabbed the handle of her carry-on. "Well, I guess this is it."

Sarah took charge of the remaining suitcases, one in each hand, and pushed the screen door open with her shoulder. "I'll carry these things out. You'll have your hands full protecting the driver from your big, bad dog."

"Thanks. I'll just be a second." She checked herself out in

the hall mirror. Most people wore jeans when flying, but she still had enough of Mama in her that she'd opted for a nice summer dress.

But before she could step outside, Sarah had burst back in, her eyes wild, her cheeks flaming.

"He—he took your luggage from me and put them in the back of his car!"

"The cabbie?"

"No. It's Jase! Jase Redlander is out there, and he's arguing with the cabdriver, trying to pay him off and make him leave!"

Dropping her carry-on to the floor and handing off Hugo's leash to Sarah, Laurel hurried outside.

Jase's Cadillac was parked at the curb, blocking the driveway, and, just as Sarah said, her two big suitcases were sitting in his open trunk. She charged toward him. "Jase, give me back my luggage and go back to Dallas! Why are you here?"

Jase turned and gave her the dazzling Redlander smile. "Because I love you."

"No, you don't!" She glared at him, wishing her hair was writhing Medusa snakes that would turn him to stone. "You just thought you did because you admired my father! And now that you know about Daddy, you don't want me anymore!" She started toward the driveway. "I'm getting my stuff out of your car and putting it in the cab!"

Hugo barked from behind her, and Laurel realized Sarah had followed her outside.

Jase followed after her. "Laurel, can we talk inside?"

She stopped and turned on him. "No, anything you have to say, you can say right here!"

The cabdriver stepped forward. "Need me to call the cops, lady?"

"Don't you dare!" Sarah yelled, advancing toward him. "Let them work this out for themselves! Put that cell phone away, or I'll sic Killer Dog here on you!" She snapped Hugo's leash, and he growled.

Jase reached for her hand.

"Let go of me, you—you Neanderthal!"

But he reeled her in, and his voice dropped into a whisper as he leaned close to her ear. "That wasn't what you told me to do when we were rolling around on the front room floor."

She tried to keep her voice steady. "Biggest mistake of my life."

"Laurel, I'm begging you to listen." He loosened his hold. "I was an ass. I admit it. I think I was in shock after that night at the Bosque Club. It took me a while to process everything, but I finally got it all together when we were in San Antonio. It's like what I told Lolly—your father, my father—good or bad—they don't matter. You and I are what matter. Love *is* enough—that's what it's all about, and I'm lucky enough to love the most wonderful person on the face of the earth."

"Look, folks," the cabdriver called out. "I don't know what's going on here, but I'm charging you for every minute that car's blocking the driveway."

Jase turned on him. "You'll get your money! I'm not done yet!"

His eyes clouded as he turned back to Laurel. "I apologize for not keeping in touch, but it's been a hard couple of days. Lolly held out till we got home, then went to pieces. She's going through some pretty intensive therapy right now, and I have to be part of it. The next afternoon, Marguerite died, and I grabbed a red-eye to San Antonio to help Nyquist with the funeral arrangements—he was a basket case. When I got home the next day, Maxie was sick with the flu. The office hasn't seen me in four days, and I may be contagious even now."

Laurel gasped. "Is Maxie okay?"

He nodded. "Her fever is down, and Lolly is mother-henning her under the supervision of a nurse who must have been an army general in her past life."

He took her hands in his. "I love you, Laurel, and I want you to be my wife and Lolly's mother, to make a home together. I was hoping to roll down the highway in a gilded coach pulled by eight white horses to claim the hand of the princess of Bosque Bend, but I had Craig keeping an eye on you for me, and when he told me you were heading out, I realized I'd waited too long. Instead of Prince Charming, you've got Jase Redlander, who drove down I-35 like a bat outa hell because he didn't want to lose his last chance with you—although, to tell the truth, I would never have given up. If you'd made it to Brownsville, I'd have been right behind you."

The cabdriver stepped forward. "Hey guys, I'm behind schedule."

Sarah and Hugo advanced toward him across the yard. The cabbie scrambled into his car and locked the doors.

Laurel gave Jase a considering look. Her voice was quiet. "Jase, I've signed a contract with the Brownsville School District. Besides, now that everything is on the table, I think you and I need to get reacquainted with each other. For now, pay off the cabbie, drive me to the airport, wish me well, then visit me in Brownsville when you can. We'll take it from there."

After a long, appraising look, he raised her hand to his lips and pressed his lips against her palm. "Agreed."

Epilogue

She'd accepted his ring at Christmas. Now, a full year after Jase had shown up at her front door searching for his missing daughter, she stood inside the glass patio door of his sprawling, single-story home in North Plano, bouquet at the ready, waiting for her cue to walk out onto the patio and down the crushed granite path across the lawn to the pavilion Maxie had arranged to be erected beside the pool.

Jase's house was full of modern luxury—the ultrahigh ceilings, the newness of everything—and she reveled in it. No stern grandparents governed her from the stairway walls. No heavy mahogany furniture demanded its monthly polish. She was *free, free, free* . . .

And what she chose to do with that freedom was love Jason Redlander with her whole heart.

She reached up a hand to be sure that the strong-scented lilies Lolly had woven into her elaborate chignon were still secure, then smoothed the skirt of her gown. The lustrous silk was gathered at each shoulder, then crossed down to an intricate inset waistband, below which it had been wrapped and draped to the side to continue the Grecian-style line of the bodice. Gramma's pearl necklace was looped four times around her neck, and long, ornate pearl earrings dangled from her lobes. They'd belonged to one of her wild great-aunts, she seemed to remember.

Something old, something new, something borrowed, and something blue. The earrings were old, the dress new, the necklace borrowed, and the "blue" was her lacy garter, supplied by Sarah, who'd driven up from Austin that morning.

She glanced over at her honor attendants. Sarah was stunning in a brilliant green creation with an asymmetrical neckline, while Maxie had chosen an aqua-beaded outfit, and Lolly was prancing around on frighteningly high heels in a purple minidress she'd picked up in a high-priced teen boutique. It was cute, stylish, and very short. Jase disapproved of it, which was probably why Lolly had chosen it.

Sarah peeked through the drapes. "Jase is walking through the crowd, chatting everyone up," she reported. "God, Laurel, he should wear a tux every day of the week. That man is gor-gee-ous!"

Lolly joined her at the window, pressing her nose against the glass. "They're all sitting down at the tables now, and Dad's finally stopped glad-handing. He's making for the pavilion. I think I see Pastor Richter and Uncle Doug too."

The opening chords of the wedding march sounded, and Maxie picked up her bouquet, slid the glass door open, and stepped outside. Lolly and Sarah followed her at ten-second intervals.

Laurel stepped out onto the patio, her heart beating so loudly that it set up a jarring counterrhythm to Wagner's wedding march. Blood sang in her ears. This was it. She moved down the path between the pool and the flotilla of tables set out on the lawn. Thank goodness Maxie had arranged to board Hugo and her elderly dachshund for a couple of nights. Sir Frederick was more of a sedentary kind, but Hugo would have had a field day with all those helium-filled silver balloons bobbing from the backs of the chairs.

Sarah took her bouquet, and Jase walked forward to join her in front of the pastor. Bless Jase for arranging for Maxie's minister to perform the ceremony. Laurel knew she'd never have felt truly married in a civil ceremony. And Jase knew that too.

Once the pictures had been taken and the marriage license signed off on, the party began. The caterer's crew popped open champagne bottles, lifted the lids off bins of food on the long tables, and set up a serving line. Loosening his bow tie and unbuttoning his jacket, Jase led Laurel into the thick of the crowd.

The first person he introduced her to was his best man, who'd arrived at the house from Austin a scant fifteen minutes before the ceremony. Laurel had seen Doug Shumate on television and knew he was a powerhouse politician, but up close and personal, his charisma was overwhelming.

"It's a pleasure to meet you at last, Laurel," he announced in a mellifluous baritone as he took her hand. His eyes twinkled, and his teeth gleamed, and his brown hair caught gold highlights from the setting sun. "Known Jase for ages."

She couldn't help but back up a little.

A snappy brunette nudged him in the ribs. "You're scaring her, Doug. Turn it down a notch."

He laughed and reached over to give the woman a brief hug. "You always know how to bring me back to earth, Connie. If you ever want to leave Jase, there's always a place in my office."

Then came the deluge, everyone trying to talk to her at once. Most of their guests—Jase's politician friends, business associates, and longtime employees—were strangers to her, but she was happy to see that Ray Espinoza, Art Sawyer, Mrs. Bridges, Craig Freiberg, and Rafe McAllister had been able to make it.

Ray reported that he had arranged for a large, splashy wedding announcement in the *Retriever*, and Art made a big ceremony out of handing over an engraved silver bowl from the city council. Before Marilyn Bridges left, she got Laurel aside and presented her with a subscription to the Dallas Symphony Orchestra and a congratulatory card signed by everyone on the block, even the Carrolls. And Jase opened an envelope from the Bosque Bend Museum committee certifying that Rafe McAllister and Craig Freiberg had contributed a ten-by-ten block of pavers to be inscribed with the names of Jason and Laurel Kinkaid Redlander.

To top it off, Pendleton Swaim, uninvited, had FedExed them a Kinkaid genealogy.

As the evening deepened, the guests wandered around the pool with cake plates and champagne glasses in hand.

Sarah was among the first to leave. "I've got to make it back to Austin tonight because Keith has surgery tomorrow morning," she explained. "I wish I'd been here in time to arrange a bachelorette party—you know, maybe a visit to a male strip club for comparison purposes." She winked at Laurel, giggled, and saluted Jase with a flute of champagne.

Another hour, and all the guests had gone. Jase and Laurel remained outside even after the caterers had packed up, Maxie and Lolly had left, and the outside spotlights were dimmed. Resting her eyes on the dark woods beyond the yard, Laurel leaned back against her husband and breathed in the silence and the starlit night. His arms embraced her shoulders, warming her in the cool night breeze.

It was full dark now. The smell of honeysuckle was on the heavy summer air, votive candles in silver dishes floated aimlessly in the pool like enchanted lotuses, and the helium balloons glistened in the moonlight. Further back, she could see the silver-bowed hurricane lamps that marked the edge of the turf to warn guests away from the dangers beyond, and above the lamps, thousands of tiny lights strung in the wide-armed oaks extended the horizon into the stars.

She could almost pretend they were lovers from long ago, united at last on some supernatural plane of existence. In a way, that was true. So many years lay between them, years of pain and denial. Years that they had the rest of their lives to make up for.

Jase bent his head to her ear. "I love you, Laurel Elizabeth. I love you and always will."

The oaks rustled in the distance, and the lights hanging from their branches shimmered like a million fireflies.

"And I love you, Jason Redlander—forever and ever."

* * *

Laurel was totally sated and totally exhausted. Her libido was all used up. They'd taken the edge off with a quickie on the family room couch as soon as they'd gotten back to the house, and then there'd been a couple of replays once they reached the bedroom. Good thing they'd packed their bags early for the Disney World honeymoon.

She glanced over Jase's shoulder at the genealogy chart he'd picked up from his nightstand. "What about that Pen Swaim thing? Do you think you and I really are distant cousins?"

"Could be. Swaim lays out a good plot for the book he's working on now. An outlaw gang attacks your Auntie Barbara and her architect as they're eloping. Snake-oil salesman Asa Redlander scares the bad guys off before they kill her like they did her lover. Asa's squaw nurses Barbara back to health—except for the brain damage, of course—and six months later, Barbara gives birth to a full-term baby girl who grows up to marry Asa's son when she's old enough—or maybe when she isn't, judging by the number of generations the Redlanders managed to squeeze into one hundred and thirty years."

He replaced the chart on the nightstand, and Laurel felt the mattress sink beside her as he leaned over to caress her bare belly. She moved her arm to give him better access, but didn't have the energy to respond to his gentle touch.

He ran his fingers back and forth across the pearls that looped around her neck and down her body.

Laurel tilted her head in consideration. "The weird thing is that Pen saw some woman on that TV antiques show who had traced her family history back to the jade pendant, but couldn't go any further. Her got in touch with her and worked everything else out."

Jase's hand followed the path of the necklace down the valley between Laurel's breasts. "Jade is okay, but I prefer pearls."

Her shoes had come off on the way to the bedroom, the lilies Lolly had woven into her hair were now crushed beneath them on the sheets, and her beautiful wedding dress was now just an ivory heap beside the bed. But the pearls—the long necklace and the heavy antique earrings—had remained.

Jase lifted the rope and started winding it in a lazy circle around her right breast. He was playing with the pearls, she realized, decorating her breast.

His voice deepened. "Tell you what, babe. You'll never want to give these sweet beads back to Lolly when I'm through with them."

Laurel watched him maneuver a second row within the first, but she was too tired to react. "They're hers, Jase. I just borrowed them back for the wedding."

"We'll see." He circled her breast one more time, then another.

Laurel took a deep gulp of breath when the edge of his thumbnail touched her nipple. "I'm glad Doug was able to make it to the wedding. It was n-nice to meet him."

Jase smiled at the stutter in her voice. *Good.* But he wanted more than awareness from her. He wanted her burning hot.

He twisted the rope and moved to her left breast, laying down a careful first row. "Nearest thing I have to a brother."

Laurel's head was swimming. The familiar heat was racing through her veins. Jase carrying on a seminormal conversation with her while he wrapped her breasts in pearls was incredibly erotic, like a French movie she'd seen, where the heroine's sophisticated lover paused a couple of times for a puff on a cigarette while he was making love to her.

He ringed her breast again, and she could feel her passion rekindling with each pearl he nudged into place. She tried to rise, but he pressed gently down on her shoulder.

His voice was guttural. "Not yet. Artist at work." He circled

Laurel's tightening nipple a third time, then draped the last of the pearls down to her stomach.

Damn, she is beautiful, like a pagan love goddess. He gazed at her for one long moment, at her pale, luminescent skin, her gray eyes turned to smoky slate, her swollen lips, the long strand of beads, the barbaric pearl earrings. He swallowed hard and his eyes narrowed. Taking her face in his palms, he covered it with soft, tender kisses, working his way down across her throat to her beaded breasts, sucking first one turgid nipple, then the other until they gleamed with moisture.

Laurel gasped as the air-conditioning hit her warm, wet nipples, slamming her sex drive into high gear. Her breath came in quick, shallow pants. She was on fire.

"*Jase...*" Her voice was a feverish whisper. She grabbed at his arms, to pull him closer, but he pressed on her shoulder again.

"Not yet, baby. Trust me."

He unwound the pearls one round at a time, rolling them against her tender skin, then let them fall in a loose line down toward her belly.

"*Jase...*" Her voice was thready. She couldn't keep up her end of the conversation. She didn't even remember what they'd been talking about.

His hand pressed against her shoulder yet again.

"Not yet," he repeated.

He moved the line of pearls down to the darkness at the juncture of her legs. A rush of desire rang in her ears and thudded along her veins. "*Now*, Jase, I'm ready! Now! Now! Now!"

His voice was a soft whisper. "That's the idea, baby." He separated her weeping folds with one hand and lifted a single shining pearl with the other. "This is for you, Laurel, only for you."

He moved the bead against her, pearl on pearl until, with a high-pitched, sobbing cry, she spasmed into his waiting arms.

Then, with the hard line of the pearls still rolling between them, he entered her.

And they were one.

LOOK FOR JEANELL BOLTON'S NEXT NOVEL

WHERE THE HEART LEADS

Available Spring 2015

Chapter One

Moira drove into the asphalt lot across the street from the yellow brick building and swung her six-year-old Toyota into a marked space.

Panic crawled up her spine.

It's just another audition, she told herself. *You know the routine—you've been auditioning since you were a kid. No big deal. You either get the part or you don't, and if you don't, there's always another audition around the corner.*

But this wasn't Hollywood or New York—it was small-town Texas, and she wasn't a kid trying out for a role as the main character's tagalong little sister anymore. She was an adult, twenty-six years old, and she was auditioning on a three-month trial basis to be herself, Moira Miranda Farrar, with no safety net whatsoever. The Bosque Bend Theater Guild had hired her to direct their upcoming production, and if she could pull it off, they'd keep her on permanently.

And if they didn't? No, that wasn't an option. She *had* to keep this job. Everything depended on her success, not only for her, but also for her family, just as it had since she was four years old, when Gramps had discovered she had a freakish memory and a gift for mimicry. With his disability pension stretched to the limit, she'd become the major support of the family, although Kimiko, her mother, occasionally sent a check to help with expenses.

She draped her arms on the steering wheel and stared at the gold building gleaming in the bright October sun. It looked like an old high school, but Pendleton Swaim, her contact with the theater group, had called it the town museum and said the board met there.

She glanced at her stylishly oversized wristwatch. She was early, which gave her time to get the lay of the land before she met with her new employers.

She'd been hired, sight unseen, at the recommendation of Johnny Blue, who'd starred in the last show she'd worked in before she'd met and married Colin all those years ago. Well, it wasn't entirely sight unseen. All of America had watched her grow up as an assortment of third-banana little sisters on TV sitcoms, and then, when she was too old for the bangs-and-pigtails roles, as Johnny's robot assistant. Of course, now that he'd moved on to films, Johnny was on the showbiz A-list, while she wasn't worth a Z.

She rubbed the scar on her upper left arm and compressed her lips into a determined line, then opened the car door, stood up, and smoothed the skirt of her belted safari-style dress. Even now, a member of the theater board might be looking her over from one of those dark windows in the yellow building. She glanced down at her sensible pumps. Was she dressed conservatively enough for a small Texas town?

Just in case, she adjusted her portfolio under her arm, segued into her no-nonsense persona, and, despite there being no traffic, waited for the light to turn before she marched across the street. As she walked up the wide front steps of the yellow building and through the imposing front door, her heart pounded with fear and excitement, just like it always did before a performance. There was no turning back. Now to locate the meeting room before anyone arrived.

According to the directory on the wall beside the stairwell, she was on floor two and the Bosque Bend Theater Guild met on the third floor, in Room 300. She hurried up the stairs, passing a group of schoolchildren wielding plastic branding irons, who were being herded along by a trio of anxious-looking adults.

The door was locked, but she could see through the window in the door that there was an elevated stage at one end of it. She nodded. The room was an appropriate place for a theater guild to meet, and it would be a good place to practice too. The performances, as Pen Swaim had told her, would be in the big auditorium in the center of the building.

Since she had a little extra time, she might as well spend a few minutes checking out the local scene. She walked back down to the second floor, looked around, then wandered into a display room. One wall featured an interactive history of the Indian tribe that had been the area's first settlers, but grimy-looking fossils dug out of the Bosque riverbank dominated the space. Moira moved on to the next room, which featured rotting saddles, wicked-looking branding irons, and ambrotypes of squinty-eyed cowboys, all donated, according to the legend beside the display, by Rafe McAllister of the C Bar M Ranch.

She checked her watch again. Eight minutes till blastoff. A leisurely stroll up the stairs and she'd still be five minutes early, the perfect statement for a new hire who was ahead of the mark.

She turned the corner toward the front of the building and collided with a fast-moving freight train.

A flame-haired man the size of a building, who was holding a strawberry blonde child by the hand, steadied her with a light touch on the arm, his eyes twinkling. "Didn't mean to mow you down, ma'am. We're makin' an emergency run for the ladies' room."

Ma'am? He was calling her *ma'am?* Like John Wayne and Gary Cooper in the old westerns? Did small-town Texans really do that, address all unknown females as *ma'am?* Holy Hollywood! Did Red have a horse hitched up to a parking meter outside?

Moira tried to smile back—her real smile, not the clenched-teeth grin she'd been taught to use for character shots—but Big Red was halfway down the hall before her lip muscles could get themselves coordinated. She stared after him in awe and wonder. Maybe there was more to Bosque Bend than a last-ditch job and a boringly tame history museum after all. Red had the most beautiful eyes she'd ever seen.

Red and the little girl stopped in the middle of the hall.

"Come with me, Daddy. I don't want to go in there by myself. It's big and dark and honks like an angry elephant." The child was dancing with purpose, and the high pitch of her voice echoed off the hard walls.

Red bent down to her. "Delilah, Daddy can't go in there. It's only for girls."

"Then I'll go with you to the daddies' bathroom, like when I was little."

"That's not gonna fly, baby. Tell you what. Daddy will stand right here by the door, and if you yell, he'll come a-chargin' in and rescue you."

Moira approached them, making sure her smile was properly adjusted this time. "May I help? I was just about to use the restroom myself." She turned to the child. "Delilah, my name is Moira."

The little girl gave her a hard stare, then broke into her own smile. "Okay. I like you. You're pretty."

Which made Moira want to suggest that Red hustle his daughter off to an ophthalmologist ASAP. Having grown up on the Hollywood scene, she knew what *pretty* meant—tall and willowy, blond and busty, languid and lovely—none of which she was. On the other hand, while short, small-breasted, and hardworking might not win any beauty contests, it was very good at opening restroom doors. Delilah charged into the nearest stall, talking the whole time.

"I have three aunts and three uncles. Aunt Rocky comes to our house to take care of things, but she really lives with Uncle Travis in his house. Aunt TexAnn and Uncle Wayne live in Austin most of the time because she makes laws that tell people what to do. Aunt Alice and Uncle Chub don't talk to us 'cause they're mad at Daddy. Oh—I have Aunt Sissy too, but she's not a real aunt. She works for Daddy in his office."

"Um. That's nice." Moira had no idea how many aunts or uncles—make that half aunts or half uncles—she herself had. The only siblings she knew of were her half sister, Isis; and her half brother, Arne, but there were probably more in the woodpile. Her mother's exes did tend to get around.

Delilah flushed the toilet and scurried out of the stall as the pipes trumpeted. It sounded just as she had said, like an elephant on the rampage. Moira helped her wash her hands, then escorted her back to her father.

Red shot her a slow, sexy smile. "Thanks, ma'am. Delilah's

not happy with the restroom, but it came with the buildin'. This place used to be Bosque Bend High School before they built Eisenhower Consolidated to pull in all the kids at this end of the county so we could play in the Interscholastic League A-division."

She looked at him blankly.

He laughed, a rumbling basso. "It's football, ma'am. Bosque Bend lives for football, like all the rest of Texas."

His drawl was getting deeper. "Ma'am" was two syllables now, and the first syllable of "football" rhymed with *boot*. "Like" was pronounced *lahk*, and the *o* in "town" sounded like the *a* in *cat*. Her old vocal coach would have had a field day with Big Red.

Delilah wound her arms around his leg. "Daddy, I'm tired. Can we go home now?"

The overhead light sparkled off the gold wedding band on Red's left hand as he lifted his daughter into his arms. "I've got to stay in town to take care of some business, sweetheart, so I'll have to take you over to Aunt Sissy's. You can play with Baby Zoey and take a nap."

Delilah pulled away from her father, and her lower lip pushed out. "Don't wanna stay with Aunt Sissy and play with Zoey! Wanna stay with the pretty lady!"

Red looked at Moira and raised an eyebrow briefly, like the reverse of a wink, and his deep voice turned to velvet. "Honey, I'd like to stay with the pretty lady too, but I can't stay with either of you right now. Got some work to do." His gorgeous eyes focused on Moira, and his voice took on a warm lilt. "Maybe the pretty lady could meet up with me later this evenin' over drinks and we could get better acquainted."

Moira gave him her best arctic stare. "I don't think so." Pivoting on the heels of her sensible black pumps, she marched back down the hall.

What a creep! Making a pass at her in front of his innocent child. She wouldn't want to be his wife!

Cool it, Moira. It doesn't matter. According to Google, Bosque Bend had a population of almost twelve thousand, so the odds were that she'd never see Big Red again.

She walked up the stairs, and glanced toward the auditorium doors across from Room 300. Pendleton Swaim had told her they were kept locked, but he'd get her a key. It didn't matter. The stage wasn't going anywhere anytime soon, and Pendleton Swaim had written the new show for this particular venue, which meant there shouldn't be any wicked surprises.

"The holiday season is our big moneymaker," he'd told her when he interviewed her by phone. "Everyone wanted to do a musical, so I wrote one. Lots of singing and dancing. Lots of kiddos too. We try to get the whole community involved. Little actors grow up to be big contributors."

"What's the plot?"

"Well, I've always been partial to O. Henry because he's a distant relative, so I decided to base the play on his most famous short story, 'The Gift of the Magi.' It's the one about the husband pawning his watch to give the wife a comb for her hair and her selling her hair to give him a fob for his watch. O. Henry was living in Texas at the time, but I never thought the story had a Texas feel to it, so I switched it to London, which allowed me to use a lot of kids in the play—guttersnipes, bootblacks, flower girls, and the like. Never did like the way it ended, so I expanded the story to two acts, wrote a libretto, and gave it a happy ending."

"Sounds good to me." She was all for happy endings. In

fact, she was in search of one of her own. God knows, she'd seen enough of the other side of the coin.

* * *

Moira paused outside the door of the Room 300 and murmured a few calming *om*s, then smoothed down the skirt of her dress again and fluffed up her new, short hairdo.

Costuming makes the character, as the wardrobe mistress of *The Clancy Family* had told Moira when she'd rebelled against the pink-and-white dresses Nancy Clancy always got stuck with, and now she wanted to look like a competent, complete professional. No pink and white, no ragged jeans, no resemblance to the scatterbrained Nancy Clancy, smart-mouthed Twinky Applejack, or any of the myriad other roles she'd played. That part of her life was over. She was herself now, Moira Miranda Farrar, and she'd be the one directing not only the show, but her own life as well.

Setting her jaw, she turned the doorknob.

An awkward, white-haired Ichabod Crane of a man rose in old-fashioned courtesy and pulled out the chair next to him. "Come sit by me, Moira. I'm Pendleton Swaim."

Moira gave the assemblage a confident smile, then walked briskly to the table and took her seat. *Pretend like you've done this a million times before.*

Pen beamed at her. "So nice to meet you in person. I must confess that I never watched *The Clancy Family*, but I hope I redeem myself by saying I did catch a couple of episodes of Johnny's sci-fi show."

"*Quark Kent, MD.*" Johnny had been a teenage Martian doctor with comic-book-hero powers, and she'd played his mechanical assistant. It was the nadir of her acting career, clanking around in a tin suit and pretending to have a robotic crush on Johnny, but she kept the smile pasted on her face.

"I had a wonderful time as a child actor, but as an adult, I prefer being behind the scenes." What choice did she have? Her acting career was down the drain.

Pen nodded. "Johnny said you would be perfect for us. I understand that, as well as years of practical experience, you have a drama degree from UCLA."

"Yes, when Johnny left *Quark Kent*, I decided to take a break from acting and go to college." Theater seemed the logical choice of major.

A short-necked, muscular woman with over-rouged cheeks and unbelievably black hair leaned across the table. "I'm Xandra Fontaine, and we're so happy to have you with us, Mrs. Sanger."

Moira gave Xandra her best fake smile. "Farrar, please. I've reverted to my maiden name—for professional purposes, of course." As if she'd ever get a role again. She'd turned down the right roles at the wrong time after marrying Colin, and her acting career had wilted and died on the vine. Giving up her career hadn't helped her marriage, and in the end, Colin had passed away a few years ago. "And I don't want to trade on Colin's name."

Xandra's eyes glistened with interest. "I just adored Colin Sanger. And he was so right for the role of Rhett Butler in the remake of *Gone with the Wind*. Tall, dark, and handsome—and that voice! It sent shivers down me every time he spoke."

"Everyone tells me that." Yeah, Colin was a heartthrob. The women wanted him, the men wanted him—she would have had to sweep a pile of adoring fans off the doorstep every morning if they'd lived in a normal house rather than massively built mansion with an eight-foot-tall wall around it. The wonder was that Colin hadn't dug a moat and stocked it with alligators.

The long-necked, long-beaked woman sitting next to Xandra, who seemed to have dyed her hair out of the same pot as her neighbor, moved her head forward like a hissing snake. "He died so young."

Moira lowered her eyes, struck her best grieving widow pose, and softened her voice to a whisper. "It's been two years, but I miss him still." Damn this Method acting. She'd convince herself if she wasn't careful.

Xandra took over again. "Too bad there were never any children."

The twosome stared at Moira pointedly.

Who were these women? Were they tag-teaming? Moira sighed dramatically and gave the same crap answer she'd given countless tabloid reporters. "We were both busy with our careers and thought we had all the time in the world."

The door opened, and the people seated around the table looked up long enough to identify the newcomer, a tall, angular woman in a peacock-blue squaw dress cinched at the waist and a copper-medallion belt. Her flyaway hair looked like a stray mockingbird had tried to make a nest in it.

Pen motioned toward her. "That's Vashti Atherton, our accompanist. Musical genius. She scored the *Gift of the Magi*. Her younger daughter, Micaela, will play Della, the wife. Phil Schoenfeldt—the man at the end of the table who's waving his hands around—has been cast as the husband. And Travis McAllister will sing the dream sequence. He's the one talking to Vashti right now."

"Pen, I really do need to see the script."

"As soon as our chairman gets here, my dear. He's bringing photocopies for everyone."

The door opened again and an attractive brunette entered, nodding at Pen as she took a seat further on down the table.

"Rebecca Espinoza. Her husband is a city councilman, and they're very supportive of civic theater. Both of their children have appeared in our productions."

Xandra leaned across the table again. "Lucinda Jane and Melody have been taking dance classes with Sister and me since they were toddlers. Clarette and I choreograph all the numbers and train all the dancers—even the ones who don't patronize our studio."

Pen beamed at the duo. "The Fontaine sisters have been very generous in contributing their talents and expertise to our theater productions."

Moira commented the only way she could. "Wonderful!"

Vashti Atheron, Phil Schoenfeldt, Travis McAllister, Rebecca Espinoza, Xandra and Clarette Fontaine. She repeated each name to herself and glued it to a face. She didn't want to accidentally snub anyone in the grocery store—these people would determine whether she stayed in Bosque Bend in triumph or slunk back to Pasadena in disgrace.

A masculine voice rang out from the end of the table, where most of the men seemed to have congregated. "Hey, Pen, what's holding up Chairman Mao? Rafe's photocopier broken again?"

The room roared with laughter. Apparently a running joke.

Pen gave him a quick comeback. "You know more than I do, Travis. He's your brother." He turned to Moira. "We're not very formal—no elections or anything—but Rafe McAllister runs the show. Great guy."

"Rafe McAllister? I saw some items in the museum that he'd donated on behalf of the C Bar M Ranch."

Pen nodded. "Josiah Colby established the ranch in 1855, but couldn't make a go of it until Gilbert McAllister came on the scene right after the Civil War. The Colbys have pretty much died out, but the current generation of the McAllisters is going strong and has been quite generous to Bosque Bend. Now that Rafe's got the museum up and running, he's negotiating for us to buy the old Huaco Theater just off Austin Avenue and restore it as a permanent home for the theater guild. He thinks we can get a historical marker for it too."

Moira's eyebrows went up. "That's quite an undertaking."

Pen shrugged. "Rafe's an architect, so he knows what he's doing buildingwise. The plan is to move us onto a more professional footing so we can draw audiences from Waco and some of the smaller towns around here. That's where you come in. Carolyn Gomez-Sweeny, the Eisenhower Consolidated drama teacher who started us out four years ago, said that we've reached the point where we needed to hire somebody full-time."

Moira glanced around the table. "Is Ms. Gomez-Sweeny here today?"

Pen retrieved a card from his shirt pocket and handed it to her. "Carolyn's having to step back—school stuff and the new baby—but she wanted you to have her phone number in case you want to ask her about anything."

The door opened again and all the heads bobbed up again, but this time, they stayed up. A smile spread across Pendleton Swaim's face. "Rafe!"

Moira turned to see a tall redhead with a cardboard box under his arm enter the room. He gave the group a familiar, easy smile, and his eyes twinkled like summer sparklers.

Nooooo!

Big Red started passing scripts down the table. "Sorry to be late, folks. It was that dang copier again." Moira froze in place as his gaze moved down the table, then traveled back up and settled on her. "Glad to see our new director made it."

She forced the corners of her mouth to curve up, but her blood ran cold.

* * *

Wet autumn leaves slushed under her tires as Moira backed her six-year-old Toyota out of its parking space in the asphalt lot across the street from the museum. The mid-October temperatures in central Texas seemed to be as mild as back in Pasadena, but this intermittent rainfall was driving her crazy. Pray God it wouldn't get too cold later on. She and Isis didn't have a heavy coat between them.

Her fingers tightened on the steering wheel as she waited at the street for a break in the traffic. *Damn!* That was Rafe McAllister standing at the curb in front of the museum, and he was looking her way. She'd like to run the jerk down. *No, Moira, play the game. Isis is depending on you. Arne is depending on you. Gram and Gramps are depending on you.*

Moira thought she was off the financial hook when she married Colin Sanger and he arranged for a monthly allowance to help support her family. But when Colin died, not only did the allowance cease, but Moira also learned that he'd hadn't changed his will after they were married. That meant his ex-wife was now enormously rich and the Actors Guild's coffers were overflowing. All Moira's family had to live on was the sale of the jewelry Colin had given her, the yearly stipend she received from the father she'd only met once in her life, and residuals from *The Clancy Family* reruns.

She was still better off than Isis, whose father had never bothered to contact her after Kimiko left him for another man. But then, Bennie Birdsong had been their mother's second husband—or maybe her third. It was hard to keep track. Her mother was currently preening herself as Kimiko O'Donnell, Lady Eglantine. That wouldn't last long, but at least she'd sent a couple of checks back home to Pasadena this time. Not much, of course—it cost a lot of money for a fifty-two-year-old woman to maintain her looks enough to compete with the latest wave of twenty-year-old honeybuns.

Moira mulled over her meeting with the theater guild as she drove onto Bowie Avenue, then cut over to Austin Avenue, Bosque Bend's main drag. Apparently the major purpose of the get-together had been for everyone to look her over. Accordingly, she'd smiled like a demented dolphin and shaken everyone's hand, even Rafe McAllister's.

And his gorgeous eyes had sparkled at her the whole time.

* * *

Rafe gave Moira Farrar a wave as she drove out onto the street, but she didn't respond. Probably didn't see him—or didn't want to.

What was going on with the woman? He'd felt an immediate connection with her in the museum and followed up in kind, but she'd gone cold on him. Maybe he shouldn't have made a move on her right off the bat, but she was such a cute little thing. The sitcom camera had never caught those high cheekbones and exotic eyes, the eyebrows that looked like they'd been painted on with a feather, the fanlike lashes, the sweetness of her smile. And that rasping voice, which had been used for comic effect in *The Clancy Family*, had sent shivers down him to right there where it mattered.

He watched her car turn the corner at the end of the block. Colin Sanger had died two years ago—dived into a half-empty swimming pool was the story. Did Moira Farrar have a current boyfriend? *Boyfriend*—a stupid term for an adult male. *Say it out, Rafe—does she have a lover?*

A red Mustang pulled over to the curb, and Rafe's brother lowered the passenger window. "Hey, Mao. You gonna stand there all day holdin' down the sidewalk?"

Rafe bent to rest his arms on the rolled-down window ledge. "Trying to think what else I can do to fix that damn photocopier."

Although actually the machine worked like a charm. The real reason he'd run late was that Delilah had pitched a fit when he'd tried to drop her off at Sissy's. Only the promise that he would invite "the pretty lady" out to the ranch over the weekend had reconciled her to stay with Baby Zoey, but he wasn't about to announce that devil's bargain.

Travis laughed. "Guy, give up and buy a new copier. You got the money—if you haven't driven yourself into bankruptcy paying for that cutie-pie little director to come to town."

"You noticed?"

"I'm married, not blind."

"Speakin' of being married," Rafe smiled, "I hear tell Rocky's not happy about the amount of time you've been spendin' with Micaela Atherton lately."

Travis snorted. "Rocky's on my back if I so much as hold the door open for a little old lady."

"Rocky's your wife, Trav, and Micaela's not a little old lady. Half the town saw you cuddlin' up to her at Good Times last weekend."

"Lay off, Rafe. Micaela and I were singing a love song and had to make it look good. For God's sake, we had a spotlight on us and everyone in the damn honky-tonk was singing along."

"Just be careful."

Travis grimaced and ran a hand through his hair. "You don't know how it is. Rocky's after me again to hang up the band. Hell, all I need is a decent break and I could hit the big time, maybe make the Grand Ole Opry." His face lit up. "Hey, how about you corralling Ms. Farrar and bringing her out to Good Times tonight so she can hear me? That woman has showbiz connections up the wazoo, and I want to be in her address book."

"Don't think she likes me, Trav."

"Rafe, every woman on the face of the earth likes you. It's those eyes of yours. You hypnotize them." He glanced around as the light turned and the traffic started moving behind him. "Gotta go before I get myself rammed."

Rafe stepped back from the curb. "Later, guy."

Good Times. It just might work, for him as well as Travis. He'd tell Moira he needed to discuss her ideas for *Gift of the Magi*, and maybe he could warm up the ice princess after all.

About the Author

Jeanell Bolton is an active member of the Austin chapter of Romance Writers of America. She has three children, one husband, and one dog. She lives on five glorious wooded acres in the boondocks of Georgetown, Texas. In past lives, she has been a teacher, an activist, an artist, a journalist, and a chorus director, but she is now settled into writing about deep, dark romances that end up happily ever after, which is how it always should be.

Learn more at:
Facebook.com/Jeanell.Bolton